TRUST ME

A Novel By

Paul Slatter

This book is entirely a work of fiction. References to real people alive or dead, events, establishments, organizations, or locales are for the intended purpose only to provide a sense of authenticity, and are used fictitiously. All other characters, and all incidents and dialogue, are drawn from the author's imagination and are not to be construed as real.

TNCS - Publishing Edition

CreateSpace Edition

ISBN: 9781794504615

First Trade Edition:

1103027 B.C. Ltd.

Also by Paul Slatter

Burn

Rock Solid

For

Jean and Bob

Semper fortis

Contents

The Vancouver Series

Book Three:

Trust Me

Chapter One

Mazzi Hegan could still hear the clicking of the small stunt bicycle as it freewheeled around and around somewhere in the distance behind him. The guy had passed him earlier trying to look tough, once then twice, riding the bike with his knees up around his chin, giving Mazzi the eye, sizing him up as he'd passed. hoisted

Now he was out there still, cruising around somewhere in the background, the rear gears ticking as he coasted. He took a left, then a right—the roads quiet at 3 a.m. on a Tuesday morning in downtown Vancouver. He saw the steps for the small park just west of the convention centre that would take him down to the seawall and Mazzi Hegan took them quickly. If the guy on the bike was following him then he'd think he'd have gone straight on; and if somehow the guy'd seen, then he'd have to come down the steps. And if he did that then Mazzi himself could disappear into the darkness and wait it out, let the man go and then take the seawall back to his place that looked out across the city at the bottom of Davie Street.

Moving quickly, he reached the bottom of the steps. It was clear down there—well lit on the seawall, that is. The park where he'd hide if need be was dark against the silhouette of the street lights and apartment blocks on the other side. Mazzi carried on, listening as he looked around, hearing only the faint lapping of the water on the wall as the gentle swell hit home having travelled across the globe.

There was nothing, no clicking, no young man with a hoodie trying to look cool riding his little brother's bike. Mazzi continued, thinking about the night—this guy he'd met earlier causing trouble like he had because Mazzi liked to drink, throwing a beer Mazzi should have already drank in his face, then leaving with Mazzi's wallet while Mazzi stayed, alone with his phone sending drunk texts to anyone stupid enough to reply until the music stopped and security asked him politely to leave.

He carried on along the seawall, looking behind him at the steps as he went. Another man was there now in the distance, halfway down the wall looking through the telescope to North Vancouver on the other side of the inlet with its streetlights and industrial sodium burning light back across the blackness. Mazzi moved forward, looking behind him again at the steps and at the empty warmth of the trees lining the way. If the guy on the bike had followed on foot, sneaking down when his back was turned, he'd be trapped.

He continued on, the man ahead more visible now in the faint street light as he pulled his eye from the scope and looked back to Mazzi as he drew closer. The man young, in his teens, with a newspaper delivery bag slung over his shoulder, stared at him as he drew ever nearer. He looked to the ground, knowing too well he shouldn't and then looked up again just in time for the teenager to smile as their eyes met and say clearly, "Howdie partner!"

Mazzi carried on, passing the kid and looking to the ground again for another twenty feet, wishing he'd stayed up on the road, feeling for the phone he knew he'd lost when they'd thrown him out of the bar in his drunken state. Quickly he looked back over his left shoulder for the young man with the bag—he was gone now. Then looking over his right into the darkness, Mazzi saw him moving, following, hiding in the darkness. Feeling the knot in his stomach tighten, he spun around. In front of him at the end of the park just above the yachts all moored up and sleeping, the kid on the bike was waiting under a lamppost.

The *fucking prick* had corralled him he thought, steered him onto the steps, pushed him down them with his presence. Now he was trapped.

He slowed almost to a stop looking quickly down the bicycle path again, the kid with the bag nowhere to be seen. He looked back, the one on the bike doing nothing but sitting low in the saddle waiting, pushing him further into the darkness of the park again with his presence.

Turn, he said to himself, *turn and walk back—head for the steps*. The kid with the newspaper bag was no bigger than him, but what was in the bag?

He carried on, feeling the sweat on his back under his shirt—don't go into the dark, he told himself, walk up to the guy and carry on past him, that's what you do—walk up, stare him down and let him know with your eyes he's in big fucking trouble if he decides to get off his little brother's bike.

That's what I'll do, he thought, I'll say that as I get to him, say, hey fuckhead, come near me and you'll wear that bike like a hat.

He could do it; he'd done it years before when he'd been bullied after school, passing a whole gang of older boys every day as he walked home. Mazzi thinking they were cute and wondering why they were calling him *fag-boy* and *cocksucker*. Way back then, when he was all confused. Then one day he'd come home with his mother, walking the same path and forgetting about these guys who always hung at the same corner trying to look cool. Seeing them and hearing them call him names as they always did, shouting out *dogface* and *fagboy* and asking if his mother was a dyke as they passed, Mazzi all tough like he should have been before when it had started, instead of there and then when it was too late on that hot summers afternoon, when the sun was setting and he'd lashed out blind and hit his mother in the nose by mistake.

But this time he didn't have his mother's honor to protect and could lash out without her getting in the way like she had. All he had to do was go for the guy, kick the fucker off the bike, thump him if he could land one and keep going till he started crying like his mother had after the gang of pricks had seen how hard he could punch.

Then the blow from the baseball bat the kid kept in his bag hit him across the side of his head and knocked him off his feet. His elbow hit the paving stones hard as he landed on the ground and felt the power of the kid's foot hit him straight in his chest, winding him as the kid followed through with his other, spinning Mazzi's head around towards the boats in the marina just in time to see the blur of a figure of a woman dressed like a guy running along the dock, clearing the gate just as the kid on the bike arrived. The woman screaming out at them both, "Get away from him you pricks—I'm a cop." And she was, and her name was Daltrey.

Chapter Two

Daltrey stood above Mazzi Hegan and watched as the kids disappeared across the park into the darkness. The man now half up and back on his feet in his tight leopard skin trousers, stinking of booze, with blood running from his mouth.

How long has it been since she'd ventured outside, Daltrey thought as she stared at him, days or weeks? How long had she spent holing herself up in the boat she knew would be empty with her face and hands burned and what felt like half the hair on her head gone. Locking herself away, sitting there, crying for hours, feeling her hands shake, knowing she was a coward.

What had she been doing thinking she was so brave? Following the Russian like she had and failing herself, failing the street woman who'd been the brave one, the woman trying to protect her and being burned herself. The woman, without fear, doing everything and a terrified Daltrey had done nothing, except run. And run she had, like a kid running for their mother on the first day of school, with her face and hands burning from the flames the Russian had poured down upon her. Running both from him and from her shame.

Day after day, hour after hour, she’d sat locked away from the real world, too frightened even to look in the mirror as her delicate fingers felt her burnt hair. Waking from dreams of him coming at her spitting death, seeing this woman beneath him, who should have been her, dying, feeling the boat rock on the water in the dock as people passed, clonking the wooden planks with their feet, she’d hid and watched them looking in as she looked out at the world through portholes of pitted brass. Until one day, as if it couldn't have gotten any worse for her, she'd felt her hands shaking as she saw something across the water, something that could only make her question her sanity—a poster of Dan standing there in a pair of silver underpants.

How could she have left her there? How could she have run as she did, Daltrey asked herself again, as she walked over to pick up a phone and handed it to the guy who should've know better than to walk alone through the park at night?

****

It was around three in the morning when Chendrill, the private eye who used to be a cop, arrived back at Dan's mother's house and, using his key, crept inside and took a shower before climbing into bed.

A lot had happened over the last few days or so, and he was wondering if things could get any worse. Nearly burned to death, electrocuted, almost drowned, beaten in the ribs by a baker, kicked in the throat by a Sikh.

Things needed to start settling down.

Dan's mother, Tricia, was stirring now, her body smooth and warm beside him. He could wake her and make love, but why, what was the point? All he'd do was be thinking about how long the wannabe gangster he'd just sent swimming out into the dark sea only hours before had taken to drown?

Then he heard his woman say, as she turned naked to him and feeling her light touch upon his chest, "I was beginning to worry again."

Chendrill lay still and said, "There's no need."

But there was and Tricia knew it. This man who was

big and strong and took no shit from anyone, the guy who used to be with the force but now was paid handsomely to keep an eye out for her son, who, despite his newfound fame as a supermodel/actor, still lived downstairs in the basement.

Chendrill watched over him and had been staying with her since they'd become lovers. The night before, he'd disappeared and come back in the early hours with his hair full of salt, smelling of the ocean, with his shins ripped up and calves bruised.

He had been a mess—now she'd sensed the sadness after he'd returned again. She said as she leaned up and placed her head on his chest, "Something's upset you?"

God, Chendrill thought, she was right but how could she tell that just from him walking in the room? But she had sensed it, heard his breath, his silence. The way he lay himself next to her and didn't move. She asked, "Is it about last night?"

It was—a man with a diamond in his front tooth had tried to end his life and almost succeeded, and only a few hours earlier Chendrill had turned it around giving the same man a taste of his own medicine. He took a deep breath and, lying, answered, "No, it's all good."

But it wasn't good, not by a long stretch. So already knowing the answer, but changing the subject, he asked, "Is Dan home?"

Dan wasn't; his red Ferrari absent from its usual spot outside his mother's small stucco covered two-bedroom home.

The truth was Dan had gotten back home from work and without showering jumped straight into his speed restricted racing car and headed into town to climb back into Adalia Seychan, who was now riding herself up and down on his cock with just enough light on in the hotel suite for her to see him but him not to see her.

Not that Dan cared.

He could have had the lights on full blast or the suite could have been pitch black and he'd have been happy. All he wanted was to feel her pushing down on him, her stopping as she felt him about to come every minute. He'd wondered what a woman's pussy felt like for years and now he knew—with hers all smooth and shaven and still tight for a woman in her fifties—or sixties, but who was counting—and all courtesy of a combination of yoga and a very talented surgeon who'd also done her neck.

Smiling as she looked down at him holding her waist with one hand and with his other in a packet of family sized Cheesies, she said, "You like that do you—when I ride you like this?"

Dan grinned and stuffed another handful of Cheesies in his mouth, the Rock Solid brand tablets he'd been given earlier in the day still living up to their name.

"If we're going to be working together and you're going to love me in the movie Dan, then I want the chemistry to be real—you'll need to know what I like, and I like this."

And she did, she liked riding him and staring at his tight stomach as she let her thigh muscles bring herself up and down, feeling his dick on her cervix. She said, "You know what you're rubbing inside me don't you?"

Dan did, he knew all about the sexual reproductive organs of a woman on paper and for the last few years had been trying his best to get as close to the real thing as possible, so he said, "Yeah, when I was a kid, the cat next door got in and started playing with one of my mum's mice."

Adalia stopped and looked down upon him, this young lad, sexy enough for her to dream up a bullshit excuse and leave her heart-shaped California swimming pool for Vancouver in the hope she could meet him. This guy, now inside her bareback, whose photo in a pair of silver undies had made her come her silk panties in the back of her blacked-out limo on Rodeo drive—her calling out to her driver through the communication device to make another four lefts so she could see him again. She said, "Oh!"

"Yeah," Dan said, "Mum got all embarrassed, pretended it was the real thing, and chased it out into the garden with a broom."

Then as Adalia pulled herself almost off of him and slowly dropped back down, she said, "That's not the best thing to be talking about when you're making love to a woman, Dan."

And that's what he was doing at last, making love, or fucking and eating Cheesies—depending on who's perspective you took. He heard Adalia carry on, saying, "You need to be telling me how beautiful I am, how much I mean to you. Make me feel like a beautiful woman. Tell me I'm special Dan—tell me what you want to do to me."

Dan gave it some thought as he looked up at this woman he could barely see in the faint light coming in from the hotel suite's minibar that he'd left open, then said, "I wanna fuck you in the ass."

That, he thought, was what she wanted to hear—as it was all this other older woman who'd picked him up in the street and sneaked back to his basement a couple of nights back had kept saying. That is, before his mum burst in the room, turned on the ugly lights, and kicked her out.

"Really? Don't try to run before you can walk Daniel," Adalia said with a grin to this kid who'd obviously spent too many late nights on the internet as he'd said it like a porn star. This same kid who could act and ad lib like a natural and with whom she was about to make a movie. The same kid who she was going to show to the Western world and turn into a star, so that when he was just that and the people had begun to forget her, she could let it slip they'd been in love and ride the tabloid wave until no one longer cared.

Leaning down she felt her breasts touch his chest as she gently kissed him on the mouth and said, "You think you can do that to me, do you big boy? Well why don't you start by fondling my breasts then, since you've got your big hard cock where it's supposed to be—try holding me down on top of you and give me everything you've got before you start fantasizing."

And raising her buttocks a little to meet him, Adalia pulled Dan's hand from her waist and whispered in his ear, "Go on Dan, I'm waiting—touch my breasts, feel them, caress them, hold me down and fuck me as hard as you can and try not to come whilst you pound me until I have."

Dan reached up and began to touch Adalia Seychan's breasts with his right hand, feeling their softness as her nipples grew harder beneath his fingertips. He watched as Adalia closed her eyes whilst he lifted his other hand up and began rubbing both breasts with both hands, squishing them, tugging them, stretching out her nipples, pulling them away from her until Adalia worried he'd undo all the work she'd had done and asked him to stop, "Oh Dan, please be gentle with me."

And with her own hands she pulled his hands up, placing them onto her shoulders. Then she said, “Hold me down Daniel, hold me to you,” as he looked up at her breasts, seeing them all covered in orange Cheesie stains and sticky crumbs from his fingers.

Adalia looked at him staring up at them as Dan panicked, leaning up quickly before she could see the mess he’d made; he took her breasts in his mouth and began to lick them all over. Closing her eyes in delight as she felt his tongue sweep across her breasts, his teeth nibbling at the crumbs around her nipples, Adalia saying, “Yes Dan, do that. Oh yes, Dan. Yes! Do that and fuck me, Dan. Fuck me hard.”

And he did begin to fuck her hard as he licked all the delicious flavored Cheesie grease from her million dollar breasts as she ground down, filling herself with his cock as Dan lapped like a dog with his paw on the edge of a ripped open empty bag of chips, getting every sticky morsel with long hard strokes of his tongue. Adalia moaning, Dan in double ecstasy and unable to speak, and eventually in the heat of passion they both came together, Adalia feeling every inch of her body shudder as her muscles tightened and the nerves along her back and down her legs tingled calling out to her as her wetness flowed out onto Dan’s balls. Dan feeling himself involuntarily unload as the muscles in his groin pumped his sperm into her the same way they had each time his mother had treated him to a papaya and he’d taken the whole thing to his room.

It was about the second time Adalia had come that night when Chendrill got the phone call as he lay asleep back in Dan's mothers bed in the suburbs on the other side of the city. Not knowing the number, he hoped it was Archall

Diamond calling to taunt him, telling him he'd survived as Chendrill had himself the night before.

And as he lay there feeling Tricia's warmth beside him, listening to the breathing of whoever it was on the end of the line, nothing could have surprised him more when after a few seconds of picking up the few words she spoke through the tears he realized who it was and sitting up said, "Daltrey?" as she cried harder through the earpiece.

He got up again and walked naked to the window and looked outside on the off chance she could be sitting there. Then wondering what the hell was going on, he said, "Where are you?"

"On a boat, hiding—like a coward."

It was hard to work out, this girl who he'd used to know intimately and who he believed, like everyone else, had burned to death just over a week before was now crying to him down the telephone. He stayed calm trying not to ask questions, yet still said, "Let me know where you are and I'll come see you."

"I'm on a boat."

"In dock?"

Then there was silence for a moment before he heard her simply say, "Yeah."

Then even though he already knew she wasn't, he asked, "Are you okay?"

"I've been better," Daltrey answered as she choked back the tears.

Chendrill asked, "What's the name of the boat you're on?" And again heard Daltrey's silence. Then he said, "People think you're dead. There was a body in an…"

"Alley," Daltrey finished for him. Then she said, "It should have been me but it wasn't… It wasn't and it should have been."

****

Charles Chuck Chendrill walked through the darkness of the park, dropping further towards the water's edge. In the distance, he could see the sun silhouetting the mountains as it lifted the morning sky from darkness. If he was right, Daltrey was sitting on one of the hundred odd boats tied safely to the floating wooden docks held tight by the steel posts smashed firmly into the seabed below.

He stepped out onto the dock, feeling it move as the rig adjusted itself to his weight, and headed into the maze. In amongst the tears and words she'd tried to speak she'd said that the boat was blue, but in the darkness blue could also mean black or brown or green. Then in the distance, he saw it with its twelve-volt light burning dimly in the galley.

He sat on the edge of the small bench in the yacht's galley and stared at Daltrey as she used the sleeve of a man's fleece she'd found in the closet to wipe snot from her nose. Small droplets of tears were falling on the formica table, her hair on the side of her head burned, old bandages and ointments from the contents of the boat's first aid kit were still strewn across the small counters alongside opened tins of salmon and empty water bottles.

Daltrey not seeing the mess, Chendrill giving her time.

"He came at me out of nowhere with this flame gun. I felt my hair go first and covered my face, then somehow pulled my jacket over my head, then for a second it stopped and this woman was there and he was burning her face away… she must have been in the alley… She must have been trying to save me, she fell at my feet and all I did was throw my jacket at his face and ran. I ran and tried to get my phone, but it was gone and my gun and everything and

I just ran and ran and I could hardly see."

Then she went silent.

And that's how it had played out that evening in the alley at the back of the luxury condo building where a realtor named Patrick watched women walking naked from his window. The man had come at her from behind, taking her by surprise. This Russian, who spat fiery death from his fingertips, throwing out a wall of molten flame, singeing her eyelashes and what was left of her already plucked eyebrows. She'd gone down, crawling on her hands and knees, as he'd walked behind her spitting death onto the back of her hair and the thick leather of her jacket. Then she'd curled into a ball as the Russian's victims always did, covering their faces with whatever they could while the rest of their bodies burned.

Then the girl had come out of nowhere, pushing his arms away and, in the last moments of her sad life, saved Daltrey's before the monster had stood above this heaven-sent angel who'd spent her life on the streets, selling herself for heroin and sending poison flowing through her veins, ended her harsh tenure in this unforgiving world.

Chendrill said, "The Russian's dead. His past caught up with him before I could get my revenge for what I'd thought he'd done to you."

Daltrey looked up, her eyes red and bloodshot.

"He did to me, what do you mean?"

"We all think you're dead, Daltrey. Everyone thinks it was you in that alley. They found your gun there, your phone, your ID, everything."

She sat there staring out the side of the small porthole at the picture of Dan lit up in his silver underpants out there in the far distance. Then taking a deep breath, without looking back, she said almost to herself, "Well maybe I am dead. I keep seeing things."

"You look pretty much alive to me," Chendrill answered, carrying on straight after with, "you're upset yes, but your hair will grow back, your burns will heal."

"What about the girl though, the one who died for me, will her hair grow? No it won't."

Chendrill stared at her, this girl who he used to date and who had been scared of no one but who'd hidden herself away in fear and shame. He still couldn't believe he was here though, here and talking to her when only a few hours before he'd been wondering why he'd not heard about a funeral date. He said, "Can I ask a question?"

Daltrey turned away from the porthole and just stared, the morning sun catching what was left of her hair.

"Why'd you take so long to call?" Chendrill waited for the answer he already knew deep down. The girl needed time, time alone to come to terms with what had happened, time to process her shame and her fear of a man who was never going to rise again—not from the grave, as Daltrey had just done.

Then out of the blue, Daltrey took him by surprise, "I didn't have a phone—but there were these guys, I was watching them and I could see they were going to fuck with this, this man, and then one hit him across the head and I just burst up and out of here on what must have been instinct. I got to them before the other could join in. Funny thing is, after the fuckers had gone and left the guy on the ground with a fucker of a sore head—I found this phone. He said it wasn't his and when I got it back here, I found Sebastian String's number in it and right below his was yours."

****

It was just past 6 a.m. when Chendrill got Daltrey to the hospital emergency at St. Paul's and as they sat and waited to be fast tracked through the junkies asking for ice, Chendrill said, "The Russian you're frightened of was chopped to pieces."

Daltrey stared at him, feeling her skin tighten.

"He was?"

Chendrill nodded, stretching out his legs as he did, feeling the pain in his shins, "Yeah very much so, I saw him lying there up in his flashy suite, so you can forget about that fucker."

For the moment that is, Chendrill thought, she was still a cop and there was little chance of her not getting torn apart with questions once the world caught up with what had happened—even if she was still in shock.

He said, "I'll put a call in this morning to that thief Ditcon and straighten things out for you best I can, but there'll still be questions."

Then he heard Daltrey say with a sigh, "I can't see myself doing the job anymore anyway—not now."

And to Chendrill, it seemed that she wasn't wrong.

****

Chendrill got back to Dan's mother's home just after seven to see Dan's Ferrari sitting outside and the light on in his mother's room. Letting himself in, he walked along the corridor, hearing his weight creak the old wooden floorboards beneath his feet. He opened her bedroom door softly to see her sitting up in bed reading with her knees up and her small delicate feet with her toenails painted red poking out from under the duvet. Looking up for a second, she briefly said before returning to her book, "I'm starting to get worried about you."

And she wasn't kidding, in her eyes the man could keep better hours, even though it was painfully obvious sometimes it wasn't his fault. But she drew the line at nighttime phone calls from women. *Especially if they're crying*, she thought, and still looking at her book she said, "This woman who called all upset, it was so important that you had to go right there and then to help her with her problem?"

It was, Chendrill thought, but kept it to himself, instead saying, "I'm sorry it could have waited I agree, but, you see it was the girl Dan was seeing who everyone thought had died."

Trish sat there taking that one in, staring at her book, the words now just a blur, this mysterious girl who Dan was seeing who'd been murdered and who recently Dan had suggested she meet for the first time at her upcoming funeral.

"And she called you instead of Dan?"

Chendrill nodded, then sitting down said, "Yeah, it's complicated."

"And you've slept with her in the past have you, you and my son have both fucked her I suppose?"

Wow, Chendrill thought, he wasn't expecting that one coming at him from left field. There was no point in lying, so he just said, "A long time ago yes, but it was nothing."

And regretted it the moment he heard her snap back, "Dan's nineteen now and was dating her—so you're saying you left my bed and run out the door for some girl, twenty years your junior?"

It wasn't getting any better.

****

It was almost an hour and a half later when Chendrill took the Aston into the flow of traffic and headed back towards the city still ruffled by what had been their first fight and for the first time ever he had been happy that Sebastian had called him with another 'emergency.'

A fight with Dan's mother, if you could call it that, an argument more like, comprising of him keeping quiet whilst his new woman vented and threw stuff. Like her son had warned him, the woman had a temper.

He took a left off the highway onto Hastings, passing the PNE on his right, the place looking deserted now with its empty rollercoasters and rides. Years before when he was a cop, he'd been called to meet a man at the exit of their biggest ride—designed to make you puke. A man who had somehow managed to get all his clothes off throughout its duration, throwing them into the air as the carriage twisted and turned until he arrived completely naked and sated to meet a young Chendrill at the bottom. The man saying it was an accident and how he just loved the ride as Chendrill covered him with a towel, declined the offer of them both going around once more, and put him in cuffs.

He hit the lights, trying to remember the man's name and then remembered seeing him only a few days prior lying unconscious face down on the man's living room floor. Now though there were other issues, like what he'd say to Ditcon as he'd promised Daltrey he would. The man who'd built his career off the backs of others' careers was almost the sole reason Chendrill had given up on his. Wondering why he still had the guy's number, Chendrill pulled out his phone and hit 'The Thief' on speed dial, waited for a moment, then heard Ditcon's voice on the other end.

"Ditcon here."

Taking a moment, relishing the words in his head before omitting—*you stupid fuckhead*—Chendrill simply said, "It's Chendrill, I think you fucked up again—I just had breakfast with Daltrey."

And hearing the silence as Chendrill's words churned around and around in the mind of the most incompetent man he had ever met, Chendrill followed it up with, "Oh yeah and she's decided she's not interested in working with you guys anymore."

To which Ditcon, gathering himself, replied, "Thank you for your information. We already know the welfare of Officer Daltrey and we are not at liberty to comment further regarding ongoing investigations."

Chendrill hung up and let out a long breath, half throwing the phone down onto the soft leather of the Aston's passenger seat, he said out loud to no one but himself, "Not at liberty? The fucking idiot." Then he laughed. *Why should I be surprised*, he thought, the man had worked his way this far up the ladder without getting his hands dirty, so why should things suddenly have changed?

It would take about another thirty minutes for the phone to ring again asking him to come down to the station on Main Street for an interview and about another thirty for someone to look into all the hospital entries over the last week so they could prove they'd done some work and say to him, "We are fully aware of your and Officer Daltrey's movements this morning," or some other form of bullshit like it.

He reached Yaletown and parked up on the meter outside Slave Media and took the elevator up to the offices. The place was now a hive of activity since the company's owner, Sebastian String, had decided—on a whim—to indulge Patrick, an old real estate friend's desire for a life time makeover, giving him the go ahead to make a film only the writer could understand.

Chendrill reached Sebastian's office situated in the corner of the building, knocked once on the stained window of the door, and stepped in to find Sebastian tickling the stomach of his dog Fluffy with a duster, who with the slightest movement of his head just looked at him.

Smiling, Sebastian said, "Fluffy loves it when I do this Chuck. Why don't you see if you can make his leg kick?"

Chendrill shook his head and walked to the window putting his backside against the sill and watched this advertising media wizard in his bright yellow trousers and Italian shoes trying to send his dog into ecstasy. Then he said, "Is this the emergency you mentioned?"

It wasn't, but there was one—at least in Sebastian's eyes—and putting the duster down on his desk he said, "Mazzi's called in sick."

Chendrill looked at him, waiting for more. Then when it didn't come he asked, "Is that it?"

"No. I think a sash window came down and banged his head last night when he was working late. Either that or he made it up and fell over because he'd been drinking."

Chendrill waited again, this news being nothing new when it came to Mazzi Hegan, who he knew from past experience to be a party boy—and falling down drunk came with the territory. He said again, "Is that it?"

It wasn't. After waiting in vain and wondering if Chendrill was going to ask if the man was okay, Sebastian carried on, "Well last night I was all alone and I didn't want to bother you because I know you're tired, so I let it go, but I'm not sure if you'd heard on the radio about this man who crossed the border a few nights back? Well, I've had this thought and its worrying me, it's about the situation with the company and Gill Banton—you know, with Slave taking over the contract she had with Marshaa. Anyway, I was worried because I heard some noise outside my door last night and I thought it could be this guy who crossed the border, maybe he's come here to hurt me."

Chendrill stared at him for a moment, taking it in. He'd not heard on the news about the man stealing a U.S. Customs officer's 4x4 and crashing it across the border two nights prior, but he did know about the incident more than anyone, because it was him. He said, "I can tell you, Sebastian, you have nothing to fear from this man."

"But how do you know Chuck?" Sebastian asked, wanting to believe Chendrill.

"Because I know the guy who did it and his problem is not with you or connected in any way with you."

Sebastian stared at Chendrill with his mouth open, then he said, "You know him. How? How do you know him?"

"It doesn't matter, just relax and know you're cool with this guy. However, if you're worried at night at your place call the police, it's what they're there for and then call me."

"I don't want to be a pest Chuck, you know what I'm like. I'll only ever call if it's important."

Chendrill did know exactly what he was like and at times wondered if the $1000 a day plus expenses was worth the 'emergencies' he had to deal with every other day—

after all incidents such as 'someone's looking at my bicycle' hardly categorized as an emergency. He did, though, get to drive the Aston Martin which was looking good below the window as all the pretty girls were passing alongside it.

He felt the side of his face, which was still sore, and thought of Dan's mother. Chances are she'd have calmed down by now, but you couldn't tell. Like she'd said after she'd slapped him, 'at least you know I care.' He looked back to Sebastian, held up the phone Daltrey had called him from a few hours earlier, and said, "I've got a question for you though Sebastian. Last night a man was mugged around the marina close to your place and he dropped this; strangely though it has yours and my phone numbers on speed dial."

Sebastian looked at the phone then asked, "A man?" And before Chendrill could answer, he carried on with, "You see—I've got this friend."

"The man who was mugged, you think?" Chendrill asked, as he saw Sebastian start to blush.

Then Sebastian stood saying, "No, not like that, you're misunderstanding what I'm saying, we're talking about a woman Chuck, a woman I met."

"Oh?"

"I haven't got a man, I haven't. I've got no secrets Chuck, there hasn't been another man in my life since Alan."

And there hadn't, Alan had been the sole reason Sebastian existed and since he was gone there could be no other who'd come close to filling his shoes. Except for Charles Chuck Chendrill of course, but that was a secret fantasy as he played for the other team, which in its own way only made it all the better. He carried on, "I'm friends with this woman Chuck, no kinky stuff though, so don't get any ideas."

Kinky stuff? Chendrill thought, male and female together, that's the way he sees it.

"She's so sweet, I met her in the park, we chat and she's got such a wonderful family."

"And?" Asked Chendrill, waiting.

"And she doesn't have a phone… so I bought her a phone. And put yours and my number into it," Sebastian said, smiling like a guilty child who was lying to his mother.

"And?" Chendrill asked again.

"Did I do wrong Chuck?"

He hadn't, but in his mind what was wrong is that the woman took it. Chendrill asked, "What's her husband do?"

"She said he's looking for work Chuck that's why I helped out."

Chendrill took a deep breath; it was getting better by the minute. The next thing Sebastian was going to suggest was either the husband come and work with Chuck or Sebastian was going to buy the guy a car so as he could get to work.

But for once, he was completely off the mark, as Sebastian carried on saying, "No Chuck, I just bought them a house."

Jesus Christ, Chuck thought—the man was a sweetheart and generous to the bone but who was this woman? He said, "What's the woman's name?"

"Oh I don't know."

Chuck took a breath, fuck me, he just bought a house for a woman and he doesn't know her name, so he asked,

"She has a first name?"

"Oh yes—Suzy."

"Suzy? Right. And how old is Suzy?"

Sebastian thought about it, staring down at his dog as Chendrill waited—this man who was worth a fortune and could see through any level of bullshit in his own world was now talking like a fool.

"Maybe forty, but she looks younger."

"Where does this friend and her family live?"

"They used to live on the East Side, but not in a home with a nice garden on the East Side. They were in sheltered housing Chuck, right in the East Side."

Chendrill asked, "Where?"

As he picked up his duster again then put it back on his desk, Sebastian said, "Right plum front and centre to that nightmare Hastings Street with its drug and social problems."

Chuck sat quietly for the moment still staring at the dog laying on his back showing off his dick. Then as he was about to speak, Sebastian said, "Oh, and she used to be an erotic dancer."

A stripper? Chendrill thought, as he wandered around Sebastian's office at Slave. Then turning said, "Used to be?"

"Yes Chuck, she used to be."

"Why, is she too old now?"

Sebastian shook his head; this wasn't the case, far from it. "Oh no Chuck, the girl's still got it, she has a medical condition that's all and I think it's best we leave it at that."

A medical condition, Chendrill thought and not taking the slightest notice of Sebastian's hint at protecting the woman's privacy asked, "What is it?"

"She's got a bag Chuck. So like I said, let's leave it at that."

Well chances were high he wasn't referring to Burberry or Coach, Chendrill thought, so he put it out there, "What type?"

"There's more to it, Chuck. She's unemployed now because she's wearing a colostomy bag. And I don't want to betray the woman's privacy, so please let us leave it at that," Sebastian said back in the kindest voice he could muster.

Okay? Chendrill thought as he found his way back to his usual spot by the window and carried on asking Sebastian, "Why's this girl not taken a real job then, one where she can keep her clothes on, like everyone else?"

For some reason unknown to Sebastian, Chendrill had become hostile, he'd seen it building in him, ruffling his red Hawaiian which clashed with the car, then saw it run through him the moment he'd mentioned the lady used to be an erotic dancer. He'd said to Chendrill, "There's nothing wrong with that Chuck, I've known a couple of friends who danced burlesque. They were completely sane; it's an art."

But it wasn't art for this woman—that was for certain. Chendrill could feel it. It was a business, and in his eyes strippers were one short step away from laying down for a few dollars more than they could stuff into the lining of their panties when they left the stage.

Someone was coming after Sebastian and him being gay only meant that they were coming from a different angle. That was all, playing on the man's softness and generosity. But how the fuck had whoever it was gotten this far so quickly?

Chendrill sat outside Slave at the wheel of the Aston thinking for a moment before pulling away. That one had taken him by surprise. He had asked when they'd met, and Sebastian, getting candid, said he'd been sad on the day after the fireworks when he'd seen Chendrill trying to be discreet holding Dan's mother's hand. Then the next day he'd been for a walk in the park and seen this beautiful lady crying and explained how he'd sat with her on the bench and heard her pour her heart out and how he'd got on the phone without a thought and bought this woman he didn't even know a home, doing it on a whim. He'd told Chendrill how beautiful the place was with its big bay windows and how they met now occasionally in the park. Chendrill had stood there by Sebastian's own window, no longer looking at the dog's bollocks but shaking his head in disbelief.

Trying to justify himself, Sebastian had said, "Oh, I'm just letting them live there, Chuck—I'm not stupid."

Sebastian snapped back at him in the kindest of ways, and heard Chendrill ask, "For free?"

"For now, yes. Until the family gets back on their feet. I did it because I was feeling sad Chuck and it made me feel good.

"It's just a cheap place Chuck, old and cheap."

Old and cheap? Anywhere in Vancouver old and cheap these days was going to be around a million dollars regardless if it was on the East Side. Chendrill had said, "Vancouver's not cheap Sebastian."

"Neither's making a film Chuck, but I can tell you, buying that house and telling that beautiful lady she and her family now have a proper roof over their heads has given me more satisfaction than I'll ever have shelling out on Patrick's movie."

It was a family of four, the unemployed stripper, her unemployed husband and their two boys, probably the same two 'wonderful' boys who'd stolen their mother's new phone and who Daltrey had stopped from mugging the guy in the park.

Probably.

He took the flyover passing through the sports stadiums and headed towards Strathcona on the East Side of town with its trendy wooden houses full of aging hippies and families in rentals.

The address on the piece of paper Chendrill had squeezed out of Sebastian read, 2123 Salsbury Street. And just as he pulled up along the road from the newly purchased property which made his employer feel good, he got the phone call he was expecting from the Vancouver Police Department—a message politely asking him to come in for an interview.

Chendrill estimated that the house was at least a hundred years old and looked like any other on the street with its steps leading up to the front door and big bay window, except for the sold sign sitting in the front garden and the stacks of new furniture boxes and cellophane thrown down the side alley—from the extra twenty thousand Sebastian had splashed out to fit the place out.

He got out and walked along the road and stood outside, feeling the wind heading south away from the mountains, hitting the trees with purpose like an invisible ghost rushing away to nowhere.

Walking up the short stairs, he knocked on the door and waited until he heard a stir and then knocked again and moments later saw the silhouette of a slim woman with big fake titties walking towards him through the stained-glass window of the front door.

She opened the door and before she could speak Chendrill said, "Suzy?"

Suzy looked up at him, this big guy in a red Hawaiian and, still clinging to the front door, pulled her long hair from her face, tucked it to her shoulder, and asked, "Who are you?"

"Sebastian asked me to come over, see if you have anything you need sorting out?"

"Sebastian?" the woman asked, her face as blank as an empty cinema screen. Chendrill stared back at her in her tight top, clinging to her stomach and oversized bosom, and wondered if Sebastian had been correct about this bag.

"Yeah, Sebastian. The guy who owns this place."

That did it, Chendrill thought, that jogged the memory as he saw the lights go on in her eyes as she remembered Sebastian, the nice kind hearted gay guy who just forked out over a million on a whim for this place because she was crying, kitted it out with furniture so the family could get away from the drug ridden neighbourhood where the woman probably used to work twenty-seven days out of thirty in a strip club.

"Oh Seb? Yeah Seb, he's so cute."

"Cute?" Chendrill asked and was about to carry on speaking when he heard the voice of a man call out unseen from the living room.

"Hey! Tell this Seb guy to get his ass over here and get rid of all that shit piled up in the alley for fucksake."

Chendrill looked to Suzy and smiled, raising his eyebrows as he did and said quietly, "Okay, I'll pass the message on."

Then he heard the man, whose big boots were by the

door and who did not bother to get up, call out again, "Tell him if it ain't gone tomorrow, I'll be doing it and he'll get the bill."

He'll be doing it, Chendrill thought, this unseen unemployed man who'd just been given a home. Telling the guy who'd bought it for him to shift his ass or he'd be sending him the bill. *Take it out of the rent*, Chendrill thought, before he placed his hand in his pocket and handed her back the phone she'd also been given for free.

Suzy's eyes lighting up, saying, "Oh my God, where did you find this?"

Chendrill looked back smiling and said, "The police found it, came round and said they wanted to speak with your two boys."

Which in a roundabout way was half true, although in Daltrey's mind she was no longer a cop.

Chapter Three

Ditcon sat in his office and fumed. So far he'd had everyone he could think of in there with him, one after the other and he'd shouted at them all. Now his throat was sore.

How the fuck could anyone in this day and age let something as simple as checking the DNA of a corpse slip through the cracks? Now he had to deal with it and on top of that he'd have to look that smug fuck Chendrill, who still wasn't returning his calls, in the eye somewhere in the process.

It hadn't been that long though and he'd be able to skate around the borders of truth like he did, hiding behind a closed door which only the Mayor could open. But there was an election coming up soon, so chances were that the sweaty prick would be gone and there'd be another guy he could bamboozle with the bullshit he had become so good at preaching.

Tell the guy what he needed to hear, bore the fuck out of him with charts and so many statistics that the man just stopped listening and started thinking about pussy or worried about the parks and bike lanes and looking good to the small percentage of people who'd bothered to get off their asses to vote in the first place.

He walked to the corner of his office and opened the small drinks cabinet with its secret bottle of vodka at the rear, cut a quarter lemon, reached down, pulled his underpants away from the crack of his ass, and poured a drink.

Chendrill, the big fucker, gone from the force but not

forgotten. Still out there sticking a thorn in his side like he'd never left. A legend when he was here and even now, after he'd left, he somehow carried it on. Even driving a fucking spanking new red Ferrari, which Ditcon had managed to have towed. Now though he'd heard a report that the prick was cruising around in an Aston Martin.

Nonetheless, the guy was a mini Che Guevara in the local legend department. *Minus the stupid shirts*, Ditcon thought as he took a huge hit on the vodka bottle and sunk back the lemon. Walking to the window, he looked out, almost hoping to see Chendrill pulling in to the carpark like James Bond with Daltrey at his side looking all sexy like she did so she could explain to him herself just how she'd pulled a Lazarus and risen from the dead like she had. The woman was now well on her way to being a bigger pain in the ass and too smart to manipulate into the sheets the way he'd have liked to.

This woman, who didn't sleep and who got results that he was never able to twist into being his own, where the hell had she been for the last week or so? Pretending to be pulling some barbecue action in the morgue that's where. But what had she been doing in the background while everyone was asleep and who was the crispy-crunch impersonator waiting in the freezer closet in the meantime? It was all he needed, especially with what seemed half the Border Security workforce calling him every five minutes asking bullshit questions.

He picked up his phone and, finding Chendrill's name, held his thumb just above the screen—one half of him wanting to push the button and to get a start at sorting the mess out, the other wanting to go back and reopen the fridge.

Maybe he should do both, he thought, and did the latter.

If he called, he thought, as he took another huge glug and followed it with a lemon, the big fucker will get all smug and say something back to him like 'I thought you were the detective?'

Or some other shit like that.

Then he'd have nowhere to go but to eat humble pie. He closed the fridge door and felt the taste of the lemon on his tongue as he heard a slight knock on his office door and a female officer in full dress uniform—just the way he liked them—stepped in and said, "We've found her sir, she's at St. Paul's. Chendrill brought her there this morning."

****

It wasn't often Ditcon rode in a squad car with the sirens on, but when he did he enjoyed it. The same young woman driving, nervous as hell, with her hair up and jacket pulled tight—it put the icing on the cake.

He leaned into the corner, enjoying the feel of the inertia squashing his body tight into the door as they hit a red and took a left onto Burrard as the lights and sirens screamed out. Fuck, he thought, this was what it was all about as he looked at the civilians holding their ears and staring at him looking cool in the back of the car.

It didn't matter that he'd been told Daltrey was asleep; he wanted to be there when she woke so he could say something clever like, 'You may think you've been hiding but I've known exactly where you've been the whole time.'

Then he'd give a little look to the girl driving the car with the sweaty palms after he'd ordered her to park illegally right in front of the hospital and insist she then join him upstairs so he could show off.

Or better still, he'd simply pretend the whole thing was part of a bigger plan that was in operation and, while Daltrey was weak, convince her she'd been used unwittingly as a pawn in a massive scheme and award her with a medal or something like that.

That's what he'd do, Ditcon thought, as they smashed through the lights at Georgia, destroying the eardrums of anyone not smart enough to cover up.

It was all part of a bigger plan. And Daltrey had done such a fantastic job in her part of it all.

They entered Officer Daltrey's room on the ward, Ditcon being noisy, making sure that he wouldn't have to wait long for her to wake. As soon as she opened her eyes, Ditcon was right there—front and centre in his suit applauding, clapping his hands together with a smile as big as the window as though the girl had just blown the socks off a panel of judges in a singing contest, and with one fist clenched in victory he said, "You should be proud of yourself girl, real proud, we've got them now!"

And he'd left it at that, turning abruptly and exiting the room before Daltrey could make sense of what had just happened, let alone respond.

As they rode the elevator down to the ground floor of St. Paul's, he turned to the young police woman hiding her titties underneath her heavy jacket and said, "Let's just say 'illegal border crossing' shall we? That'll give you some sort of clue as to why we burned all that extra gas getting here today."

It was absolute bullshit, of course, but it sounded good and was actually completely feasible; after all, it was little bullshit gems like the one he'd spat out that had got him where he was today. Never let the truth get in the way of a good story, as they say, especially one that moves you forward.

Yes, at some stage they'd be a very high ranking official arriving in his office from both the U.S. and Canadian Border agencies once this young and sexy number dropped that juicy bit of gossip to the eight or so other officers who'd be sitting around her with their tongues out in Starbucks, but by then he'd have worked the end bit out and until then he was looking good.

So Chendrill could fuck off and suck his dick, he thought.

Ditcon stepped out first as the elevator doors opened and, seeing his car still sitting there in the street with the lights going, realised what a fuck up he'd just made. As cool as it was for him to have this fit young female officer with her hair up Starsky and Hutch it out front with the lights going so he could whip out the rear and hit the front doors with meaning, why oh fucking why had he not done exactly the same but at the other end of the hospital?

Then he could have carried it on, looking cool and tough, staring at all the sexy nurses as he went marching down the corridor crashing through as many double doors as he could with his badge shining brightly on the front of his lapel.

If he'd really thought it through he could have had two squad cars pull up full of cops and formed the diamond formation as he had on big occasion's such as the Olympics, when they'd moved through BC Place like a flock of geese heading for warmer climates—him in the centre flanked by burly officers with attitude and dark glasses.

They reached the car and, opening the rear for himself, Ditcon got in and pulled out his phone, waiting for the young female officer to get in and thinking that what he needed to do now was avoid another sexual harassment issue like the last time and play it cool with this beauty.

He found Chendrill's number on speed dial and, putting himself on speaker phone, began to rub his neck and shoulders; despite the huge traffic problem the car was causing, he signaled for the young police woman settling into the driver's seat to hold off a moment on starting the car.

This time around he hit the button with no hesitation and, on hearing the legend that was Charles Chuck Chendrill answer, he said so that the young girl in the driver's seat knew exactly who he was talking to, "Chendrill… Chief Superintendent Ditcon here, thanks for the enquiry earlier. We have Detective Sargent Daltrey fully secured at St. Paul's but request that you hold off on making contact with her at this time while we deal with this border fugitive issue."

"Really?" was all the girl heard Chendrill say as she sat in the driver's seat of the squad car and played with her computer pretending not to be listening. Then she heard Chendrill follow it up with, "You're telling me Daltrey was fine and working on this issue with the illegal border crossing two nights back—you've known this all along?"

"This is Police and Government Border Security business and I'm not at liberty to say at this moment," was all Ditcon replied with the usual air of superiority he kept in reserve and pulled out whenever he had no idea what he was talking about.

"But I presume you know the identity of the suspect

currently at large?" Chendrill asked.

Ditcon gave the officer a knowing look as their eyes met in the rear-view mirror and turned to look at the congestion he was causing outside, and said, "I can let you know yes, that we're fully aware of the individual and his whereabouts."

Then they heard Chendrill say, "Fuck me you're good," and begin to laugh, slowly at first, growing louder with each guttural roar building from deep within. Then settling himself, Chendrill said, "Are you going to continue to be a complete and utter cunt all your life?"

****

Chendrill stood on the opposite side of the road and watched Ditcon pull away from the hospital and disappear through a red light in the distance with the siren blaring.

He'd wondered what the hold up in the traffic was on the way to see Daltrey and, after switching back, had parked the Aston alongside the forecourt of the Wall Centre Hotel. He slipped the concierge a tenner and spotted Ditcon sitting in the back of the squad car. Then his phone rang.

Fuck, the guy was so full of shit, 'yes, we're fully aware of the individual and his whereabouts' when in fact he was talking to the very same person to whom he was referring.

He crossed the road and found his way to the room where Daltrey lay in bed recovering as she should have been doing two weeks prior. He opened the door to Daltrey's room and sneaked a look inside to see her lying there all bandaged up with her eyes closed and heard her say, "You're supposed to knock."

He was—he knew that only too well—and suddenly

embarrassed by his own behavior, ran his hand across the top of his head and then his neck, “I’m sorry.”

“Don’t be,” Daltrey said, “you look more tired than me.”

She was right; he was. It had been a busy week and he was hurting all over, but more than anything he was hurting inside from the spat he’d had with Dan’s mother earlier that morning. He said, “You’re the important one right now.”

Then lifting herself up, Daltrey said, “Ditcon was just here.”

“And?”

“And he woke me up with his presence, then when he saw I was awake just gave me a standing ovation, said some shit about me being great, doing a great job, and left.”

“You tell him you’re out?” Chendrill asked as he sat on the end of her bed, and saw Daltrey look away towards the window as if the problem was somehow just outside.

“It’s hard to do anything with that man the way he takes over the room.”

“Take your time,” Chendrill said. “Don’t go crashing the door down like I did.”

And he had done just that when he’d had enough of Ditcon and left the force, crashed the door open with his right foot and stuck his resignation letter straight to the front of Ditcon’s sweaty forehead.

But that was years ago.

Daltrey said, “I don’t think I could carry on now, you know I’d always be that girl.”

“What girl.”

“The one that ran away and left a girl to die.”

Chendrill looked at her, this girl who was as tough as old boots but who was now distraught beyond belief with herself for doing nothing other than acting on basic instinct and surviving. He walked across to the small chair at the side of the sterile room and sat down, taking his weight off of his lower legs and said, "There're only four people in this world who know the truth and two are no longer with us. For one, this is a blessing; for the other, a tragedy—which was not your fault. And if anyone ever hears about it it'll have come from you and not me, and that's a promise."

"There's this guy, though. I was up in his place watching before that Russian guy attacked me, maybe he saw?"

"Patrick, the realtor?" Chendrill asked butting in.

Daltrey looked up at him, "How did you know?"

"I'm a detective, you know that. As soon as I'd heard you were gone, I was all over it and was onto the fucker within a few days."

"Which fucker?" Daltrey said, showing the slightest bit of her old self before sitting there staring into nowhere for what seemed an age. Chendrill noticed and gave her time, looking at the floor.

Then she asked, "So, you met him then?"

"I met them both. The Russian in a café where he got away and Patrick—along with his teeth—except he wasn't smiling a few days back, he was shitting himself."

"Why?"

"Because he saw you in trouble and didn't pick up the phone."

Daltrey looked up, the news of this guy she'd kind of liked betraying her seemed to hit a nerve. Then she said, "Worried the bad press would hurt home sales no doubt."

And Chendrill looking up smiling said, "No. Houses are not his thing anymore. He saw a picture of himself looking back at him like an idiot and didn't like what he saw, so now he's a film producer and they're making his film over at Slave and your old boyfriend Dan's in it."

Chapter Four

Patrick DeSendro, who used to be a realtor, walked thought the now crowded offices of Slave Media teeth first with a smile saying, “Hey how you doing?” and “Hey here he is! Here she is!” He reached Sebastian’s office without a clue as to who the people were or what they did—all that mattered was they were going to be helping him in his quest to be famous. Opening the door to Sebastian’s office as though it was his own, he saw Sebastian holding his dog Fluffy up towards the ceiling and held out his hands and said, “Put that dog down, you don’t know where he’s been.”

Ignoring him, Sebastian simply said it as it was, “I think he’s got worms Patrick, what do you think?”

Patrick moved closer and joined Sebastian staring up at his little dog’s backside, then said, “Is he rubbing himself on the carpet?”

He had been, that’s what had been bothering Sebastian. He replied, “Maybe, you have experience with dogs do you Patrick?”

Patrick didn’t; in fact, many a multimillion dollar property he’d been ready to show had been disastrous because of them, despite having his team go over the place, cleaning from top to bottom, getting rid of miscellaneous furniture by stuffing it into a truck that parked miles away—getting the place perfect, only to have some prospective buyer step in a stinky coiler left out on the lawn to ruin the magic.

“A little, and, trust me, you need to be careful!”

“I think I’ll call the vet, Patrick,” Sebastian said.

Patrick nodded in agreement, as though it was the most important decision of the day. And to Sebastian it was.

Patrick walked to the window and looked down.

"Did I see Chuck here awhile back?"

He had and had been coveting the guy's car. Sebastian had been in such a generous mood lately that Patrick was up here hanging about, not knowing what was going on around him, but still fancying one for himself because they looked so cool. The fact he could easily afford to go to the showroom and smack down enough cash for two was beside the point—there's no fun in that.

Putting his dog down and watching Fluffy walk, Sebastian said, "Why?"

"I just thought it would make us all look so cool if we all had a sports car."

"How's the script Patrick?" Sebastian asked without looking up.

It was a good question, and one Patrick was still unable to answer because he had yet to read it. Megan Rawlis, his friend the writer, who used to be a cocktail waitress, had said it was incredible, though, so what was wrong with that? Yes, she may have been a raving lunatic flower child from LA, but she looked hot with no clothes on and seemed to like working him and milking his dick as much as she enjoyed living the dream. So who was going to upset the apple cart with that one? Not him, that was for certain.

Holding his hands out in a gesture impossible for Sebastian to ignore, he said, "Trust me—it's fantastic."

Sebastian stared at him and said, "That's it? That's all you've got to offer? No plot points, story line, perhaps, even, possibly an idea of your own?"

This line of questioning wasn't what Patrick had been

expecting. Maybe it was a bad time to come in and mess about with the man, especially since he was worried about his stupid dog's ass. So he said, "Oh, trust me Sebastian, I know the script from top to bottom. I just don't want to ruin it for you when the latest draft comes through. Why kill the magic hey? If you want though, I'll have Megan come over and sit down for an afternoon and break the whole thing down after she's given you a personal reading."

That'll do, Patrick thought. He knew how much the Joni Mitchell-singing hippie chick drove everyone crazy in the office with her long skirts and wild hair and Sebastian would rather put needles in his eyes than suffer that. And right on cue after just a moment's thought, Sebastian said, "Sure, bring her in and all three of us can sit down and go through it together."

****

Ditcon was still rubbing his neck and shoulders when he'd arrived back in his office on Main Street and turned the heat up. His driver *de jour* still with him, now wandering around the large room with her fingers unconsciously trailing across his large wooden desk as she looked at all the photos of the big guy receiving medals and playing golf with celebrities.

He'd left the hospital and had her gun it right through town with the lights on all the way to his favourite Italian restaurant near Boundary Road. They'd stopped off for an early lunch with some wine, at which he'd told her how good a driver she was and how her handling of the corner earlier on Burrard was so precise he'd cricked his neck—not her fault of course, his entirely for not having expected such acumen. She'd just been too good for him—taken him by surprise.

Now they were up in his office, waiting for an important phone call coming in that she could listen in to as long as she didn't let on that she was there. After all it wasn't often that you're on a conference call with the head of the CIA. In the meantime, she could watch him work, see how the big boys do it, learn some stuff that the ego maniacs at cop school, with their fuck you attitude, can't teach you because they don't know it themselves.

Oh, and if she was getting hot, she should take off that tight-fitting jacket and fix them both a drink from the bottle he had stashed at the back of the mini bar.

Ditcon watched as the young police woman unzipped the front of her jacket and let those titties out. *Fuck she was nice this one, apart from her ass being a little too big*, he thought. She seemed to like him, giving him that little look when they were eating at lunch, laughing at his stupid jokes. Him not touching her, her getting tactile with him instead after the glass of wine, grabbing his arm and punching him really hard when he teased her, telling her she was going to make detective.

Looking up as he watched her pour them both a vodka from his little minibar, he said, "I've got some blow if you want?"

"Sorry?"

He smiled at her.

"You're kidding, right?"

He wasn't. Blow was easy to come by when all the alleys that surrounded your police station sold drugs—and women, but that was another matter. It was the moment of truth with this one, either she was going to start to play or she was out the door with the knowledge that her superiors may hear about her drunk driving—which was not good, especially since it was in front of the boss.

Ditcon looked at her with that big, stupid grin on his face, trying to remember the girl's name. *Dorothy—that was it*, he thought. He was good with names, it was his strong point and partly the reason he'd moved up the ladder so fast—that, and meeting, by chance, the then teenage boyfriend of a now long-forgotten Mayor.

He said, "What do you think Dorothy, am I playing with you?"

He heard her say back, "My name's Stephanie."

Shit.

"Just playing with you Steph, I knew that," Ditcon confessed.

Then he heard her say, "I never thought I'd be offered that up here."

Ditcon leaned back in his chair and, still feigning his neck injury, said, "Yeah well, life's strange."

Then she looked at him and totally serious said, "Is this a test?"

"Maybe?" Ditcon said back with a smile.

Stephanie stared at him, unsure of what to do. The guy she'd seen walking around the station with purpose, looking all serious and kicking ass was not the same man who was sitting there grinning like a fifteen-year-old and rubbing his shoulders. Yeah, she'd done a bit of coke in her day, back in her late teens during Stampede week in her hometown, Calgary. She'd been trying to be cool, then lied about it in her confidentiality report when she applied to be a part of the Vancouver Police Department. She'd even taken a line an hour before the polygraph test they put her though to straighten herself out.

The wine had already been going too far, but now vodka while on duty—and cocaine? *Jesus*. But who knows, she thought, the guy is the top dog around here and partying with the boss could do no harm. After all, he's the guy who'd be firing her, either out the door or further up the ladder if she played it right.

Turning to him and holding both glasses to her chest, she said, "How do I know you're not a cop?"

Ditcon laughed, that was a good one. He said straight back, "How do I know you're not a cop, hey? Could get dangerous, here in my office, both of us carrying guns and all."

Your office. Stephanie thought, your office on the top floor, away from it all with its huge desk and sofa and view of the mountains.

Then taking him by surprise as she handed him his large vodka with a little piece of lemon, she said, "When you take this call later from the big shot in the U.S. about this guy who stole one of their cars and crashed it across the border, why don't you tell them you've heard from a good source that it's Charles Chuck Chendrill they're looking for? That'll set him straight for disrespecting you the way he did this morning."

****

Megan Rawlis sat in the chair opposite Sebastian with Patrick flanking them both from the side in a manner that showed without a shadow of a doubt that he had absolutely nothing to do with this read through meeting.

Moving his chair out purposely, making a circle, and holding a notepad and pen, Sebastian looked at Patrick and said, "Patrick before we start, why don't you give us both your thoughts on the script, and then tell us, maybe, how the plot points could be strengthened and, possibly, if you think there are any weaknesses in the plot or sub plots."

Patrick stared back at Sebastian sitting in the middle of his office in his yellow trousers like a king. His ass was still aching from the working Megan had just given it, the way he liked her to do. Megan milking him onto the nice clean sheets on her king-sized bed in the suite Sebastian was paying for at the Sutton.

For once, he had gone over there to go through the script as they had a meeting that afternoon and the flower child had surprized him with the offer of giving him what he liked. And this time she hadn't gone easy.

He said with a grin that had sold a hundred condos, "Trust me Sebastian this script is just fantastic! Adalia's going crazy about it."

Asking in a clear and precise manner that left no doubts in the mind of anyone in the room that it was Sebastian who was paying for this project and in charge, and definitely not Patrick, despite the man's front and bravado, Sebastian said, "Like I asked before. Tell us how maybe the plot points could be possibly strengthened and if there are any weaknesses within the plot or sub plots?"

And Megan piped up for the first time since she had sat down and despite being nervous ever since Chendrill had given her a talking to regarding her behavior said, "I think we should scrap the ray guns altogether and put all the emphasis on love and bringing peace to the world, let's be different."

Smiling and holding out his hand with the gentlest of touches, Sebastian held it to the young girl's arm, stopping her in her tracks and said, "Megan love, we'll get to your thoughts soon enough, please let Patrick have his turn."

And he turned to Patrick, waiting.

Patrick shifted in his seat, his ass still burning inside, wishing he'd looked at the script at some stage or known a character's name at least. But then he remembered he did, there was Dan's character's name the one Dan was on about when Dan had humiliated that guy with the ego who'd written the script in the first place. Dan had told him about the binoculars and how it was impossible for them to work the way it was scripted. He said, "The binoculars, they've got to go, maybe use a laser system—you know get ahead of technology same as Star Trek used to do. Let's make incredible gadgets up that scientists can latch onto after the movie's been released. Same goes for the ray guns as Megan just mentioned, I'm all for that 100%. Trust me, it's what this script needs. It'll make all the difference. Oh, and I was also thinking maybe we introduce a pet for the kids to love, you know like a little dog that can save the planet. Maybe even a really cute one like your little Fluffy. Trust me, kids'll go crazy. How is he by the way?"

****

Sebastian watched from his window as the producer and new writer of the film he was indulging Patrick with left the building and hailed a cab out front. The man obviously had no idea what was going on, but he'd seen worse—at least the guy could sell. Once the thing was finished that's where he'd be coming into his own, and truth was he liked the idea about having little Fluffy in the movie. Even if Patrick had used it as a deflection like he had.

Fluffy would like that as well, and he'd be able to get

him all shampooed for the film and double up the glam for the premier, bring him there in his own limo—give his little dog the red-carpet star treatment. This would be amusing.

But for the moment, the little dog had other issues. The biggest one being the fact he was leaving tiny skid marks on the rug. He picked up the phone and called Charles Chuck Chendrill, “Chuck! It’s Sebastian, what are you doing? I’ve got an emergency.”

****

They drove slowly across the Granville Street Bridge, Chendrill at the wheel of the Aston, Sebastian in the back discreetly blowing on his dog’s backside to keep it cool as they went.

Two emergencies in a day was a record for Chendrill. Sebastian waking him again happily—this time in the middle of the afternoon—pulling him from a dream where his mouth was taped up and he was drowning while he was sprawled out on his oversized sofa back at his condo.

As they took the right exit towards 4th Street, Sebastian said, “I know when he’s not well Chuck, I always have."

Chendrill looked in the mirror, just nodding on the way over and doing the same on the way back as Sebastian said exactly the same thing but in reverse, “I always know when he’s feeling better Chuck, I always have.”

Feigning interest, but not wanting to know about what had been going on behind closed doors at the vet’s, Chendrill kept quiet. Sebastian nonetheless telling him how Fluffy hasn’t liked it there at the vet ever since he and Alan had the dog shaved after they’d found a flea. Keeping it up, Sebastian carried on and said, “You wouldn’t believe it Chuck, it was an infestation!”

"Really?"

"Alan was beside himself, kept scratching all day at work, thinking he had them also. We had bites on both our ankles."

Telling him it comes with the territory if you have a pet, Chendrill joked, "They can lie dormant in the carpet for years you know."

They parked out front of Sebastian's building as the sun was making its way towards the west, Chendrill picked up Fluffy, carrying him to the door—the dog making the most of the fuss, seemingly half asleep in his arms.

As they rode the public elevator up to his penthouse suite, Sebastian said, "Patrick's saying Fluffy should be in the movie, Chuck."

Chendrill looked to the dog lying almost comatose in his arms. The dog had star quality, that was for sure. It spent enough time at the doggy spa to qualify. They reached the top floor and the doors opened. Seeing a man standing in the corridor looking to them both, before then getting into the elevator himself and closing the door behind them, they stepped into Sebastian's suite as Chendrill said, "What's Patrick's after?—Besides, how do you know Fluffy can act?"

"Oh, he can act, Chuck. Look at him now lying there as though he's dying when all he's got is a sore backside. I don't know who was worse today, Fluffy or Patrick with the way he could not sit still."

Chendrill didn't want to go there—he'd seen the photos of Patrick being taken by the Russian woman and that had scarred him enough. As he stood by the window looking down to the road below waiting for the man who'd stepped into the elevator when they got out to appear, he asked,

"That guy who was just up here, you know him?"

Sebastian stared at him confused. Then answered curiously, "The one up here, who got in the lift?"

"Yeah."

"No—Why?"

"Because he's just appeared downstairs and he's now sitting on a park bench."

Sebastian walked over to the window and looked down. The park below his place was packed with people laying, sitting, walking, running, riding bikes, each enjoying the last of the afternoon sun as it sneaked through the trees. He said, "There's got to be a thousand people down there, Chuck."

"The one on the bench."

Sebastian stared down trying to see who on earth Chendrill was referring to. He said, "You've got better eyes than me Chuck, I can't see a thing."

Then Chendrill made it only too clear.

"The guy looking up at this place."

At first he couldn't tell and wondered if Chendrill was going crazy, then, looking down to the man, Sebastian said, "You even sure it's the same person, Chuck?"

"One hundred percent."

Sebastian moved to another window and, calling out unseen to Chendrill, said, "He might be looking at the other building's penthouse suite at the back, Chuck."

"He's not."

"Maybe he's just looking at the birds in the sky."

"Maybe," Chuck answered, not wanting to get Sebastian any more alarmed than he already was or he'd be asking him to stay overnight on the couch or in the guest room. The guy was no bird watcher, nor was he looking at the neighbours.

Three minutes later, Chendrill was outside, leaving through the parking garage and nipping across the road to stand in the park as the general public passed him by.

The man was still there, looking up, looking down, scratching his head, rubbing his eyes. The man in his forties with darkish skin, making him look almost Italian, the guy trying to look younger in his turned-up jeans and cowboy boots.

An hour later, he moved on with purpose, his head down, hands in his pockets, stopping for a piss at the public toilets on English Bay, then up the steps and across the road onto Davie Street, then up the hill to the top where the rainbow coloured shops and bars screamed out at him making their own sexuality statements until they faded back into the vanilla yuppiedom of Yaletown and the offices of Slave.

And there he stood as he had at the bench, looking up at nothing from a doorway, this man with thinning hair whose youth had long past, waiting and watching while Chendrill watched him.

It was almost an hour that passed before he checked his phone and moved off again, Chendrill sitting in the bar three doors along watching the man through the reflection of a hat shop window next to Slave.

He kept on heading east, crossing the boundary where rich become poor, and where the poor came home to rest their heads in sheltered housing and the cheap hotels, feeding off welfare and selling their infested beds in cramped damp rooms to these poor, emptied souls stuck in a cycle of poverty.

From what Chendrill could see, this is where he was

from, this man who'd been waiting up in the corridor outside Sebastian's home. The man whose up-market clothes didn't match the people who knew his name.

From the diagonal direction the man was heading, it was odds on that he was on his way to the strip club at the top of Main Street. By the time he'd reached it and paid the cover, Chendrill was already sitting inside watching him through the long thin legs of the girl on the stage as she pranced about, hanging onto the pole that would be hers for the length of five songs.

He knew them and they knew him was all Chendrill could tell as the man sat down at the corner of the stage ordering a beer as he watched the girl's shoes and felt her pink boa whisk past his face. An hour passed along with five more beers and five other women on the stage dancing and trying to look keen, the man banging the flat of his hand on the stage as his spirit loosened with booze as he watched the legs and tits of the girls on stage and the perky asses of the lap dancers roaming the room seeking their prey.

By the time his hand was sore and his sixth beer was half done, the lap dancers moved in, sidling up using their sex and the smell of their soft skin to entice him until they lured him away to a room upstairs where they could all take turns rubbing themselves into his crotch as his hands hovered inches from their wiggling tits as they floated in tantalizingly close, touching his lips for the length of one song and another and another until he could take no more and staggered away with the smell and feel of the girls still fresh in his mind, down the stairs to lean his giddy spinning head against the stall wall of a piss stained toilet, pull his erect cock from his pants and stroke it until he came. It was what he liked to do and what did he care what people thought of him as he heard them chatting bullshit as he jerked himself silently, breathing heavy as his hand ran. What did he care if the door was half open? What did he care of their laughter and their taunts? They were nothing in his world—after all, how many people had they killed?

He walked out staring down the young men in the rest room and checked himself in the mirror. He still looked good even if his hair was messed and his cheeks were red. He opened the door and walked out, hearing the music blaring now as he passed through the crowd and back towards the stage towards the big guy in the Hawaiian now sitting on his stool. Reaching him, the man sat down and, leaning in, retrieved his beer.

"Sorry, am I on your stool?" Chendrill asked.

The man answered, telling him it wasn't a problem and looking at the girl on the stage with half the interest.

"You're good, you're good."

Chendrill got straight to the point, saying, "Now that you've jacked off, you can tell me what your interest is in Sebastian String and Slave?"

The man stared at him, the girl on the stage now right there with her snatch out in his face. The man turned his head and looked at it for a moment, her skin shaven all around with a tiny stud in her clit. Looking away and back to Chendrill he said, "Can you imagine doing that to your dick?"

Chendrill stayed quiet, waiting for an answer. The man continued, "You the guy who got out the elevator with him then?"

He was, they both knew that. Then the man said, "How about I just get up and walk away and we leave it at that.

Pretend neither of us ever met? Then we can both grow old."

"How about you answer my question so you can come back in here again without feeling embarrassed," Chendrill answered.

The man turned away looking back at the stage to the girl, on the other side now, and took a deep breath. Did he need this bullshit right now from a big fuck who couldn't dress properly? No. He looked at the girl for a second longer and then to one of the lap dancers who'd just ruined his hair and, turning to talk to her, leaned down pulling a gun from his cowboy boot and stuck it quickly in Chendrill's stomach. Smiling as his other hand dropped a wad of twenty dollar bills next to his unfinished beer, he said, "How about the last thing you see is that girl's crotch?"

"I could think of worse," replied Chendrill quick as a flash with a smile as he watched the man get up and slowly back away with the gun tucked up the sleeve of his top.

Calling out as he went, Chendrill said, "Next time, you'd better have two."

****

The name of the guy who'd pulled the gun after wacking off in the shitter was Mattia, Chendrill discovered from one of the lap dancing girls as she dropped the hundred dollar note into her purse while Chendrill did his best not to look at her breasts.

"Says he's Italian and from Calgary," she said, "and he worked as a drover until he fell and found Jesus. But that's bullshit, because he ain't no cowboy. And yeah, he does this thing, takes two or three of us upstairs at a time then goes down and wacks one out in the stall, but there's nothing new there. Oh yeah, he's got a big dick and he smells."

"What of, sweat?" Chendrill asked. The girl shook her head and said straight back, "no, more like death," as she watched the door for prey as it opened. Chendrill looked at the girl's shoes, wondering what would happen to her ankle if she missed a step. She was a good-looking woman though, despite the shoes, perfect in almost every respect, her hair long, lovely shoulders, face, breasts, flat toned stomach, tapered legs, what the hell was she doing here he thought. But she was there, her and the others who floated about looking sexy. As he pulled out another hundred-dollar bill, he said, "Is he with the Angels?"

She shook her head again, looking about, there were a few here in the crowd sitting in groups, feeling special in their VIP booths along the wall. She looked back to Chendrill.

"No, he doesn't run with that crowd. I've heard he lends money though. He comes here and gets it on with us, but I've seen him alone with one of the other girls if you get my drift." He handed her the other hundred.

"What like he's fucking one of them?"

The girl, not giving a shit, said straight back. "Yeah but not here though, if you know what I mean, people have relationships, even us."

"If he comes back in here, send me a text before he goes upstairs and I'll give you another one of these," Chendrill said.

The girl looked at the cash and took it before saying, "Make it three and you've got a deal."

****

The first thing Chendrill did when he got back up to Sebastian's penthouse was to ask Sebastian what was going on. Sebastian sitting there, not wanting to look up at Chendrill, holding little Fluffy in his lap on the verge of tears with his tea shaking in its porcelain cup, Chendrill telling him straight as he looked down upon Sebastian saying, "Sebastian, I can't help you unless I know everything."

Sebastian stared back at him with watery eyes, shaking his head and saying in an unsteady tone, "Chuck, I'm telling you I don't know. Maybe the guy just wanted to rip the place off."

Shitheads like that don't carry guns and blow two hundred on three lap dancers at a time, Chendrill thought, they're opportunists—this guy wasn't.

"Have you done anything illegal?" Chendrill asked as Sebastian stared back at him with a look of astonishment on his face.

Sebastian simply replied, "You know me Chuck, I don't even walk in the bike lane in the park."

It was true, he didn't, thought Chendrill. He'd seen him struggling through the crowd on the seawall when the bike lane was empty. Then looking about the room to the art and pictures on the wall spanning the man's life, Chendrill said, "May I ask, Sebastian, what about Alan? Is there anything there that may be an issue?"

And that's when Sebastian started crying.

"He was a man's man Chuck—you know, like you are," Sebastian said once the tears had stopped and he'd been able to breathe again. "He really was, just like you Chuck."

Like me, Chendrill thought, and wondered how that could be at all possible as Sebastian carried on, his face brightening as the memories came flooding back.

"He loved to go to the races, it was his thing, you know? I didn't really care, but I went anyway. Every time one of the big stallions came strutting past and its penis would drop down, you know like they do, Alan would say, 'Oh if only I could take the weight.' Oh, he was so funny Chuck, it was like his own little catch phrase—he never missed the opportunity."

It wasn't what Chendrill wanted to hear and, rubbing his hands across the top of his brow, he said, "And?"

"And, you know, it's the way he was."

What is going on? Chendrill thought, what was this little secret Sebastian wanted to let out but was having such a hard time doing? He stared at him waiting, watching as the bubbles inside Sebastian floated towards the surface.

Then taking a deep breath and suddenly letting go, Sebastian said, "There was this man, Chuck. Alan liked him, see he was really into horses and Alan—bless his soul—wanted to have a stake in one. So, he could feel part of it all instead of just one of the punters watching. This man was selling his stake in a thoroughbred from the Island who'd won this and that cup and they wanted to go the whole hog with the horse, hire jockeys and such."

"And you paid?" said Chendrill in the softest of voices.

Sebastian nodded, "Yes Chuck, I was doing well then and it wasn't such a huge amount to put a smile on Alan's face."

"How much?" Chendrill asked in a tone so firm Sebastian had no choice other than to answer.

"Just two hundred and fifty thousand."

Just! Chendrill thought, wondering how much the man actually had made in his life. Then he carried on saying, "And?"

"And Alan bought his share of the horse and it raced and won and…and then it died."

"How?" Chendrill asked in a similar tone.

"It was strange Chuck, in an around about way it was killed by a mosquito."

"It caught a disease from one?" Chendrill replied, wondering if he'd ever heard of a disease horses could catch from a mosquito.

Sebastian stayed quiet for a moment and then taking another deep breath said, "No, Alan was taking the horse to a race out on the island. Alan was driving the vehicle which was pulling the trailer. Anyway, Alan said there was one in the Range Rover around his legs and he freaked out, started swatting it because he was wearing shorts and they went off the road and into a ditch. He said the trailer twisted over and ended up resting against a tree."

Chendrill stared at Sebastian for a moment. A mosquito took them off the road? It didn't sound right. He asked, "And were they hurt?"

"Alan was okay because he was wearing his seat belt—this other guy was knocked out though, Alan said he thought he was dead."

"What about the mosquito?"

"Oh well, who knows if it survived Chuck. They only live a week or so anyway."

Chuck waited a moment, then asked, "No, what I mean is it true about the mosquito?"

"Yes Chuck, they can give a nasty bite, you know that."

"What about your horse?"

"He said it was ok, but when he got to the racecourse, the horse was dead."

"So you lost your stake in this horse?"

"Yes Chuck."

"And anything else?"

"Like what Chuck."

"Like who was this other 'Partner'?"

"No, nothing like that, he was straight, Chuck—though I do admit I was jealous as hell. But no, nothing like that. Alan was so upset Chuck, I remember him calling me and crying."

"And?"

"And, that was it, apart from Alan being sick with worry about it, and then not long after he started getting sick, Chuck. I think it was the stress of it all. Then he got really sick and the man disappeared and I thought that was the end of it. But at Alan's funeral, when I was in a daze, someone came up and shook my hand and I didn't know who he was until he said quietly in my ear, 'you still owe for the horse.'"

"The same guy who was downstairs?" Chendrill asked quietly.

Sebastian shrugged, shaking his head, saying, "It's a blur Chuck, the whole thing—maybe?"

"And Alan passed on eight years ago?"

Sebastian nodded, closing his eyes, as the whole event replayed in his mind like a nightmare.

Chendrill gave him a moment before saying, "Well it looks as though this is what it could be all about."

And as always Chendrill was correct, but just how far things were about to go, he could never have imagined.

Chapter Five

Dan made it home and for the first time in his life, he didn’t stop off at the fridge before tiptoeing down the stairs. The last thing he needed right now was twenty questions from his mum, especially with his dick hurting the way it was.

Quietly so as to avoid the squeak that always gave him away, he opened the door to his room and slipped inside to see his mother sitting on the bed looking at him with red eyes. She said, "Have you seen Chuck?"

He hadn't. After a moment, he said, "Why, did you hit him?"

She had. Maybe it was a hit borne from any one of the old movies she’d sat up watching in the early hours in the morning when insomnia was a part of her life, a slap that had come hard and sharp right across the face.

She said, “Why would I?”

“Well he ain’t in here, so somethings gone on,” Dan answered as he walked past her wondering if she’d been nosing about the place.

He sat at the bench Sebastian had bought him so as he could carry on with his electronics while Sebastian’s company exploited his looks, picking up a circuit board and staring at it for a moment as he heard his mother say, “So what have you been up to?”

“Rehearsing for this stupid film your boyfriend has got me involved in.”

“Really—where?” Tricia said, perking up at the thought of her son being in a movie.

Dan didn’t look back, saying only, “It’s stupid Mum, so don’t go phoning all your friends or you may get egg on your face."

"Who were you rehearsing with then?"

A tricky one this one, Dan thought, as he looked to the desk. Maybe someone had called and told someone at Slave and they'd called his mum, telling her he'd been sleeping with a sixty-year-old who still had nice tits.

He said, "Why'd you ask that?"

Tricia stared at her son sitting there in his room with his back to her, all hunched up the way he used to be when she knew he'd been raiding the neighbour's kitchen and they'd been over to complain.

She said, "What have you really been doing—have you got a girl?"

"Yeah."

"Really?" his mother asked with a smile. Then she said, "Do you think I'll get to meet this one— how old is she?"

From what he could work out, Adalia Seychan was sixty-two, so if he reversed the order he'd just be able to claim dyslexia like he used to at school when he got bored.

So, as he turned and faced his mother, he said, "Twenty-six."

"That's a little old for you, don't you think?" And for a moment Dan thought that in the process of trying to be clever, he'd actually said Adalia's true age—until his mother, putting his mind to rest, said, "Well I should be grateful for that, at least she's not the same age as the one you brought home a few nights back."

Then she asked her name and Dan sat there for a moment thinking, his mother sitting there still on the bed now with a smile saying, "You telling me you don't know her name?"

And Dan answered, "It's not really that kind of a

relationship."

"Really—what kind is it then?"

Dan thinking quickly and saying straight back, "What are you doing in my room anyway?"

Tricia stared at him, this son of hers, who was now getting fan mail and drove a Ferrari, but still lived in her basement.

"It is my home you know."

"Yeah well it's my room."

Tricia stood and headed for the door, she'd been down this road before and knew the argument off by heart and the only reason she was down there in the first place was because for the first time in a long while she felt lost and alone and wanted to be close to the one person who belonged to her 100%, the one person she loved unconditionally even if she had just found the nice soft rayon sock she'd been missing for weeks all crispy under his bed.

She reached the door and, turning as she opened it, said, "If Chuck calls you, tell him to call me please."

Dan nodded, then without looking up continued as he heard the door close, saying, "Promise that if he doesn't then you go put an order in for a box of pastries at the bakers so as you can give that guy with the van another shot."

Dan picked up a circuit board and stared at it for a moment as he listened to his mother's footsteps head up the stairs, hearing her call out as she reached the top, "Fuck you, Dan."

Dan waited. It was at this point when his mother would either let it go or come back down the stairs like a swat team leader and, if she could get in the door, start throwing stuff. He looked to the door—the lock still broken from the other night when it had not had his weight behind it, as it usually did, when his mum was in a rage, and all because he'd had a woman heavier than him sitting on his face. If she was here now, hiding under the bed like he used to fantasize about, then it would be ideal and he'd have her guard the door so he could get on with working his way around this electronic governor Sebastian had installed on the Ferrari.

After all, he was taking Adalia out on the weekend in it and could do without being the slowest car on the road.

****

Mattia the Italian sat in his big empty house out at the edge of Deep Cove and wondered if his ex-wife would be making it impossible for him to take his kids to the football game in the afternoon as he liked to do.

That fucking bitch, saying to him every fortnight how they have a cold or a sore throat or they've got dance or whatever shit she could dream up just so she could fuck with him. Then the kids would see him and love their dad because he let them run riot and put on his big sovereign rings. But that was a whole three days away and, in the meantime, all he could do was wait. They'd lived on the coast out east before, and he would travel west to make his living and cause trouble when necessary. Then she'd started fucking his friend who raised chickens, and then later the guy at the restaurant who pretended to be a surfer but didn't have a board.

Mattia had had enough of it and one day just did not come home, his wife arriving later with the kids and setting up a home again and after a while continued being a bitch.

Then the lawyers came, hers giving it out in court—the man trying to look like someone he could never be, with his bad acting and fucked up monologue, demanding to know where he earned his money, trying to destroy him any and every way his ex-wife could think of, asking for the world as she sat there in her fancy dress and stupid shoes and pleaded poverty to the judge who saw right through them both. Mattia had sat there quietly listening to his ex's lies and her accusations of cruelty, planning how he'd make her weasel of a lawyer eat dog shit.

And on a summer's day, as the birds circled high in the sky above the park next to Mattia's new home, the court's divorce process all done and long forgotten, he'd done just that. Hitting in the kidneys the man with the acid tongue who wished he could be more than the ambulance chaser he was, he said to him in a mimicking tone the same words he'd heard him say, "And I put it to you sir, you are not reputable, you are not a business man, you are nothing more than a thug, a degenerate, a parasitic man who lives off the need and discomfort of others."

And as his ex-wife's lawyer lay there distraught with pain from the blow to the kidney and the knee in his back, he felt the sovereign covered fingers he'd looked down upon with such disdain hold his mouth open and force foul smelling dog's shit onto the tongue that had spouted a full week's worth of vile accusations. The man who had so much wanted to sound like Tom Cruise, squirming and unconsciously kicking his feet as he choked and gagged and vomited as his body ejected the grass and faeces whilst he listened, hearing his own words coming back at him and knowing right there and then that there could be no recourse because everything he'd said about the man who held him tight to the soggy wet ground beneath him suddenly appeared very true.

****

The stripper at the club had been correct as Mattia did lend money and his rate was good he felt, decent enough, fair and only a little above what the banks charged for a fancy credit card that would let you fly somewhere nice for free as long as you kept on spending—except such privileges were long gone for the people who came to him. For Mattia's banking plan was as simple as the rules which defined them. You could borrow as much as you want for whatever you want, be it to pay the rent, or for drugs, or booze, as long as you paid it back along with his fees.

The math clear and understandable to all. Money was available to anyone and was paid out in $100 blocks, each $100 cost $25 which came straight off the top of the $100 just borrowed, if $100 was actually needed then two $100 blocks could be purchased at a price of $25 for each, getting the customer $150. On top of this was another $25 a week fee per $100 block for the next eight weeks, including an additional $25 fee payable on the eighth week when you were due to payback the $100 block to close the debt—rounding the last week out at an even $50—then you were done and clear, unless you couldn't meet the $150 repayment and had to just keep paying the weekly $25 fee until you could, which many did.

No point in strangling someone when you can just choke them slowly time and time again. After all, they'd always fuck up in someway or need another fix. Let them borrow. Let them pay back three and a half times what they'd borrowed, and let them come back and do it again.

Better that way than spending the day frustrated and breaking legs, chasing your own greed.

Those days of chasing and beating were all long gone now though, days spent when he was young, working the street, learning the ropes as a side kick to a guy who thought he was connected because he had a friend who truly was—a guy in it more as an excuse to hurt people than for the money. This guy with his tattoos and arms like legs from steroids that made his dick shrink, crying like a baby and pissing his pants as he hung from a meat hook up in the attic of Mattia's uncle's pool hall after calling Mattia a *wop* and a *spick cunt* once too often and over stepping the mark. The guy whose name Mattia sometimes forgot even though he was his first kill, the muscled up Roid Monkey crying as he bled to death and disappeared from this world unnoticed.

****

The heroin addict who once fronted a band and thought he was cool now played the guitar in a doorway these days outside Granville Street station told Chendrill pretty much the same regarding the Italians's pricing structure, except he'd left out the bit about the $25 he'd started paying to the guy for one block—though he couldn't remember why.

Chendrill had seen the Italian in his cowboy boots reach into the ex musician's guitar case at the same spot the day before as he'd followed the man to the strip bar. The Italian helping himself to a wad of change. The Guitar player happy for the $100 in cash Chendrill had dropped off, not because he liked the tune but because he wanted info. It was a quick $100 the heroin addict had already spent in his mind as soon as he'd seen the note hit the inside of his guitar case, paying back the loan shark and taking out another two blocks to convert Chendrill's $100 and the change he'd gathered whilst banging out a shitty version of Purple Rain straight back into a quick $150.

The heroin addict happy, taking the hundred bucks but wishing Chendrill would fuck off now, as he could feel the ground move underneath him because a train was coming in. Not looking Chendrill in the eyes now that he had his money, the man spoke fast in a manner that would suggest that Chendrill was little more than shit on the heel of one of his second-hand shoes.

"Listen the guy doesn't keep books okay. Keeps it in his head you know. Mental stuff, like he's got a Chinese accountant stuffed behind his ear. But look, if you need more, go look, you know, because there's a lot of people know him better and I don't know much else and I got fans that needs to hear me okay."

"Really, you've got fans?"

"Yeah,"

"You're saying you've got people getting off that train down there just so they can come up the stairs and listen to you bang out a load of nonsense?"

And before the man could answer, the first of the commuters came out from the swing door. Chendrill watched as the man's head went down and like magic his grimy fingers blasted out the opening chords from 'Stairway to Heaven' from a small battery powered amp that had seen better days. Raising his head, the musician quickly glimpsed the commuter as he walked away and looked to Chendrill. Chendrill said, "Maybe he doesn't like Led Zep?"

Then the door to the Skytrain that now went

underground opened and not missing a beat, the musician who'd once played at the Yale went straight back to the beginning. Stepping back almost in a vain attempt to shield himself from the noise, Chendrill watched as the commuters came and went without a glance or a care for the man who held onto the chords just a little too long.

Chendrill pulled another two twenty dollar notes from his wallet, stepped back over and dropped them in the musician's empty guitar case. Then just as the man finished, said, "You've got to be kidding, why do you keep playing the same song?"

The heroin addict saying straight back, "People love it." Then the guy said, "The man you're after, he's loaded—I don't think there's a person I know who doesn't owe that fucker cash."

Chendrill stared at the musician thinking how they were similar ages and lived in the same city but were both in different worlds.

Then the guy said, "Do us a favour though and don't fuck with him as there ain't no one else around who gives his rates, others'll fuck you if you're late but he won't, all he does is make you go stand in line and buy tickets at the arenas for his friend who's a tout. Unless you just don't pay or even do that, then I think you're in trouble."

Unable to take 'Stairway to Heaven' for a third time, Chendrill left the guy and carried on. The big man moving through the streets in his Hawaiian looking like a canary feeling cool. The stadium was not far away and the football was about to start in an hour. The Whitecaps would be heading out there to get frustrated with the ref as they played their rivals from Portland in the south. The touts were all standing around like sharks in a crowded sea on a holiday long weekend, holding their tickets like geishas. Chendrill knew most of them and told each one he'd buy four in a row at centre pitch if anyone could tell him where the Italian with the rings who sells money in blocks lives.

One of them waited and, leaning in, said, "If you buy them from me you won't need an address because he'll be sitting ten rows down from you."

The kids were already there with Mattia the Italian, all in primo seats on the sideline when Chendrill sat down at the edge of his empty four in a row. The Italian watching every kick and screaming at the Whitecap's coach, as his kids, not watching the game, took turns running up and down the stairs with ketchup on their chops still holding their fries.

Chendrill sat there in amongst hundreds of fans, watching the Italian who sold money in blocks of a hundred losing it over the goings on of the game, the crowd oohing and applauding every shot their heroes missed and shouldn't have. Despite his big mouth, Chendrill could tell the Italian knew football, and, forgetting about the kids, kept telling the ref to fuck off and the strikers to get a real job, or to get back to the Roxy.

Chendrill waited till halftime and for the Italian to pass him as the man came back down from the concessions and sat himself down, loaded with pizza for the kids and two beers for himself. Waiting for the Italian to stuff half a pizza slice into his mouth, Chendrill then got up and moved down the aisle to the bottom, taking one of the kid's empty seats and slipping in next to him. The Italian taking a moment to notice that the big man was there and then just as he clued in, Chendrill said, "So how many blocks does Sebastian String owe?"

The Italian stared at him for a moment before saying back, “If you’re here to talk about the game then fine; otherwise fuck off because you’re sitting in my kid’s seat.” Chendrill looked out across the pitch, its artificial turf lit from the open roof above and calling out to anyone who’d ever kicked a ball and enjoyed it. Turning back Chendrill smiled and said, “We can talk now since it’s halftime or I can come back when they’re in bed.”

Chapter Six

Daltrey waited until morning before she checked herself out of her private hospital room and headed home to her apartment in a cab. The place was a mess as she stepped inside. Curry powder was on the floor of the kitchen and all her toothpaste was gone in the bathroom. She looked at herself in the mirror and wondered now why she had not come home sooner rather than hiding herself away as she had on that boat. Twisting her head to the side, she looked out the corner of her eye to the mirror, trying to get a side view. *Nope, nothing's changed, you're still a wreck,* she thought as she looked at the bandages around her head hiding the burns and her scorched hair. She felt like crying but what was the point in that? She'd done that enough for a lifetime. She walked out from the small bathroom back into the kitchen and looked to the curry powder on the floor. Maybe she'd dropped it before she'd got herself into the mess she was now in. Maybe? But really what did it matter? It wasn't like she was about to knock out a chicken tikka masala anytime soon.

She was getting stronger now though, not crying at the state of her place was a good sign. Stuck on that boat, too frightened to go anywhere, she'd cried at anything, especially the huge billboard of Dan posing in the same underwear he'd snuck into the last time they'd been together—when she'd been sneaking around Mazzi Hegan's apartment and found Dan on the bed wearing only those silver undies and a stupid grin. There was that one and the others she'd seen on the way over too, Dan with a busted nose in the elevator looking frightened, Dan with that dumb model with the tits, and Dan getting his face licked by some guy. *What had Chuck said?* he's now an international superstar model driving a Ferrari. *What the hell had happened?* No wonder she thought she was going crazy.

Daltrey walked back into the living room and then into her bedroom and sat on the bed. Everyone had thought she was dead but no one had bothered to come over and sort her stuff out. But who would have, who did she have? No one really; her family were all gone, ravaged by sickness and the ones who were still alive lived far away on the fringes and were long forgotten in her life.

She could have been burned alive and the only people at her wake would have been the people she rather be dead than socialize with anyway, except for Chendrill that is, so maybe it would have worked out perfectly.

Now though she had a dead girl a lot braver than she was to thank for the fact she was back home with the rest of her life ahead of her. She walked back into the bathroom and stared in the mirror, her head bandaged up, her cheeks still blistered. Unclipping the bandage, she began to unravel it until it was completely off and laying crumpled in the sink. Very slowly she took off the t-shirt she had stolen from the closet of the yacht she'd holed up in, hiding from herself, and stared at her reflection in the mirror.

Her face and hands were taut and red from the Russian's flames, but now in the bright bathroom light the injuries didn't look half as bad as they had when she'd glimpsed herself in the half-light of the boat's cramped washroom. Her hair on one side was partially gone, the skin on her shoulders peeling. Then as she stood in the shower feeling the cool water on her skin, the house phone rang and for a moment Daltrey carried on, ignoring it and wondering who it could be.

Stepping out, Daltrey answered the phone and for a moment, the person on the other end of the phone sounded like a man, as she heard the voice in a familiar tone say, "Hey, you're a hard one to track down."

Running her fingers through her wet hair, Daltrey said, "Who are you and what do you want?"

And the girl on the other end of the phone, who wore leather and rode a Harley, got straight to it, saying, "Don't play games, you know who I am and I want you over here giving me a piece of your pie."

Knowing now who it was and worrying about her hair as she sat down on the sofa. Realizing her hands were shaking, Daltrey looked to one of the Monet prints on her wall for comfort. The woman in the painting framed against a wispy blue and purple sky. Standing amongst a field of flowers clothed in a white dress and hat looking down at her. The woman from another era, beautiful and now long gone, clutching an umbrella to shield herself from the afternoon sun. Holding herself with perfect poise and femininity as she posed for the artist who maybe she was in love with. A woman who Daltrey knew she could never be. She said back, "I've had some trouble, my hair's not the same."

"So?"

"I've had a bad burn, my face… it's burnt and my shoulder. I've just got out the hospital."

"So that's where you've been?"

"Kind of," Daltrey replied, thinking of the amount of time she'd spent crying and eating tinned salmon.

Then the girl, who lived out on Commercial Drive and

who drove a Harley and hated men because she wasn't one, said, "You fit enough to meet for lunch?"

She changed into some jeans and a top she'd forgotten she had, wrapped a scarf around her head and wondered where her Audi was now as she sat in the back of a cab watching the meter rise.

The biker girl was already there when she arrived, sitting there at the curb with her ass side saddle on her bike with straight pipes. Kissing her on her good cheek and looking at her other, the girl said, "It's not that bad."

Daltrey saying straight back, "You should see my hair."

Trying to look cool, the girl said to her, "Hair grows back, that's why we get those hot bitches working the salons."

They sat on the patio of the restaurant that had been bought and named after the owner took a holiday in the South Pacific, the biker telling Daltrey how she'd really enjoyed their time together before and how she'd been out there trying to find her since, and Daltrey knowing she'd been feeling the same way—but that was before someone had tried to kill her.

Then the biker, who liked to be called Sam, said, "I know the line of work you're into so I won't ask you what happened, but you can tell me if you want when you're ready."

They were both eating the salad with raisins in it, which came free with the meal, and stopping for a moment Daltrey stared at the plate. How could she explain what she'd done? Someone had tried to kill her—another girl coming out of nowhere, saving her, but getting herself burned to death in the process and Daltrey doing nothing about it, just running and hiding. Really, how could she explain that?

Changing the subject, Sam took a swig from her beer and said, “Seen any nice pussy lately?”

Smiling, Daltrey looked up and shook her head.

Then Sam took her by surprise saying, “What about that guy with the busted face everywhere in town in those undies, he getting you going is he? I heard he was from Vancouver. I can tell you, I think that skinny fucker is out there for the sole purpose of doing a conversion job on hard ass bitches like me. If I ever see him in the flesh, I hope he hasn't wasted his time getting that nose of his fixed as I'm going to be breaking it again the first chance I get.”

****

Around noon, Chendrill parked his Aston up outside Slave and didn’t say anything to a soul until he reached Sebastian’s office. As soon as he opened the door, the man who paid him a grand a day to look after their new star and gave him the Aston to drive asked, “Is Dan okay, Chuck?”

Chendrill didn’t know, as he hadn’t been there since Dan’s mother had caught him hard with a slap to the face which she now regretted. Without lying, he said, “Don’t know.”

What he did know though was that Sebastian didn’t owe money to the loan shark anymore–the Italian telling him earlier at the stadium only after it was too plainly obvious that Chendrill wasn’t going anywhere in a hurry.

“You can let that faggot know he owes me for a new car,” Mattia had said. Chendrill hitting him straight back with, “I thought this was about a horse?”

“Yeah and the horse.”

“What’s the deal with the car?”

"Ask your friend; his boyfriend smashed it up."

"I heard it different."

"Well you heard it wrong."

Then Chendrill had asked, "You were there, were you?'

The loan shark who had a thing for big titted strippers coming straight back with, "No, my brother was."

Chendrill had took a chance and said, "What your brother does in his personal life is his business."

Then after looking up the aisle for his kids, the loan shark had taken a deep breath and said, "Your friend who's got the penthouse, his boyfriend led him on."

"From what I heard your brother's the one who had something in his mouth when he got knocked out, not Alan."

The loan shark had looked at him, that statement and Sebastian's old love's name seeming to sting the loan shark's inner being.

Chendrill carried on, "What does it matter now though—the guy you're talking about is long gone from this world."

Then the loan shark took a look at the ground and in almost a whisper said, "Well at least he'll have company."

"You talking about Sebastian?" Chendrill said.

"If he doesn't pay up then yeah, sure, I've got a place he can hang out in."

"How much he owe?"

"Not sure."

Remembering the junkie guitar player's words, "the man doesn't carry a book he remembers everything," Chendrill raised his eyebrows and said, "Well when you've figured it out then come see me because what you feel he owes you is now, according to street law, my debt because

I took on what he owes a while back."

The loan shark who'd filled his ex-wife's lawyer's mouth full of dog shit had sat there for a moment, staring at the subs out on the artificial turf, practicing kicking the ball about, wishing they could make the team and trying to look as though they were alone in the park and didn't have 28,000 people watching them, then he smiled and looked at Chendrill and said, "Good then you can tell that little poof he doesn't owe me a penny, but before you get your ass out of my kid's chair you need to know you now are on the hook to me for $250,000."

"$250,000—for what?" Chendrill snapped back, almost laughing.

"For his boyfriend, distracting my brother while they were driving over there on the island—for sending my car down the ditch and killing the racehorse in the back of the fucking trailer, that's what."

Chendrill stared out across the soccer field, still trying not to laugh at the man. What had gone down with this guy in his personal life to make him so angry after all these years was anyone's guess. Chendrill knew though that whatever it was wasn't his problem and just from the snooping about he'd already done, he knew the man was not stupid. For the moment though he was being just that and it was a waste of time arguing a solid point with stupid people. Even if they were just going through a phase. Either way, he'd heard enough.

Looking the man straight in the eye, Chendrill said, "I suggest you and I call it quits and part company so you can carry on earning a living off those junkies like you do. Because if you want settlement for something that happened years ago and I know you had nothing to do with financially, you now have to come see me. But I'll tell you, if you do I'll be telling you straight away to do to me what I'd say your brother was doing to Sebastian's boyfriend when he crashed your car."

****

"Now," Chendrill said to Sebastian as he parked his ass against the window ledge as he liked to do, "this guy who's been sniffing about is a loan shark, works on the East Side feeding off junkies."

Sebastian stared at him for a second, then said, "There're junkies here Chuck?"

There was—they were everywhere. Chuck looking at himself in the big mirror on the wall said back, "Yeah, you need to get out more—maybe you'll see them. Keep your eyes peeled; they're floating about in amongst the poor people and look like shit."

Sebastian nodding, he knew the type having seen enough out there with their hand out looking dirty and beaten, then he said, "You think that some of those poor guys in the shop doors are that way?"

"Almost all," is all Chendrill said, then carried on with, "And if you've been dropping them any cash then chances are it's been finding its way back to that Italian guy who was here the other day."

"He's Italian? I thought he was Persian," Sebastian remarked. Chendrill said straight back as he moved from the window and sat down without being asked, "No, the Persians deal in furniture, fruit, and cut hair. They also think they can play soccer."

"Oh?"

"Yeah, and the Italians have cafes and buy commercial

property and do a few other things."

"Like what?"

"They lend money."

"Oh, well I do that Chuck."

Chendrill smiled at Sebastian, wondering if Sebastian was half the fool he pretended to be. He said, "Yeah but these guys always want it back. Except in this guy's case, he didn't lend you or your Alan money and you were right, it was about the horse—don't worry though its settled and he's told me you don't owe him anymore."

Then Sebastian said, "As far as I know I didn't owe him anyway, Chuck."

"Well in his eyes, you did, but not any longer. I think he's got some personal issues going on and wasn't focusing properly."

Sebastian stood there for a moment, then he said, "Yes, I heard this guy who was driving the car died Chuck, maybe that's what it is?"

"Could be."

"But it's sorted?"

Chendrill nodded, then smiled, knowing by some instinct that, from the man's reputation, it was a long way from over—but now without Sebastian's involvement.

He said, "Yeah don't worry, it's sorted."

Sebastian smiled, and for the moment Chendrill thought he could see the relief come straight off Sebastian's shoulders. He asked, "How's Dan?"

Chendrill wondered again if Dan had been up to mischief again and Sebastian knew something he didn't. He replied, "Dan's good."

Then quickly and, trying to sound sincere as he watched Sebastian reach down to pick up his dog, said, "How's the movie? Patrick causing problems still?"

"Fluffy's going to be in it."

"Yeah you said."

"And Campbell Ewes, Adalia's favourite director is coming up here to speak with me. He's such a talent, Chuck."

For a moment, Chendrill wondered what movies the guy had done and, deciding not to ask in case Sebastian suddenly thought it would be a good idea for him to hang about so they both could meet, he said, "Great, well I'd better get going."

Then he heard Sebastian say, "Oh really, well since you're off and Dan's fine, why don't you go down to the airport to meet him? I'm sure he'll love the Aston."

****

It had been a little over two minutes since Ditcon had put down the phone and had begun to laugh harder than he could remember doing in a long long while—with Stephanie next to him doing the same, both of them writing a fictitious text earlier in the morning over coffee, then sending it to Ditcon's police phone. Ditcon had received it and sent it to the head of Border Protection down at Peace Arch, who then passed it on, sharing the information with the powers that be in the U.S. And a half hour later, Ditcon got a call on speaker phone from a bunch of irate big shots, sitting, no doubt, in some board room in the States wanting to know all about this Charles Chendrill who'd been disrespecting their line in the sand.

Ditcon listened at his desk with a grin, Stephanie standing next to him leaning over doing the same, as all the bullshit she'd instigated spewed back at her out of the speaker phone. Ditcon the King, playing it cool, sitting in his office telling them he knew this guy, he used to be a cop, and now he's just a washed up P.I. pain in the ass.

"How reliable was this source though?"

They'd both heard someone call out, trying to make himself heard from what sounded like the back of the room, as Ditcon was telling them, "If we take it on a scale of one to ten, you're looking at an eight."

Then after five minutes of bullshit, during which Ditcon had managed to get his hand in a friendly grab just up above Stephanie's knee, he'd forwarded Chendrill's photo and stats to the U.S. Task Force and was off the phone convulsing in tears with his right hand covering his face on the desk and his left hand still there slowly working its way up the inside of Stephanie's thigh. He was laughing, Stephanie laughing with him and at the same time wondering if this bad boy in a man's body with a bald head had the guts to take it all the way and hit the sweet spot at the top. Stephanie standing there, having fun and feeling Ditcon's hand on her thigh, knowing if it got any higher he'd find himself unleashing the spirit the young lady held within, and once he had there would be no turning back. Ditcon being Ditcon knowing the top was exactly where he was always heading, be it his young driver's inner leg or a seat at the Mayor's luncheon table. The man playing the big shot boss, bold and sleazy enough to fill his day with booze and drugs and then give it a go with his new driver de jour. But once he did cross that line of common decency, he would soon discover that little miss Stephanie had games of her own she liked to play, and itches she liked to scratch.

****

It wasn't the first time since he'd taken the contract with Slave that Chendrill had felt like a chauffeur. Chendrill wondering if he'd see this latest hot shot director running through the streets away from Slave in the early morning light, the same as he had the last one. Chendrill, the big time P.I. now knowing this new director guy's name off by heart because he was feeling stupid standing there at the arrivals with it written on a piece of paper.

Campbell Ewes, who had an Oscar, saying as he sat in the back of Chendrill's Aston Martin, "You're a lucky guy driving me about in this machine for a living hey! They ever let you take it home?"

Chendrill sitting there behind the wheel, thinking it'd be the last time he drove this guy anywhere and answering back, "Yeah, I'm a lucky guy."

"I got a black guy like you back home, except he has a hat and a uniform, wouldn't have him wearing your get up though. After this project I think I'll get him an Aston, but I don't know about the shirt."

Chendrill sat there, the guy in the back asking sarcastically what the speed limit was as Chendrill moved quickly through the traffic onto Granville Street. Chendrill chewing through what the man in the back, who'd expected him to lift his matching crocodile skin suitcases and golf clubs into the trunk and not saying thanks afterward, had said before, '*I got a black guy like you back home*,' the pretentious prick, talking like a slave owner. Then giving it to Chendrill about the shirt he'd just ordered up online.

Fuck off—was what Chendrill wanted to say, so as soon as the man got all passive aggressive with him again about not stopping on an amber light, saying, "I heard you guys up here in Canada took traffic lights a little more seriously than the Mexicans," Chendrill did just that.

The director saying straight back, "I'm sorry?"

Chendrill staying quiet as the director who liked to watch his trophy wife deep throating him in the mirror said, "Did you just tell me to fuck off?"

Looking at him in the mirror, nodding, and smiling as he did, Chendrill said, "Yep, sure did."

Moving back away from the centre console and half leaning back in the brown leather seat, Campbell Ewes said, "You know who you're talking to?"

"Yep."

"I'll have your fucking job. This'll be the last time you drive this car."

With one eye on the road, Chendrill watched the man growing more and more red in the rear of the car as they went, sitting on one hand, rubbing his neck with the other, pulling out his phone, dialing then hanging up and eventually saying, "You're fucked, you speak to me like that… You know who I am? I want to speak with your boss right now… This'll be the last airport run you do, that's for certain."

Liking what he's hearing, smiling in the mirror, and hearing the man ask again if Chendrill knew who he was, Chendrill answered, "Yep."

When they reached the offices of Slave, Chendrill got out and opened the trunk, then walked away without speaking, leaving the new director in the street with his crocodile skin bags and clubs open in the Aston's trunk.

Hearing the man calling out to him as he crossed the road, "What about the hotel?"

Yeah what about it, Chendrill thought, as he entered the

glass front door to Slave and skipped the elevator, hearing Sebastian say as he walked back into Sebastian's corner office, "That was quick Chuck, is he at the hotel?"

Sitting down on the sofa and almost hitting the dog, Chendrill answered back calmly, "No, he's here, downstairs; he wants to talk to you."

Sebastian smiled and walked to the window, saying as he went, "Well the man's keen, it's a good sign—how nice."

Then Sebastian looked outside and saw the man at the back of the Aston red in the face and struggling with his bags. Minutes later he was upstairs and puffing his fat gut along the corridor, asking noisily for Sebastian String. Sebastian met him outside, disarming him with his warmth and a smile and taking him into his office.

The director, who had an Oscar, and had given a fantastic speech about Darfur after he'd received it, even though he couldn't give a fuck and had never been there, calming as he went, hearing Sebastian ask, "Everything okay, Campbell? Did you have a good flight up?"

The director saying as he walked through the door, "All was fine until your man picked me up, then told me to fuck off. The guy was driving like a lunatic and I asked him to slow down because he kept running red lights. I said he needed to be more responsible like my guy in LA. Wouldn't take me to the hotel, wouldn't help with my bags, wouldn't do a thing. The man is rude, arrogant and to be honest, I can't see myself being here if he's still around."

Chendrill sat there to the side in Sebastian's office listening to the heavily exaggerated string of events, letting the guy's mouth run. Standing there with his mouth open, Sebastian looked to Chendrill sitting behind him with

Fluffy on his lap not giving a shit.

Looking back to the director, Sebastian said, "Oh!"

The director stood there in front of him, letting his temper build again, now with his hands on his hips, not letting up and throwing his weight about before he's even said hello, saying, "Quite simple, bottom line, he's not driving my Aston anymore. If I see him again, I'm out."

And as sweet as can be, as the director turned shocked to see Chendrill sitting behind him, Sebastian said, "The car's not for you Campbell, it's Chuck's personal car. He was doing you a favour—let me call you a cab for the airport."

"Sorry?" the director said, Sebastian's voice so soft he wasn't sure if he'd heard him properly.

Sebastian said it again, "Chuck owns the Aston, it's his vehicle—you're not happy so I'll have someone call you a cab for the airport."

Half an hour later, he was gone, picked up in an Aston by a guy in a Hawaiian, dropped off by a Sikh in a Hyundai wearing a Hawaiian.

Sebastian was pissed. As he walked back and forth in his office, he said, "Chuck, I don't have you here to cause trouble." Chendrill now leaning with his ass against the window like he liked to, feeling guilty and watching Sebastian, who for the first time was getting really upset.

"No, you have me here to stop trouble, not do pickups."

"All I wanted was a favour."

"What's wrong with that woman Belinda?"

"Belinda's a man Chuck, we all thought he wore a dress."

Chendrill already knowing this and half laughing as he said, "I thought you were all cool with that around here."

Sebastian moved back behind his desk and sat down. It was obvious there was going to be no taming this wild beast of a man. How many times had he tried, and the truth was he was half expecting a call from the airport telling him that Chendrill was a no show and had gone AWOL. As things had turned out, Sebastian would have been better off with that scenario, as now he needed to find a new director, and, even worse, tell Adalia her friend and 'favourite' director was heading back south.

He said, "Not in that sense, Chuck. We just thought Belinda was a girl because Belinda's a girl's name."

"Not in the Punjab it seems," Chendrill said, happy Sebastian had sat down as he was wearing out the rug and making him and the dog dizzy. He carried on steering Sebastian further away from the subject of the director he'd just managed to piss off, saying, "I always knew she was a he. Anyway, I thought guys were your thing?"

And as soon as the words left his lips, he saw Sebastian's face redden as Mazzi Hegan walked in the room without knocking, ran his fingers through his frosted tips, and said, "Was that Campbell Ewes I just saw come in?"

With Sebastian saying back quickly, "Yes, and that was Mr. Ewes going out as well. Chuck told him to fuck off on the way over."

"That's what you get when you use the help," Mazzi Hegan looked at Chendrill, who still could care less, as Chendrill looked back at Hegan's get up—the guy all in purple except for perfectly ironed green socks.

Looking away, Mazzi said on the fly, "Well that's great, well done, two for two on directors coming in and straight out again. So far no one's made it further than the office. If your friend's so clever, then maybe he should direct."

How are your feet? Chendrill thought, remembering the last time he'd picked up Hegan and then kicked him out the car barefoot. Watching Hegan walk away down the corridor, he heard the man spit out, "But he'd probably do better with traffic," as he reached the safety of his office. *What am I doing here*? Chendrill thought, *I used to be a police officer, a revered detective.* Now he was being spoken down to by egotistical maniacs.

And as though Sebastian could read his mind, he heard him say, "I've told you before, Chuck, everyone who works here is of value, even Mazzi. And you Chuck are more valuable to me than that Oscar wielding prick I just sent back to LA for coming in here, not saying hello, and throwing his weight about. And as you know I'm not one to lie, the Aston's yours, I was going to put a nice bow on it for you on your birthday, but there you go, you've gone and ruined your own surprise. Let that be your punishment for being belligerent and not holding your tongue."

Chapter Seven

Suzy stood in the bay window of the house Sebastian had bought her after he'd found her crying on the park bench he liked to sit at along the seawall. She had been worrying about her life and this angel of a man sent down from the heavens was there to help her. She looked at all the new furniture he'd bought her and the TV, which her husband, who'd been out late, then up all night watching movies, was addicted to. The guy upstairs in bed sleeping, when he should be out at work now that she no longer could because of the colostomy bag attached to her stomach.

She needed to get into a new line of work, she thought, as she moved and looked at herself in the mirror Sebastian had bought online. She still had it, long legs, nice boobies, which she may as well get reduced now, her stomach still sort of flat. She was in her thirties now, steaming towards the big four-zero—but who'd have guessed with all the wolf whistles and the stares and comments as she passed. Not that her husband would notice, when was the last time he looked at her like he had when they were young. When he'd been fun and told her she was beautiful. Sebastian had—he'd told her straight away as soon as he'd sat down and she'd felt his presence there with his little dog sniffing the air. He'd told it to her straight in a way that felt true and genuine, told her she was the most beautiful girl he'd ever seen, handed over his silk hanky with its embroidered initials, Sebastian String letting her know he wasn't an asshole with a smile.

The guy genuine and pure with no hidden agenda, just wanting her not to cry and to be happy. For her it meant mccting someone she hadn't seen in a long time, a decent man and if the man had liked girls, despite his age, she'd have left her husband for him in a heartbeat.

Picking up the phone, she dialed his number and when Sebastian answered she just said, "Hey."

Chendrill was still parked with his ass against the window when the call came in. Sebastian had looked at the display on his phone and smiled before he answered and Chendrill knew exactly who it was when he heard him say, "Are you all settled in?"

Chendrill watched him on the phone, this man who'd just gifted him an Aston Martin because he'd insulted some big shot. He heard the voice of the woman on the end of the phone who used to be a lap dancer and who worked the circuit. Her laughing, Sebastian smiling being polite, knowing Chendrill could hear her cackle, giving little looks as though he was embarrassed to be talking in such a way with a girl.

Putting down the phone, he looked straight over to Chendrill and said, "We're just friends."

"It's none of my business," Chendrill retorted quickly.

Then he stared at the floor and to Sebastian's dog, still playing with its behind, and looking up again said, "What I am worried about though is you wasting money."

"Wasting money on who?' Sebastian asked, half laughing to himself.

"Me."

"Thank goodness for that. I was worried you were going to give me another lecture about the girl. No Chuck, don't go worrying about the car, or that pompous man Ewes. He was a promise to Adalia, which I fulfilled, and now I can't be to blame if he isn't wanting to be here." He took a deep breath and, shaking his head, continued, "you know this little whim of Patrick's is becoming a pain now, especially after speaking with that man's agent. He was asking the world. The reality is, Chuck, you just saved me a fortune, and if it wasn't for little Fluffy being in the film, I might just pull the plug on the whole thing."

Chuck asked it straight, "How much did the prick want?"

Wide-eyed, Sebastian said straight back, "One and a half million USD. Plus 10% of the gross." Then he smiled and said, "Oh Chuckles, you don't know how happy I was when he said to me it was you or him."

****

Dan sat on his bed and stared at his dick. Adalia had called twice and he'd not answered; so had Marshaa, who'd gotten the same treatment, and the same with Melissa. Then after he'd gotten the strangest one from Daltrey, who hadn't left a message, which was very confusing. Now though he had an erection which had come on as soon as he'd seen her name—which was odd. Why would his body have feelings like this for a dead girl, even if she had been hot? Maybe that was it, he thought, after all his fantasies over the years weren't just limited to a sex maniac who lived under the bed, there'd been the odd hot ghost too who'd paid the occasional visit and maybe this time it was real. After all, they'd never got it on and perhaps in the afterlife her spirit was realizing there was something it had missed out on and her spirit was there now with him in the basement wanting him. That's why his phone had rang with her name on the display; it was her way of telling him she was there.

Looking up to the ceiling he shouted out, "You want it,

come get it," and his mother called down, "Sorry?" Then quick as a flash she was clumping down the stairs and opening the door and staring at him, naked except for his socks with just his quilt across his lap.

She said, "Did you call me?"

Dan saying quickly, "Yeah, you want me to call Chuck, see what he's doing?"

Charles Chuck Chendrill had just left the offices of Slave and was heading out of town when his phone rang and he was surprised to see it was Dan for once.

He asked, "What have you done now?"

"I should be asking you the same question since my mum's been moping around the house all day and won't stop pestering me in my room," said Dan.

"She there now?" Chendrill asked, as he pulled up at some lights and looked to another woman looking at the car and then to him.

Wondering whether it was the shirt or the car, sitting there feeling cool, he said after not hearing an answer back from Dan, "Well?"

But Dan, getting bored, had already gone.

Dan sat on his bed, threw his phone to one side and lifted the duvet off his lap, looked to the door to see if his mum was still there, and then back to his dick. *Fucking Chendrill*, getting his mother all upset and messing up his first ever real paranormal sexual experience.

Looking around the room he called out, this time not so loud, "You still there?"

Nothing.

He said it again, "You still there? You feeling horny?"

She was, he could feel her in the air, feel Daltrey's presence, she was there in his room wearing those tight jeans she always wore. She was staring at him in his socks with his dick all hard, there with him watching him make it twitch up and down the way Adalia Seychan liked him to do, she was there with him… Daltrey unbuttoning her shirt, letting her hair down as her titties fell out, opening her jeans as she began to bend over towards his cock as he twitched it over and over making it jump up into his belly, summoning her to him like a finger.

Then his mother said from just outside the doorway, "What on earth are you doing Dan?"

Dan quickly grabbed the duvet cover back up towards his groin, covering himself again, not wanting to look up, hearing the door open and his mother ask, "Who are you talking to?"

"Chuck."

"What did he say, did he ask about me?"

Wanting to say, 'Yeah, he wants you to go meet him now' then he could get her out the house so he and Daltrey's spirit, which was feeling horny, could get some action, Dan looked up and said, "He wants you to meet him," seeing the relief in his mother's eyes as her mind registered that he'd asked Dan to tell her this. There was still the possibility that Chendrill was about to deliver some bad news though.

Dan told her, "Yeah, he wants to meet you at the cinema."

This way she'd be out the house long enough to use up half the butter left in the fridge.

His mum stared at him now, confusion on her face.

She said, "Really?"

Dan nodded, wondering if Daltrey's spirit was still in the room with her top off.

"Yeah, you need to be quick, the movie's starting soon."

"Which one?"

"The one with Adalia Seychan, it's on downtown."

His mum saying, "Oh?"

Dan nodded, knowing at least that much was true—as it's all he'd heard the woman talk about all through the night and into the morning in those spare moments she'd had when she hadn't had his dick in her mouth or been telling him what to do to her.

He carried on, "He said to be quick or you'll miss the start."

****

Almost an hour later Chendrill pulled the Aston into the road where Dan and his mother lived. He'd been sitting for a while across from the house Sebastian had bought for the family of losers and was contemplating going straight to the door and telling them they had a month to make their excuses and leave or he'd be back with the police and begin pressing charges for extortion. But one thing was bothering him and it was that Sebastian was certainly no fool. The man cut through bullshit in his own Machiavellian way. This time though it was almost as though he was blind.

Chendrill pulled the Aston up outside Dan's mother's, parking it an inch from the back of the Ferrari that couldn't go over 90kph, feeling his ribs twinge as he got out. He walked up the steps to the door, pulled out the spare key Dan's mother Tricia had given him, and opening the front door heard Dan calling out Daltrey's name from the basement.

Daltrey was here he thought. That was quick, but she was supposed to still be in the hospital. Then he heard Dan call out again, “Get over there and get back on the bed.”

And moments later, “Don't—don’t you try and escape, get your ass in the air—I'm not done with you yet.”

Then, “Get away from the door!”

Chendrill called down the stairs into the basement towards Dan's room.

“Dan! What the fuck are you doing?”

Seconds later, the door to Dan's bedroom opened, Dan popping his head all red and sweaty out as Chendrill heard him say, “You what?”

Chendrill stood leaning against the wall at the top of the stairs, staring down at Dan, seeing a piece of the duvet peeking through at the bottom of the door.

Then Chendrill said, “Leave her alone, if she doesn't want to be down there with you then don't be a prick.”

Now Dan was confused, how could the big fucker in the shirt know he'd just made love to the spirit of Daltrey with the help of what ended up being all the butter from the fridge upstairs. He said, “There ain’t no one here.”

Chendrill saying straight back, “Then who are you talking to then?”

Dan looked back into the room as if there's someone there and nodding, then looked back out again and quickly said, “Mum’s waiting for you at the cinema, you'd better be quick.”

Chendrill frowned, wondering what the international sensation was going on about now. Then heard Dan carry on saying, “Yeah, she's waiting for you, she wants you to watch Adalia Seychan’s latest film. She said since you and her have had troubles, it could be kind of bonding.'

Oh, Chendrill thought, *that film*. Adalia Seychan was supposed to be good in it. He remembered hearing about it—it was about a woman who, in the autumn of her years, goes back in time and kills every one of her boyfriends and husbands. He said, “The one where she plays the axe murderer? Sounds great.”

Then he asked, “So, who's in there then?”

“None of your business,” said Dan, who quickly heard back, “Really?”

“Yeah!”

“It's normal for the youth of today to keep people imprisoned in their basement rooms is it?”

Dan telling him again, “Mum's waiting.”

Chendrill smiled at the kid who could be as sharp as a tack one minute and one dumb fucker the next. He said, “Your mum picked that film as a nice couples movie did she—thought we could cuddle up?”

“Yeah that's exactly what she said.”

“And that's how you got her out the house was it? Gave her a bullshit line about meeting me at the movie theatre so as you could have a girl back here?”

Fuck, Dan thought, how did this prick always seem to be able to see through his bullshit—even if Daltrey wasn’t quite here in a physical sense.

Wondering if Chendrill knew he was naked, he said, “Why you keep talking about me having a girl down here?”

“Because you were telling her to get away from the door, and other stuff.”

“Well yeah, you were right, but she’s gone—she ain’t here anymore.”

“Well unless I’m deaf and didn’t hear her climb out that little window, she must still be in there with you.”

“She’s not.”

“So why you giving her shit then?”

"Just pretending. I'm rehearsing for this movie you've got me in… That's what."

"I've got you in?"

"Yeah, you're the one who came here knocking."

"Oh, ok? So you're rehearsing?"

"Yeah, it's important. Sebastian said I had to."

"And that's why it's two in the afternoon and you've got no clothes on, is it?"

Fuck, Dan thought, wondering how this prick with the moustache who was screwing his mother could tell.

He said, "Haven't you got better things to do than hang around here?"

Ignoring the question, Chendrill just said, "Why's there butter on the door?"

"Dunno. I had a sandwich."

Chendrill said again, "Well like I just said—unless I'm deaf and I didn't hear whoever you've got in there climb out that little window, then whoever you were bullying is still in there."

"I told you—no one's in here."

"What are you doing then, having sex with a ghost?"

Smiling and looking back at Chendrill, Dan wondered now how he'd managed to work that one out. Tilting his head to the side, Dan said in a sarcastic tone, "Maybe!"

Hearing the minute inkling of truth in Dan's voice, Chendrill laughed inside. He looked to the streak of butter smeared on the door. Raising his eyebrows, he said, "Really?"

"Yeah, you need to get out more. People do stuff like that these days."

Then as he turned and began to walk away, Chendrill said, "Well if it was Daltrey's ghost, you're just wanking as normal."

Leaving Dan in his basement, Chendrill headed to the cinema downtown so he could 'get out more' and found Dan's mother standing alone in the foyer. Walking to her, taking her by surprise with a squeeze of her arm he said, "I heard your son's been recommending couples movies for us."

Then he heard Trish say, "I'm sorry I hit you."

As she turned to him, Chendrill looked down at her, smiled, and said, "Forget about it."

Then she replied, "I take it coming here was all Dan's idea. He must have sensed there was trouble."

"Yeah, he's really deep."

They sat at a restaurant just down from the cinemas, Chendrill ordering for them both. Tricia not liking the chicken on a bun and wanting a salad instead, but not saying a word.

Chendrill carried on as though it was normal to have his hair pulled and to be slapped in the face. Then out of the blue, just as the waiter had walked away, shuffling his way through the afternoon crowd, Chendrill said, "You're my girl—I haven't got another woman and I'll let go what happened the other morning but you need to know if it happens again for whatever reason, it won't happen a third time."

Tricia looked at him, getting it no problem. She knew what she could be like and wondered if she should just end it now. She said, "It's the one thing I hate about myself, Chuck, somethings are just there, but I will try."

It was just there, thought Chendrill, *just there as it was in a lot of people*, just there under the surface of men who lashed out when they felt angry or threatened or frustrated by their inability to find an answer to their wife's quick tongue or emasculation; just there in the woman who did just that to the one person who truly loved her, hitting their partner they pretended to love or their children with their venomous words and crying after to hide their shame.

They headed home to Tricia's place, Tricia quietly listening to Abba in the passenger seat of the Aston, her right hand out the open window playing with the air, her left unconsciously stroking Chendrill's leg, hoping she could control her temper, wishing they could be forever. Three cars behind them, the guy from the U.S. Customs and Border Protection followed along, wishing he'd listened at school so as he could drive an Aston Martin as well and be like James Bond.

They reached the house and parked outside behind Dan's Ferrari, which hadn't moved. The pair of them still holding hands as they went up the small steps to the front door and headed for the kitchen. Chendrill sat in his usual spot, as he always did, Tricia wondering where the butter had gone, Chendrill wondering if the guy who'd been following them was a Pap.

As he watched his girl making a drink, he asked, "Do you think your kid will ever get out of that basement?"

Shaking her head, Tricia said back, "He likes it down there. Sometimes he doesn't come out for days."

"I see that," he said, and then, "This girl he was kind of seeing, the one I told you had died, the one who called me…"

Deciding to let it go about Chendrill having slept with the woman, Tricia asked, "Have you told Dan?"

Chendrill shook his head, then carried on saying, "I tried to mention it earlier, but he was busy."

"Oh?" said Tricia, wondering what her son had been busy doing. She said, "Well should we tell him now?"

Chendrill shrugged, then said, "Sure." Tricia walked to the top of the basement stairs and called down to her son, her voice like that of an angel who had something important to say.

They both waited, Tricia looking down the stairs, Chendrill looking at the floorboards in the direction of Dan's room almost as if he had some sort of superhero powers. Dan's mother tried again, "Dan?—Dan?—Daniel love?" Tricia waited then looked to Chendrill, saying, "Maybe he's asleep?"

"Yeah, he's probably tired, the way he's been rehearsing for this film."

She tried again, this time louder, "Dan—Daniel—Daniel—Dan—Daniel love."

Then they heard him stir slightly and something fall over, and then his voice say, "Fuck." And then again, "Fuck," and then once more in complete irritation, "For fucksake—what?"

Chendrill looked to his girl as he heard the door to Dan's room open, and then heard Dan himself wade up the stairs, appearing up the top in his underpants with one sock on.

He said, "I'm trying to sleep you know."

Chendrill and Dan's mother just stared, keeping quiet as Dan carried on saying, "You know, I'm a model, I need my sleep so I can look good. It's important."

Chendrill said straight back, "I thought all the appeal came from you looking like shit?"

"Speak for yourself," Dan said, snapping straight back.

Then as he began to turn and head back down to his

cave, he heard his mother say, “Dan, Chuck’s got something to tell you.”

And Chendrill said, “The police made an error. Daltrey is still alive, I saw her last night.”

Dan stared at him for a moment, putting it all together, the calls, the fact that having sex with a ghost hadn’t really felt anything different from any other ‘special time’ he’d given himself on a Saturday when his mother was out—or in, for that matter. It all made sense now.

He said, “Yeah I know she called.” Chendrill stared for a moment, wondering why. Then said, “And?”

“I didn’t answer, I thought it was a ghost.”

Chendrill smiled and looked to Dan’s mother, everything making sense now—Dan in his room downstairs, doing what he’d said Chendrill should do, only there was no spirit in his room to reciprocate.

Chendrill said, “I guess it was a bit of a waste of time then this afternoon, now that you know the facts.”

“Depends which way you look at it,” replied Dan, grinning ear to ear.

****

Stephanie told him he wasn't allowed to use any of his fingers as she sat on the edge of Ditcon’s desk and held him tight by the ears. It wasn't the way his tongue licked her that was making her excited, it was more the way she was making him lick her that was making her excited. Ditcon, doing it kind of okay—but she'd had better guys down there, ones who cared about what they were doing more than simply getting off on the scent. Ditcon there, sitting in his big office, on his big chair with her on the edge of his big desk, out to lunch in more ways than one by the way he was gnawing on her vagina. His head felt good in her hands even though it didn't have much hair, and his ears were turning red from the way she'd been pulling him into her.

What a fun start to her shift week it had been, getting the call to drive the big guy about like she had, listening to his bullshit, then having him sucking on her pussy in a little over 48 hours without the guy even trying to get his cock out. Not that she would ever let him; after all, she did have a boyfriend.

Ditcon looked up and wiped the dribble from his nose, which hurt. He said, “I could sit here and do this all day,” which is pretty much what it felt as though he had been doing from the way his neck and jaw ached.

“Well you'll have to stop soon because I need to go to the toilet,” said Stephanie. Ditcon going in for afters then pulling back, stopping, without a thought for her. He said, “You're good yeah?” She wasn't, far from it really, but what the hell, the way he was going about it there was little hope anyway.

She had him now where she wanted him, there was no doubting that. Long gone were the days of sexual manipulation or harassment for this girl as domination was Stephanie’s thing.

It had all started a few years back when a friend who kept a cat suit in the closet and a dungeon in the basement had asked her for help and male sexual subservience had quickly become Stephanie’s little secret.

Nowadays any sleazy, power crazed man, such as Ditcon, who saw her as easy prey would soon find themselves quite literally sucked in and feeling abused. So, with all the booze and drugs Ditcon had been plowing into Stephanie along with his wandering hands, her boss Ditcon had deservedly just gotten his first taste.

She said, “We going anywhere today?”

Ditcon thought about it. They'd had breakfast, then coffee, then some wine over lunch, then some tequila and a couple of shots of brandy, then out had come the cocaine again along with another tease and some more inappropriate touching and suddenly Ditcon had been eating another lunch in the office.

As he watched Stephanie straighten herself out so quickly that even he wondered if the last hour had been his imagination, he said, “Yeah get the car ready, there's a nice cafe on the other side of town which needs looking into.”

They moved fast, the traffic parting as though Moses himself was sitting in the back of the Buick town car he’d picked this time with its souped-up extras. Ditcon feeling good, but a little pissed now, wishing he'd stopped what he'd been doing 20 minutes earlier so as he could snag one of the glazed pastries from the cafe before the kids got out of school. *Sometimes they split them*, he thought, as he stared out the window at the cars pulled over at the side of the road. If they did and there were two left, he'd have them both, tell them one was for his driver.

He said, “When we get close, turn off the lights and siren so as no one knows what we're up to.”

They pulled up outside the café. Ditcon was first out, coming in at the back end of a bunch of schoolkids just hitting the door. Pulling his ID, he said, “What school you guys from?”

The kids looked nervous for a moment, saying, “Kits”.

Nodding as if knew something they didn't, Ditcon ducked in front.

They sat at a table by the window, Stephanie looking at

him with a smile wondering if one of the two pastries he'd bought was for her. Ditcon was in a bit of a dilemma because of this. Then the phone rang and it was from the U.S. Customs and Border Protection. The guy on the end of the phone said, "Do you have a reason for thinking this Chendrill character is our guy? He seems clean, has a valid passport, why wouldn't he just use that?"

Ditcon looked at his new driver, who was now sexually harassing him. Raising one eyebrow, he said, "You want us to bring him in to see what he has to say?"

The guy on the phone sitting up the road from Dan's mother's home wondered about the time because he'd been on the phone to a place he knew from old called Happy Feet and booked a foot massage. He said, "Let's give it a bit—see how it all plays out."

Ditcon sat there with frosting on his upper lip, putting the phone on speaker so he could look cool, and said, "Be quick, or you'll need to get a work visa."

The guy sitting in the rental thinking about his toes said straight back, "Don't need one, I'm a Canadian, eh!"

Chapter Eight

He'd been there before, this little place just up from the Sutton on Burrard with its signs on the wall telling anyone who'd listen to respect the girls who made his feet feel good.

Kaio wasn't there anymore, the woman at the desk had told him, the girl there instead though sorting him out with her magic fingers looking just like the one before who he used to see. The Asian girl squeezing his big toe at the top just like Kaio had when he'd been up before cruising round town looking for bad guys.

He smiled and said in almost a whisper so as the fat woman three chairs along couldn't hear, “You're really pretty.”

The girl who looked like Kaio smiled back at him as he tried to hold in his gut. Then he said again, “I'm not kidding, what's your name.”

“Maio.”

The girl answered louder than he'd have liked as he caught her fingers with his oily splayed out toes and gently shook her hand and, still whispering, said, “My name’s Basil and I'd love to take you for coffee.”

They met after her shift finished; she was all smiles and so, so shy. Basil's feet slipping in his socks as he walked—same as they had the last time he'd been in town. He looked at her over the top of his latte as he spoke, asking her what the little wooden tool she'd been digging into the pressure points at the top off his toes was for. She told him it came from her grandparents, the same as Kaio had the last time he'd been in that same cafe.

He said, "Really, that's so nice."

She was from Hiroo, one of the many residential districts of Shibuya, right in the heart of Tokyo—this little beauty with hands of steel who was still having trouble with English and the words which came spitting out at her fast and furious, just as her sister Kaio had a year earlier when she'd been in town.

Basil sitting there telling her about his place just across the border with its view of the sound and boring her with the new granite topped kitchen he was putting in, Maio getting confused, just answering with a "Yes."

Basil lying, saying his feet had never felt so good and how he liked the squishy feeling in between his toes. Maio saying 'yes' again.

She looked at him, this girl whose great-grandmother had spent the duration of the WWII using her little wooden tool to massage the feet of the officers in Beppu Prisoner of War Camp in Japan while they starved Basil's great-grandfather to death. This guy who needed to clip his toe nails, talking to her about workmen building a chicken. The man looking and acting the same way as the guy her sister had met.

She looked to the clock on the wall. Time was getting on and she was becoming worried about getting back to work. The manager being such a bitch as she was, giving her those dirty looks with her beady eyes and checking her watch when she was a few minutes over on her break. Then making her work late rubbing stinky feet even though she knew she would be walking home on her own in the dark and hoping the lady with the snotty nosed kid she rented a room from would be up.

Basil looked at her, still remembering the way she'd

dug her fingers into his heel.

Putting down his coffee, he asked, “You like what you do?”

“Yes,” Maio replied.

Basil carried straight on, saying, “You've made my calves ache.”

“Yes.”

Then he said, “Maybe tomorrow—I've booked up another massage—after we could go for dinner?”

And Maio said, “Yes.”

****

Things could have been better. Sebastian and Fluffy were at home trying to relax, Sebastian with his feet up on his cashmere sofa talking on the phone with Adalia Seychan, who was having a breakdown.

“I'm not sure if I can give you what you need if Campbell isn't on board,” she said. Sebastian hoped she'd walk so he could get his life back to normal.

Waiting a moment, he said, “Adalia love, it's important you feel comfortable.”

She said, “Campbell said your driver told him to fuck off, Seb?”

Seb? Sebastian thought, it had been a while since he'd heard himself called that. Alan had used it sometimes, and earlier when he was a kid a friend who lived in the house next door to his mother’s—whose father kept budgerigars—had also.

Changing the subject, he said, “It’s been a while since anyone's called me that Adalia, you're making me feel old.”

“It's been a while since I've had a director quit on me whilst I've been preparing for a role,” replied Adalia

Preparing, Sebastian thought, for what? A bullshit script about space travel?

He said, “Yes, I understand—I know, this script it's really deep.”

“I've put so much into it—so much, Sebastian, I'm living the part, please give me the guidance I need.”

A seeing eye dog could guide you on this one, he thought, then he said, “I'll call him and calm him.”

“And you'll fire the prick who was rude, won't you?”

No, Sebastian thought, he'd fire her first then drop the project and have Patrick back selling condos to the Chinese before that would happen. He shifted himself and sat up wondering what Adalia Seychan was doing calling him mid-evening, worrying herself silly over a space project well below her standing.

He said, “I'm not one for feuds—let's see how it goes shall we? I'm sure everyone will be happy in the end, and in this big world we live in, that's what's really important isn't it?”

Adalia stayed quiet on the end of the phone, and in this silence Sebastian could feel her annoyance at not getting an immediate response to what she wanted, where in the past a studio executive would have just said ‘don't worry that fucker’s toast’ or something along those lines. He had heard about her in her early days, Adalia having her people take photos of crew members she didn't like and having them fired, then referencing them on future projects if she thought she'd seen them pass her on the studio lot.

He said, “Live and let live, Adalia darling.”

Then, surprising them both, without another word, he shut her down and simply hung up.

He got up, carefully moving Fluffy so as not to wake

him and walked to the window and watched the kids huddled together smoking dope down below, kids hanging having fun while they could before life came along and took their fun away. He looked at the bench where the guy Chendrill had chased off had been sitting earlier, when Chendrill had luckily been there. The man with his big sovereign rings now long gone, but somewhere inside he wished he was there again looking up and scaring him the way he had before. The man had brought Alan back to him in some strange way, he thought. Or maybe it was as simple as it gave him an excuse to call Chendrill. And with that thought in mind, he pulled out his phone, fiddled with the settings, and did just that.

Chendrill lay on Tricia's bed with her head on his chest and heard his phone buzzing in the pocket of his jeans. Tricia looked up at him as he heard her say, “No it can't be, it's not possible?”

But it was and Chendrill knew it, it had happened so many times now in the past that it just had to be. The pair of them laying together or in the throes of passion and Sebastian would call right in the middle with an emergency.

Slowly, he moved Tricia reluctantly off his chest and, reaching down, scooped his jeans off the floor and pulled his phone from the pocket. He leaned back onto the pillows and looked at the display that said unknown and answered it.

“Hey Sebastian,” he said.

Sebastian was surprised, “How did you know it was me?”

“I'm a detective.”

“I thought I'd call to see if you are on your toes. God,

you're good."

Being polite, Chendrill just said, "What's up?"

"That guy's not here Chuck, he's not outside!"

Chendrill smiled, then said, "So that's a good thing then."

"And there's a group of kids smoking dope on the beach."

"So?"

"Well the police will be along soon."

"And?"

"Well I was thinking they're not doing any harm, they're just talking and smoking and I think there's some beer also. I've seen it a lot here you know over the years, they sit quietly. Then the cops show and then there's trouble."

"And?" Chendrill said, looking at Dan's mother getting up off the bed, wrapping her slender frame in a dressing gown.

"Well, I've been thinking and it's not nice."

"Tough being a kid sometimes. Remember when you were young Sebastian, sometimes having a beer and smoking a joint on the beach when you're not supposed too is half the fun."

Sebastian stood there and looked out, thinking Chendrill was right as usual. He said, "Well I hadn't thought of it like that Chuck."

Then without a word to Tricia, Chendrill suddenly said to him, "If you're a little bored and wanting some company, Sebastian—it's not late, why don't you give Belinda a call and come on over to Dan's mother's place and I'll see if I can get her to whip us up something nice to eat?"

****

Dan had just finished working out the algorithm and binary code that would isolate the governor Sebastian had fitted to his Ferrari so it would only do 90 KPH when he thought he heard Sebastian's voice upstairs. *Maybe*, he thought, after their incident, Chendrill was out of the picture and his mum had moved up to the top of the totem pole—and that had been Sebastian up there in her bedroom poking her all evening. No, that wouldn't work though, he'd have heard the dog, and the guy was gay—but you never know. He was about to open the door and shout up the stairs, "Who you fucking now?" to his mother when he heard Sebastian call down the stairs to the basement.

"Daniel dear, are you down there?"

They all sat around the table in the kitchen and ate spaghetti. Dan looking at Sebastian's plate, wondering if the man was going to finish his because from what he could see, he didn't like the cheese.

He said, "Sebastian if you're full, then leave it to me. Mazzi's not here so I can eat."

Sebastian smiling and not lying in the slightest when he said it was wonderful—not wonderful in the sense of taste so much, because he could already feel wind coming on, but wonderful in the sense that he was sitting with people he wanted to be with. People who for once, despite working for him, didn't have a hidden agenda. Except for Tricia that is, who didn't work for him, though he could still see she had her eyes set on Chendrill.

So, he said to her, to make her smile, "Tricia, I really love your home."

And for a moment Chendrill half thought Sebastian was

going to either offer to buy her a new one or just clear the mortgage.

Then Sebastian surprised him by saying, “You’re very lucky living here. You know where I live, no one even talks to you unless they’re on the building’s strata council and want something.”

No one talked to her around here anymore either, Tricia thought. Everyone of them had been pissed at her son for some reason or other over the years, especially the neighbour directly next door who hadn’t spoken to her ever since she’d come home and found Dan sitting on her sofa with no trousers on. Dan pleading at the time that he must have been sleep walking in the middle of the afternoon and had no idea how a lesbian DVD from 1985 happened to be playing on the TV.

She said, “Yes, they’re very sweet around here, they especially love Dan.”

“Well we all love Dan, don’t we?” Sebastian said as he smiled to Dan, who wasn’t interested in returning the gesture. Chendrill, though, begged to differ.

He said, “Sebastian, why don’t you ask Dan about what he was up to in the basement all afternoon?”

Dan did not let Sebastian speak before he said, “Chuck’s just jealous Sebastian because I get to sleep all day because I’m a teenager and he’s old.”

Sebastian said, “If he’s old Daniel, then I’m ancient.”

Dan saying back, as quick as a flash, “Yeah but you’ve still got your looks. And your hair.”

Sebastian smiled. This was great—Dan and Chendrill were seemingly getting along now ever since Chendrill had punched him in the face for stealing his car.

Then Sebastian said, “Why don’t you all come over to

my place sometime for dinner, and I promise Mazzi won't be there."

Chendrill grinned—it was obvious Sebastian was enjoying himself. The guy for once almost forgetting about his dog, which he'd left in the back of Belinda's car outside wrapped in a kiddie's duvet.

Then he said, "Fluffy would love it."

"I'm sure he would, Sebastian. It would be the highlight of his week, he'll get to tell all his friends at the dog park about it in between sniffing each-other's backsides," Chendrill said.

"Oh Fluffy's not a dog person, Chuck; he's a people person," Sebastian said. "The only ass he'd be sniffing at the park would be yours."

Nice one, Chendrill thought, as he squeezed Tricia's hand under the table and gave her a slight smile. Then Sebastian said, "I'm sorry, Tricia, for being so vulgar in your home."

Tricia, not offended in the slightest, said, "It's all good. I'll slowly get Chuck under control, if he'll let me." And she hoped with all her heart he would.

Then with the briefest of pauses and the slightest of looks to Chendrill, she said with pride, "Dan's really keen about becoming an actor, Sebastian. He's been rehearsing with Adalia a lot lately."

Oh, so that's what's been going on, thought Sebastian, wondering why he hadn't seen it earlier. *The dirty bitch*—coming up here and wanting to be in a stupid Sci-fi flick, fighting to get a big-name director in so as she didn't look too stupid—well she'd definitely be doing the timeless airline campaign, he'd yet to spring on her now—or he'd feel obliged to let it out and she'd look like some kind of monster for fucking a teenager.

Smiling, he said, “Oh how wonderful. Well I bet she's a great teacher Daniel—what is she now about 70 or 75; she must be like a grandma to you?”

That was pretty funny, Dan thought, as he took the last of the bread at the table without asking. He didn't care how old Adalia Seychan was, after all she had great tits and he’d even got his dick in between them with some baby oil. Then she’d let him get up above her and stroke himself off until he came on them, just like he'd seen one time in a movie. Adalia there, staring up at him, playing it full on like a porn star and rubbing it in with her fingers and then licking it off whilst pretending to be turned on when all she really wanted to do was clean her teeth.

Dan said, “Yeah maybe something like that.”

But Sebastian was now only half listening while he fiddled with the pasta that was giving him wind, his mind whirling away like it did when he suddenly felt inspired. What airlines were out there that were at the top at the moment? There was Cathay or Emirates, Virgin. He’d push it now definitely. He’d give the heads in their media departments a personal call in the morning, maybe even give Richard a call himself, although it had been a while since they’d last chatted on a flight back to the U.K. from New York.

They could now fly all around the world and the campaign would pay double what the film was costing, he’d use a private jet with nice seats so Fluffy could come, and he’d hire a vet. He’d make Mazzi Hegan go a week ahead to prep so he didn’t have to listen to his dialogue.

He’d make a huge donation to the director at the hospital where Tricia worked. Then when the time was right, he'd ask for a favour, tell them he needed a nurse, so Tricia could come too.

Putting his fork down, he said, "Tricia if there was a place in the world where you'd really like to go, where would it be?"

Tricia stared at him for a moment, then looked at Chendrill for an answer. Chendrill didn't really know himself and said the first name that came into his head, "Bali."

Clapping his hands together in delight, Sebastian said, "Oh yes Bali, I love Bali. Anywhere else?"

Tricia then remembered a holiday program she'd seen years ago and said, "Oh the fjords of Norway." She'd loved the documentary, seeing the fjords dropping like sheer walls of granite rock from the heavens into the ocean. She had always wanted to go, even though all she had to do was take a self-drive motor boat up the inlet in Howe Sound thirty minutes outside Vancouver to see almost the same view.

Sebastian knew this only too well, but said anyway, "Oh, how wonderful. What a fantastic place."

Then Tricia said, "Oh and the Pyramids, and Paris, and London, Bucharest and Ayers Rock in Australia."

****

Basil—the Canadian who had a thing for Asian women with strong fingers and worked for the U.S. Customs and Border Protection—sat along the road and watched the kitchen lights of Dan's mother's home. So far he'd tested out all the electric windows of the car, the locks, all the functions of the adjustable seat including the heat, seen how horizontal the seat would get twice and played with the auto tuner on the car's radio so much that now he couldn't get it to work at all. He looked at the mirror—like they had taught him in border security training—no one there. He looked again, no one there. He looked forward towards Dan's mother's house—just the lights on. No one there either. *Fuck me, this is boring*, he thought, *maybe it's drugs*—these guys living small but driving huge cars and leaving their bodyguard outside in a Mercedes. They were probably in there now working out their next run. Maybe they had a small rocket and they were firing the drugs over the border, or maybe they were using a drone that looked like an eagle. Maybe the drone fucked up and the thing went down in a field and they had to sneak into the field in the dead of night to get the drugs back.

That's probably what had happened. It would explain why there was mud on the floor of the stolen 4x4 this Chendrill had supposedly used to jump the fence like he did. The guy was probably on a deadline and supposed to deliver and the drone broke. So, he came out and hung about in the shadows, then incapacitated the guard and crashed the border with a knapsack full of drugs. What they were doing now was working out how to get the drone up and running again. The lawn was badly cut at this shithole where they were all hiding out, and there was not a lawn mower to be seen—showed they were using a drone. That's what's been keeping the lawn trim without a mower; those blades are sharp and no different from a trimmer. He'd seen a guy using one on an infomercial once on late night TV.

He sat up, adjusted the seat for the 100th time, and shook his head. Maybe though, he thought, it could just be a load of nonsense and they could all be in there now eating dinner, which was what he should be doing right now with

Kaio or Maio or Mayo or whatever her name was. If she wasn't at work that was, at work until nine or ten she'd said—or, her boss had said when he'd called. Late yeah, but worth the indigestion if she'd put out in the end like the last one had.

He closed his eyes and twisted his toes about and thought he should just go see if he could get a foot rub right now before the end of her shift, then take her out. He picked his phone up off the passenger seat and dialed the number for the massage shop. Yes, Maio was still there; sorry she was busy at the moment. Yes, he was the guy who'd called earlier and was going to take her to dinner.

Fuck, he thought, as he blew out a big breath that almost steamed the window. She was there now, rubbing another guys toe's, getting out that little wooden tool she carried on her belt and making whoever was at the end of it feel special. Maybe though it was a woman there getting all relaxed. That would be cool. No though, it would be a guy, a big one at that, some fat cunt, with some form of foot fungus between his toes or under his toenails, the incurable sort he'd watched infomercials about on late night TV.

He called again and asked, "Is Maio working on a big guy right now as I'd recommended her to a friend who had fallen arches."

"Yes."

Fuck, he thought, now wishing he hadn't checked.

Then the woman said in her broken English, "She be done soon, you want make appointment?" Basil looked at Dan's mother's shithole of a home, which wasn't much better and worth three times as much as the one he'd recently bought in Bellingham just across the border. This was a tough one. He could sit here another hour like he was supposed to, or he could make up some bullshit about following the suspect down to Happy Feet and risk catching some sort of skin disease off the hands of his new girl who didn't know his name yet.

It was a tough decision.

He started the engine and put the seat back to the right position and pulled away, cruising past half a million dollars worth of cars. Their bodyguard-lookout was fast asleep with his mouth open in the front seat of the Mercedes. The big guy with the Hawaiian shirt there now, standing with his back to the window.

Basil reached the massage parlour, which specialized in feet, and parked right out front on Burrard Street. He walked in, heard the lady on the desk to the right of the door tell him he was early, and signalled to her that he was going to use the toilet. Then with a quick look over his shoulder, he carried on past the lavatory and sneaked a peek through the wicker fence put up so as the clients could relax in privacy while they had their feet rubbed and listened to the whale music.

Maio was there on the end, working away on some guy's right leg which was lying on her lap and looked bigger than her entire body. Her delicate little fingers rubbing up and down the calf and then between the fat flaky toes of this overweight guy with psoriasis. *Fuck that looks gross*, Basil thought, as he looked at the man sitting there in the big comfy chair almost asleep with his mouth open. He stepped back, thinking as he walked towards the toilet that there was no way he was going to let her near his feet now, not after the way she'd been digging her thumbs into that guy's open sores. What he'd do was make an excuse and say he'd changed his mind and needed a back massage instead, then he'd get her to bring him some tea, but what he'd do was have her drink it for him and be the nice guy and sit there in his undies and give her a break like he used to do for Kaio.

As he arrived back at the counter, he said to the lady, "Can I change my mind and have a massage instead? You see, I think I've pulled my back at work," which wasn't actually a lie after all the mucking about he'd been doing with the seat in the rental car.

The woman behind the desk saying straight back, "No massage, too late, you book feet, yes?"

"Yeah," Basil said and followed it up with, "but you see I hurt my back on the way here."

"You book feet, with Maio. You want other girl do back?"

No, he didn't—unless she was hot. But from what he'd seen so far, Maio was the cream of the crop for the moment down at Happy Feet.

A half hour later he was sitting there with his trousers rolled up to his knees in the same seat the fat guy with psoriasis had been sitting five minutes before and he was certain he could smell the man's dribble and BO on the pillow. Maio looked up at him smiling as she rubbed oil into his calf then all over his feet and toes. She liked him coming to see her again, seeing the unconscious smile he always gave when his eyes were closed and she gave him a little bit extra. She wondered if he had a little dick like the guy her sister had told her about. The one who used to come see her all the time when she'd worked there a year before. Basil at the same time wondering what kind of sterilization lotion they used on their hands in between foot rubs. Then as it had many times before the sensation of her hands took over as she moved from his right foot to the left, her delicate but firm fingers melting away all thoughts and concerns of disease as quick as a sailor's mind emptied the moment he stepped though the doorway of a whorehouse.

Maio pouring on the oil as she rubbed and squeezed her way around Basil's feet, releasing magic from her little bottle and squirting it all over his toes, then getting one foot in each hand and squeezing all of her fingers between each of his toes, she began rubbing all the oil into the curved underside of his arches with her thumbs as she went. Basil closing his eyes again in ecstasy and whimpering as she did, hoping it would never end and wondering whether they taught this trick in foot massage school in Tokyo.

Then opening his eyes again, he saw Chendrill sitting next to him on the other comfy chair looking right at him. The big fucker sitting there in his flowery Hawaiian smiling. Chendrill asked, "That looks nice, you enjoying it?"

As quick as a flash, Basil panicked and like a rat caught in the larder he was up and trying for the door as his feet slipped around beneath him on the shiny tiled flooring. Chendrill watched as he slithered about, saying, "If you're going to try and run for it you better put your shoes and socks on first. Either that or sit back down and let the girl finish. Then once she's done you can tell me what you're after."

****

At first Alla didn't know where she was as she woke in a daze in her hospital bed. The sound of traffic in the distance being similar to back home on the outskirts of Moscow. Back east, where cars were driven hard and fast and some by men looking for her—or others like her—

stopping on impulse as the sudden urge in their groins took over their senses and rational thought. No, this wasn't home, this wasn't the morning sun that came in low from across the Russian steppes, crashing through the faded curtains and drying the black mold on the walls that made her clothes smell. These walls where she lay now were white and lined with soft pastel, and there were tubes in her arms and Dennis was sitting in a comfy chair next to the bed sleeping.

Then she moved her feet and everything came rushing back. She said quietly, as she looked to him, her voice almost a whisper, "Dennis?"

Dennis opened his eyes and looked at his wife. She lay there looking beautiful, with her hair like ragged straw and her make up gone. Seeing the drip in her arm and the wires tug as she tried to move to touch her legs, she heard him say softly, "Stay still love, stay still."

He moved to her, pulling himself from the recliner that felt so nice, and touched her hand as she looked at him through her newly formed tears. How had he found her, she wondered. She had left him to be with the man who had money and little sense. She said, "Dennis, I can move my feet, I can feel the skin on my legs."

And seeing his smile as she felt his skin as she touched him, she said, "I'm sorry Dennis."

Then she lied straight after, saying, "I did it for us."

"I can only hope this is true," Dennis replied as he looked at the floor.

Then he heard himself say, "I'll do better for you from now on Alla. I promise this." But just how he would do it he really did not know.

How had she done it? he thought. He already knew

she'd arrived at the reception in the early hours with a bag full of cash. He looked up, stared at her porcelain skin, and saw the faint hair he loved on the top of her forearm as it laid outside of the sheet.

Then before he could speak, she asked, "How did you find me?"

"I know people," was all he said. And he did know people, once upon a time he'd been wealthy, successful, and respected. And it was this respect that had earned the call from an old colleague who'd once worked on the front desk at his surgery. She liked him, seeing him there in his white coat at the top of his game. Now though she had called and let him know that this wife of his, of whom she had been so jealous, had just been operated on under mysterious circumstances.

"Oh?" Alla said, still feeling groggy, but not caring because she could feel the warmth of her blood flowing through her legs again.

Then she asked, "Has that guy with the diamond been around?"

He hadn't. Dennis shook his head and asked straight out, "Did he bring you here and pay for this?"

Alla said back, "No, I came on my own with the money. It was a gift, he wanted, he said, to surprise you, and all he wanted was for me to go to the hockey with him so he could show off." Then after the briefest of pauses she said, "Dennis, he meant nothing to me. If someone offers a gift of health, of being able to stand and walk, it's impossible to turn down. You have to understand that? You are the man I love."

Dennis understood, kind of. But there were still unanswered questions.

He closed his eyes for a second then opening them again asked, “How am I to know if you were going to come back, you know, with the way you’ve been before?”

Alla let go of his hand and reached up, touching his face gently as he leaned in to her. She said, “Dennis, I know I could have been better, I could, I really could. I had my reasons though, I had some growing up to do and the reasons mostly revolved around my brother, but all the time I was away from you, in my heart I never left. I was always with you. I acted stupid yes, but I’m young and I see it now, everyone acts stupid in their life at some point and I’m no different, except my stupidity ended up getting me hurt. Dennis, I know I’ll walk again and that man, that idiot, whoever he was, was sent from God above. He came to us for a reason, he gave us the financial head start to get us here so as we can get on with our lives again. You’ll have your licence back soon love, we’ll make sure of this and we’ll be on our way back and we can get away from here love, go up north like you said and spend time in the snow and have a small house and make love on Sunday afternoons and at night when you’re away from the surgery. We can be together properly. Truth is there’s only two things I want in life now Dennis, to walk again and to be with you and have children.”

Dennis looked down to see the newly formed tears in her eyes and said gently, “That’s three things Alla.”

Alla stared up at him, squeezing his hand, and smiled as she carried on, “I’m sorry, I’m just mixed up, I’ve got my words and numbers jumbled like I do.”

But she hadn’t jumbled and mixed up anything, except the truth, because of the three things she’d said she wanted in life, only the first were true and her empty words so tender and so full of love and hope that had come after were, as usual, nothing more than deceit.

Chapter Nine

Basil sat there with his feet back up again on Maio's lap and felt her hands rub into the soft bits between his toes the grit the oil had collected during his attempted escape. It was a different kind of interrogation this one, he thought, not quite the same as the ones you see in the movies where the guy would be tied to a chair or an overhead pipe and be taking a beating from some big guy who had not listened at school.

Chendrill sitting there next to him with his feet up on the lap of another girl from Japan who Basil didn't fancy because he thought she had a funny chin. Chendrill saying, "We all have jobs to do and the best thing for you to do is let me delete the pictures I've got of you with your eyes closed so you can carry on doing yours. After all, no one wants anyone to get fired."

Basil kept quiet, wishing he'd stayed sitting outside the shitty house Chendrill had been in. *What pictures did this big guy have?* he thought. *What had he been doing wrong?* He was just having a foot massage. He looked at the clock on the wall that let the girls know it was time to start wiping the oil off. It was 9:30 in the evening and he had yet to file a report. After all, he was entitled to his own time, he had his own life, no one could deny him that. But what if the pictures did end up in the office of someone who mattered? What if they stayed with him for his entire career, coming up every time he looked for a promotion and he had to answer questions about how and why he had his eyes closed and mouth open? There was nothing bad, but people had a tendency to make anything bad—

especially in the world of border security services. He said in a whisper, "Why would I get fired—I'm just sitting here?"

"Because you're supposed to be watching me and I'm sitting next to you whilst you get your feet rubbed."

"Yeah, it's called doing my job, I'm undercover remember?"

Good point, Chendrill thought. He said, "Yeah but usually when you're undercover, you're not asleep with dribble coming out of your mouth, I've worked undercover as well you know, I am a detective after all, but you know that already don't you?"

Used to be, Basil thought, but kept his mouth shut and said instead, "Why don't you just let me walk out of here and we can forget we ever met?"

"Why would I do that?" Chendrill said straight back.

"Because I'm the only one who knows you're running drugs across the border and holed up in that shitty house on the East Side."

"Really?"

"Yep," Basil said back, nodding, "you're drone fucked up and you had to steal the border guard's car to get your ass back here, because you were on some sort of deadline."

That one took Chendrill by surprise, the guy being half right. How the fuck could the guy have known that, unless they'd managed to get a finger print or a photo, but that was almost impossible.

He said as cool as a cucumber taken straight from the fridge, "You reckon eh?" Basil nodded with a grin and looked at Maio so as he could feel cool, then he heard Chendrill ask, "And I've got a drone?"

"Not anymore so you'd better go buy a lawn mower."

Chendrill laughed. *What the fuck was this guy going on about*? It was a good one, the guy out there on his own following Chendrill about like he must have been for a while, putting two and two together and getting three.

He said, "Who told you about my drone then?"

Basil chancing it and bullshitting, saying straight back, "We picked it up on a listening post, and it led us to you."

Chendrill laughed, thinking, *what a crock*. He said, "The post on 205th Street?"

Basil smiled, laughing to himself and lying as he closed his eyes and said, "Yep."

Chendrill laid back and closed his eyes for a moment also, taking a second to feel the Japanese girl's fingers as they dug into the balls of his feet. Then he said, "Maybe you should just go fuck yourself with these little fantasies and theories you've concocted and start thinking about your career. And once you've done that, you can tell me who it was who gave you my name in the first place."

****

Mazzi Hegan was having fun, despite his head still being sore. Not that he'd ever been shy of having fun before in his life, but this time it felt different and was different. Slave was taking a new direction in heading into movies and he was ready to accept change as it came. For not accepting change brought with it complacency and with complacency came death. Now though, he'd made friends with this great guy and found himself introduced into a totally different club scene, one where the sexy women weren't guys who were taller than him, but girls his new friend Einer just happened to know and who just happened to like fucking and sucking Einer's dick—which was exactly what one of these girls had been doing while in a crazy drunken stupor only ten minutes before.

Now though she was riding some other cool guy she didn't know and had just met. The woman looking at the man's tight stomach and chest, feeling his cock slipping in and out of her as she leaned down and licked the inside of his ear. This girl feeling the guy buck and fuck her as she eased off him. Then, feeling him all the way in, she pushed back down again on him, stretching her spine and her neck back so she could look at the art work on the ceiling and so Mazzi Hegan could look at her titties with her nipples all hard and wonder what the fuck he was doing—but enjoying it just the same, just like Einer had told him he would.

Mazzi liked the girl's skin which was almost as soft as his, liked the natural moistness of her pussy and the way it ran along his cock and onto his stomach and dripped down around his balls. He liked her hair and the way its layers fell back into place and her perky tits jiggled as she moved whilst he pounded her hard. But then he came, and as soon as the shiver had run its course though his body, down his legs and out the tips of his pedicured toes, he hated himself.

Oh my God, Mazzi Hegan thought as he headed for the bathroom, locked the door, and started to cry as he looked at himself in the mirror. Saying out loud in the faintest of whispers, "What have I done, oh my God, what have I done?"

Then he heard the girl on the other side of the door saying to him through its carved wood, "Hey baby, can I come in, I need to pee."

Mazzi Hegan spun around to look at his oversized toilet and felt the woman's sticky juices going cold and stinky around his cock. Mazzi in a panic saying, "Hang on please."

"I need to pee!" she said.

In a fluster, Mazzi wiped his eyes, then, still naked, he took a towel made from the finest Turkish cotton from the bar and opened the door to see the girl rush in and squat down over his toilet and spray piss like an elephant into the bowl just below the rim, she looked up at him at the same time and said, "God you really got me going there, I loved it when you ate me out."

Mazzi then remembered that he'd done just that, laying there all drunk and high on E, her squatting above him naked as she rubbed her wet vagina across his lips. She finished messing up the toilet and began to wipe herself with a tissue and asked. "You want to do that to me again?"

He didn't and it was a while before he'd gotten her out of the bathroom, her there what seemed like only moments before, still naked trying to seduce Mazzi, getting close, pushing her tits into him, as he unconsciously wrapped himself in all the towels he'd picked up in Istanbul. Mazzi being unnaturally polite as she began getting all cozy and trying to kiss his lips as he tried not to puke. But she was out of the bathroom and away from his bedroom now, walking down the corridor calling out to Mazzi's friend Einer about how she'd just taken Mazzi's girl cherry while Mazzi sat with his knees up on the bathroom floor with its under tile heating, feeling violated and crying again as he wondered what the fuck had just happened.

An hour later, after he'd heard the same woman come again, then giggle after as she and Einer fucked, both Einer and the woman had gone. Mazzi having showered three times had yet to leave the bathroom, the man still sitting in the same spot, hearing them leave and her calling out her goodbyes through a locked door as Mazzi stayed quiet and heard her say, "Let's do it again sometime."

****

It was just after ten in the morning the next day and just after Chendrill had gotten out of the shower when Sebastian had called and told Chendrill there was an emergency at the office. Chendrill getting up earlier in the morning with his feet feeling good but wondering now if this loan shark had been around again bothering Sebastian and how it was Ditcon had discovered he had crossed the U.S. Canadian border illegally a few nights back. Basil having let him know everything and giving away his secrets in exchange for Chendrill keeping the pictures of him getting his toes rubbed to himself. That and a half promise from Chendrill that he'd keep his ear to the ground for anything which might just lead to something big.

Chendrill pulled the Aston into a dedicated slot outside Slave, still wondering how the thief Ditcon had managed to find out about the border incident and how he would deal with it. Under normal circumstances he'd have gone over to the station and near on booted Ditcon's door down. Then he'd have told him to fuck off had it not been true, but this time it was, so how the fuck had the guy known?

He reached the top of the stairs, entered the office, smiled at the cute girl Sebastian had working the front desk and wandered down to Sebastian's office. He knocked on the door once and stepped inside almost as if it was he who owned the agency.

Sebastian looked up and almost immediately Chendrill could see he was really worried. It had to be the loan shark again—the guy obviously not listening to Chendrill when he had told the Italian he'd taken on Sebastian's debt. The guy had been around, either to Sebastian's penthouse or the office. The man coming on strong like he did with his intimidating manner that gave even Chendrill cause for concern.

Without even as much as a hello, Sebastian said in a hushed voice as he stood up, "Chuck, I'm really worried. Thank God you're here."

Chendrill looked at Sebastian as Sebastian came around the big desk, closed the door firmly, and sat Chendrill down on the sofa before sitting next to him.

Then taking a deep breath, he said, "There's a real problem Chuck. Mazzi's come to work this morning and his socks aren't pulled up,"

Chendrill stared at him, taking in what he'd just been told, then he said, "Sorry?"

Carrying on speaking quickly and saying in a hushed tone as he looked towards the now closed door, Sebastian said, "Yes—they're all saggy and I can see his ankles."

Chendrill stared at him as Sebastian waited for an answer that wasn't going to come, then he said, "I've known him eight years now Chuck and he's never done this."

Chendrill looked to the floor for a moment, then noticing Fluffy sleeping on an old Alexander McQueen sweater in the corner said, "Maybe the elastic's gone, it happens you know."

Then Sebastian stood, looking down at Chendrill, and said, "I'm serious Chuck. He's not himself, he hasn't been since he hit his head."

Chendrill looked at him. He said, "He did?"

"Yes, Chuck don't you remember, he didn't come into

work the other day, he said a sash window came down all the way, slammed down and nearly took his head off, you'd have thought the French were here."

Chendrill frowned; he remembered Sebastian calling and leaving a message saying there'd been an accident. "Did it happen here?" he asked.

"No Chuck, I've had all these ones checked. He won't say where. He's been acting so strange ever since, I thought it was the new friend, but maybe he's got a tumour."

Chendrill shrugged then said, "Well call the doctor."

"No, I called you," Sebastian said straight back, "I want you to go chat with him first and see if he's ok."

Chendrill took a deep breath—this was all he needed. He couldn't stand talking to that fruit cake at the best of times, but going into his office and asking him about the elastic on his socks was the last thing he needed. But as he looked at the concern on Sebastian's face, he knew he hardly had a choice in the matter, so he said, "I'll look into it and if there's any trouble, I'll let you know." And look into it he did. As he walked back along through the office, he stopped at Mazzi Hegan's door and tapped on it twice before walking in.

Mazzi Hegan sat there looking as cool as ever, even if his socks were down. Chendrill got straight to the point, asking, "You got anything you want to tell me?"

Mazzi snapped straight back like a bitch, "If I ever do you'll be the last to hear."

And Chendrill replied just as quickly, "Pull your socks up; you're upsetting people."

That was that then, Chendrill thought, as he walked away from the office. He'd done his bit, whatever was making the man not iron his socks was his problem—if he had one in the first place that is. He reached his car and got in. He sat there for a moment, wondering, as he did almost every day, why he wasted his time working for them. Then as he started the engine of the Aston, he heard it purr, and instantly remembered why. He could see Mazzi standing in the window above looking down, probably too scared to put his head out like before in case there was an earthquake and the window came down again. Shifting the car into drive, he pulled away.

****

Basil sat on the end of the hotel bed and wondered what the fuck had just happened. One minute he'd been in control and getting his toes rubbed and the next his whole career in border security was being questioned, and all this before he'd even got to asking Maio if she was still up for a late-night meal.

This Chendrill guy was smarter than he'd thought, seeing him leave and then tailing him the way he had. Now, though, he'd have to wait and bullshit his superiors and hope that the big ape had something up his sleeve so he could still come out of the whole trip looking good instead of coming back with a negative. What he needed would be someone with drugs, or—even better—a crazed terrorist group on their way across the border, who were about to wreak havoc on his country. *Maybe I could find one*, he thought, infiltrate some mosque or some group who hated the Yanks. Maybe if he was lucky, he'd follow one and find the terrorist getting his toes rubbed one last time before committing jihad, just the way that big fucker had found him, and then they both could start blabbing while in the middle of having one of those Japanese sticks dug into the side of their toes.

He could say something like, "If you ever need into the US then for a price I know a way where they don't ask questions," then he could set it up and have a bunch of agents—who by then would all now know his name—waiting on the other side along with a couple of waterboard specialists in tow. *That would be good.*

He got up and looked at the clock on the bedside table. It was now 11 a.m. Maio would be there because they started around that time, all depending on when the woman on the desk got in. *I could get one in*, he thought, maybe a 45-minute special that would take his mind off what had happened last night. Then he could go cruise around in the car down on Zero Avenue so he could make it look like he was doing something while he worked out a new game plan.

Half an hour later, he was leaving the massage parlour after the woman behind the desk had just told him Maio wasn't working, even though he could see her shoes in the spot where they always kept them. Basil having considered the offer of another girl from the woman behind the desk, but there was always a chance Maio could arrive—or be there, as he thought she was, and come out of one of those little booths where they did the massages to see him there with another girl rubbing his feet. Maybe it would make her jealous though and do the trick, moving him up a notch or two in the overall game plan. He hit the highway and headed towards the border, everyone driving slow on the huge road like they did up here.

He reached the border at Peace Arch, turned left onto Zero Avenue, and wondered what he'd be doing if he wasn't working undercover right now—stationed back there at Peace Arch instead, no doubt, checking passports, sniffing for drugs, and looking for any signs of bullshit.

He kept driving, working his way east, cruising, watching the border, and looking at the farms and the way they spread down to the border road. It wouldn't be easy for someone with an agenda to cross with all the cameras on the other side watching. But he was there, working, looking at stuff, and some ding-dong in an office somewhere, bored as shit from looking at the ground, would be following the car because he's got nothing else to do and then zooming in and saying, "Hey I know that guy, he pushed in front of me in the canteen. What's he doing over there in Canada?" Then they'd all be watching.

Looking up at one of the cameras mounted high 100 feet in the air on the other side of the open border, Basil reached up and spun the car's visor to obscure his face before stopping the car. He'd give it a bit of time, so the cameras could find him, then he'd open it up again so the cameras could catch his profile. He pulled out his phone and called Maio. Three rings later she answered, her soft accented voice barely audible against the breeze running up from the south and squeezing itself through the crack at the top of the window.

"Hello."

"Maio?"

"Yes."

"It's Basil."

"Hello?"

"Are you at work?"

"Yes."

I knew it!, Basil thought, as he reached his finger out and, without looking, found the button to close the window completely. Then he asked, "You want to meet for lunch?"

"Yes."

"Great, I'll come meet you and we can go for sushi if you want."

"Yes."

Great, Basil thought, as he repeated the same word over in his head and looked in the distance along the border that, maybe, in the future was going to make him famous. Pulling the visor back, he sat there for a second, then he got out and walked right to the border itself and stared south into the U.S. with purpose. The camera on the other side would be on him now, snapping away.

He walked along slightly, then crouched and picked up some soil, as though he'd found what he was looking for. Then spinning away so no border security lip reading expert could be brought in to analyze his words, he said, "I'm at work right now, you know, doing some really important stuff for the U.S. Government, what time should I pick you up?"

"Yes."

"You want me to pick you up or should we meet?"

"Yes."

"Which one?"

"Yes?"

And on it went.

****

Chendrill hadn't been sitting down on his sofa for more than ten minutes when Sebastian called again. Chendrill picked up and without any reason said, "What's the emergency?"

"There isn't one Chuck, not this time," Sebastian

replied straight back. "I thought you were going to come back and tell me what Mazzi had said."

"Well, what he did was he told me to fuck off and he hurt my feelings so much I came home," Chendrill answered just as quickly.

"He actually said that?" asked Sebastian.

"May as well have."

Then out of the blue, Sebastian said, "I've bought you a bicycle Chuck. I told you that didn't I?"

"I can't remember," Chendrill answered, as he picked up his drink of orange juice from the coffee table and took a sip, hearing Sebastian say, "Oh I think you do, you're just trying to avoid going with me down to see the house I bought that lovely lady and her family to live in. I thought it would be nice."

"Today?" Chendrill asked, then said straight back, "I think it's going to rain."

On the other end of the line, Sebastian said back, "Don't be so silly Chuck, stop trying to get out of it, it's a blue sky out there. Get here after lunch, my bicycle has a little basket at the front, Fluffy's going to love it."

Only Fluffy didn't like it at all. The dog all upset and trying to escape every time they stopped on the cycle path—Chendrill still in his jeans and Sebastian looking fabulous in spandex getting in a tizz, worrying about the traffic whizzing by and trying to keep little Fluffy in, calling for Chendrill to help and not getting any.

The man hearing Chendrill instead say sarcastically, "He might bite, Sebastian." Then they hit the East Side with all its drug problems, and that's where Sebastian stopped worrying about the dog. They passed the first run of homeless in their drugged-out state with shabby clothes and their few life's possessions, spread out for sale across the path.

Crazy men screaming in the street at unseen terrors—when they should be in a hospital—others high, shooting up, or having just shot up as ambulances came and went. These lost men and women hanging out in alleys where they themselves and others pissed and shit and sold and bought the drugs that kept them there.

Sebastian came to a halt and said straight away to Chendrill, "We've got to help these people, Chuck."

"I thought we were going to visit this house you bought?" Chendrill said as he looked around and stared down a man whose teeth had long fell victim to the crack pipe he carried and who was about to approach Sebastian.

Unconsciously covering his dog, who by instinct now knew it was good to stay put, Sebastian feeling frightened said it again, "We need to help these people. Not right now, Chuck, but in the future."

And that's the reason Chendrill got to meet Clive Sonic in person.

****

Clive Sonic had a new girl now, all sweet smelling and fun, a million miles from the ex who still kept his balls on the mantle. She was different, this one, in almost every way—the way she dressed, the way she smiled as she ate, and the way she liked him fucking her dressed as a gladiator.

Clive on top in his chest piece and leather skirt with her calling out 'Maximus Maximus' as she looked up at him holding a sword and feeling his other one inside herself. Then when the time was right, she'd pull a move like she always did, the one she'd picked up at yoga, and thrust out her hips so she could feel him touch that spot that made her insides change and her imagination slip away, making her eyes close as the visions of men kicking up dust in the arena swirled around her mind, seeing herself all nice and trim with her muff shaved, waiting below the Colosseum's killing ground. Listening to the chants and the screams of the citizens of Rome as her man left the huge arena, walking away from the blood he'd shed, across scorching sand, hearing the clanking of his armour against his shield as he came to her laying there in the real world with her eyes closed. Clive sliding in and out of her all sweaty and feeling like an idiot as she saw Maximus in her mind standing strong, looking at her through the bars of his cell as she waited for him on his straw bed and then, and only then, as she saw herself laying there naked and anticipating she would call out, "Fuck me Maximus—fuck me." And Clive would fuck her hard and fast, pounding his sword into her with all his fake armour clanking and listen to her scream and orgasm as she clung onto the imitation leather outfit she'd sneaked out from the fancy dress store where she worked. Her loving it all. Clive only liking the bit at the end as he let go and felt the shiver run through his body for the briefest of moment where he could forget about it all—before he'd have to stop and hold still like he did and push back the gladiator helmet that had fallen across his eyes so he could look at her and feel stupid again.

Then he heard the phone ring and it was Chendrill. It hadn't been more than two hours since they'd gotten back and Sebastian had sent Fluffy off with the receptionist to the dog spa for a bath when Sebastian had handed Clive's name over to him and asked him to track him down. Trying to sound tough, and still wound up from his brief trip into Vancouver's East Side, Sebastian had said in a firm voice, "Go skip trace this fucker and we can get things rolling."

Chendrill stared at the name and seconds later clued into the fact that the guy was a rock star—or had been until he'd lost some fingers. Looking up and smiling Chendrill asked the obvious question, "The guy's a guitarist with no fingers; what's he going to be able to do?"

Half an hour later, Chendrill had skip traced him—as Sebastian had liked to call the act of finding someone who'd gone off the radar. That is, of course, if you could call living in a small house on the water in Deep Cove in North Vancouver going off the radar.

Clive listened on the phone and looked towards the bedroom door and wondered if his girl was rubbing herself off again, Chendrill saying, "There's a guy downtown who'd like to talk to you, his name's Sebastian String, he runs a media company."

Clive shook his head, wanting to take the gladiator outfit off. He said, "I'm out of all that now, tell him thanks but no thanks. I'm no longer in the music industry." Then Clive bullshitting said, "I've kind of got my eye more set on other things these days."

"Yeah we know. That's why Sebastian String has had me call," Chendrill replied.

****

They met that night at Sebastian's house. Clive there on his own without his girlfriend who wished he was someone else. Mazzi there, half drunk, still all messed up with a sore lump on the back of his head. Sebastian worrying about him because his colours didn't match. Patrick also there, uninvited, but there anyway in case they were there to talk about him. Chendrill sitting there also at the end of the table, armed with a bread roll in case this ex-musician went crazy.

Sebastian holding court, smiling and saying, “It’s so good of you to come Clive. Mazzi loves your music. So does my dog Fluffy. Patrick told me only this afternoon he has all your albums and Chuck! He loves your music too.”

Chendrill didn’t like his music though; in fact, when asked it was always hard for him to put his finger on what he did really like or not—unless it was Queen, he liked them. But Freddie was dead, so that was the end of that—kind of, unless you considered Queen still alive because Brian May was still knocking everyone over with his guitar like he did, just as Clive Sonic had before when people used to know him like that, except now he was known as ‘that guy,’ the one who could no longer play guitar anymore because he’d lost some fingers.

“Thanks for inviting me, it’s a pleasure,” said Clive, who was once on his way to being one of the all-time greatest guitar players and now lived well off the royalties of a list of songs he’d written and which Chendrill was having trouble remembering.

Sebastian still smiling said, “I loved ‘Boom Boom Love’ Clive.” And so did Clive, it was the song he’d written and known as he was doing it that it would go worldwide and had until the news of a kid saving his life in the sea off Grand Cayman had gone bigger.

The truth was though, the day he’d been saved by the kid, Clive had wanted to die out there—two and a half miles off shore in the Caribbean on the shallow reef called Stingray City. Clive Sonic standing there in the sunshine with his heart pounding, holding a Stripe, studying the kid snorkelling happily in the water, watching the stingrays beneath him as Clive did the same from his motor cruiser. The kid below in the warm, crystal clear water and Clive Sonic nice and safe and dry above, leaning on the deck's rail. Both of them there years before watching as the rays lay swishing their tales on the beautiful shallow sand bank. Clive up there waiting for just the right moment when he could leave the sunshine and dive down off the boat to save a child and allow himself to be killed in the process.

But it hadn't worked out the way he'd hoped it would that day—that day, when one of the world's greatest guitarists since Hendrix should have died a hero saving a child. For when the moment came and everything lined up just right, Clive had called out to the child's parents, "The kid's in trouble—the kid's in trouble!"

And before they'd put down their beers, wondering what the hell was happening, Clive had dived in off the side of the boat into the calm and crystal-clear Caribbean water to save the life of a child who was perfectly fine. Knocking the boys mask from his face as he passed by next to him, he'd pulled himself through the clear blue water and, reaching out, grasped the peaceful stingray with each of his hands, attacking it with such force that he'd hoped it would whip up its tail and sting him in the chest so he could float away unconscious into the warm tropical waters and immortalize himself forever.

But the stars of fate were not quite aligned that day in the tropics when Clive Sonic's life was supposed to end. In the frenzy of sand and swirling water whipped up by Clive as he held on, with a vice like grip, to either side of the bucking ray. The kid and the rest of the startled rays fled this predator in tight shorts with a death wish and a number one hit record around the world. Swishing up its tail, the ray caught Clive Sonic's chord hand as he wrestled around and around, twisting and pulling under the water, purposely sucking seawater and sand into his perfectly healthy lungs until he himself passed out. He lay there alone in a soup of sand, seaweed, and blood—a scene of his own creation. His lungs without air and three fingers on his left hand somehow gone. Then, without a thought for himself, this kid whose life Clive had so courageously set out to save had swam back down and saved him.

It wasn't until the next day when Clive had woken in the hospital that the world discovered they'd almost lost the creator of "Boom Boom Love," which was, at that very moment playing in the sleepy resort island's reception, and that somehow this brave and daring boy, who'd grown up surfing in Venice Beach, California, had fought his way through a plethora of deadly stingrays and approaching reef sharks to pull the international superstar from the grips of death. The boy was a hero.

Sebastian, leaned in and offered Clive some more wine without so much of a glance to Clive's missing fingers as he held out his glass, saying, "Well I'm so glad you've decided to stay here Clive when you could easily afford to live anywhere in the world."

Patrick took this opportunity to chirp in with his patented line. "Trust me," he said, letting it hang for a moment, then added, "there's no better city in this world."

Smiling, Clive answered back, "How could I leave, it's so lovely," which just happened to be the lyrics from another song he'd knocked out that always did well at Christmas.

Not picking up on this at all and agreeing nonetheless, Sebastian said straight back, "Oh, that's why Alan and I came here in the first place. You know he used to love your songs. We had your first album."

Clive nodded, not sure who Alan was or why he was there himself, but as always, he'd done his homework. Sebastian String, the man who can make you famous if it takes his fancy. He said, "Alan?"

Sebastian apologized, then said, "He used to live here with me, but sadly Clive, he's passed on now."

"Oh, I'm sorry," said Clive as he looked around at all the matching plates and wondered if the big guy in the red and blue Hawaiian or if the effeminate guy who wasn't speaking was Alan's replacement.

As if he himself could hear the thoughts floating around in Clive's pickled brain, Sebastian said after a pause, "Chuck here's not into guys sadly, he's my bodyguard. We were out today with little Fluffy on our bicycles in a real rough part of town and as much as we love the bike lanes, we feel the city really needs a change. Don't we Chuck? In fact, this lady I know, this spiritualist, palm reader friend I see, she's been telling me that it's only going to get worse."

Chendrill didn't have a clue as to what this guy, with the dog who sold stylish product and could make you a star, was talking about, and it was the first he'd heard about Sebastian visiting soothsayer type women who read palms. He did know that Keith Richards tuned his guitar so all he needed to do was lay one finger flat across the strings so as he could hit a chord on stage when he was out of it on tour, and since Clive still had a thumb and a forefinger, he was wondering why he couldn't just do the same.

Looking up at Sebastian and then to Clive, Chendrill

said, "I'm not a bodyguard."

"I'm just teasing, Chuck," Sebastian said with a wave that dismissed everything he'd said before.

Then he said, "Sorry Clive, Chuck does security and he's the best detective in the city. We're lucky to have him, aren't we Mazzi?"

Raising his eyebrows and knowing he would normally just say 'No' in a tone that left you wondering whether he was joking, Mazzi opted instead to say nothing.

Sebastian carried on, "Anyway Clive, we've been thinking and we feel the city is choking and we were thinking it would be great if you would run for Mayor."

Not expecting that one and not particularly liking the one they had now since the man had personally stopped three developments he had his hands on, and despite his prior ignorance to the suggestion, Patrick said, "Trust Me—it's something we've been talking about for almost a year now."

Both Chendrill and especially Mazzi Hegan knew Sebastian liked to drop unexpected bombs, but this one took them both by surprise and made Chendrill wonder when Sebastian had actually come up with the idea in the first place. It couldn't have been just pure coincidence that they'd been out earlier that day on the bicycles touring the bike lanes with Fluffy sitting in the front basket and Sebastian had seen the chaos that was Main and Hastings first hand; he couldn't have just had an epiphany. The guy was calculated. There was no way he could have been so successful any other way.

Lying in the same way Sebastian was, so as to let him know, he said, "Yes, it's all Sebastian keeps talking about. He's been driving us crazy with his planning. He said that if you're not interested in doing it, he was going to ask Mazzi here."

Mazzi stared at Chendrill thinking, *go fuck yourself, you big fucking ape!* And what the fuck was he doing here anyway with this guy, who should be wearing a glove. *Fuck*, this was nonsense, Sebastian making him come to dinner with these morons so he could show off with his 'surprise' ideas as he liked to when all Mazzi wanted to do was be at home watching Sissy Hypno.

He said, "Yes Clive, we think you'd be great."

Sebastian carried on, "The city needs a change Clive, and I remember seeing that lovely interview you gave from your bed in hospital in the Caymans after that brave boy rescued you. And that stupid idiot, insensitive reporter guy asked you what you'd be doing now after you'd lost your hand. And you'd smiled and said, 'well, I guess I'll run for Mayor.'"

Clive couldn't remember this. In fact, he could barely remember being in the hospital. He did remember the long flight home he took via Miami where he'd got stuck in a small seat because of a mix up and was having trouble carrying his bag and eating. But being Mayor? Now he was in his late thirties, so *yeah*, *why not*? It was a way to get out there again and be noticed. Be someone. Be the guy who was going to go far and change the city first, then the country second after he'd gotten into politics. Just like the way he was going to be the guy who could have been the greatest guitar player ever had he not been killed trying to save that kid from drowning.

All Mazzi Hegan had to say at the end of the evening after they'd said their goodbyes and Chendrill had walked Clive down to Belinda, who was waiting in his Mercedes and had forgotten to take the dog, as Sebastian had asked, was, “I heard he likes to dress up as a gladiator when he fucks.” Ignoring it at first as he cleaned up in the kitchen and hearing Patrick agree, then unable to ignore it anymore, Sebastian asked, “Really, how do you know that?"

Sitting down and looking out of the window to the lights on the other side of the water, Mazzi replied, “Just heard it—you know, friend of a friend, people talk.”

Patrick agreeing, like he knew it for a fact, then saying, “People talk Sebastian, trust me.” Sebastian ignored him and wondered when the man was going to leave.

He said to Mazzi Hegan, “People do strange things Mazzi, you know that.” Mazzi did, only the night before he’d fucked a woman and it was still annoying him because deep down inside he knew that a little part of him had liked it. He said, “If you’re famous, nothing’s forgotten. You know that.” And Sebastian did, as the gladiator thing was already worrying him. He said, “What did you think about him?”

“Shorter than I’d expected,” Mazzi answered. “To tell the truth though, I do remember seeing him in a bar years back rocking out surrounded by an entourage, the way those guys do.”

“A bar?” Sebastian said back, already thinking that this latest venture was going to be a waste of time if there was ‘stuff’ out there and this bar just happened to be one of the ones Mazzi frequented. He said, “When you saw him Mazzi, did he have girls with him?”

Thinking straight back to the night before when that girl who was Einer’s friend with the tight dress had kissed him in the club, sticking her tongue into his mouth as the lights had swirled around him and the half-naked dancing guys had watched as they spun about above him on their podiums, he said, "I'm not sure."

Sebastian said, "Do you think he's gay, Mazzi? You know you can't tell these days, can you? You know a lot of guys mix it up. And if he's going about dressed as a gladiator, then you never know?"

Fuck, what is going on? Mazzi thought as he wondered for the first time in his life if he was 'one of those guys who mixed it up'. Before it would never have entered his head, not even as a teenage kid in Stockholm. Then before he could speak, he heard Sebastian say, "Well it's early days, we'll just have to see won't we."

****

Clive sat in the back of the limo and thought about the night that had just been and the offer Sebastian String had just proposed. An unlimited resource budget that would put his name up on the billboards across town again promoting him just the same as they were now promoting some scrawny kid in silver undies. *Mayor*, he thought, *Mayor Clive Sonic—Clive Sonic, Mayor*. It sounded good. This happy and sweet gay man looking to do what it took to get him there as long as he put in the effort and agreed to do three things once he was there. *What about Clive Sonic, Premier of British Columbia?* he thought as Belinda drove the car up and over the Lionsgate Bridge towards Vancouver's north shore. What about Clive Sonic, Prime Minister of Canada? Could be, it had a nice ring to it, but it would be tough to accidently kill yourself when you had the RCMP's finest watching your every step and trying to do the opposite. What he'd do, he thought, was exactly the same as he was going to do before, but on a different scale and this time it would be better. He'd go from Clive Sonic, the guitarist who lost his fingers, to Clive Sonic, the guy who was going to put Vancouver back on the map and change the city—the guy who could have done so much around here but who sadly, after such a tragedy, was with us no more. Just like that he was back on track; destiny awaited.

He hit the other side of the bridge, the lights on Grouse Mountain brighter now, lighting the ski run that was yet to get snow. *Yeah, that's what I'll do*—with this gay guy helping he'd get the people to love him again. He would get them to love him and trust him—*trust me, yeah.* 'Trust Me'. *Trust Me!* Just like that stupid guy who was at the dinner party and had his picture on the buses all over town always says—but on a bigger scale. He'd say that all the time, 'Trust Me'. It would be his catch phrase. Then, when everything was lined up and the people loved him and *trusted him,* he'd leave them speechless with some incredibly tragic end, but this time he'd do it properly.

****

Chendrill arrived back upstairs just in time to go out again, this time, though, he was with Sebastian and the dog. Sebastian happily wandering slowly through the park, taking in the night air, watching the groups hanging around, smoking dope, still trying to dodge the police. Couples together sitting quietly and not speaking, just being, breathing the night air and in love. Chendrill with him, walking slowly alongside Sebastian with little Fluffy in between and wondering if people thought they were a couple, feeling conspicuous, but not caring. He said, "What's this all about making this guy with half a hand mayor?"

Sebastian sat himself down on a bench and asked Chendrill with his eyes to join him. The light from the moon and the street lamps near the water tailing off across the wet sandy beach. Sebastian smiled to himself as he waited before answering. Then he said, "It's something that I want to do, Chuck."

"I thought you were making a movie?"

Sebastian laughed to himself, then said, "Paying Chuck, paying, not making. But you know me, I'm a super multitasker." Then Sebastian asked, "Chuck, are you happy?"

"In what?"

"Everything."

It was a good question, Chendrill thought. Was he? Kind of. Looking up, he said, "Is anybody really? You see some people who have everything and they look miserable."

"I'm not talking about everyone, Chuck, I'm talking about you."

Chendrill looked back out across the water then to Sebastian's dog sniffing out something in the grass. He said, "Yeah I'm good."

"What about work, are you happy at work?"

No, he thought, *not really*, apart from the money and the car, of course, and for the fact he got to hang out with Dan's mother. He said, "Yeah, I love it."

"You see, Chuck, I love having you on the team, but when you're at work, I always feel you wish you were somewhere else. And my gut instinct tells me that you wished you were back in your old job—you know, back on the police force, as a detective."

Chendrill looked at Sebastian and frowned; was it that obvious? He said jokingly, “But if I did that, I'd not be able to keep the car.”

Sebastian smiled and looked out across the beach to a guy letting his dog run free when everyone around knew it was against the rules. Then looking back at Chendrill, he said, “Oh, the car’s yours Chuck. I’ve told you that before.”

“Then why are you asking if I'm happy? Are you wanting me to leave?” asked Chendrill, suddenly wondering if this nonchalant attitude he'd been carrying around had suddenly come back to haunt him, and if so it was best to know now.

Then Sebastian smiled and said, “Oh no, Chuck; I'm not letting you go anywhere. I like to see my friends happy so I'm getting you back where I know you want to be, and to do that Clive has to become mayor, then once he's there he'll be dealing with me and the first thing he can start doing once you have your old job back on your own terms is start cleaning up the East Side.”

****

The first thing Mazzi Hegan did when he got back to his penthouse suite was have a beer, then another, then one more, followed by a double Macallan scotch that stung his throat—which was fine, as he’d had worse land on his tonsils. *Fuck,* he thought, *what a waste of an evening it had been, going to a dinner party at Sebastian’s was painful enough without having to be pleasant to some has-been loser who couldn't hold his fork.*

Sebastian was now getting himself into politics for some reason or the other. *Probably so he wouldn't have to pay for the meters outside the office*, Mazzi thought. They did cost a lot, though, he knew that. He sat down on his leather sofa and thought about the bill he'd seen a year prior and remembered Sebastian saying he'd done a deal for $200,000. He would be after eliminating that or reducing it, and, knowing the man like he did, he'd be happy to part with 4 times the amount to do so.

He leaned back and put his feet up on the coffee table and looked at his Mauri slow movers. *Fuck me*, he thought, *what was going on*? He sleeps with one woman and forgets to take his shoes off at the door—and his socks were down. *What the hell was going on?* All this… this fucked up, upset feeling he'd had ever since that bitch with the nails had talked him into eating fish. He let out a deep breath and thought about having a cigarette, not that he smoked or had ever smoked—he just felt like it. That chick with nails, long and red on the end of those slender fingers she'd dug into his ass. Yeah, he'd liked that bit, that and the feeling of her tits on his chest when she'd leaned in and licked his face after he'd been down there. The dirty bitch. Not that he could talk with the shit he'd done, but that was natural—at least for him and some of his friends.

Mazzi Hegan looked at the time. It was almost midnight and there was a meeting in the morning about this stupid film. He screamed out, "Fuck," just like he always did when he didn't want to do something. *What was the point?* he thought, *what was the fucking point, making a movie when the producer hadn't even read the script, wasting everyone's time*? What he should be doing is calling up one of his 'friends' and that girl so he could put on a show like she'd tried to get him and Einer to do. But that was never going to work, not with Einer, even if the guy had dipped his toe in the water when they'd met a while back.

Yeah, he'd do that, he thought, *get her over and show her how it's done. But no, how could he?* He thought, what was he going to do, call a guy and say, "Hey it's Mazzi, wanna come over and suck my dick so this hot babe can watch and join in?" The first bit wouldn't be a problem, but if he mentioned the bit with the girl then that would be weird shit and people would begin to talk.

****

They all met in the morning, all of them wrapped around the boardroom table. Patrick was at the head, talking bullshit about how this was going to be the most fantastic movie ever made. The director, Campbell Ewes, agreeing to a reduced rate and back on the scene as a favour for Adalia—for a fifth of what his agent had asked for and with a stipulation in his contract that he could never be driven anywhere by Chendrill, which wasn't a problem for anyone. Mazzi was also there looking hungover sitting next to Megan, the flower child, and hating the way she smelled. Sebastian watched it all and listened with his dog on his lap, worrying about the pair of steel toecap work boots Mazzi was wearing.

Sebastian looked at the door and wondered when Chendrill would be in so he could also take a look at the plaster on Mazzi's boots. It looked real and he wanted to know what the hell was going on, the guy looking like shit the way he did and all. Then he heard the purr of the Aston pulling up and parking in one of the expensive bays down in the street below. Chendrill making light work of it, killing the engine quickly instead of turning the whole operation into a day time soap opera the way Mazzi Hegan always did. Except today there was no Ferrari for Chendrill to outshine and squeeze in next to, as it looked as though Mazzi had walked.

Chendrill shut the door to the Aston and crossed the road to the offices of Slave. He'd been asleep in Tricia's bed when his phone had gone off and wondered what the emergency would be this time around. "Mazzi's wearing a pair of boots and they're not clean," were the first words out of Sebastian's mouth. That, along with a quick question about Chendrill's whereabouts, to which Chendrill had answered, cool as a cucumber, as always, "I'm at Dan's."

Sebastian asking him straight back if he'd just arrived. "Yeah, just got here," Chendrill answered, which he had—if you counted having been there since leaving Sebastian's place the night before. Then Sebastian asked after Dan and then his mother, knowing deep down there was a high chance the guy was laying next to her as they spoke. But what did he care? After all, all that mattered really in life was that they were both happy.

Chendrill reached the reception for Slave and was once more greeted by a huge smile from the pretty girl at the desk who had two guys on the go and only saw one of them on the weekends because the other worked. Lying, she said, "I really like your shirt, Mr. Chendrill." Chendrill did also, it being the camo Hawaiian he'd picked up at The Bay. His prize possession having been on the missing list for the last few days and he'd been wondering where it was until he'd discovered Dan had been wearing it down in his basement. "Mr. String said to go straight into the meeting, he's saved a seat next to him for you and asks if you could not make eye contact with the director."

The room went silent as Chendrill walked in, stared down the director, and sat himself down next to Sebastian.

Sebastian whispered in his ear, "Did you not get my message?"

"Why's the mouthy fuck back?" asked Chendrill, just loud enough for the director to hear. It was just how he was. He looked to the script and some other paperwork that had been placed neatly for him on the table to read. Ignoring it, Chendrill looked up. Patrick was back talking, telling everyone what a great project he'd developed. Chendrill listening for about 5 seconds and then stopping. Like an animal penned in a cage, he looked to the door, then leaning in to Sebastian, he whispered, "Why am I here?"

Clasping Chendrill's arm ever so softly and guiding his eyes to Mazzi who was also not listening as he sat at the end of the table looking out the window, Sebastian said, "Look under the table; he's wearing workman's boots, Chuck. And not only that—they are filthy."

Chendrill looked under the table. He was, there was no doubt about it. The boots hugely big with steel toecaps, all ruffed up, showing steel and covered in caked on muck, making Mazzi's feet look like a circus clown's at the end of Mazzi Hegan's skinny silk trousers. Chendrill looked back at Sebastian and said very quietly, "He's stolen some plasterer's boots."

"Really?" Sebastian replied, confused.

Chendrill nodded, then asked, "Can I go now?"

Sebastian smiled. *Chuck, you are a devil,* he thought. The guy, sitting there all buff and tough in his camo, never wanting to be part of his world when it came to work, but who would sit comfortable chatting in a park on a summer's evening or out on Sebastian's penthouse balcony. He said, "Is it really that bad here, Chuck?"

Chendrill laughed quietly to himself for a moment. Then leaning over, he said, "This is your world, Sebastian."

And it was. Sebastian, sitting there half listening but not missing a beat; Chuck there, still not listening at all. He said, "If you're not here, who will I be able to have fun with, Chuck?" Chendrill thought about it. This guy, who was so rich he could entertain making a movie for a fair-weather friend who he knew would take your watch if you held his hand to long. The man just wanting to be a kid at school again. He nodded towards Patrick, who was still spouting bullshit, "Why do you indulge this guy?"

Sebastian laughed. Chendrill was there with him getting it like he always did. He said, "I get bored, Chuck, and doing this stupid film gets me one of the world's top models and, if I'm lucky, a huge corporate promotion where we can all travel around the world for a bit with Adalia."

Chendrill said straight back, "What about the dog?"

Sebastian sighed and looked under the table at Fluffy who'd settled at Chendrill's feet. The big guy was right, what about the dog? It was the only little minor detail he was having with putting this bigger deal together on the back of Patrick's ego trip. He said, "I'm hiring a vet, Chuck. He can come with us if he wants as long as Fluffy likes him."

Chendrill answered, "I thought dogs didn't like the vet." Sebastian thought about it for a moment. The last trip to the vet's had been a bit traumatic with Fluffy snapping at the guy for lifting his tail. He said, "I'll find one he does like, Chuck; you know how I am."

Then Chendrill surprised him by asking, "Where are we going?"

It was a good question, he had been thinking of Europe first, for a week or two and only the other day he'd come across a video on the internet with a cool guy from Kenya who was there singing about Zagreb, except he'd called it Zahaa in a cool way and slapped his hand down as he'd said it like he couldn't give a shit—except he obviously did or why else would he have made the video in the first place? He said, "Zagreb in Croatia, I should think. There's this guy out there singing about it. He's a rapper, it's very in right now. Some guy called Chunky."

Chendrill raised his eyebrows, and said out loud, "Croatia?"

Sebastian nodded, as Chendrill thought back to Archall Diamond's rap, the one he'd heard him singing as he'd walked along the corridor from the toilet in Rasheed's old place. The East Indian gangster's words not making any sense and cut short as Chendrill's clenched fist had smacked the rapper straight in the mouth and shut him up. He said, "I didn't know you liked rap Sebastian?"

He didn't, not really, but it was good to keep up with the times—otherwise you became Patrick. He said, "I like all sorts of things, Chuck. There's a lot of things out there to keep you amused if you just look; even right here with Patrick pretending he's read the script."

Chendrill looked up at Patrick almost standing now and gesturing with his hands. Then he looked back to Sebastian and said quietly, "He sounds like he has."

Sebastian smiled. Then he said, "That's what he's good at, that's why he's been so successful in real estate—it's because he's creative with his words. Listen we'll see just how much he's read."

Then without missing a beat, Sebastian raised his right

hand, stopped Patrick in his tracks, and said, "Patrick, tell me, how do you feel we can build on the fundamentals of this story to give it more strength?"

And as quick as a flash, Patrick deflected the question over to Mazzi Hegan by saying, "That's a good question Sebastian, and a question I feel we should be asking Mazzi, as I feel he's always got such a fantastic take on things and if I was to answer first we may just lose something brilliant."

But Mazzi Hegan wasn't listening. His feet were hurting and he wanted to go to the toilet because his dick was sore.

They made their excuses and began to leave. Sebastian standing up and halting proceedings with his hands, then he told everyone how sorry he was and how he had important business to deal with and headed straight for the door and, with a serious face, held it open for his dog who was two steps ahead of Chendrill. Then as they walked back along the corridor towards his office, Sebastian said, "You see what I mean? He hasn't read it."

Chendrill looked at the girls in the booths looking sexy and said, "But you already know this?"

Sebastian, all in a fluster, still carrying on, said, "He should know better, though." Chendrill reached the door to Sebastian's office, wondering what it would be like to sleep with the brunette in the last booth who was busy doing God knows what at her computer, and opened the door. As Sebastian passed through followed by the dog, he said, "Why don't you get one of these young ladies here to sit down and read it to him if you're that worried?"

Sebastian reached the corner of the room and, dropping down to make sure Fluffy was watered, said, "Oh, I'm not letting him near any of those girls Chuck, not now that I've seen the photos that guy sent over. Not that I would have before, in any case, except if one of them had some cash come their way and they needed a condo."

Then sitting himself down, Chendrill said, "Anyway—I thought you liked it that he doesn't have a clue and is bluffing?"

"Oh, I like it Chuck," Sebastian said, working himself towards the window in a fluster, "but I have my limits."

Chendrill began to smile, wondering if he'd ever be able to go off like this and get himself in a flap over something he had knowingly orchestrated in the first place. He said, "Well, just say fuck it. Shut it down and stick the 5 million into the guy with the missing fingers."

Sebastian looked at Chendrill leaning back in the sofa with his left foot up on the $2000 coffee table like he owned the place and said, "You're not wrong, but don't be calling Mr. Sonic that. He has a name you know and it's not his fault he lost his fingers. Besides, you know I'm looking at the big picture because on the back end of it all is a massive advertising campaign—but really, truth is, that could all disappear as soon as Adalia's drinking from the fountain of youth gets shut down. So, after listening to that nonsense in there, I ask myself is it worth it. I think Mazzi feels the same way, you know. I've never seen him so bored; normally he's bouncing off the walls with ideas and the guy's sitting there and not even listening." *Join the club*, Chendrill thought as he recalled Patrick and his dialogue as Sebastian began to carry on.

Then without as much as a knock, the door opened and it was Mazzi Hegan all red in the face with his hair a mess, and all he said to Sebastian was, "Seb, I need help. I've been doing something terrible, I don't know what to do, I can't control myself anymore, you have to help me, I can't stop thinking about sleeping with women."

****

Leaving, Chendrill got back into his car and looked up at the window to Sebastian's office and wondered if the pair of them had stopped crying yet. *Fuck me what a morning,* he thought, could it have gotten any stranger? *Maybe this was normal though*, he thought, as he put the Aston into gear and pulled away. Maybe this is just the way it was in advertising and everyone was all fucked up—neurotic and weird—with sexuality issues to boot. Fuck it was strange. He hit the end of the road and took a left onto Cambie. There was something that wasn't sitting right though, something he was about to snag onto when Hegan had burst in and polluted the room with the disgusting news that he'd been sticking his dick into the one place it had certainly been designed to fit.

Turning right, he made his way north until he hit Hastings and took a right, driving past the junkies and homeless who lined the streets less than a minute's walk from the police station. He carried on without a thought for the Italian who fed off them and Ditcon who simply pretended they weren't there. So Adalia had been drinking from the fountain of youth and, according to Sebastian, was about to be shut down. But if Dan was the fountain he'd been referring to, then how had he missed it? And if he had, he hadn't been doing his job.

He pulled up outside Dan's mother's place and parked in the spot which was seemingly his these days and walked inside. The Ferrari was still there, so unless Dan had gone for some exercise, which wasn't likely, he'd be in his basement. This seemed to be the case when he'd heard him stir right after he'd pulled his lips away from Dan's mother in the kitchen. Getting right to the point he called down the stairs to Dan's room, "Sebastian's told me you're not allowed near Adalia Seychan anymore."

Tricia's jaw dropped as what she'd just heard sunk in and, turning to Chendrill mouthed, "No?" without actually speaking.

Chendrill looked at her and with a shrug of his shoulders whispered, "Maybe? According to Sebastian, she's been drinking from the fountain of youth and we're about to find out if Dan's got control of the tap."

Before she could say another word, Dan was up the stairs, saying, "We ain't doing nothing except acting."

Chendrill saying straight back, "I'm sure at her age she's the only one acting, Dan."

Then confirming the speculation Dan simply said, "Yeah well from what I can tell she loves it."

Dan's mother stood there, unable to say her son's name for a moment in shock, then as soon as the name she'd christened him with when he was a soft and loveable baby made its way from the pit of her stomach, the rest followed in quick succession. She said, "Daniel, you disgusting freak, what is that woman, 65? What the hell do you think you're playing at?"

And Dan said straight back, "No actually Mum she's 68, but what does that matter, she's got better tits than you."

And that's when his mother hit him straight across his face.

Chendrill took his new girl to the bedroom and held her

while she cried as he looked at his watch. There's no doubt about it, he could have handled that better instead of baiting the kid in front of his mother.

It was almost 2 p.m. and from what he could work out she'd been crying since midday. There wasn't much he'd said that had helped; in fact, the more he had said the worse it had gotten. Especially the bit about older women being attractive these days, which had just seemed to make things worse. 'He wouldn't have been interested if she hadn't had surgery' also hadn't gone down too well either. So now, for the moment, he was keeping quiet and in this quiet he couldn't help but wonder what it would have been like to fuck Adalia Seychan himself.

Another 30 minutes or so passed before he heard Dan appear from his cave below and open the fridge in the kitchen and, making his excuses, he left the room to find Dan digging his teeth into a slab of cheese whilst he wiped the remnants of cooking oil from his right hand onto the dish cloth by the sink. Dan looked up and said with a full mouth, "I thought you'd gone?"

"No, still here."

"Guys don't usually stay that long once the water taps turn on. If you know what I mean?"

Chendrill did and, truth was, he could do without the history lesson. So he just said, "Well, times have changed," and followed it up with, "and so should you Dan if you want her to take you seriously now you're doing your own thing—so to speak. Why don't you start by going in there and apologizing?"

Without looking up, Dan said, "You're the one with the big mouth not me, so why don't you stop trying to be dad and mind your own business."

He has a point, Charles Chuck Chendrill thought, and felt hungry as he watched another slab of the cheese disappear into the void that was Dan's mouth. After all, he wasn't Dan's dad. As quick as a flash, Dan carried on with, "And its just as well you're not. Because if you were, I'd have gotten your looks and with that chances are high I'd never have gotten a multi-millionaire superstar sucking my dick." And just as he passed him heading back down the stairs to his cave, Dan heard Chendrill say back, "Yeah, I get you, no teeth can be good!"

****

Daltrey sat on the edge of her bed and pulled off the bandana she'd been wearing to hide her burns. How long had it been now, she thought, as she felt her burned skin which she hoped would heal soon. She'd been on the boat hiding and done the same in hospital and now she was back at her apartment hiding again—except for when the biker had managed to drag her out. Which had been nice, but out was as far as she'd let it go for the moment. Not until she was used to the way she now looked at least.

What would she have done if she'd not found that phone and called Chendrill like she had, she thought. Would she still be there? Maybe, but the food and drink that belonged to whoever owned the boat had been getting sparse, just as the toilet paper had also. She looked at the nails on her hands—they were getting long now, longer than she could remember them ever being before. But what did that matter with her hair being the way it was at the moment?

It was time to get back to the real world—this she had known for the last while. If she'd had the guts to take on those two kids armed with baseball bats, mugging that man, she was strong enough to start looking into the identity of the brave girl who had saved her life.

So, for the moment, she needed to speak to the one guy who could find out pretty quick—even if he was an idiot.

She picked up the phone again and was surprised at the speed she was put through once she'd mentioned her name.

"Ditcon here," was all she'd heard, the guy sounding like he had a thousand other things to do at that precise moment rather than talk to her, which in reality couldn't have been further from the truth.

Daltrey said, "It's Daltrey, I need you to find out who you've got in the morgue wearing my name tag."

"I'm busy, why don't you call them yourself and ask?"

Daltrey took a deep breath and felt the rush of blood she used to feel when someone had pissed her off and whoever it was, was about to get an earful. The man was a thoughtless pig. She said, "If I'm right in thinking there's only two people in this world who know you're full of shit, maybe three if you include your mother. So, I'll ask again if you can get me a name or I'll start telling everyone I meet you had no idea I was on that boat."

"What boat?" Ditcon snapped back.

Jesus, Daltrey thought, then she said, "Just get it done, so as you can keep up your bullshit charade." Then she hung up.

Ditcon sat back down in his office chair and stared at his phone thinking now of all the things he should have said. Such as, 'unless you're Mayor, then you can get it done yourself you fucking bitch', or 'do your damn job', or 'I just saved your ass, so cut the attitude?' *Yeah*, that's what he should have said. Told it to her just like that. That's part of the job though, diplomacy, being able to know when to keep quiet. After all, she'd been undercover and he knew how straining that could be—so he'd been told. He picked up the phone and said to the person on the other end who he thought he knew but didn't, this guy who always offered resistance when all he needed to do was say 'yes'.

"I want the name that goes with the body you thought was Daltrey. We let your incompetence down there go for a while because it suited us. But no longer, so no back talk, the girl's been undercover for me and she needs a name."

Then he looked up and saw Stephanie was just waking up, the girl sleeping in his comfy chair by the window after she'd just managed to rebuff another approach. She said, "You want me to drive you to that place in Deep Cove so as we can get a coffee?"

That was the ticket, Ditcon thought, he'd have her grab one of them Dodge Chargers from the pound and whip him over there. Then when he was done he'd phone that guy from the U.S. Customs and Border Protection and see what was happening with that fuckhead Chendrill. After all, why should a guy who'd busted across the border illegally be driving around in an Aston Martin?

Ditcon finished his muffin and his hot chocolate and wondered why Stephanie only ate half of hers when they came here. She was probably thinking about her weight, as girls did. Catching her attention as she looked out the window to the inlet that could easily have passed for a lake, he said, "You know this isn't Hollywood, you can finish that."

"If you want it you can have it," Stephanie said, then raised her eyebrows and gave him that cheeky smile to finish it off at the end of the sentence to imply a double meaning.

Fuck the little bitch, Ditcon thought, flirting with him all the time and giving him a sniff but not letting him have sex with her properly like she should have been doing by now. She was fun though, even if his neck was starting to ache, this time, for once, for real. He said, "You know, I'm thinking this Chendrill's being a bit flash, cruising in an Aston when all we've got is a Charger."

"Yeah I was thinking the same," said Stephanie, when in reality was she had only been thinking about how she had to walk her boyfriend's dog that evening because he would be working late—the same "working late" as she had been doing for the last couple of days, except he hadn't been holding off because he was in a relationship. "Why don't you call the guy the Yanks have up here sniffing about and see what he's found out and we can take it from there," she suggested.

The phone had almost rung off and went to voice mail when Basil answered. Ditcon and Stephanie sat there staring at the phone on speaker propped up on the table.

"Hello," Basil said, waiting silently long enough for Ditcon and Stephanie to hear the whale music in the background.

Ditcon looked strangely at his new driver who wouldn't give him any, then asked, "Where are you?"

Basil asking straight back.

"Who is this?"

Ditcon always liked this bit whenever he was given the chance to lay out his full credentials, even if it was over the phone or otherwise, and being the egotistical prick he was he wasn't going to let the opportunity pass by—especially when he was so close to nirvana with his new sexy driver de jour. Taking a deep breath, he said his name and rank slowly and surely into the phone, laying it out as if he was in fact hearing it himself while being honoured for bravery, which was not going to be happening any time soon, "Chief Inspector Ditcon of the Vancouver Police Department. Please answer the question."

"You don't even know who I am, I haven't even identified myself," answered Basil from the other end of the phone.

Ditcon said back quickly, "Basil Setter, working undercover with the U.S. Department of Homeland Security. That's who you are. So cut the bullshit."

Basil said straight back, "Get to the point, I'm busy."

Ditcon looked at Stephanie sitting there next to him raising her eyebrows. He'd have liked to have gone over to wherever this idiot was, pick him up, then throw the disrespectful prick back across the border. But he couldn't, not without there being an international incident, so, eating it, he said, "Tell me how you're doing with Chendrill?"

"Chendrill's great."

"And?"

"And what?"

"And I'm asking so you need to tell me."

"My wages are paid in U.S. dollars, not Canadian."

"I'm thinking you want to keep getting paid, so cut the shit or I'll have you sent back home."

"I am home, I'm Canadian, remember."

Ditcon looked at Stephanie; the conversation wasn't going well and he could feel his temper building and that wouldn't look good, not when he was pretending to be cool. The fucking prick was getting smart with him, pulling the Canuck card when the fucker was probably from

Quebec. Then as soon as he was about to tell the guy to go fuck himself and send a car to some unknown address where they played relaxing fucking shitty whale music to have him arrested, Stephanie leaned in and said, “Basil. Please tell us anything you may have found out about Chendrill and in return we’ll happily make the call to your superiors to tell them what a great job you’re doing up here.”

And that was all he needed to hear.

****

Mazzi Hegan opened the front door to his penthouse suite and, without a thought, wandered down to the living room and put his feet up on the glass coffee table. His boots were still on and still felt heavy, but putting it out there to Sebastian, who he knew would understand, had been a bigger weight off his chest. That ape Chendrill had been there, yes, and heard his confession, but what the fuck? He’d have found out anyway. His type always did. He looked at his phone and played with it for a while, doing nothing, checking this and checking that, and flipping through the pictures of the night before, after he’d given in to temptation and messaged, ‘Hi!’ to the woman who had only hours before made him puke.

The photos were there now on his phone, telling him the story about what he’d done and who he was now becoming.

He had been in the bar with a chick who normally hung around with Einer. The pair of them were getting wasted, then there was a plasterer there with them with his arm around her neck. Then the three of them were doing green shooters, her in the middle of them, then there were flaming

Sambucas, and they were looking all pie-eyed. Then another girl was with them with nice teeth and big tits with eyes that matched. Then another girl and Einer, who didn't look drunk. All of them were popping selfies as quick as they were knocking back the drinks. Then they were back at this guy's place with shit all over the floor and half eaten bags of chips in the kitchen. All of them were in his little bedroom, then all of them were naked and fucking, except, for once, it wasn't him being spit roasted in the middle, taking it from both ends—it was a girl he remembered now who was screaming too loud and the guy whose place it was was trying to keep her quiet with his dick in her mouth, and the guy was not looking Mazzi in the eye, let alone kissing him. Einer was there watching it all and laughing at Mazzi as Mazzi Hegan fucked one girl, and then the next, as Einer fucked the girl with the teeth and made her tits wobble.

Then he'd woken up still drunk and alone, not knowing where he was, with his face on a sheet with a shitty thread count which needed to be washed, his shoes gone, and only when he'd stepped outside with bloodshot eyes into the cool morning air, wearing the only things that he could find that would fit on his feet, he'd realized that he was just around the corner from Slave where there was a room full of people waiting for him in a meeting he didn't want to be at.

But now it was all out in the open and chances are his Mauri slow movers were gone. But what the hell. It had been worth it, getting wasted and feeling free, seeing a straight construction worker naked—going at it and making weird faces like he had. But the girls, they'd smelled nice, and he'd liked the feel of his dick inside them, liked the way they could just go and go, orgasm after orgasm until none of the guys had anything left to give.

He stared along his legs to his boots and smiled; he hadn't had a pair on like it since he'd gone out with his friends years ago all dressed up. They were quite cool really, all covered in white stuff, and even if they were a tenth the price of his Mauri's, they were worth the trade. All he needed now was the construction hat and a safety vest and he could have gone dancing. But who with and where? With a bunch of fags? No, he wasn't feeling that. There was no doubt about it, pussy was what he was feeling for the moment, and sexy pussy at that, so he may as well go with the flow.

Mazzi stared at his phone, looking at the pictures of the girls and their long hair and nails the same as he'd once tried to grow. Yeah girls were it, really sexy girls with softer skin and better hair than his. Girls with sexy legs and shoes whom he could go out in his new boots, dressed as a construction worker and pick up. Girls he could lay out some coin on and take them cruising in the Ferrari, then, if he was lucky, he could fuck them at the point in Stanley Park, just like these other hetro guys seemed to do.

Chapter Ten

He found some old jeans, a t-shirt, and a construction vest some closet case had left behind a year before, stuck the boots back on, and headed out into the night in the Ferrari. He hit Granville Street, heading north off the bridge and instead of turning left onto the rainbow coloured streets of Davie he carried on up the road to where the bars were and the straight people got their kicks.

For the first time in his life, he parked the car with ease and strutted in his big boots and vest into the first bar he saw. Throwing the keys to the Ferrari on the counter he asked the girl with the nice ass behind the bar for a beer. That should do it, he thought as he saw her clock the emblem on the keys and pick up a glass. He'd seen it work before in a movie when an actor had pulled a bar maid. The actor all macho in the movies and pretending to the world to be straight but Mazzi knowing from personal experience, that the guy wasn't, because of the way he'd kissed him once at a party. Then he heard the girl say, "Six dollars twenty-five."

"Sorry?"

"Six dollars twenty-five."

Not even a 'hey good looking' or 'nice car', or anything, just the bill and he hadn't even seen let alone wet his lips with a beer yet. So just as the girl turned around, he said, putting it out there the same as he would have a few blocks down in the old neighbourhood he used to frequent on Davie, "Nice ass."

"Fuck you."

That was all he got back as a reply, no sly look or grin

or sexy wink as a thank you like he'd seen in the movies. Just 'fuck you'. *Well fuck you too*, Mazzi thought, as he handed her a stack of twenties and walked away without a drink. He reached the shooters girl cruising the room, grabbed two, knocked them back, then another one, and, putting the glass back down on the tray, said through the music, "Go see your friend, I gave her $400, keep $100 for yourself and the drinks flowing for me and the girls baby."

Then he grabbed another shooter and headed off into the room with the glass and the waitress in tow, rocking from side to side to the music, as she handed out the first ever drinks he'd bought for women and letting them know they were from him. He walked on, strutting his stuff, the women were fine, but despite the free booze they were still keeping to themselves, talking in their little groups or lost within their phones and not saying thanks. He walked over to the first who looked in his direction and as soon as he got there said, "Hi I'm Mazzi Hegan." The girl just looked up and nodded back, not even bothering to speak as she watched Mazzi moving his head from side to side to the music. Then again as he normally would in this situation if he was a few blocks to the west on Davie, he said, "You wanna see my dick?"

The girl just stared, wondering if for the moment she'd heard this guy dressed in construction clothes correctly. "Sorry?" she said. Mazzi Hegan said it again, but this time pulled out his phone, not waiting for an answer.

He moved on to the next, "Hey?" and then the next, "Hey, what's up?" Then to another, "Hey!"—but this time he added 'baby' then said, "Man, you're hot, wanna come blow me in the bathroom?"

He walked across the room and stood alone at the edge

of the dance floor. *Fuck, this isn't easy*, he thought. The straight to the point approach he was used to wasn't working with these women. They just weren't as receptive as the guys were around the corner on Davie. Normally, he'd have had sex at least twice by now, especially given what he was wearing. All he'd have to do was put it out there and next thing he'd be out back in a sword swallowing competition. But that wasn't going to work here it seemed. Mazzi looked out through the crowd, the girls were still doing the same as they had been—some dancing, mostly together with other girls, though some were with guys who seemed to have this straight thing under control.

The shooter girl passed by again and he took another, then one more, knocking them both back. Then he caught her again on the way back. The music was weird here also, almost rave-like, but not, some sort of rave/techno/lounge mix that didn't seem like it knew what it wanted to be. He watched the DJ up on his small plinth, the guy really tall in his beanie cap, with only one ear in his big puffy headphones, fiddling with the knobs on his little machine. DJ Raffi, the man grooving to his own sounds with three girls on the go. The guy looking up and wondering why one of the Village People was looking at him, and also wondering what Mazzi was about to do now that he was entering the dance floor alone.

Mazzi Hegan hit the centre of the dance floor and started to loosen up, feeling the music. In amongst it all there had to be some raw bassline to hook into, and a second later he had it. Boom Boom da Boom Boom da boom boom. Yes, Mazzi had it now. He looked at a circle of girls all dancing around their handbags and with his elbows out at chest height and his fists at both nipples with his left arm up and his right down he began to strut across the dance floor, rocking his hips, lifting both arms up and down alternating each of his fists up to below his chin to a rhythm only he could hear.

He reached the girls, staring them each in the eyes as he passed around and around—the girls looking at each other wondering what the fuck was going on. Then, on his third pass, and just as he'd gotten them all under his spell, he called out in his deep Swedish accent to DJ Raffi on his plinth, "Hey DJ, let's get this party started baby, give me some ABBA, give me some Pet Shop Boys, where's the Frankie man!"

It was going to be a tough transition.

****

Adalia Seychan had a problem, and it wasn't one her plastic surgeon could remedy; though in the end, it came down to almost the same thing. The problem was she needed time, time to relax, time for people to faff over her so as she could feel special, time to fuck, time to recover, and time in between Patrick and Slave's incredible sci-fi flick and the next film she'd just been offered. She needed time.

This new film had come from out of the blue after its leading lady had walked from the project, and the producers were now delighted to go with Adalia—that is, if she was interested, because after all she had not been their first choice, but truth was they'd said she had 'actually' been their first choice from the start, had the studio not stepped in. Which was a complete crock of shit, which Adalia knew, but, being cut from the same cloth as the people who had fed her this line, she went along with it anyway. The only problem now though was that the producers on the next job had done the math and lined up a new shooting schedule to start two days after Adalia would be taking off her space suit in Vancouver.

But this wasn't enough. She needed at least six weeks to prepare, and since the new offer was better it was Patrick who was going to have to make the changes. And all Patrick, being Patrick, had said to Adalia's agent when he'd called with the proposal was a completely naïve and ill-informed, "no problem, we'll start shooting next week."

The first person to be woken up about this emergency was Chendrill, who couldn't care less, and who'd been keeping Dan safe while sleeping over with Dan's mother again. The second was Mazzi Hegan, who'd gone to bed early but hadn't been to sleep—for only an hour after he'd entered, on his own accord, the first bar where the majority of its patrons ran the risk of procreation if they had sex, he'd met Einer's girl again. And after watching him clear the dance floor, all she'd had to say was, "Why are you hitting on kids when you've got real women you can please?"

But unfortunately for Mazzi, the 'pleasing' wasn't altogether in the variety expected as part of his new sexual awakening, as it would only be offered at a price and one which had no actual monetary value.

"What do you say about us all having some fun, Mazzi?" was the first thing Einer's girl had said the previous evening when Mazzi had sat down and automatically put his arms around her two friends, who were sitting in the corner booth section of the bar drinking free shooters from the waitress.

"See, we've been watching you strut your stuff. Now we want to get naked so you can watch us at your place below that painting you've got on your bedroom ceiling. We want you to watch us making love underneath it, then if you've been good you can join in, but you can only do that if we can watch you first."

Mazzi stared at Einer's girl, then looked from side to side at the two girls he'd sandwiched himself in between—just the same as he'd seen DJ Raffi sit down and do after he'd had enough of Mazzi's dancing. He asked, "What is it you want me to do?"

And Einer's girl had said straight back, "what we want is this: you and this guy we found to put on a show, and no it's not Einer, because he's a flake." Mazzi looked around the bar as he took it all in and said back, "You're not talking about the DJ are you? Because I don't think he likes me."

"No Mazzi, we found a guy from somewhere deep in Africa—Congo, or Sudan, or somewhere like that. He's on this web site and claims to make fantasies come true—he's waiting for us to call him back."

They left the Ferrari to get towed eventually and all jumped in a cab and were back at Mazzi's pad within the hour. Mazzi still rocking the boots and jeans. The girls making themselves at home and leaving the fridge door open, wandering around the place, drinking wine and smoking thick spliffs of BC dope, half naked in their knickers.

Then the buzzer went and it was the African gigolo. *Fuck me!* Mazzi thought as he followed the girls as they ran excitedly towards the entry phone. All three of them there giggling at the sight of the guy outside. Mazzi stared at the guy as he watched him on the screen. With the amount of guys he'd had up in his place, the chances are he knew him anyway. In the old days, he would have been first to the phone, but somehow now it felt different. Gone were the usual feelings of his dick stiffening at the thought of a black guy coming over—though now it still was already semi-there because of the girls in their knickers and bare feet running about the place. They liked the pad, that's what it was—he could see that. It was a cool place to hang out and party and take selfies. But having to deal with this guy being brought in suddenly seemed to change the equation.

The door opened and in he came, carrying a smile as wide as a long weekend, arms open, hugging the girls like he'd only left them a week earlier even though he'd never seen them before in his life. He high fived Mazzi as he passed in the hall, sizing him up—the guy he'd have to fuck. The man not gay, just a walking fuck machine who'd do anything or anyone for money. And Mazzi Hegan the opposite and all confused, doing anything for fun.

He reached the living room and walked straight out onto the balcony to take in the view, as people always seemed to do. Then he turned and said, "Hey Girlfriends, who's got my money?" The girls ignored him and grabbing him by the hand, pulled him back inside. The man laughing as he followed them in and, in his African accent, said happily, "Easy baby we have all the night." The girls wanting to see what he was working with, wrenched on his jeans to pull them off, and for the first time ever Mazzi was hoping it was small. *Jesus*, he thought, when it wasn't.

Very quickly he said, as the girls took the man's dick in each of their hands, feeling its weight, "Well you can put that away." His own voice that, for a moment, didn't sound like his own.

Walking them both like prisoners and carrying their wine as they did, the girls marched the two men towards the bedroom with the painting Mazzi had commissioned years before on the ceiling. The male prostitute from the Congo now naked with his huge dick swinging as he went still asking about the money. Mazzi with his top off, still wearing the labourer's boots and jeans—his mind all over the map.

They hit the bedroom, the girls cuddling up against Mazzi's silk covered pillows, readying themselves for a show as the man from the Congo began to take control, saying to Mazzi, "You need to take off your trousers, I am strong, but I cannot break through denim."

Mazzi stared at the man as the guy from Kinshasa unconsciously stroked his dick, getting it somewhat ready to perform. Getting lippy back, Mazzi looked to the girls at the head of the bed and said, "If he was worth the money you girls are paying he could."

Then all of a sudden, the man from the Congo was up, standing on the bed holding Mazzi's hair with one hand and his dick with the other, slapping it across Mazzi's face from one side to the next as Mazzi kneeled before him and called out with every swipe.

"Where my money?"

Mazzi looked at the girls for an answer that didn't seem to be coming as the man's dick hit him again across the side of his face. "No cash, no show," he said to the girls. But the show had already begun and there was no way they were looking for an intermission.

Frustrated, the man from the Congo hit Mazzi again

with his dick, from the left and again from the right. Then like a baseball player lining up to hit a curve ball, he took a huge swing, hitting Mazzi Hegan so hard in the face it sent him spinning off the bed.

Mazzi stood up from the side of the bed and felt blood tricking from his mouth, he had a thousand dollars in cash in his sock drawer but there was no way this fucker was getting any of that. Looking up at the man standing naked on his bed, still holding his dick, he shouted, "Get the fuck out of here."

"We had sex man—money first, then I go."

"That wasn't sex, that was like meeting the fucking Gestapo," said Mazzi, spitting blood with every word and wondering at the same time what was going on with him as he heard himself say out loud again, "Now get the fuck out and take your dick with you." When not too long ago, had he have been in the same situation, he would have been on his knees with his head back, like a stork swallowing a huge fish. But no, here he was, standing in builder's boots and jeans with three beauties half naked and curled up, hiding behind his silk pillows with their backs against the headboard of his bed, watching this black guy standing naked at the other end of it with what looked like a third leg that had been cut off above the knee. Then the man, who used his dick for a living said, "I thought you gay guys liked it rough?"

And Mazzi screamed out for the first time in his life, "I'm not gay okay—I'm straight!"

In a fit of rage that would normally have instinctively sent him pathetically slapping at the guy's legs, Mazzi stepped up onto the bed, not caring for a moment about ruining the immaculately stitched Mulberry silk sheets with the plaster from the dirty boots he'd stolen. Swinging out with his right arm he bought up his left, aiming for the man's chin in just the same way he had years before his hormones had kicked in and he'd started liking *Wham,* the same as he had when he'd aimed at the bully and punched out his mother. Only this time he didn't hit anyone and missed.

With his head snapping back, dodging the ill-aimed strike and getting his feet all twisted and tied up in amongst the expensive bedding, the man from the Congo fell back away from Mazzi standing there in his jeans and dropped down off the other side of the bed. Quickly the girls stood up on the bed, still holding their glasses of wine, and joined Mazzi looking down at the man laying naked, knocked out cold from hitting his head on the $74,000 Persian carpet Mazzi had just shipped in from Iran.

"Is he dead?" asked one of the girls, as she looked towards Mazzi.

Mazzi stared at the guy for a moment then he shook his head, "No, he can't be, it's okay—the vein in his dick's still pulsing."

****

Not long after Sebastian was on the phone wondering where Mazzi was because there was an emergency. The only emergency Mazzi could see was that he had a promise with the three girls he had sitting next to him. He said to Sebastian, "Can it wait Sebastian? I've got something going on right now?"

"What?"

"It's been a busy night Seb, this guy came over with a huge dick, he called me a fag and we had a fight. I took quite a beating, but in the end I knocked him out and an ambulance came and he's gone now. Oh, and don't worry, the secret's out now. I've come out—or in—or whatever you'd want to call it. You know, best thing is though, is that I'm not confused anymore. I'm telling the world I like pussy."

Sebastian String sat down at his desk at Slave and looked at the clock. It was 7:01 a.m. and maybe Mazzi was right to be more concerned about his life than a stupid film he'd allowed a guy who sold him his penthouse to run amok with. But work was work, and Mazzi should be in when asked, so fuck him and fuck the girls he was apparently fucking now because they had work to do. He said, "I'd appreciate it if you were able to make it into a meeting we are having at 9 a.m. Thank you."

Sebastian looked at his dog and then to the window. He walked to it and stood at its side looking out. It was still early out there, the shops selling designer wear were not opening for another couple of hours or so. And some cafés were still only just flipping their open signs on, ready for the day. That guy was out there again, holding a coffee.

He called Chendrill and heard him answer after a couple of rings.

"What's up."

"That guy's here Chuck, drinking coffee."

"What type?"

"Looks like Starbucks."

"How long's he been there?"

"I'm not sure I just looked out."

Less than ten minutes later, Chendrill was downtown and walking away from the parked Aston with its engine still crackling from the caning it had just received all the way over from Dan's mother's home on the East Side. The Italian was still there, waiting in a doorway just outside Slave's office. Not looking up, but staking out along the street for whoever it was he was waiting for to come in to work within the next hour or so. Approaching from his blind side, Chendrill stopped right next to him and, before the guy felt his presence, Chendrill said, "I thought the kind of people you did business with didn't get up until the afternoon."

The man turned seeing Chendrill, not flinching whatsoever, he said, "Some people I do business with have normal jobs."

"Maybe I'll come down to your place and watch your kids go to school."

"They don't live with me anymore. I just get them every other weekend."

Ignoring him and turning away, the Italian looked at Slave's offices. Chendrill watched him for a moment, wondering what was going on inside the man's head, he said, "I told you before that whatever debt you've dreamed up in your mind, it's with me now."

The Italian reached into his pocket for a cigarette and remembered he no longer smoked. This guy was good; it was early and he wasn't even finished with his drink and the fucker was onto him—even caught him unaware. He said, "You got a quarter of a million dollars spare have you?"

The man was right, he hadn't. Chendrill said, "Why are you chasing rainbows?"

The Italian looked at him, surprised. Then he said, "Is that what you call it?"

"That and a few other things." Then Chendrill said,

hitting the guy with a little taste of reality, "If you're feeling the crunch because your usual clients are dying from fentanyl before they get a chance to make good, then maybe you should be looking at who's mixing the shit and talk to them instead of getting up early and coming around here?"

Mattia, the Italian who leant money to people who couldn't pay back, looked at Chendrill and then back away towards the offices of Slave and took a deep breath. It seemed like almost every day now he was hearing of someone who owed their death, or near death, to fentanyl. Whoever was mixing it in the dope was out of reach, at least to him. Knowing Chendrill wasn't wrong, he said, "Go speak to social services if you're worried about the community."

Chendrill shrugged; what was going down out there on the streets was pretty shitty and now more than ever if you took any drug on the streets—from good old-fashioned hash to heroin—it could be laced with fentanyl. If so, there was a chance it was check out time—unless you happened to have someone nearby who had the tools to bring them back or an ambulance arrived quickly. A lot were not that lucky, and the problem was becoming an epidemic. There was little he could do—unless he wanted to take on the Triads and the Angels and whoever else was playing in the shadows. Chendrill said, "Like I say, if times are hard, go get a real job. Otherwise, fuck off and leave me and my friend be."

And the Italian said straight back, "And like I said, you've got till the end of the month to start paying."

****

They sat upstairs in the darkness of the reception, Sebastian on the sofa holding his dog, Chendrill on the reception desk with his legs dangling like a kid in the class at school when the teacher was out of the room. Sebastian all concerned and red in the face said, "Let's just pay the man Chuck and get him out of our hair. After all, Alan did smash up the guy's trailer and stuff."

Sebastian had a point—it would be easier—but deep down he knew the guy he'd been talking to downstairs was full of shit. After giving it a bit of thought, he said, "Truth is, I feel as though time's have hit hard for this fuck—this and the fact he just discovered his brother was gay. And because of this he's putting the two together and coming up with us."

"No, Chuck. Me."

"US," said Chendrill, making sure Sebastian 100% understood that he was never going to be alone in this.

"Okay, us."

Then in a tone that left no doubt as to what Sebastian wanted Chendrill to do, he stood up, bent over to drop little Fluffy to the floor and said, "I've got better things to do than worry about this man Chuck, and so have you—I'll have a blank cashier's cheque for you by midday. Give it to him, and if he comes back for more, then go find someone and have the prick put in a hole."

****

Two hours later, the movie making team were all back around the table, and from what Chendrill could tell they had a week or two to get it together and go into production or the job was over—unless they recast, which wasn't going to happen. Not with Adalia Seychan headlining, even if she was, according to Dan, sixty-eight years old.

As usual, Chendrill was wondering why he was there and why Mazzi was sporting two black eyes. The rest was as per the norm, with Patrick blathering on. When Chendrill wasn't staring at his phone and not listening, he was looking out the window and not listening—except when Sebastian, who was acting the most serious he'd ever seen him, had leaned in for a second and whispered in Chendrill's ear, telling him Mazzi had told him he was definitely out (or in) the closet and had gone straight.

There was no doubt the man's attitude had changed, and he still had those plasterer's boots on, but how the hell could that have happened to a man who was such a flamer he almost caught fire Chendrill wondered? Then he heard the name which had been a constant throughout pretty much all of Chendrill's life, Rock Mason.

Rock Mason had been a star in the 70's, 80's, 90's, and well into the new millennium—if you believed the guy's agent that is. Regardless, he was up there in the Hollywood elite and Chendrill had seen pretty much all the man's films. He'd missed all of the first part of the conversation, but from what he could tell, the prick of a director was, for the first time, starting to make sense. They needed Rock, and Rock was available.

"He's a has been," Sebastian said as soon as they were out of earshot.

"Yeah well aren't we all sometimes Sebastian?" Chendrill replied, as he sat down in Sebastian's office which was slowly becoming his own.

Sebastian said straight back, "I didn't know you were a fan Chuck. Well we'll definitely get him now then won't we? And there's another guy who'll be around this afternoon, Roger's his name. I spoke to him last night after a call from Patrick. He's an old friend of Alan and mine—used to live with us in the first apartment we ever rented in town here. He was an office PA back then, but the man's a producer now—and a heavy hitter, takes no shit Chuck."

Chendrill asking straight away without even thinking, "So, what team does this guy play on then?"

Sebastian looked at him for a moment, then sitting down said, "And that matters, does it?"

"No."

"Let's stop it then please Chuck, I've got enough trouble going on with Mazzi at the moment."

Chendrill smiled, loving it. Then he said. "So how did he get the black eyes?"

"He had a fight, with a huge black guy, Chuck. That's what he said."

Chendrill started to laugh, then stopped and said, "You're kidding, right?"

He wasn't. "No Chuck, he said he won as well, knocked the guy out. Mazzi told me all about it. He said that he'd been to the Roxy and picked up three girls."

"Three! Not one? Not two? But three!?"

"You know Mazzi, Chuck, he doesn't do small—he took them back to his place, then this guy shows up, said he knew one of the girls and it got physical. Mazzi knocked him out and they called an ambulance."

"What happened after that then?" Chendrill asked, wondering at the same time about the bit where Mazzi knocked out the huge black guy and if this guy was gay as well, and he heard Sebastian say, "Well what happened after that Chuck, the guy's saying he's straight, he's got three girls he's picked up at a bar with him in his penthouse, you work it out for yourself, I'm sure if you get close enough you'll smell fish."

"Oh?" said Chendrill and wondered why Sebastian, and Mazzi for that matter, had always associated sex with women with fish when in reality it was just a rare hormonal issue some girls had to deal with on occasion. But to them it seemed it was a constant almost as though in their mind making love to a woman was pretty much the same as entering an Alaskan cannery for the first time. He said, "What is it with you and fish Sebastian?"

Sebastian stared at Chendrill for a moment with his eyebrows furrowed, and he said, "Don't get me started on that one, Chuck. Besides you're the expert. I'm sure Mazzi will be banging on your door for advice soon on the subject since he's now come out—or in, as he put it."

"I know, you keep telling me," Chendrill answered, as he began to smile.

"Oh, he's definitely gone straight, Chuck. Although truth be known, I've always thought deep down he liked girls, but you never know, maybe it's from when he hit his head—people change after head injuries. I knew a kid when I was growing up who wouldn't eat sausage and then he fell off the swings as a teenager and afterwards couldn't get enough of them in his mouth. It happens."

****

With a blank cashier's cheque in his pocket for a quarter of a million dollars that he hoped the Italian guy who lived off the back of addicts would never see, Chendrill made it back to Dan's house and sat in the kitchen as Tricia got ready for work. Dan was downstairs in his cave, playing heavy metal as loud as he possibly could.

Through the noise Chendrill asked why.

"He does this sometimes, always has. I used to fight it but in the end I discovered he gets bored of it before me if I don't react and just leave him be," replied Tricia.

Chendrill smiled, it was the same approach the cops used in the cells on a Saturday night when the drunks were getting mouthy. Let them shout and scream and question who's fucking the cop's wives while they're here at work and if they ignored it, it stopped quicker. Some police officers liked the drama, though, so it could get loud.

He said back to Dan's mother through the noise, "This film Dan's in is going to have Rock Mason in it as well."

Tricia turned and stared at him, then said in astonishment, "No?"

Chendrill nodded as he fiddled with the buttons on his Hawaiian.

"Yeah, how about that, who'd have believed it?"

"My son in a Rock Mason movie?"

Chendrill nodded again, "Seems that way. Sebastian says he's going to make sure Dan's name is there right next to Rock Mason and grandma Adalia."

Thanks for that, Tricia thought, having just managed to forget about the woman for the moment. She said, "Do you think we'll get to meet Rock? He's so lovely. You know years ago when Dan was young, he used to put on one of Rock's movies when I was feeling down and I'd always cheer up."

Chendrill smiled; it was hard to think of this lovely woman being down about anything, but she was human after all. And, of course, she had her son to deal with. Through the din, he said, "They're going to start filming next week with a splinter unit, they'll get as many scenes as they can with Adalia and Rock Mason on blue screen. You know, get the close-ups because she's leaving and then they can use a double for the rest once she's gone."

Tricia stared at him for a second, then said, "I thought you told me you went to these meetings but never listened to a word?"

Chendrill shrugged, then said, "Well I'm bound to pick up a bit—you can't help but not, besides Rock Mason's in it now." Then he said, "Tell Dan, see what he says."

Tricia took it in, "It'll be interesting. I know he likes him, you see he watches his films through to the end, which is rare because usually he gets bored." She walked to the top of the stairs and leaning with both hands on either side of the wall as she had many times before called down through the racket to Dan's cave in the basement.

"Dan—Dan—Rock Mason's going to be in this movie you're in." And then she waited and called again. And waited. And again, and again. This time though the music went off.

Taking a deep breath, Tricia waited then she called down for the fifth time, "Dan, they're having Rock Mason in this movie you're in." A second later the music was back on, blasting through the floorboards and out onto the street. Tricia walked back to the table and, sitting herself on Chendrill's lap, smiled. Then she said sarcastically, "He's such a great kid."

****

In between having to dress up, Clive had been doing even more research, tapping out on his keyboard with one hand and what fingers he had left on the other. It turned out Sebastian String was an even more rich and powerful man than he had first discovered. Powerful in the sense that he could change the way people thought and influence their behaviours without even knowing in the slightest it was him pulling the strings. This was a talent which only became more apparent an hour later when, after a game of dress up, he'd looked down to see a used BlueBoy hanging from his dick.

Since then the idea of him being Mayor of Vancouver had been growing—there was prestige to that. But you had to do something great before you could be known for not being able to do something, or many spectacular things for that matter, because the world had been robbed of your presence due to your untimely passing. It couldn't be bike lanes or outdoor movies in the park, it had to be more than the odd jazz festival like the current guy was doing. It had to be that, plus more, something special—and helping people was special.

He called Sebastian String and congratulated him on his BlueBoy campaign and felt embarrassed straight after as he heard Sebastian ask him, "Did buying them make you feel dangerous."

"Yeah, they did; it's why I bought them," he'd said. But they hadn't really, in fact all he ever really felt after having sex and dressing up like Russell Crowe was stupid.

Then he heard Sebastian ask, "Would you like me to send over the limo so as we can sit down and talk about making you famous again?"

From the corner of his eye Clive sat in Sebastian's office and watched as Sebastian's dog rubbed its ass on the carpet. Sebastian was saying, "I've looked at all the dates and we are a little late but sometimes that can be a good thing. We can let the opposition spend all their money then we can blitz them. I think there's only about 10% of the population who do actually vote, so if I make it trendy to vote for you then that will be that."

Clive looked away from the dog and back to Sebastian, who was looking at him and smiling. Sebastian continued, saying, "He does that. I think he's got worms."

Clive smiled, the man was nice and honest and it almost felt a shame to lead the guy up the garden path like he would be. He said, "If I get in, I don't want to be doing just the norm—I want to do something special, you know like helping people."

Sebastian smiled and said straight back, "Oh, there's so much we are going to do Clive."

"We?" asked Clive, suddenly worried about how much of a puppet this guy was going to make of him and, if so, despite how generous he was being, would he get to the level of fame needed to be really and truly missed?

"Oh yes we, Clive. When I say 'we' I'm talking about myself, but I can't do it—being gay and all, even in this day and age, else I should think I'd be there now. It would give me something to do on the weekends."

Then standing suddenly, Sebastian clapped his hands together and with a beaming smile carried on, saying, "We are going to build parks, improve roads and beaches, make it so people can park again for free after 6 p.m. and have a real steam train that takes people around the city—maybe even resurrect the Royal Hudson? Reduce the fees for the cruise ships so as I can walk to the top of the Lionsgate Bridge in the evening and wave them goodbye. Plus, we'll make sure there's free medical for the elderly and sick. Oh, and sort out the East Side—you know, where there's all these drug people."

Clive stared at him, everything he'd said so far made sense and if he thought it out for a while it was all doable. But the East Side. Over there, you were going up against gangs and corruption. He said, "The East Side?"

"Yes," Sebastian said smiling, "What we'll do is designate an area over near the docks, maybe reclaim some land so people don't moan, and we'll make an island that's about a half mile square and open it up as a bar, drug, and prostitute zone. Just like they have in Amsterdam. All the people who want their vices can still do their thing, but they'll have to do it there instead. Or, they go to prison if they do it out in the open. Then we can watch out for the girls on the street and give them health care and rehabilitation. And we can weed out the ones who are too young Clive. Oh, and the street guys that keep arriving from Montreal, we can send them back on a bus if they want to go with a $5000 contract saying they can't come back unless they have a job and a place to live, then we can separate them from the people who have real mental health problems, and give them the help they need. We can also reopen some of the hospitals they shut down and Patrick and his friends sold as condos. On top of all this, I think that if you're retired and need help for whatever reason, you should be able to get it Clive—healthcare transportation, housing, food, clothes. Anything, regardless of how much you have in the bank."

Clive stared at him wondering when the man was going to stop. In the end, he just said, "Oh my God Sebastian, this is exactly what I need to do!"

"Oh, I haven't really given it too much thought yet—it's just a couple of ideas, but it's something we need to start looking at once I put together a campaign so as I can get you in the position where you can start making a difference. So, it's up to you, Clive—we are going to do great things. You up front and me quietly working anonymously in the background with Chuck. I want to make you great Clive, not just here in this town but as far as we can stretch it—it's what I'm good at."

Perfect, Clive thought, it couldn't be any better.

****

Chendrill sat at the kitchen table at Dan's home which was now quiet and looked at the blank $250,000 banker's draft Sebastian had given him with no name attached. If he lost it, anyone could put their name on it. Sebastian knew the name of the man who he was giving it to, but he had left it blank. *Maybe it was a test*, he thought. But why would he do that? Maybe he was leaving it up to Chendrill's discretion and had given the money to release the burden of debt however ridiculous it all seemed. Either way it seemed odd.

He looked at the clock, it was almost 7 p.m. and chances were the prick would be at the peeler bar getting his rocks off—although the girl he'd been speaking to hadn't called like she said she would. But that didn't mean much.

Twenty minutes later he was parking the Aston in Gastown and heading back east towards the bar. He opened the door and paid the cover, walked in and the first person he saw sitting on G-row was Dan. Moving in next to him he said, "What are you doing here?"

Dan looked at him and then to his shirt then said, "What are you doing here? I'm surprised they let you in with that shirt."

"Well they did." He asked again, "What are you doing here?"

"Same as you I should think, looking at chicks."

"You're not old enough."

"Your too old," said Dan straight back, as he looked up to see a bare ass pass by right above him.

"You're supposed to be 21 to get in here."

"I got ID."

"You're too young for an ID card."

"I didn't say it was mine, besides they recognized me and let me straight in, no cover either. Not like you."

Chendrill thought about it, the kid had to have guessed, he'd seen Dan as soon as the door opened and the kid hadn't looked around at the door once.

"How do you know I paid cover?" he asked.

"I see you in the mirror."

Chendrill said straight back, "How about I see you leave in the mirror."

"How about I don't tell Mum you was here and you leave."

"I'm working."

"So am I."

"Doing what?"

"Learning dance moves."

Chendrill laughed, the kid was funny even if he was a pain in the ass. He said, "Nice music this afternoon."

"You like that do you, make you feel young again, I can see you as a head banger."

"You still here?"

Then the girl who'd taken him for $300 from before came over, this time dressed as a schoolgirl in a short skirt with her tits hanging out, smothering herself all over

Chendrill with her hands and arms. Some people liked that kind of thing, to them it was fantasy island, to Chendrill it wasn't though. She said, "Hey Chuck. Your friend's just gone upstairs, you got that $300 you promised?"

And all Dan heard through the bumping and grinding of the mixtape the DJ was playing for the young girl onstage as she bent over, picking up fives and change off the floor so as she could try to pay her way through veterinary school was, "Chuck—upstairs—you got that $300 you promised?" Which to even Dan translated directly to 'you're a fucking pervert', which, of course, Dan could care less about, but nonetheless he told him anyway.

Unfazed, Chendrill replied, "Make sure you're not still here when I come back down."

Mattia the Italian sat up top in a dark room on a sofa so dirty and stained that even a blind guy wouldn't sit on it if the lights were on. As per usual, he had three girls on him, one on either side and the other on his lap in the centre, all with their tits in his face as they rubbed their hard, lithe bodies into his. The Italian lost in the moment as he always was. The girls who should have known better, somewhat lost themselves in their lives, looking at the clock. He had six hands on him, two with their palms flat pushing and rubbing the sweat on his chest, another two stretching down to his groin and the other pair combing through his hair. The Italian wondering how long he had left and the girls wondering who the guy in the red Hawaiian was sitting alone on the chair in the corner was. Then as the music stopped, and so did they, leaving the Italian sitting there with his mouth open and feeling embarrassed as the girls left the room. Then he saw Chendrill sitting in the corner.

"Once you've settled down we can talk business."

The Italian stared at him taking the time to smooth out his hair and compose himself. All agitated he asked, "Couldn't it have waited?"

"If I liked you I suppose it could."

"Get the fuck out of here you perverted cunt," the loan shark who lent out money in blocks said to him in a curt voice.

Not giving a shit, Chendrill said straight back, "You come to see my friend when it pleases you, I'm doing the same—besides, I'm not the one here with the tits of three girls half my age in my face."

"Fuck you."

Chendrill shrugged, still not caring what this man who lived off of the backs of the weak and dying had to say. He said, "You want this money you've been harping on about or do you want me to leave?"

"If you have it all, yeah."

"How much is all?"

"You know."

"No, I don't, see I think it's a figure you picked from the tree because you found out your brother was sword swallowing my friend's boyfriend when he crashed your car and you always thought he was straight and preferred to play the same games you play up here."

The Italian loan shark stood checking his fly, his hard on long gone and forgotten, and as soon as he felt comfortable with himself again he said, "Maybe I'll stick a sword in you?"

Chendrill laughed to himself, smiling, not bothering to get up off the chair and said, "Given how horny you were only seconds ago, maybe with a comment like that, there may be a little bit of your brother in you after all."

And on those words, the Italian felt the blood rush away from his stomach and up into his chest as his temper took over and, pulling his hands from the top of his trousers, he went for Chendrill across the other side of the room, pulling a blade from out of nowhere.

Quick as a flash, Chendrill was off the stool and moving to one side, slapping his left hand down on the Italian's knife hand spinning around it as it came at him. The blade hit the floor at exactly the same time as the side of Chendrill's other hand caught the Italian right in the throat, rendering the man with the sweaty chest unable to breath.

Quickly Chendrill picked up the man's knife and hoping it would stick into the drywall wall, threw it hard across the room and seeing the wrong end hit and the knife smash and spinout across the floor said to the man gasping for breath, "I thought you carried a gun?"

And as soon as he said the words, he saw it coming up in the Italian's hand from a holster on his lower leg. Again, Chendrill was quickly on him, grabbing the back of the man's shirt and pulling him off balance enough to distract him as he brought his foot up, kicking the gun away and then again bringing it up into the man's stomach, sending him rolling across the floor.

Chendrill moved away, picking up the gun, he said, "From what I remember, you said it was $250,000. And if I'm wrong I don't care."

Pulling out his wallet, he pulled out Sebastian's cashier's cheque. Then holding the loan shark's nose he pulled the man's head back until his mouth opened and he stuffed the whole thing in.

"Don't swallow because there's a cashier's cheque for a

quarter of a million in your mouth. Don't spend it all at once, especially in here."

Then he stepped back and, standing above the loan shark who had a thing for dirty young girls, said, "If you come near me or my friend again, I'll use every means I know to put you away for 10 to 15 years."

And with that Chendrill was gone, down the stairs, passing drunken men, red with excitement, hand in hand with scantly clad girls who, on a given evening made almost the same hourly as the odd lawyer they were grinding their pussies against. He reached the bar and passed it, moving through the crowd towards the brightly lit stage in the centre of the room—now occupied by another beauty who wasn't going to be a vet, and who was dressed as a cowgirl but soon wouldn't be wearing much of anything. He found Dan, still on Gynecological Row with another beer, banging his hands on the stage along with the rest of the guys who should be at home with their families. Dan shouting out just as Chendrill reached him, "Show us the peach baby."

Grabbing him by the scruff of the neck, Chendrill pulled him from his stool past the bouncers and through the entrance out of the bar with Dan shouting as he went, "I need to go back to pay for the beers."

Not letting go, Chendrill said to him as they walked, "Leaving without paying is a good thing, now you won't be allowed back."

They reached the Aston and in one swift move the rear door was open and Dan was thrown into the back. "Don't think about trying to escape I have the child locks on," Chendrill said as he opened the driver's seat and started the engine.

He pulled away into the flow of traffic and into Gastown, passing the streetlights of an era long forgotten, passing the crowds, passing the homeless looking for a handout, passing the drug dealers hiding in the alleys, passing the park where the people did smack on one side and the girls sold themselves for it on the other. Dan spitting out as they passed, “You should have come here, they’re cheaper. How much you spend up there for 5 minutes?”

Still pissed and not listening, Chendrill just looked in the rear-view mirror until he heard Dan carry on saying, “Maybe Mum would be interested, you know with you spending up there what she earns in a shift—what was it, $200?”

“Actually it was $250,” Chendrill replied without missing a beat.

They reached Tricia’s house and, without speaking, Chendrill opened the rear door of the Aston for the supermodel who still lived in his mother’s basement, then watched as he walked up the short steps and opened the door, went inside, and slammed the door behind him.

Dan walked straight to the kitchen and opened the fridge. Grabbing a knife from the sink, he cut away half of the new slab of butter his mother had just bought from the supermarket and pulled out a carton of milk. Opening the cupboard, he pulled a two-pound bag of sugar out and opened it, spilling the sugar all over the counter. Dropping the butter into the bag of sugar, he shook it up, spilling more onto the kitchen counter, then reopening the bag he pulled the butter out and, holding the slab to his mouth, began to scrape and lick the sugar from the butter until there was no butter left. Picking up the milk carton, he took a swig straight from the opening at the top, dropping more mess down his front and onto the counter and floor. He then repeated the process again until there was just enough butter left to use to dab out the mess he'd made on the counter.

Dan wiped hands on the curtains and headed down the stairs to his room and locked the door. It was time to knock one out, there was little doubt about that—those girls at the club getting him all revved up like they had, with their sexy asses and legs, showing him that bit of extra snatch and attention because he was the 'BlueBoy' guy. But then Chendrill had turned up looking like a peacock and ruined it all—the fucking asshole. Had the prick not, he'd probably have managed to get one of them back here to his basement so he could fuck them—just the way Adalia had been teaching him. Except a stripper would be naturally young and tight, a new experience, not like what he'd been getting it on with lately. Then afterward he could have driven the Ferrari over to the Sutton and fucked Adalia from behind as well, which is the way he liked it best because he could watch TV. Then maybe he'd tell her what he'd done—fucking a stripper and making her come. Maybe she'd like that. Maybe?

But that fuckhead Chendrill had fucked all that up and the Ferrari with the governor which no longer worked because he'd over ridden its circuitry was still at the strip bar's carpark. But that was not his problem, that was the big ape's problem—after all, he was the big boss for shit like that around here.

He turned on the computer and typed in the name of the girls he'd seen that afternoon. Seconds later they were up on the screen looking all sexy and seductive, staring back at him from the computer screen. Reaching down, he pulled down his trousers and whipped out his already hard dick and looked at it. *Perfect*, he thought, *Rock Solid*. This was it. He was there, he thought, there was no hard-assed stripper coming over for him to fuck but that didn't mean his mother's late shift was going to be wasted. In actual fact, he may be better off, he thought. He could please himself all evening and then when he was done, he could look at wiring circuitry or whatever else he fancied without having to listen to a load of blah about how the girl felt or some shit like that, the same way he did with Adalia.

He reached down to the bottom of the computer desk Sebastian had bought him and pulled out the small bottle of expensive olive oil his mother had thought she'd forgotten to buy and began to unscrew the top, but with the butter and sugar he was unable to remove with the curtain still stuck on his hands it was proving difficult. *Hang on*, Dan thought, as he set the bottle of olive oil down on the desk and looked at the streaks his slimy hands had left on the dark brown bottle. Butter, sugar, olive oil? He could use all three, why not? Maybe he was in for a new experience after all, especially with that full packet of sugar and half a slab of butter still left in the fridge. He was hungry after all. Now he could wank and eat, it couldn't be better, the evening wasn't wasted. He was back on track.

****

The Italian couldn't remember being this upset even when he'd been married to his bitch of a wife. This guy Chendrill had come into his private space and humiliated him. The fucking prick.

Now people were disrespecting him, laughing at him

when he'd gone and found them asking for the money they owed. Word was out—he was a pussy. Chances are though it wouldn't have been the big guy, who had been faster than he'd expected; he was too cool to go shooting his mouth off. It had to have been one of those whores in training calling themselves lap dancers—although he hadn't seen one dance yet. Them or maybe one of the meathead bouncers who had been too lazy to get a real job. The guys knew who he was and liked it that he'd taken a slap. They were outside the door, at least one of them was anyway—had to be to protect the girls from maniacs.

"Fuck you," he shouted out at no one in particular as he walked down the alley for a chat about money with one of his regulars. He kicked him once, then again, and then again. The prick moments before telling him he couldn't get any money this week and refused to take another block to cover what he owed because he was back with his family and clean now and wanted to stay that way for his children. The man promising the Italian he'd get the money but that it would take time as he wasn't going to break into cars anymore and received a head-butt in the face for his troubles.

Now the Italian was kicking him while he was down and holding his nose, kicking him, and thinking about Chendrill. He was pissed. He was supposed to be the tough guy loan shark around town and, despite that, this prick in the loud shirt had still insulted him. First, he had come into the private room where he knew he was with his girls. Second, he had told him straight to his face that he sucked cock the same as his stupid fucking brother had, and he may have well have done just that for the way he'd tried to kill the prick for telling him so, not once but twice, and the fucker had still made a fool of him in the process.

How long would it take for his new girl to hear about it from her coworkers, he thought. How was he supposed to make her his after this?

It wasn't good.

And now there was this fucker on the ground who didn't want to pay because he wanted to support his family, word was definitely out on the street that he, Mattia, was a pussy—but pussies don't kick guys who owe money and leave them for dead. Pussies talk about it without actually making good on a promise. *But not me*, he thought, as he continued relentlessly kicking the man's body for wanting to make it clean. Not now, no way. This fucker below him now, who used to be a good payer, a guy who'd do whatever necessary to get a fix, who would now either die or survive, and who would then have to pay later or go through another beating. Either way it didn't matter, all he wanted now was for word to get back around town that he was still the man—even if Chendrill had stuffed a $250,000 cheque into his mouth like it was his dick. That cunt doing that when truth was he should have been begging him for his life instead—just as the man below him who wanted to start afresh was.

And that's exactly what the big fuck would be doing soon, the Italian thought, as he saw the man below him beginning to lose consciousness, curled up in a heap at the side of a dumpster. The big fucker who'd been quicker than him was going to die. That's right, he'd kill the fucker, then when he was lying down in a gutter he'd lean over him and look down and see him with his eyes all watery—just like those of the guy below him now as he kicked him. Then doubling his power, like the crescendo to the fireworks he'd watched with his kids on the beach only days ago, the Italian kicked again and again. Saying to the man who he wished was Chendrill as he did, "Tell me what it was you were saying back there in that room. Yeah, the bit about being a cock sucker. Tell me again, you fucking piece of shit—tell me again. Tell me again. Tell me again. Tell me again. Tell me again."

****

With the light fading quickly, Chendrill drove the Aston deep into Burnaby and wondered where Dennis was. He'd passed twice since he'd last seen him at the house when he'd been there watching a man with a diamond in his front tooth who thought he could sing. *He could call*, he thought, but on the end of the phone he wouldn't be able to look into the man's eyes and that's what he needed to do. There was a problem and it wouldn't go away. The problem being that Patrick had been asking to find Alla, which was almost impossible to do. He wanted her in the movie because she was the most beautiful woman he'd ever seen—though from what Chendrill could gather it wasn't exactly as though the man had seen a lot of her face when he'd been in her company. But now Sebastian had gotten involved, saying almost out of pure curiosity, "Well let's see what she says, Chuck."

He got out of the Aston and looked around, then walked along the road to where Archall Diamond had been parked with his truck and stopped. He carried on to the now empty basement. From what he could see there was oil on the driveway that hadn't been washed away by the rain and there were no cobwebs on the door. Dennis was still living there, but just wasn't there at the moment. As for his wife

Alla, the most beautiful woman in the world according to Patrick—and no doubt Dennis—with the doors all being shut and her in a wheelchair, then the odds were that she'd left and not come back.

He headed south and reached Archall Diamond's place and on opening the door could see the slight tracks of a man and the tracks of a wheelchair in the dust of the cocoa pops that were all over the floor. If they were there to stop anyone sneaking up on him because of the crunching then it hadn't worked, he thought, as he walked around the house and then up the stairs into the bedroom. Last time he'd been there, the bed had been covered in cash and pills, but now the bed was clear and the tires tracks at the bottom of the stairs led to the ramp at the front door. Alla, it seemed, had left and not come back.

****

Well I looked for Alla and she's vanished, Chendrill thought as he looked at the clock on the dash of the Aston which read 11:00 pm and knew he could do a lot more. Then making a mental commitment to search out Dennis sometime soon, he forgot all about it and began to wonder if he should call Dan's mother. He could have picked her up from work, but he'd learned over the years of finding and losing women that sometimes less was more.

He reached the end of Dan's mother's road and looked down the street. Dan's Ferrari wasn't there but his light in his basement cave was on. Parking the Aston in its usual spot, he got out and walked up the short steps to the front door. Inside through the door he could hear Tricia was crying. With a soft knock on the door's small window he pulled out the only set of keys to her home she'd ever given to a man and opened the door.

As soon as he was inside, Tricia was on him running down the corridor and when she reached him, Chendrill could see her tears were a mix of pure anger and worry. She said before he could get a word in, “Chuck, call Sebastian and tell him he needs to get him out of here.”

Placing his arm around her slender back, Chendrill walked her to the kitchen and as soon as he entered he could see the mess. He said, “What’s the problem?”

Pulling away from him and screaming as she pointed to the counter, the floor and the curtains, Tricia said, “That’s the problem, look what I’ve come home too!”

Chendrill looked around the kitchen—it was a mess. The butter was everywhere, sugar, flour, some sauce, but he’d seen worse. He said, “Has someone been baking a cake?”

Almost as quickly as Chendrill could finish his words, Tricia replied, “No one’s been baking a cake okay! You don’t bake a cake and not use a bowl, and you don’t bake a cake in the fucking bathroom or the hallway and you don’t use the fucking curtains either.”

Without a word, Chendrill walked away from the kitchen and into the bathroom. The light was still on and as soon as he entered he could see butter and sugar all over the sink and mirror, and what looked like blood. He walked back out and into the kitchen and asked, “Is that blood in there?”

“It’s not food colouring Chuck, okay? Of course it’s blood.” Then she carried on, “It’s everywhere, blood, flour, butter, and sugar.” She walked to the top of the stairs and screamed down towards the door where her son lived, “Dan, what the hell is going on, there’s blood and crap everywhere."

Then they both heard Dan's voice calling back through the door, "Listen leave me alone, I've got a problem."

And he did—it was his mother. Calling straight back down the stairs, she said, "What the hell have you been doing all evening? Where the hell is the blood coming from?"

Dan said again, "Leave me alone. I've got a problem."

Then it hit her. It was obvious what had been going on, he had a girl back here and they'd been in the kitchen making food and they'd started screwing and there was a possibility whoever it was had her period. She said, "Have you got a girl down there?"

"No," came Dan's voice from the basement.

"Why's there blood everywhere then and where's my kitchen roll gone?"

Then they both heard Dan call up through his door, "It's Chendrill's fault."

Tricia looked to her boyfriend, whose job it was to look after her son, waiting for an explanation. Chendrill stared back, shrugging his shoulders without a clue. Then Chendrill said, "Maybe he was making some food and he cut himself?"

Tricia said back, "Some detective you are, where's the knife? You think if he'd hurt himself while cooking he wouldn't be up here? Besides, he doesn't cook, the closest he's ever gotten to cooking is putting bread in the toaster. And—what does he mean it's your fault. What's been going on while I'm at work?"

****

Sebastian sat at his desk at home with the side light on

and worked his way through the paperwork he needed to get done before he went back into the office in the morning to sit at a meeting that had been originally set up for nine but which, now his old friend Roger had come on board, had been pulled back to eight.

He liked to be busy, and busy he was now that he had a movie starting in a couple of weeks' time, but it was hard to concentrate with little Fluffy rubbing his ass on the carpet like he was. He looked at his dog as he came over settling back at his feet. Rock Mason would be in town soon and it was funny how things had changed around the office since the director, who didn't like Chuck, had gone out of his way to get him on board. Even Adalia had quieted down with her demands—at least a bit. He picked up his half empty cup and took a swig, the tea was cold now and it surprised him as it hit his lips. *Had it been that long?* he thought, and turning he looked at the clock—it was almost one in the morning, a whole two hours late for little Fluffy to have his nighttime walk. He said, "Fluffy, what am I doing, you poor thing, I should have had you outside hours ago. No wonder your bottom is itching."

He put the dog on his leash and tucked his arms into a light Merino cardigan to protect him from the night air and stepped into the elevator. The park out front next to the beach was quiet now in the early morning. They crossed the road and walked along the sloping path which led to the beach and stopped at a group of rocks separating the path from the sand. He shouldn't be there with the dog, he knew that only too well, and it was another slight adjustment to make once he became king of the city—well, kind of. He could feel the wind picking up now as he sat down on a rock and looked out over the waves lit dimly by the street lamps. Taking a deep breath he felt the fresh air fill his lungs as he listened to the gusting wind as it hit the trees behind in the park, rustling their leaves as it passed through like a ghost moving in the night—the leaves blowing, the surf breaking and spreading itself thin across the sand of the beach, the clicking of the young boys' bicycles as they circled up on the road and dropped down to pass Sebastian as he sat there quietly alone.

He watched them go almost out of sight in the distance, both of them talking as they rode together. Then, almost in sync, they broke formation, turning in an arc and headed back towards Sebastian with their faces no longer visible from their t-shirts pulled up above their noses. Reaching Sebastian, the larger of the two moved in close, punching Sebastian hard in the face as the smaller of the two grabbed his dog.

"You want some more of what you just got or shall we just shit kick the dog?" said the larger of the two kids.

Sebastian held his jaw and moved himself away from the beach and out onto the pathway that led away from the seawall and up under the trees. Holding his mouth and tasting blood for the first time in years, he said surprisingly, "I don't care about the dog, he's not mine and all he does is shit anyway."

The young boys were laughing now, at the old man with the strange voice trying to be funny. The older one said, "So, you don't care if we throw him in the sea?"

"There's no need for that," Sebastian said, as he looked up at the empty road.

The bigger kid who'd hit him smiled under his t-shirt saying, "There's no cops up there at this time of night—if you wanted them you should have been down here a few hours ago before they went looking for a Starbucks." Then looking to the dog, he said, "You want me to throw the mutt in the sea or not?"

Sebastian shook his head, he didn't. As he looked at Fluffy pulling at the lead to get back to him and away from the younger of the two boys, he said, "What do you want?"

"What you got?" answered the bigger of the two.

Sebastian felt for his phone, which wasn't there, and neither was his wallet. Remembering leaving them up in his penthouse, he said, "I have nothing."

The kids laughed together, then the youngest of the two spoke for the first time saying, "Well, looks like the dog's going for a swim."

"Take my sweater it's worth a grand, same with my shoes," said Sebastian.

"What do we look like a fucking thrift store?" said the older of the boys, laughing again.

Then taking a deep breath, Sebastian said firmly, "Well you can fight me or you can fuck off."

The two kids stared at him, this old gay guy getting tough. The older of the two dropped his trick bike to the ground and moved towards Sebastian as Sebastian took a step towards him and caught the kid straight in the eye with a left hook.

Stunned the older kid stepped back as the other began to laugh. Then without another word the bigger kid ran quickly towards the other, grabbing Fluffy's leash and pulled him out across the rocks and into the openness of the beach, calling out as he went, "Let's see if the dog can fly." As Sebastian scrambled across the rocks, the older kid began to spin, taking the dog with him, making Fluffy run at first until the poor dog with the itchy ass couldn't run any longer and his paws left the sand as the young man spun him around and around like an Olympic hammer thrower and moved towards the water, shouting out, "Woooo wooo fly doggy fly." Then just as the kid made it to the water, Sebastian came running desperately down the beach and slammed his body into the kid just as the kid let go, and sending Fluffy like a small white missile up into the air over the surf and beyond into the dark black water as they both fell into the sand.

Deafened by the sound of the surf and ignoring the kid laughing in his ear, Sebastian picked himself up off the ground and ran without a thought for himself out into the cold pounding surf. Pushing his body through the waves as they hit his groin, punching through the first set then the second as they hit his chest and then the third as they took his feet from the seabed and encased his head in the chilling sea.

Struggling in the darkness Sebastian pulled himself to the surface on the other side of the rushing waves. Out there in the darkness was his dog, swimming or floating on the water and trying to survive—just as he was now. He looked left, then right, then spun around as the swell lifted him up and dipped him back down again as the waves rolled in from the bay.

Then he saw him, his white body laying on the water as it crested on a peak, lit from the city lights miles away in the distance. Sebastian kicked once and then twice, pulling his arms above his head as he swam along in the swell watching his dog appear and reappear in the darkness of the water.

Suddenly, out of breath and gasping for air, he had reached him and was there next to the dog he and Alan had picked out of so many long ago when Fluffy had been a puppy and all had been well in Sebastian's world. Sebastian straightened his body, steadying himself in the water as the little dog yipped and clawed at his master's head, desperate for survival, his frightened eyes straining, bulging out of their sockets, as his soaked fur clung to his tiny skull.

****

Chendrill entered the office at about half an hour past nine and got a 'who are you and why are you late' look from Roger, the new producer who used to live with Sebastian. Then just as he was sitting down and looking under the table to see if Mazzi, who had not shaved, was still wearing the plasterer's boots, he heard the guy say, "If you're looking for Sebastian he's not under there, he's gone home."

No shit, thanks for the update you cocky fuck, Chendrill thought, as he then stood and turned, opened the door again and left. He was almost out the door when Sebastian's friend from old caught up with him and holding out his hand to Chendrill said, "I'm sorry I just clued in, are you Chuck?"

Chendrill smiled and, taking the man's hand said, "Yes, I take it you are Sebastian's friend."

"Roger Salmep, pleased to meet you, Sebastian tells me you are a wonderful man and a great detective."

Chendrill smiled as the thought of what kind of over the top elaborate description Sebastian would have given of him. He said, "Well you know how he can be, don't believe a word, but if you lose your cat or dog, I'm your man because that's about as exciting as it gets around here."

And with those words he saw Roger's face change, the

man looking to the floor for a moment before looking up again and asking, "Has Sebastian not called? He said he would. I'm not sure if you've heard but he's pretty upset, his dog died."

Chendrill stood there for a moment, not knowing what to say. It was just a dog, yes, but it was what the dog meant to his friend that was the problem. Taking a deep breath, he asked, "What happened?"

Roger stood there, scratching his head, then he said, "I'm not sure, he was here first thing even before me and he was quiet. He has this black bruising around his eye and scratches on his forehead and neck. I asked what had happened and all he'd say was 'it's okay,' then he told me the dog was gone. He was here for a bit but then he left."

It was just starting to rain as Chendrill drove the Aston quickly along Pacific towards English Bay and nipped through the red on both lights as he went. What the fuck had happened? The man called him every other day with an emergency that was nothing of the sort and then when he loses his dog and is injured, he doesn't say a word. When he arrived, it was the first question he asked, as he sat at the dining table with Sebastian, discreetly looking to the man's bruised eye as Sebastian watched as the rain hit the windows. Sebastian waiting for what felt like the longest time until he eventually told him everything from start to finish. The kids cruising by and then coming back to hit him and then him hitting the older one back harder. Sebastian sitting there bolt upright and serious with bloodshot eyes from crying. Chendrill saying with a smile, "And you punched the guy out?"

"Oh, just because I'm gay Chuck doesn't mean I can't throw a punch. I used to box at school you know. There's a lot of tough gay men in this world you know. It's not just you."

Chendrill knew that. It wasn't that long ago he'd taken a Russian one on himself and the man could have very easily killed him. He said, "And because of this he threw your dog into the ocean?"

Sebastian stared at the table, without looking up he said, "Yes, if not for that storm from a few days ago way out in the Pacific making its way here I think he would have been okay."

"And you went out in it in the dead of night to save your dog—you're lucky you're still here," said Chendrill.

"Am I?" Sebastian said as he looked up at him.

"It's not your fault or the storm's that the dog died; it's the kids' fault for attacking you and throwing him in the drink."

"Because I hit him."

Chendrill thought about it for a bit. The guy in his sixties, punching some punk kid then swimming out in a swell, finding the dog and bringing him back in as he swam on his back with one arm cradling the dog, riding the surf as the waves came in one after another until he hit the shore. Only when they reached the beach had he found the dog had stopped breathing. *Did the dog drown or had the kid injured it internally?* Chendrill wondered.

Sebastian saying straight after as though he could read Chendrill's mind, "I think he had a heart attack, Chuck."

Chendrill looked at him and closed his eyes for a second before saying, "Maybe."

"I think so because he started whimpering and yelping when he was on my chest and then he went still."

Chendrill looked up and wondered what he was going

to do to the kids when he found them. Kids or not they were going to learn a lesson. He said, "I'm sorry Sebastian, I wish I could have been there."

"Same Chuck, but don't get a guilt trip going because it's my fault I pushed myself so hard working late like I did. If I hadn't, I'd be just getting out of that meeting about now or in my office listening to Roger telling me what a wanker Patrick is."

Chendrill laughed, the man still coming out with one liners just a few hours after walking to his favourite spot in the park. The man doing so while he was still soaking wet and digging up the dirt next to his favourite tree with his bare hands and burying the one thing he loved more than anything in this world. Sebastian said, "How's Dan?"

Chendrill laughed for a moment then said, "He's hurt his dick."

An hour later, Daltrey was sitting in Sebastian's living room looking cool with a hat on to cover her hair along with Williams, who was in uniform and trying to be all professional. Williams asked, "Mr. String, did you manage to get a look at their faces?"

He hadn't, and with the slightest of shakes of his head he told him so. Daltrey spoke for him, "One's about 14 the other about 18, both have brown hair and are thin in the face, the older one is almost 6' and the younger is about 5'6."

"Brothers?" Williams asked.

"Maybe, high chance," Daltrey replied. "They both wore skate shoes, but so does half the town at their age."

"How do you know them?" Williams asked at once, feeling even more inferior than he had already been, being in the company of two accomplished detectives.

"Just do," Daltrey said, "they roll people late at night, drunks and such. If you want to catch them just go for a walk somewhere quiet after 2 a.m. and they'll probably find you," and this was exactly what Chendrill had already decided to do.

That same night Chendrill went out, wandering around in the darkness, sitting on benches. Then getting back in the Aston when no one was around and moving to another spot around town where it would be easy to fall victim to a couple of thugs who knew no better than to mug old men and throw their dogs into the sea to drown. Chendrill, out there, sleeping by day and wandering the parks by night, staying away from the normal channels so that no one other than his tight circle would know what he was up to.

Watching, waiting as lovers and drunks came and went and the homeless moved noisily to and from their shelters hidden in bushes and behind walls. Daltrey joining him sometimes in the dead of night, seemingly intuitive as to where he would be and telling him how nice it was to be looking after Sebastian. The young woman liking Sebastian so much after their first meeting and volunteering to cover for Chendrill by day at Slave. This beautiful girl who was still shaken, watching the offices swell in preparation for the film Patrick was producing even though he didn't know what it was about. The man avoiding Daltrey at all cost and finding ways to leave the office for a writers' conference once a day so he could talk his way into getting his ass worked.

This time though she'd found Chendrill sitting alone on a log at Sunset beach a mile to the east of Sebastian's home, and as she sat there next to him closer than maybe she should have been, she felt the night air on her face and heard Chendrill ask, "Sebastian's friend Roger still riding everyone is he?"

Daltrey nodded and smiled. The man was like a demon and ripping into anyone who fucked up or showed in the slightest that they did not care. She answered, "He is yeah, they start shooting a splinter unit in a couple of days. Sebastian's in the thick of it, quiet, but smiling."

Chendrill listened and apart from news with regard to Sebastian he could care less.

"Mazzi Hegan, still got those boots on?"

"They mention his name a lot, but all I hear is that he's at the studio. Wherever that is."

Then pausing she said with a big smile, "Rock Mason's coming in tomorrow."

Chendrill turning to Daltrey said, "Dan's mum wants to meet him—if they ask you to pick him up, don't."

Daltrey said straight back, "Don't worry, they tried that, I told them straight—I'm not a taxi. Anyway, I doubt Sebastian would ask. He told me what happened last time."

Chendrill smiled as he wished he'd done the same straight off the bat, and then laughed as he remembered the 'Big Director' getting all red in the face after being told to fuck off—and how Sebastian had stuck up for him. He said, "Yeah Sebastian's a good man."

Then she said, "There's this other man who keeps turning up also, he looks familiar and he's missing his fingers on his left hand."

Without looking up, Chendrill said, "He used to play guitar but Sebastian's going to make him mayor."

Daltrey smiled, and said, "That's it. I liked that guy, he did 'Boom Boom Love'."

He looked at her sitting there at 3 a.m. on the old log

from a different era which had drifted in off the water many decades ago and wondered what Daltrey had been like as a teenager rocking out to Clive in his tight jeans and long hair. Then he wondered what would happen if those kids came along now to roll a couple of late-night lovers and how she would handle it. He asked, "How are you doing, feeling better?"

She was, at least a bit, having been to see a private therapist she knew who loved his wife and was outside the police system. The guy helping her see things for what they were and letting her know it was natural to run and be scared. She'd also been out with the big biker girl and discovered it was natural to run from her also, at least for the moment anyhow. She said, "I'm cool, Chuck—you'll know when I'm not. Soon I'll be putting all my efforts into finding the name of this girl who saved me. Once you find these kids, that is."

Leaning down and picking a stone from the sand, Chendrill said, "If you want I'll help you with finding out who she was and anything else you need to know."

Daltrey took a deep breath, it would be good to have the big guy with her when she felt the time was right to go to the morgue and onto the streets after to find who the girl who'd saved her really was, but reality was that it was something she needed to do on her own. She said, "Thanks, but I'll be fine. I'd hate to take you out of your vigilante phase in life."

Chendrill smiled. Daltrey wasn't wrong, it's exactly what he was doing. He said, "Well, maybe if I'm lucky they'll find me tonight and mug me."

Daltrey looked at him and said, "You're too big, they wouldn't chance it. It's a predatory thing remember."

She wasn't wrong and deep down Chendrill had known this all along, but there was always that slight chance and one could hope.

He said, "Has Sebastian bought you a car yet? He likes to do that."

Daltrey smiled and leaned back on the bench. Saying, "No, but he hinted at it, we went for a spin in my Audi after work the other day and he asked if I'd seen the new ones. I doubt he will though, not with the two Ferraris he bought Dan and Mazzi Hegan sitting in the pound."

Chendrill looked at her and smiled, then he said, "I wondered why you'd come to see me at this hour."

"Yeah there's something I think you should see."

They cruised along McGill Street in the Audi. The gate was down in the entrance to the compound where the tow trucks dropped off their hauls before heading off to do their duty for the common man. The two Ferraris were now together at the front of the lot for everyone to see, lit with work lights from either side as though they were in a showroom. The guy who'd brought them both in was in the office now, using his neck for a pillow and looking at his phone, waiting around the clock to collect the $110 fee per car for releasing them from his clutches and for the opportunity to say 'fuck you' to Chendrill when he did.

As they watched from the other side of the street, Chendrill said, "Fuck me, what a loser." Daltrey smiled, Sebastian had told her all about the letters and calls he'd been getting ever since Chendrill had first skipped the barrier and not paid the release fee each time the Ferrari got towed. Now the pricks had two.

Chendrill laughed to himself, the guy was going all out this time—even working the night shift, it seemed, so he could keep an eye on the cars that were, for the moment, now his.

Big Carl the tow truck driver flipped the phone app and swiped 'like' for every new single girl on there with white skin, who he hoped would respond to his initial approach and his new profile showing the wannabe Angel standing next to both Ferrari's with their doors open. None would, unless they were insane—which is exactly what his wife was when he'd married her, but she was at home now doing exactly the same swiping right as he was but getting a better response because of the cleavage she was showing.

He looked at his two Ferraris out there in the night, sitting all lit up with pride in the centre of the pound, the pictures of him hauling both into the yard stuck on the wall next to the window with 'Fuck U 1' and 'Fuck U 2' written under each for everyone to see, especially the prick with the shirts whenever he came down to pick the things up.

Out back he heard the engine start on the big wrecker tow truck they used for bringing in heavy goods vehicles when they broke down. The towing company charging it out at $500 a pop for the privilege. *Where the fuck was the truck that had broken down and needed a tow?* he thought.

Once upon a time it would have been him driving it himself, turning up with the wrecker and its huge tow bars and crane on the back. Coming in at speed, pulling up at the side of the road, blasting his air horns and revving the fuck out of the machine like some sort of idiot superhero who had come to save the day. The big oaf getting out his cab, dropping down and shaking his head like it was the worst thing that could have ever happened to him that day in Vancouver. The man strutting about, making a meal about nothing, with his arms hanging awkwardly and his legs apart—like he'd shit himself—because of the steroids. The guy doing his best work to look as though he was the one who was going to have to fix the truck back at the yard when in reality he couldn't start the lawn mower.

There were some mechanics out back on bonus and still operating at this hour, but most would have called it a day. Reaching out and up Big Carl pointed his porky, ring covered fingers towards the ceiling and then slapped his left hand down on the large red button that opened the gate as he saw a tow truck rounding the corner from out back getting ready to head out onto the street. Its chrome bumper shining in the night as its fog lights squared up to the office window and blinded him as the huge machine maneuvered itself towards the open gate.

Then for a moment the huge tow truck he used to look so cool in stopped and the airbrakes came on. Its engine's rhythmic rumbling powering the blinding lights crashing in through the office window as it idled.

Big Carl sat there, shielding his eyes from the lights as he listened to the huge Detroit diesel engine rumble. Calling out through the office window with its little glass slot—the one he liked to slam shut when the general public whose cars he'd towed began to tell him how they felt—the man shouting out, "Come on move the fucking thing." But the wrecker wasn't going anywhere, for when he stepped outside with his hand to his eyes the truck's side door was open and the Ferraris were gone.

****

They took both the Ferraris east and then north over the Iron Workers Memorial Bridge both hitting 200kph as they reached the north shore on the other side and kept up that speed along Highway One as they headed west across the North Shore. Slowing at Capilano, they took a right through the chicane that took them onto it, hit the bottom moments later then took two more rights and a big swoop up onto and across the Lionsgate Bridge and into downtown Vancouver. And before the tow truck driver had got in and reversed the huge wrecker truck he wasn't allowed to drive anymore back into its usual spot, Chendrill and Daltrey were back in Yaletown and parked legally outside Slave. "The one you drove is Dan's, Sebastian had it fitted with a governor and it's not supposed to go past 90. I went the long way so as I could tease you on the highway, but it looks like the little fucker's been tampering with the electronics like he does," said Chendrill when they got out.

Picking up a cab, they cruised back along McGill, both of them sitting in the rear like a couple who had been together for so long they no longer held hands. They stopped in a side street at the rear of the compound and switched cars back to Daltrey's Audi. Something was bothering Chendrill and it had been from the very start, but now more so.

He said to Daltrey as they passed through the night back down to the lonely park by the water where Chendrill had staggered along like a drunk and sat down to sleep only an hour or so before, "Why would that phone owned by this stripper who Sebastian's bought a house for end up with you that night you called me from the boat?"

"Sebastian bought some stripper a house?" asked Daltrey.

"He does things like that, he's very generous."

"And you think the woman played him?"

"Initially—yeah, that's what I thought, but now no, I

think she was just lucky, meeting him like she did. I went over there and her husband told me to tell Sebastian to get the boxes all the furniture came in out of there—you know, 'get rid all that shit' is the way I think he put it."

Daltrey sat there and looked out the window, tapping her fingers on the steering wheel. Then she said, "Wow."

Chendrill carried on, "Truth is, I kind of put it all on the back burner because we had this other idiot trying to shake him down and I had Dan to keep an eye on as well."

"Dan?" Daltrey said, almost to herself.

"Yep."

Then Daltrey said, "I still can't get used to seeing him in these posters in town and at Slave. My friend says she's so sick of him she wants to punch him out."

"Punch him out then fuck him—or fuck him, then punch him out?" Chendrill asked with a smile.

"Neither, she's a bulldyke. You know that prick once tried to kiss me straight after he'd puked up oysters."

Chendrill laughed, that was typical Dan. He said, "And they say romance is dead."

He lifted his right hand up and began to open the door. Just as Chendrill was about to get out, Daltrey grabbed his left arm from across the centre console stopping him. She said, "If I didn't have my own issues right now Chuck I'd be inviting you home."

And Chendrill said straight back, "If I didn't have Dan's mother to lie next to every night these days we'd already be at my place."

Reaching out, he held her hand for a moment and then, raising it to his lips, kissed the back of it for a moment.

Closing the door, Chendrill walked away as he watched Daltrey pass by in her Audi and take a turn that would lead her to her apartment—where he could have been on his way back to also had he wished. She was a good woman that Daltrey, he thought, still sexy as hell even if some of her hair was missing.

He walked further along the road in the darkness towards the Aston, the kids on their bikes now just appearing from the park where he'd been sitting just before when Daltrey had come to visit.

Fuck, thought Chendrill, knowing he'd missed the opportunity to give them a hiding and throw their trick bikes off of the seawall into the bay. The kids heading along the road towards him, automatically sizing him up as too big and alert to fuck with.

Chendrill let them go without any acknowledgement whatsoever—their trick bikes tick tick ticking in the early morning calm. He reached the Aston and started it up, looking in the mirror to see which way they were heading home.

The boys went south for a block, then as Chendrill watched from four blocks back they went east, winding along the pathway in and out of sleeping cars and doing jumps off the curb. They hit East Hastings, cruising through the junkies and homeless almost as though they were at home themselves, standing and riding with their bodies leaning forward and hats to the side.

By the time they had reached the house Sebastian had bought for their mother, Chendrill was already tucked in along the road amongst the cars that would soon be taking their owners to work in the early morning sun.

It was almost six when he woke and looked to see if any lights were on in the million-dollar home with its big bay window that Sebastian had liked so much. At seven nothing had changed, and by eight they were all up. In Chendrill's mind, the school in Strathcona was two minutes walk away and if the boys went there they'd ride or walk. Either way, if school started at nine they'd be leaving at five after.

At 9:03 a.m. the front door opened as the boys with their skinny faces passed by on the other side of the road, heading towards the school. Chendrill now saw in the light of the day that the taller of the two was sporting the shiner Sebastian had given him a few days earlier. Ten minutes later their mother was out and heading in the same direction. Passing in her tight jeans and high heels, the woman was tall like her boys and still looking good with her long hair and breasts the way ex-peelers do.

Chendrill got out and walked along the road to the house. The husband who wanted him to clean up the shit last time he was there was now visible through the large bay window and walking around in the living room. He reached the steps and walked up to the door, knocked once and waited. Then again, and again until he saw the husband walk into the corridor and open the door. "I'm busy," the guy said immediately.

"I work for the landlord, he says you got stuff that needs doing."

"Oh, that fuckhead, come in."

Chendrill walked inside and looked around; the place was clean, but the ex-stripper's husband wasn't. The guy standing there smoking in his wife beater shirt, with his little feet that didn't match the boots sitting by the door sticking out the bottom of his track suit bottoms. The man asking Chendrill as though Chendrill was his for the day, "Where's your van?"

"It's not a van it's a truck," said Chendrill, "it's up the road."

Chendrill walked further into the house looking about and saying, "Nice place."

The husband saying straight back as they walked into the living room, "Yeah I'll be buying it right off the guy in the winter."

Knowing the man was full of shit and looking again at the size of the guy's feet, Chendrill said, "Cool." Then he asked, "What do you do?"

The guy hesitated for a moment, then said, "Freelance."

"Oh, great—in what?"

"At the docks. But now I've got other stuff, takes me down south."

Chendrill nodded, he knew the type, worked in the union, took day-calls when it was busy and went on EI until they had to go back to work. Employment Insurance or Worker's comp if they could feign an injury—or, even better, get one for real. He said, "Cool. What you doing down south then?"

The husband not answering and saying out of the blue instead, "You wanna beer?"

Chendrill looked at the clock and saw it read 9:20 in the morning, so he said, "Cool."

The husband disappeared into the kitchen and came back out with three cold Coors, handing one over and taking a huge slug of one of his two. "You got any weed or blow?" he asked.

Chendrill nodded and, lying, said straight back, "Yeah in the truck."

"Cool," said the guy, as he sat down at the same time to drink his beer and not offering Chendrill a seat. He reached down the side of the sofa Sebastian had just bought the family, pulled out a bag of dope along with a pre-rolled doobie and lit it. Chendrill watched him and, sitting down without asking, Chendrill asked again, "What you doing down south?"

The man smiled and said straight back with a wink, "Top secret shit."

"How old your boys?" Chendrill asked.

"The skinny fucker's 13 and the lanky fucker's 16."

"Was that your missus that just left?" asked Chendrill.

"Yeah, you see her? Hot hey? Girl's still got it. Bet you'd like to be banging that?" the man said back, "If it weren't for that bag now, maybe you'd be in for a bit."

Chendrill looked at him and asked, "Bag?"

"Yeah bag, you know ones they put in you when you can't shit. She used to be a peeler."

"Wow, she was a dancer?" Chendrill said.

"Yeah, real good one, travelled with it and all, all over the U.S. and Canada. You may have seen her because she was here a lot."

"Cool," said Chendrill, nodding, and wondering if he actually had seen her for real as the guy carried on.

"Now she's got herself all fucked up. All she's good for now is the kitchen so she's taking a job at the school—but she's still a good fuck. Back in the day she'd have got me to watch her take a big guy like you in her mouth, same as she should've done before when she got all fucked up."

Chendrill looked at him, still playing it dumb and not believing what he'd just heard the guy say. The man carried on, "That's why I took this gig going south, see she ain't got it no more with the stripping."

He took a big hit on his joint, held it for what Chendrill

thought was an age, then let it out, blowing the smoke into the carpet. Then almost as if he had not stopped at all, he carried on saying, "You know one time she was away a while, done a tour in the southern states, Miami and New Orleans, you know, on the stage and lap dancing like they do. When she got back she discovered she'd picked up gonorrhea. I said, probably got it off the carpets from all the shit holes she'd been working in, but truth was I was the one who give it to her cause I knew I already had it when we was fucking."

Chendrill hated the man, the guy betraying his wife like this to a complete stranger despite their history and thinking he was funny for knowingly giving his wife a sexually transmitted disease. Still playing it like an idiot, Chendrill said, "Cool," again, for what now felt like the hundredth time. Then he carried on asking, "They not like dogs then your kids?"

The husband wondered at the change of subject when he was about to tell this guy stories about the time he'd gotten his wife so stoned she'd done a gangbang. He said, "Big dogs yeah, they're cool, they're like their dad on that one. They just hate them little stupid fucking ones—the streaks of piss," he took another drag on his joint before he continued, "kids and the wife want to get a pit bull—now we have the house. I said I'm not picking up the shit in the yard."

"Yeah, you're right," Chendrill said, "Maybe that's a good thing. You know the guy who owns the place might come round and do it for you though."

The husband looked over at Chendrill and smiled just before taking the last hit on his joint, letting it out as he took another swig of beer as Chendrill watched the ash from the joint fall into the man's lap and down onto the cushions of his friend's sofa, hearing the man continue saying, "Yeah maybe he should. Fuck him, let him clean up the dog shit. But he can stay in the garden, the cunt's not coming in here."

Chendrill nodded and, mirroring the guy's sentiment, said, "Yeah. Fuck that guy."

Leaning on his knees and thinking of putting the TV on so they could both look at the chicks on the morning show—that, or one of his pornos he'd put together—he said, "Yeah, fuck him. Guy can't be telling us what's this and that—you know, it's enough with the fucking faggot calling my wife like he does."

"He does that does he?" Chendrill asked.

"Yeah, the guy pissed me off so much I sent the boys over to kill his dog."

Chendrill stared at the man for a moment, then said, "You did?"

"Yeah, but first time they did it they got the wrong faggot. Other night they didn't though, cause I told them straight—I told them, it's the old shithead with the dog, not the fuckhead with the hair—if you see the fucker on the beach and he has the little rat on him, drown the fucking thing."

And that's when Chendrill stood up and, with a huge rush of blood to his head, said, "Pick a window, you're leaving."

Then he grabbed the husband with both hands and threw the prick upside down straight through the big bay window.

Chendrill walked out through the front door and found the husband who liked to watch his wife get fucked laying in the garden in amongst the broken glass and smashed window frame still, strangely, holding his bottle of beer. Taking it off him, Chendrill chucked it back inside the house through the now smashed bay window. Chendrill then picked the man up by the scruff of his neck, dragged him along the road and threw him again, this time into the back of the Aston.

****

The husband didn't have a clue what had just happened. One minute he was having a joint and a beer with some cool dude from the seventies—the next the fucker had thrown him through the window. And now he was being kidnapped in a luxury car and the child locks were on. As he sat up in the back, he said, "Hey, where the fuck's the truck?"—saying it like it was normal to have just been thrown through a window. Then he said, "If it's about the container with the asparagus last year, then I've already said I was sorry."

It wasn't.

Then he said, "Okay, I can't tell you what day a drug ship's coming because I'm not working that crew anymore."

This was getting interesting, just like the old days except the car was a little nicer, Chendrill thought, as the man in the back with the wife who used to be a stripper started to blab, "It's about the container with the kitchenware?"

It wasn't.

"It's about the container with all the tomatoes from Chile?" asked the man as he tried the car door handle and window once more for luck as Chendrill slowed the car at a set of lights. Then he asked, "It's because I left the door open on Zero?"

Nope. But that one was interesting, thought Chendrill.

Then tired of the man and even more tired from being up every night for a week looking for the man's two shithead kids who liked to mug people, Chendrill told him, "It's about the dog."

"What fucking dog?"

"The same one your eldest boy killed."

Then he went quiet, as the car made its way downtown. Then he said, "Jesus, is that it? It's just a stupid fucking dog. Stop at the pet store and I'll get him another for fucksake?"

And Chendrill said, "It wasn't just a dog—it was Sebastian's dog." And then he waited for a response, which wasn't coming soon, and which still hadn't as they hit Vancouver's downtown core.

Chapter Eleven

They parked the Aston outside the offices of Slave right next to the two Ferraris that had yet to move. Chendrill got out in the same manner as he used to when he'd been a cop and had just caught the bad guy.

With only his thumb and his forefinger around the husband's wrist as cuffs, he marched the man across the road and only let go once they were through the doors and heading up the stairs to Slave. Then, with Chendrill guiding from behind like a teacher taking a naughty schoolboy to see the principal, they moved straight along the corridor without a word until he hit Sebastian's office at the end. He opened the door, moved the guy inside, and said, "Sit down on the sofa."

The husband looking about the room all confused. Then he asked, "Is this the police station?"

Chendrill smiled, still wondering why the man thought it was normal for police to throw people out of windows and drive Aston Martins. Then he answered, "No, I'm not a cop either, but if you give me any bullshit, you'll be with one."

The husband stood, even though he'd been told to sit, and began to wander slowly around the room, looking at the posters on the wall of celebs from old, fashion models of both genders in almost nothing at all. He stopped at the original stills of Dan cowering in the lift with blood running from his nose. Looking at Chendrill, he said, "Hey, I know this guy, I see him down Micky-D's all the time."

Then Sebastian came in looking all flustered and said, "Oh Malcolm, how nice to see you."

So that's his name, Chendrill thought, earlier the guy had been more interested in telling him he'd given his wife gonorrhea than introducing himself.

Chendrill piping up and saying, "Sebastian, I'm sorry to have to tell you this but this is the man responsible for what happened out on the beach the other night."

If Sebastian was angry inside, he did not show it, Chendrill thought. The only thing different from his normal behaviour was that he took his time to sit down. Then looking up, Sebastian simply asked, "How?"

"He had his kids do it, they were responsible for what happened on the beach and Mazzi's smack on the head that he blamed on the sash window," Chendrill said.

"Why?"

"He thinks you're hitting on his wife. But from what he'd been telling me earlier, this isn't usually a problem."

Sebastian sat there for a moment, lost in thought. Then looking up again, he said as he observed the man's bony face, ripped muscle shirt, and track pants, "Is there anything you'd like to tell me?"

The husband, Malcolm, shifted uncomfortably from foot to foot, listening to the big guy in the fancy office feeling like he was suddenly part of a movie. He looked at the clock, it had just gone 10 a.m. and by now, under normal circumstances, he'd have knocked one out to a home made porno and been asleep and dribbling on the sofa Sebastian had bought them. He said, "Yeah there is, I'm not paying for that window you know."

Sebastian looked at him for a moment completely confused. He asked, "What window?"

"The one your truck driver threw me through. The one at the front of the house."

Sebastian stood for a moment, then sat again. Then looking to Chendrill and then back to the husband, he asked, "The bay window?"

And as the old cop in him came out, Chendrill said butting in, "Actually, he fell through it as he was trying to escape."

****

Basil was doing well. In his eyes he was anyway. So far, he was getting himself down to the massage place to get his feet rubbed and meeting Maio after work almost every day—him there always wearing his suit that was looking like it needed a visit to the dry cleaner—and Maio there with him wondering now if this was the same guy who used to sleep with her sister.

They sat opposite each other in a cheap diner just off Stanley Park and watched the traffic pass by on Georgia. Maio's wrists aching from 10 hours of rubbing people's toes, Basil with a semi-on thinking about how nice it would be to have her back with him at his hotel. He said, as he had to her sister some time back, "I think you are the most beautiful woman I have ever met in my life."

Maio smiled and said back, "Yes. Thank you. Very much." Just like her English teacher had told her to say whenever someone said something nice—though it wasn't as if she got to go to her English class much these days with all the work she'd been doing.

Basil moved it up a gear and reached across the table to touch her hand, saying, "You know, if you're not busy, maybe you'd like to go to Whistler for the weekend sometime soon? You know, as a couple—boyfriend and girlfriend."

She liked this one, she got it. The guy had not shaved in the last couple of days and was asking her if she liked his whiskers and if she was busy on the weekends, but this was confusing as he knew she always was. He was right about the amount of couples that came in together and sat next to each other holding hands on a Saturday or a Sunday also. She said, "Yes, I like."

Great, *perfect*, Basil thought, *couldn't be better*. Next weekend the pair of them would be away together in Whistler. He'd woo her all the way there in his rented car and then check into the hotel at the edge of the slopes and whip her up the mountain for a couple of hours and get her all elemental and tipsy with a couple of wines on the mountaintop. Then, when she was tired and needed a rest from the wine and fresh air, it would be back to the room with the view and she'd lay down on the bed and so would he. Then he'd kiss her for the first time, the way he had the last girl who had the same tool that hit the sweet spot at the top of his toes. He said, "So, great next weekend, you and I—off to Whistler?"

Maio got that one also as she tried to dig into the super burger that he'd bought for her without asking and at the same tried not to let the ketchup dribble down her chin. The guy was going to grow his beard for a bit, just like her father did sometimes, he'd do that then shave on the weekend. She said, "Yes. And you, handsome like father."

Oh, *great*, Basil thought, this little Japanese girl had a daddy fetish. Things were really looking up.

****

It must have been three in the morning when Dan got the call—or at least that's how it felt. In fact, it was 6 a.m.

and Dan was already late—not that he could care less about that. It was Belinda who'd woke him, standing in the morning light at his low basement window with his hands cupped to the window pane, which could have done with a cleaning.

Dan had looked at him through half open eyes and said, "Get the fuck out of here."

Belinda saying straight back through the window, "They are telling me to wake you sir."

"Who?"

"Movie, sir; you are late for the movie, sir."

Oh that, thought Dan, as he pulled the covers over his head and felt his dick, which was still covered in Band-Aids. The fucking movie they've been going on about every fucking minute of the day with calls and texts from this person and that. Dan answering and just saying 'yes', but not listening. The whole thing was just a load of nonsense in his eyes. Adalia was going to be there as well, he thought, as he felt the sting of woman troubles hit his gut for the first time. She had been calling and wondering if he wanted to 'rehearse' and he'd been ignoring her, knowing he was still sore down there and with that he would've had some issues that would be a little hard to explain.

He got out of the car at the old corrugated steel works and wandered about the place looking for food, eventually finding some at the side of a catering truck. There were more people here this time than the last when he'd had his shoes screwed to the stage to stop him moving. Then he saw Adalia—the woman coming out the side of a large white converted truck surrounded by about 6 people. Slowly they came towards him, Adalia in shades and a huge puffy coat even though it wasn't cold, passing him, saying nothing.

Then someone was on him, a girl with headphones and a radio saying, "Hi Dan, you're late," talking to him as though she knew him.

What the fuck difference did it make if I'm late? Dan thought. They really needed to understand that he didn't care if he was late, not a bit. He'd been down this road before and he knew he needn't have gotten out of bed for another couple of hours. Then the girl said, "I'm Sadie. I'm a great fan. But don't tell anyone." *Of what, a fan of what*? Dan thought as he looked at her ass and asked her just that.

"Your last campaign," said Sadie.

Like there had been one before that one, he thought, as he looked at her a little closer and immediately felt the Band-Aids on his dick begin to stretch. Then just as he was about to tell her he was starving, she said, "Has anyone shown you your trailer?"

What? Dan thought, *a trailer*? Last time he was here he had a box to sit on and now he'd get a trailer? He asked, "Is there any food about?"

The girl called Sadie, who had a crush on the BlueBoy guy the size of the vibrator she kept at the side of her bed—this sex machine who was six years younger than her and still lived with his mum—said, "Yes, but as you're late they'll need you in wardrobe, you need to get your space suit on."

Three hours later, two of which where spent standing around, Dan was out again standing in front of a huge green screen dressed as an astronaut without his helmet on.

Jesus Christ, he thought, *what a load of fucking nonsense.* He looked around, there had to be three times as many people as the last time he'd been here and from what he could see pretty much all of them were doing nothing.

It was almost an hour before Adalia arrived along with the big mouthed old guy who kind of looked like Rock Mason. The people all faffing around them like they were gods and doing their hair and makeup when Dan knew that, any moment now, they'd all have their space helmets on. The guy Campbell something, who must be the director, making a show of it all, coming up and shaking Dan's hand with both of his, giving him a bunch of bullshit instructions that went in one ear and straight out the other. Patrick, looking dapper as always, sitting there amongst a bunch of TVs all grouped together where all the important people sat and talked. Mazzi Hegan in the distance wandering about dressed like a straight guy.

They rehearsed without their helmets on. Adalia not making eye contact and the old guy putting on a show. Dan just going through the motions, listening and hitting the marks in blue that he was told were his. Then they put their helmets on and then they were off again because the old guy wasn't comfortable, then they were on again, then off again because Adalia couldn't breathe. Then when she could, the old guy couldn't. Then Adalia's helmet was off again while they drilled holes. Then the old guy's needed holes. Dan stood there the whole time with his still on, feeling like a goldfish and wondering how much worse Adalia's breathing would have been in comparison to when she'd had his dick down her throat a few nights back.

Another hour passed, and then thirty minutes more before the clapper board went down and the old guy was off walking around in front of the green screen with his helmet on trying to fix something that wasn't there. Adalia standing there watching with her hands over the front of her helmet as though the world was about to end. Dan doing nothing—other than just walking to the next spot they'd told him to go to and watching the old guy wandering around.

And then they cut.

"Wow!" Dan heard someone shout from behind as he saw the guy he thought must be the director run up and hug both the old guy and Adalia at almost the same time. Saying to Dan as he passed, "Fantastic man, just fantastic."

Dan took a step back and watched as Adalia and the old guy carried on making a fuss about their helmets as the people who all looked the same took them off. Dan still keeping his on.

Then the old guy was making a drama about how hard it had been to walk and act in the suit. Dan heard Adalia's voice through his helmet, saying, "God you were terrific. Rock, just terrific."

Dan looked at the man with his hair all wet through his own visor, which was steaming up. *Fuck me*, he thought, *what a complete load of shit*. What had the man done? Not a whole lot more than Dan had done, he knew that. They all had their marks to hit. Move, look, nod, move, look, nod, shake head in helmet, move, stop. That was it. Now this guy was carrying on like he'd just banged out his own solo performance of Othello. *Fuck*, he'd seen better performances in 1980's pornos. They could have put a blind guy in the suit and sent him out there and things would not have been much different. On top of all that, from what Dan could see through his space helmet, this guy who looked like Rock Mason was making everything he did a drama. This and a few other things had also not been lost on the guy who was funding the whole project, and only halfway through their first day of filming, Sebastian was thinking along exactly the same lines.

It had all started with the room at the hotel. Sebastian had received a call from his friend who was running the show, saying the manager had called to say Rock Mason had been to front desk to complain there was sperm on the wall of the bathroom in his suite. And from what they could work out, he was right, there was. But there was a high chance that it was his own. Next there had been the room upgrade issue, and then when there wasn't one there was a compensation issue, which the man had requested to be paid to him in the form of credit to be used at the hotel bar and the restaurant across the street.

The next issue had come first thing in the morning with his trailer. Adalia had her own personal Airstream Classic XL and Rock Mason's was a standard Classic. He wanted the XL also. The difference was two feet more cupboard space—hence the XL. Until he had a XL or higher, which did not exist, he wasn't going inside the Classic he had said. And, of course, how could he? He was Rock Mason after all.

Now he sat there in the way at the monitors, two seats down from Sebastian, who had yet to chat with him further than their initial introduction during which Rock Mason hadn't been listening. Sebastian sitting there again wondering what the hell he'd gotten himself into and also when Dan would take his helmet off so his mother could see him.

Tricia was thinking exactly the same and feeling important as she sat there alongside Sebastian on a movie set for the first time in her life. Dan's mother all excited as she sat only four feet away from her favourite movie star. She said as she leant in to talk quietly to Sebastian, “Do you think someone needs to get that helmet off Dan? He could be in trouble.”

Sebastian knew the kid would be hungry soon and told her so.

She looked over at Rock Mason, who was a lot shorter than she’d always imagined, but God he was good. The guy sitting there doing a crossword puzzle in his space suit with his helmet off looking cool after working his magic out there as he pretended to be doing something she could not understand.

Tricia took a deep breath and leaned in and said to the one guy on earth she’d always wanted to meet, “Hey, eh— hi! I’m Dan’s mother. I’m so thrilled to be here and meet you, it’s my first time on a movie set.”

Rock Mason, looking back at her giving her that great big Rock Mason smile she’d seen him give a hundred times on the big screen, said, “Great!”

Tricia carried on wanting to tell him how good he was in his last movie, “He’s Got Butter,” in which he played a pastry chef who falls in love with a girl from Ethiopia who washes the dishes but really is a dancer. She said, “I see you’re doing a crossword. I love them, I try to do one a day to keep my mind strong.”

Rock Mason smiled, then asked, “You like word play, do you?”

“Yes.”

Then with a twinkle in his eye he looked at her and said, “Well if I give you a few words to play with then let’s see if you can work out the correct sentence I’m trying to say to you okay? Here we go— ready? I’m - Off – So –

Tired – Fuck."

And before she'd worked it out, Sebastian already had, and softly placing his hand on her arm he leaned in and whispered in her ear, "Darling, you are a beautiful person—don't ever believe what you see on TV." And then he looked at her and saw that as she worked the words through into a sentence she was beginning to cry.

Putting her hands to her eyes, Tricia stood for a moment, said sorry—first to Rock Mason and then again to Sebastian—and quietly left the stage. In her entire life, she couldn't remember anyone ever being that rude to her, and it having come from a man she'd admired from afar for so long, it had come as a shock. She reached her car, opened the door, and sat in it for a moment. She looked around at the trucks and people doing nothing and wondered where Dan was. Pulling out her phone she dialed his number and listened to it ring.

Dan stood at the edge of the green screen with his helmet on still and felt his phone vibrating in the rear pocket of his trousers inside his space suit. Pulling open a Velcro flap, he dug blindly inside until he reached it. Then pulling it out, he put it to his ear on the outside of his plexiglass helmet, which was now almost impossible to see out of. "Hello," he called out, his own voice sounding strange and reminding him of when he was younger and got his head stuck in a bucket.

He called out again through the helmet, "Hello?"

Outside he could hear his mother's voice calling, "Dan, Dan."

He called out again, "Mum?" and heard his mother call back, "Dan. Dan can you hear me, where are you love?"

Tricia hung up, and still holding the phone dropped her

hand to her lap. It had been awhile since she'd spoken to Chendrill because he'd said he was working and she only hoped he was, but things had felt different since this girl with the name like the singer had reappeared. There was no reason to feel insecure though and it had only been a few days since they'd both laid next to each other and cried with laughter after she'd told him she'd just found her son with paper towel and band aids around his penis. Turning the phone over, she scrolled down and called Chendrill's number. As soon as she heard his voice, she burst into tears again, "Chuck, love. This man's just been so rude to me."

Sebastian sat there at the monitors as the world on the movie set turned. Patrick was doing nothing, the director was doing nothing, Mazzi, still in the plasterer's boots, was doing what seemed like nothing. And he himself was doing nothing—besides paying for everything, as always, and worrying about Dan's mother and missing his dog. Looking over to Rock Mason, he said, "Rock, darling, do you think you could have been a little bit nicer." Not looking up or caring one bit for the words he'd just heard, Rock Mason said nothing. Sebastian carried on, "I should warn you that the young lady you just upset has a huge boyfriend who threw a man who upset me through a window yesterday—and he doesn't like me half as much as he does her."

Rock Mason turned and stared at the little guy in his cream trousers sporting what looked like the remnants of a black eye—who was around the same age as him, but not trying to hide it. He asked, "Who the fuck are you?"

"Just one of the guys at Slave," Sebastian replied modestly.

"Slave?"

"Yes, they're the ones paying you to be here."

"Never heard of them. What pictures have they done?"

"None, this is their first."

"Well when they've done 135 like me then come see me and tell me how to behave on a film set, until then go back to film school."

Sebastian smiled and, without the slightest hint of upset, said straight back, "Perhaps you should remember that not everyone in this world cares about the fact that you're an actor as much as you do."

"I'm sorry?"

"Some people don't care how many B movies you've done."

"Fuck you."

Sebastian laughed to himself. This prick who'd just done nothing but walk around in a space suit for half an hour and had been applauded for doing so by a director who was full of shit, was now telling him to fuck off. He said, "How's the hotel room?" He waited for an answer that did not come. Then he asked, "How's your trailer, squeezing into it okay are you?"

At this, he did get a response and it was Rock Mason turning to him and telling him straight, "Fuck you, get the fuck out of here—you're fired."

Sebastian looked at the man who'd just fired him off the film he was financing and laughed inside. Without the slightest display of emotion, Sebastian simply said back, "My good man. You need to realise something. I don't work for you—you work for me. You can't fire me—I am the one who fires you, if and when I want too, and I can do that anytime I wish—should the fancy take me."

And then Chendrill arrived and, without a word to Sebastian, sat himself down between the two in Tricia's director's chair—the chair's cloth and wood straining as he settled. He waited a moment, looking at the monitors, then at the green screen, and then at the guy on the edge in the space suit with the fogged-up helmet. Looking at Sebastian he asked, "Why's there an astronaut standing out there?"

"It's a space movie, Chuck," said Sebastian.

"Well where's the space ship?"

"It's computer generated, ask Dan about it. He'll know more about it than me—it's more his generation."

Chendrill looked around, then asked, "Where is he."

Sebastian pointed to the screen, curving his index finger right on top of Dan's head. "I think he likes looking at everything through the helmet."

Chendrill looking back up at the huge lights pounding down onto the set realized it was Dan standing there with the helmet on, he said, "Isn't he getting hot in there?"

Piping into the conversation that had nothing to do with him, without looking up from his crossword, and turning the conversation around to himself, Rock Mason said, "Yeah we get pretty hot out there but it's what we do."

Chendrill stared at him, smiling as Rock Mason looked back. And just as Rock Mason was about to drop a huge bullshit story about the time he'd played a fireman back in the 80's and found a puppy in the set of a burning building and walked out with it in his arms and how it had looked so cool they'd kept it in the movie, Chendrill said, "Who are you?"

Rock Mason smiled and held out his hand. It wasn't the first time he'd not been recognized straight off, but almost always after he'd introduced himself and the realization set in as to who he was, the return was worth the modesty, "Rock Mason. Movie Star."

Charles Chuck Chendrill offered no hand in return and instead said back, "Chuck Chendrill. I hear you like word play. Let's see how quick you can make a sentence out of these five words, "We – weren't – talking – to – you – so – fuck – off."

"That's eight words," Rock Mason said straight back.

"That's right—the last three were to see if you could count."

****

Rock Mason paced about in his Airstream Classic trailer, which he had refused to set foot in because it was two feet shorter than Adalia's. He wanted to call his agent, but he couldn't because he didn't have one. Nor did he have any money in the bank anymore, hence getting rid of the agent. There had been a day when he'd have told that pompous Brit and his big fucking friend to go fuck themselves and got on a private jet back to his pool in Hollywood. But now all the pools were gone, along with the four wives he'd decorated them with over the years.

Now he was here doing stupid space films with other A-listers who were holding onto their careers better than he could, along with some stupid kid who couldn't get his helmet off and had a sensitive mother. Now at the very same time he was trying to claw back something that may very well have been gone forever, he was being disrespected by mouthy boyfriends. But no one had to know that. He could keep it together and pretend he still had it all while he was here—same as Errol Flynn had until he'd died in this same goddamn awful city where it rained all the time.

Now he was roughing it in this tiny 31-foot rented Airstream Classic with its tiny wardrobe and a bullshit executive suite at the Sutton, living on a grand a day expenses which he had to use as wages instead of blowing it at the bar every night. *Fuck, how had things gotten so bad*? But you're still here doing it, he told himself, as he laid himself out on the sofa of the Classic and wondered if he'd be able to get the girl with the headset on into the Airstream with him for a bit of fun. In his day, yeah, there'd been magic with more than a few when he'd had them in the trailer to watch him masturbate. But up here, now, where everyone wore black and cross trainers and abbreviated their sentences more now than they ever had before, times had changed.

He looked around, there had to be something that he could find that he could moan about for a while instead of that big fuck being rude—get the people in the office worried that he wasn't happy. He couldn't get drunk like he used to—that had always worked, but not these days, not like in the 70's when it was pretty much expected of you. Back in the day when they'd call for Rock Mason and find him lying on the sofa of a proper Airstream trailer out in the desert somewhere he or anyone else could never find on a map again, he'd be there with his top off for good measure, with a bottle of Jack on its side on the coffee table and a crowd around him trying to wake him up—when inside he was fine, just playing the part. Acting. Always acting. Acting, acting.

He walked around the trailer and looked at the drawer space in the wardrobe. He'd looked it up, the Classic XL was better. It was bullshit, him having less draw space than Adalia Seychan, the fucking skank. Fucking bullshit, that and the fucking skinny bitch uber sensitive mother of that skinny retard kid and her big fucking small dick boyfriend getting all bent out of shape because he didn't fancy chatting about fucking crosswords. And who the fuck was that guy at the monitors, getting all high and mighty telling him he can't be fired? Well guess what pal—you can. If Rock *Fucking* Mason wants you gone, you're gone—done. Get the fuck out and get the fucking bus home. And if you don't like what you're hearing, go try acting, go try and be a fucking master pastry chef one minute and a spaceman the next. Try that and see if you've got the concentration needed. You know how much concentration I've got? More than anyone here has—that's how much.

Then he opened the door to his stupid fucking poxy top of the line Airstream Classic trailer and screamed it all out in a tone that would have even put Mazzi Hegan to shame on a bad day, "More concentration than you fucking lot!—Your gone pal!—If Rock Fucking Mason says you're out, you're gone—done. Get the fuck out—get the fucking bus home!"

Slamming the door, he paced once around his coffee table. He'd done 135 films and he was stuck here in a fucking piddly ass 31-foot trailer with no fucking wardrobe space. He'd tell them that as well, he walked to the door, opened it again and screamed out, "No fucking wardrobes!" and slammed the door shut again. *135 fucking films over 40 fucking years that's what I have and I'm being treated like some kind of cunt*, he told himself as he paced around the 31-foot executive trailer which was bigger than the one he'd had on his last film, when he'd spent all day in the kitchen pretending to be a pastry chef, then after, spent all his money bankrupting himself on six restaurants pretending to be a pastry chef. Muttering under his breath, he said, "135, me. These fucking idiots, 1—and they haven't even finished that yet. So that makes zero. Zero!" He'd tell them that as well. Let them know he was angry, let it get all the way back to LA, to Hollywood, to Century City, to Paramount, Universal, Netflix, Dreamworks. He'd let the real people who made movies see what a fucking farce he was stuck on up here. He'd let them know and let them know right fucking now, and opening his trailer door again with a bang, he screamed that one out as well, "135 movies for me—fuck all for you—the best actor in the world—ME—you lot, you guys, you fucking loser cunts—Zero!—Zeee Roooo…. Zerrrroooo! Because I'm Rock Fucking Mason—Rock Fucking Maaaassssooooonnnn!"

Rock Mason, having a tantrum like a 2-year-old, screaming so loud that he hoped he could be heard over a thousand miles away in California and that the people down there would somehow care and be shaken up enough to rush to talk to whoever was in charge. But Sebastian, the one person who was truly in charge was already there and listening, standing in the crowd next to Dan and Chendrill watching as the self-proclaimed best actor and pastry chef in the world ranted and raved, and all he had to say after the man's throat went hoarse and the trailer door had shut for the final time was, "I always thought he was taller."

****

Come the afternoon, Rock Mason hadn't come out of the trailer he'd refused to go into at the start of the day, and he wasn't coming out until he'd spoken to someone in charge, someone with clout, someone from Hollywood.

At just after two in the afternoon, Patrick was knocking on the door and after a short while, without waiting for a reply that was never coming anyway, Patrick stepped right in. Rock Mason stared at him, this man with a million-dollar smile, standing there in the doorway with his arms spread wide, saying, "Rock my man, looks as though I got here just in time. Trust me, they were about to shut the show down. And we don't need that."

Rock Mason sat there taking in what he'd just been told and for a moment wondered if someone had jumped in a private jet and headed up north to sort things out. He said straight back, "Got here from where, Hollywood?"

"Yaletown!"

"Yaletown?"

"Slave's offices in Yaletown."

"Really?" said Rock Mason as he now remembered meeting the guy first thing in the morning, along with the limey cunt with the shiner, but couldn't recollect his name either. He said without standing, "And you are who?"

"Patrick De'Sendro, executive producer."

Patrick, Rock Mason thought, forgetting his surname almost as soon as he'd heard it. *How many pictures have you produced?* he thought, as he looked at the man's teeth, knowing he could look at a call sheet later and check the guy out. He said almost with an element of pride, "They were almost shutting the show down hey?" He liked that, contracts stated that if a show collapsed he'd get fully compensated for the whole show. Then he could just get the fuck out of here and collect the measly million they'd offered and he could get on with his life.

Patrick nodded, then said, "Yep they were shutting the show down for a day or so until your replacement could get in."

"Sorry?"

"But he's not signed yet, so there's time still to make this whole thing work out. No one wants you to lose this property," said Patrick still using one of his timeless tried and trusted real estate quotes but forgetting again to adjust the phrasing to his new career.

"Property?"

"Movie."

"Who'd they have in mind?" Rock Mason asked, wishing he'd not gotten greedy and fired his agent before he'd signed the show, knowing this was not good. If a show went down because it was badly put together he still got in the news; if he was replaced, he was in the news, but for the wrong reasons. This early into a show it was easy for anyone to achieve—even this mob.

"Buffy just scored a three-picture deal with Tom Cruise, she got quite the package. I've heard he loves it up here. Adalia loves Tom, she's really happy."

Of course she is, the fucking dumb slut, Rock Mason thought wishing now that he'd not made such a fuss in the first place. She'd be on top billing alongside that prick of a superstar, and all she'd have to do was these piddly few weeks to get the accolade. He said, "Well as soon as I get an apology from that big guy and his buddy, we'll be getting on with making this movie."

It wasn't going to happen, not with Sebastian—who'd already given up on the show—and especially not with Chendrill. Patrick knew this. Not in a million years, so he said, "Sure Rock, they were just saying they wanted to apologize to you, no one here wants you to leave—you're the man! They sent me over to see if you're ok, that's the reason I'm here. Trust me."

****

Sebastian sat as his desk and wondered again what the fuck was going on. He'd opened up a can of worms with this whim of Patrick's and now they were all over the kitchen. He called his old friend Roger who he knew was smoking outside again as he could smell the cigarette smoke drifting through the window, a minute later the man was in his office.

He said, "Did you hear about today?" He had, the man was at the top of his game and he had his spies everywhere. He even knew that Rock Mason did the same on pretty much every show and had budgeted for it accordingly. He said, "It's all cool. He's back now on the set. Dan's there too with Adalia."

"Oh?" said Sebastian who was just going to pull the plug for real and take a week off while the movie people left the offices. He asked, "How do you deal with these people, I have enough trouble with Mazzi and supermodels but I feel that man takes it to another level?"

Roger looked at Sebastian and smiled, he was an old dog in an ever-changing world, much the same as Sebastian—except Sebastian was rich. He said, "If I stepped into your shoes for a bit then I'm sure it wouldn't be a whole lot different, except the shelf life is a lot shorter with the people you deal with. For me, the older they get, the easier or harder they become, but mostly they discover if they act stupid they get left behind."

"What about this guy then?" Sebastian asked as he habitually looked for Fluffy, who wasn't there any more.

"Rock Mason is an exception as he still brings people in, that's all—bums on seats, minutes watched on Netflix, you know the score. Put up with the prick for a few weeks and in the long run you'll make money."

But for Sebastian money was no longer a necessity, he already had it—what he didn't need was a mouthy prick who had none himself calling him an asshole. Then before he could tell his old friend who used to cry at Alan's jokes that he was thinking of shutting the show down altogether for real, his phone rang and it was Suzy, and from what Sebastian could tell she was crying.

They met at their usual spot on the park bench which looked out across the inlet with its view of the eastern part of Stanley Park and the float planes that came and went for as long as the sun was in the sky.

Suzy wearing tight jeans and a tight white blouse hugging her big melons, which made Sebastian wonder if they were heavy and hurt her lower back. The woman sitting there next to Sebastian asking about his eye with her legs crossed in her high heels, no longer crying but still upset about what had happened and how embarrassed and sorry she was that her husband had lost his temper and thrown Sebastian's driver through the window.

"I appreciate everything you've done for us Seb, I really do," she carried on saying as she looked at the water and leaned away, scratching her long red nails at something that was itching her right calf muscle under her jeans.

Us?—Sebastian thought, you more like, and your kids, in a round about way—even if their judgement of right or wrong was in dispute at the moment. He looked to the woman's ankles as she lifted her leg up to itch it again, stretching out her leg unconsciously, pointing the toe of her slim leopard skin shoe with its thin six-inch heel. Sebastian wondering as he watched how it could hold the weight of a woman who was around 120 pounds. Sexy shoes on a sexy woman, and from the looks she was getting from the men who passed by, there was no doubt in that.

"It's just that Malcolm, he's been so upset about it, now he's blaming me saying it was my fault. He's saying your truck driver was only there because he was looking for me, and he said I needed to start growing up and stop dressing like a slut now that I can't work my real job anymore. He's blaming me Seb, he's saying it was my fault I've got this bag, saying I entice men, that I'm oversexed and that I made him bring guys over—he said he only did it because he knew it turned me on seeing him watching me doing it with other guys. But it was the other way round, Seb I'm telling you, I could see it in his eyes, that's why he bought the video camera."

"Oh!"

"He'd do that Seb, and now since I can't do it anymore I'm sure he's been putting it online. I mean—don't you think that says it all?"

It did in Sebastian's mind. The man was a kinky fucker, no doubt—but who was he to talk, he thought? After all, how many times in the eighties had he gotten off watching Alan double fist a couple of cocks into his mouth? From what he'd seen, lust took you to some strange places. He said, "We've all done things dear."

Suzy sat back on the wooden park bench dedicated to a woman who had given her entire life to only one man. "Now he's saying I can't earn the money I used to earn stripping because I'm the one who wanted him to watch me. But I'm telling you it wasn't that way, I didn't even like it most of the time he'd ask me to do it. We could have spent time with the kids instead, you know? Why would I want guys at home fucking me after what I had to put up with at work, with them gawping at me and pawing me when I was giving out those dances and all, you'd have thought he'd have understood?"

Sebastian began to wonder who the father of her kids actually was and watched as Suzy crossed her arms in defence of her words and stressed the buttons on her blouse. He said, "Everything comes to an end dear, nothing lasts forever. You can forget about it now."

"Exactly. What did he think was going to happen, I was going to be swinging around a pole and sitting on laps when I'm fifty? Christ. Get real. Sometimes I'm glad I've got this bag now—at least it woke me up."

Sebastian looked at her and smiled, for a moment he'd almost forgotten about her colostomy bag, which, for some reason, despite the tight clothing, he had yet to see. He said, "Well, you'd never know you had one, I can tell you that, and I'm sure you won't have one for ever."

Suzy took a deep breath, it was good to get it all out. She was sure everyone could smell the bag taped tight to her skin underneath the top of her jeans. "I hope not," she said.

"So do I my love, so do I."

Then without a moment of hesitation in her voice Suzy said, "I'm going to leave him, Seb. Could you help me?"

****

It was just after ten at night when Belinda's limo stopped outside the front of the house and dropped Dan off. Chendrill and Dan's mother sat in the living room with Rock Mason's bullshit long forgotten. Both of them snuggled on the couch drinking wine and watching TV, listening to Dan huff and puff his way up the small steps outside, through the front door, into the kitchen, opening the fridge, closing the fridge, and carrying on into the living room with the attitude of a coal miner who'd spent his day down the pit and come home to find his wife doing her nails and no pork chop on the table. He said, "What the fuck are you doing?"

Trish looked at Dan, this kid of hers who'd just arrived home from work and who, from the looks of things, now thought he owned the place.

"Sorry?"

"Where's the cheese that was in the fridge?"

"Chuck's had it, he ate it with his wine."

"Oh well, that's fucking great!" Dan said as he looked to Chendrill then back to his mother and threw his arms in the air like a baby. He carried on, "That's fucking great. I'm at work all fucking day. Hot as fuck—all I've been thinking about all day is that cheese and how I'm going to eat it when I come in and when I get here, I discover you've been feeding the dog."

Chendrill looked up at him and then put his glass down, stood and said, "I'm going to count to ten in my mind and when I get there if you have not apologized then I'm either going to call an ambulance for you or I'm going to call your boss and have him take away all the food you get for free tomorrow along with that great big fucking trailer they let you eat it in."

"It ain't that big actually, ask Rock Mason," Dan snapped back with his eyes half closed and his head twisted to the side, which could only be interpreted as meaning that Chendrill was nothing more than an uninformed moron.

"Rock Mason's lucky he's still got a job, besides using

him as reference kind of invalidates your argument."

Then with the fear that her son may at any point in the next thirty seconds be picked up and thrown through the window, Trish spoke up, butting in, "Dan from what I can remember so far on your short journey through life you've done two days work and today was your second—and for the record, doing half a job cutting the lawn is not proper work. So, quit the attitude and apologize to Chuck, or call Sebastian and tell him you need a suite at the Sutton Place Hotel along with all the rest of your phoney bullshit actor friends because you'll no longer be welcome here."

He could, he thought, as he watched Chendrill smirk as he sat back down and pick up his glass of red wine. All he'd have to do was call the office and he'd have a suite with room service. But that would mean Adalia would be two doors down, along with that idiot with the big mouth. They did have a lot of chicks floating about the place though, at least he remembered that from the time he'd been there and nearly fucked Marsha—or 'Marshaaa' as she liked to be called. He said, "Chuck, you're not a dog you're a cat, and cats always find the best place to sleep and that's here, so I'm sorry for the insult—it's just that I'm tired because I've just worked a fourteen fucking hour day while you two have done sweet diddly fuck all."

And then he left, slamming the door and slamming his way down the steps to his suite in the basement two steps at a time and slamming the door behind him when he got there. Seconds later he was slamming Metallica up through the ceiling.

Trish looked at Chendrill and smiled. She said, "Well half an apology is better than none I suppose."

It was, Chendrill thought, but it wasn't over—he knew

that. The little prick thought he'd done a day's work when all he'd done was stand around in a space suit and move from one piece of tape on the floor to the next. Maybe he'd speak with Sebastian tomorrow and, in between this 'exhausting work' he'd been doing, he'd have the kid carry some of the heavy stuff about, the same as he'd seen some of the guys on set doing when that mouthy prick refused to work.

****

The next morning at 5 a.m. Belinda was back with his face and hands pressed against the window to Dan's cave in the basement, calling out as quietly as he could so as not to wake the neighbours. An hour later, Chendrill's phone was ringing.

"Are you with Dan, Chuck?"

Chendrill sat up, it wasn't that the call had woken him as he'd been half expecting it to come as for the last forty minutes he'd been lying there listening to the East Indian tapping on the basement window.

"Dan's not responding Chuck; they are trying to wake him and he won't respond."

They, Chendrill thought, *they*—meaning more than one, and from what he could tell it was just Belinda outside. He said, "Really?"

"Yes Chuck, they're trying to call him and the driver's been knocking on the door. I'm worried, you know with the way the world is and we hear all the time about celebs dying early for strange reasons, you know, same as Clive Sonic almost did! Could you go round, I'm sure Trish won't mind."

If he knew he was there he'd have not been able to

contain it in his voice, Chendrill thought. He'd have said something like 'since you're on the payroll; or, if it's not too much trouble for you' but he hadn't, he was asking if he could just go over, and he was asking nicely.

Chendrill said, "He's still alive Sebastian, I can assure you that, what he is, is a teenager—and teenagers don't get up at 5 a.m., they go to bed at 5 a.m. if they can. Don't forget you were one once. So don't worry, he's still with us—I can guarantee that. I'll sort it out and he'll be there within the hour."

"He's late, can you make it within thirty?"

Fuck, there it was. He did know, Chendrill thought. It was almost twenty minutes from his place downtown to Dan's so there was no way he could do it all with getting there and getting Dan up and out the door and to the studio in less. And of course Belinda would have told him the Aston was parked outside. *Fuck*, he was getting weak.

He hung up the phone and got back into bed and smiled at Trish who was looking straight at him. She said, "Should we just make love for a bit then go get him up. It is after all a little early."

It was a hard proposition to turn down, but knowing Sebastian's ability to continually ruin their love making, it wouldn't be long before the phone went again.

"I'll be quick."

"Oh!"

"Not in that way," Chendrill laughed as he got up again and slipped on his jeans without his underpants.

"I mean, getting him up."

Then Trish got up and slipping on her dressing gown said, "I'm his mother—I'll do it."

She reached the bottom of the stairs and knocked on

Dan's door as she had a thousand times before and said, "Dan, wake up you're late."

Nothing.

"Dan?"

Nothing.

"You're late for work, Dan."

Nothing.

Then after waiting a moment, she began to walk back up the stairs, reaching the top she called back down, "Dan, Sebastian just called and said they're eating pizza for breakfast and if you're not in soon, it'll be gone."

Dan sat in the back of the limo and looked at Chendrill sitting in the front grinning at him. "I can't believe a genius like yourself fell for that one," said Chendrill.

Dan shook his head, looked out the window, and closed his eyes, wishing he had never rushed out the door like he had. Now though, his stomach was rumbling. He said, "We should stop at Micky-D's."

Chendrill looked at Belinda, who was obviously listening as he was now shaking his head. Chendrill said, "Dan wants you to stop at McDonald's, he says there's a backlog of food there lately because he's been eating for free at work."

"Cannot stop sir, I am having orders."

And opening his eyes, Dan said, "What about a drive through?"

"No sir, it will make the car smell sir."

"Fuck."

"No sir, this will make the car smell also sir."

Chendrill laughed, he hadn't expected that one from the normally straight-faced East Indian who had a crush on his girl—this guy who was never late and always professional.

He said, "No you can't be doing that Dan, not in this limo."

Chapter Twelve

It was around about two hours later that Dan started work—if you could call it that. Standing there on the painted floor of the green screen with his space suit on fresh out of the shower because the make up girl told him he stank.

Adalia was there now also, trying to make eye contact through the helmet after snubbing him the day before, but seemingly changing her tune upon hearing Marshaa would be coming in later in the afternoon. Dan not giving a shit though and was more interested in watching Rock Mason in his suit holding his space helmet in one hand as he took over the whole stage whilst he acted out being a movie star. The guy strutting about like he owned the studio, telling the director, Campbell Ewes, how it should be, loving the sound of his own voice, saying out loud as he walked away to the other side of the green screen area and gesturing to a group of people sitting in the wings who couldn't give a shit either way.

"What I'm needing here is to be able to move, move as the character takes me and I'm feeling as though because this is such a crucial scene that's being played out here with these guys while we have tea, I feel as though my character should be right here."

The visual effects guy piped up for the first time, "Well if you are there you'll be having tea outside the ship."

Having given up listening a long time back, Sebastian had walked to the monitors where Clive Sonic now sat—the ex-rock star having joined them for the morning so he could have some photos taken and talk to Sebastian some more about how the guy was going to make him mayor. As he looked to Rock Mason still trying to explain himself, Clive said, "That guy really knows what he's talking about."

Sebastian closed his eyes and wondered if he was the only one around who could see straight through the man's insecure nonsense. He said, "Yes, it's rare to see one of the greats in action."

Unbelievable, Sebastian thought, as he watched the young man sitting there star struck. Getting up, he walked away and out of the door of the factory that once made corrugated steel. What the hell was he doing this for, he thought? Dan didn't care, Mazzi Hegan was too busy going through his own personal crisis to care either, Chendrill had come and gone and wished he was back hunting thieves and murderers, Patrick just liked the new job title and nothing else—except for flirting with Adalia. There were however a lot of people working on the show and from what he could tell from the odd conversation he'd had, some had families—so that in itself made it worthwhile.

He walked back inside, grabbed a tea, and walked back to the monitors to see Rock Mason sitting in Sebastian's chair when his own was only three feet away. The man doing his best to look like an astronaut who'd just got back from collecting moon dust. In his mind, there was no doubt that he was the superstar and with that any chair was fair game. Smiling, Sebastian said, "When you've finished in my chair, they've got a space shuttle out back that needs docking."

Breaking away from the tail end of another bullshit story in which he'd taken over a movie—first as the director, then as the producer, and then the editor and finally arranging a crazy distribution deal with a guy he'd just beaten at poker—he looked at Sebastian and finished his sentence, "… and saved a great script from being destroyed by imbeciles. Don't make me do it on this one Baby."

As he dragged the aging superstar's chair over and sat down, Sebastian said straight back, "How'd the restaurant business work out for you?"

Rock Mason sat there for a moment and stared at the little gay twat who had the audacity to be sitting in his chair—this guy who thought he knew how to make movies but hadn't made one yet. *How dare he*, he thought, how dare the fuckhead motherfucking cock sucking son of a bitch criticize him when he'd spent a lifetime reinventing Hollywood? Where was this prick when he was battling the studios for women's rights in film, fair pay, ethnic diversity?

Looking over, he said with the smile that had won over countless women and the selection committee at Cannes many years prior for his portrayal in an indie about a Mexican cliff diver who didn't like heights, "You know some people just don't know a good thing when they see it."

Or taste it, Sebastian thought. He said, "Have you met Clive Sonic?"

Hamming it up again and pointing his fingers at Clive, Rock Mason said, "Have I met Clive Sonic? I love Clive Sonic man. He's the best. You know how many times I've made love to 'Love me till I die'? You know for a while that song was almost playing 24/7 at my place in the Hills."

The one you had to sell, Sebastian thought but didn't say.

Clive Sonic was loving it and wishing his girlfriend was here—and at the same time he was glad she wasn't, as he'd inevitably end up having to fuck her dressed as a pastry chef while Rock Mason was on the TV. He wanted to speak but for some reason he couldn't get a word in edgewise with the man. Then he got his chance when he heard Rock Mason ask him, "Why'd you stop playing kid?"

And before Clive Sonic could start to tell his own bullshit story of how he'd tried to save the life of a kid in shark infested waters two and a half miles off shore in the Caribbean, Sebastian had done it for him, saying quickly, "Clive was attacked by a Stingray and nearly drowned, only he was saved by a real-life hero."

Rock Mason stared at Sebastian who'd just given him a back handed slap and obviously didn't care. Who the fuck was this guy to talk when the guy's biggest claim to fame was being the lead man in a circle jerk? He said, "You think I'm plastic, is that the way you see it? Well some people are heroes and people like me make them national heroes. Because if it wasn't for me, no one would know about Jack Carton—the guy who saved the honey bee from extinction by strapping two hives to his body and climbing to the top of Mount Denali during the honey bee virus of '72. Hey—you ever heard of that guy? Or Mak, Mak the saviour of the state of New York, as they call him now, the guy who single-handedly decoded the Nazi's one atom bomb they'd developed and took his own life strapping it to his back and diving into the depths of the cold Atlantic back in 1945! Well you never would have if it wasn't for me, yeah me, Rock Mason, playing those parts, becoming those great men who changed history. You want me to go on?"

Sebastian didn't. Truth was he hadn't heard of either of these people, who, in fact, never actually existed. Rock Mason's mind being all mixed up with the real-life heroes and fictional characters—who now all existed in the self-centered world Rock Mason now inhabited. He said, "What on earth would the world be without you?"

"That's right, be thankful I'm here."

"Oh, we are Rock, you better believe it," Patrick suddenly said, piping into the conversation after he'd just finished a little sexting session with a new hooker he'd found online—the girl with her little bubble butt who liked the fact he was open about her fucking him with a big rubber dick he'd bring over and him being a big film producer and all. Carrying on he said, "Rock, the whole world is waiting with bated breath for this movie."

"You'd better believe it is," Rock Mason answered back with a little smirk which led straight into another self-important line, "The world waits for any movie I'm in."

Then Patrick stood and with his arms wide open and most sincere smile Clive Sonic had ever seen in his life, Patrick said again, "Trust Me!" Then after just the right amount of pause, he carried on with, "Oh but more so they are waiting for this one Rock."

Fuck, Clive Sonic thought, as he watched Patrick sit back down again and go back to texting—there it was again, that catch phrase, all he needed was to take a leaf out of this guy's book. He knew what he was doing. Clive thought back to the days when he used to write songs—days when he didn't give a fuck about anything in life except that people had to miss him when he's gone—same as the world would miss this egotistical prick sitting in Sebastian's chair if he died saving some kid who had his foot stuck in the tracks of an oncoming train.

He needed a campaign line that stuck in people's minds—'I'll be there', he thought, 'I'll be there for you'. No. 'I'm there for you'. No, how about, 'I'll be there when the rain comes'. No, too long, but not bad for a soppy song title—'I'll be there for you, come what may'. Still too long.

He stared at the people all around the stage eating and chatting as he tuned out Rock Mason's seemingly endless bullshit. Then it just came to him, just as the opening lyrics to 'Boom Boom Love' had when he was taking a shower that time, and forgetting he'd already decided to steal the catch phrase after meeting Patrick for the first time at Sebastian's home. He blurted out, "Trust Me."

Rock Mason stopped talking and looked at this guy who used to be able to play the guitar and said, "Trust who?"

"Trust Me—it's my slogan for when I'm campaigning for Mayor of Vancouver. I've been using it since I was fourteen and schoolboy president."

What the fuck? Patrick thought, as he finished typing something about the girl's ass into his phone and looked up to hear Clive Sonic carry on, "Sebastian's running my campaign. In a moment, we're doing some photo stills—that's why I'm in today."

Rock Mason got it now, there was another reason the kid was here: so he could latch onto him, chumming it up for a photo op that he could use on the campaign trail. He said, "How do you know I support your policies?"

Not getting it for the moment, Clive Sonic looked over to Sebastian, who did. He said, "Clive's not looking for an endorsement, Rock."

"Well if he wants one, it'll cost."

"He doesn't."

Rock Mason leaned back in his chair and looked Clive Sonic straight in the eye, then said, "Biggest mistake any politician can make is to turn down a photo endorsement with a world-famous celebrity. It's what wins elections."

Even if he is an egotistical prick, he isn't half wrong there, Sebastian thought, but would he ever give the man the satisfaction? Not a chance.

"So, kid, are you in or out, you want to be mayor or what?"

Clive Sonic looked at Sebastian, then to Patrick, who was still on his phone, and then to Rock Mason with his million-dollar smile. He said, "I'm not sure, how much would it be?"

"For you kid, it'd be $250,000—and that's because I like you."

"Don't be so ridiculous," said Sebastian straight back, "if we spend that kind of money it'd be better to put it into a park," which now thinking about it wasn't actually a bad idea.

"Suit yourself," said Rock Mason as he turned back to the monitors to watch nothing, and then carried on with, "and when you lose the election, you can go both go sit on the swings and cry."

****

Five hours later, at just after five in the afternoon, there was a commotion at the door to the entrance way of the old corrugated steel factory and Marshaa and a small host of others walked in. Reaching the monitors with Buffy at her side and carrying a huge Prada bag, she hugged Patrick first, air kissed Sebastian, ignored Adalia and Rock Mason, looked at Clive Sonic, then said, "I'm sorry I'm late, I got held up in Chena."

And she had, held up in Guangzhou, China, because she'd seen the same Prada bag she now held on sale in the window of a shop in the departure lounge, which had cost her $550 plus another $20,000 in first class tickets because she'd missed the plane. Completely ignoring the fact Buffy was standing right next to her, she carried on with, "And Buffy let the real plane go without me, so we had to get some Chena one that didn't speak English."

And it was true, Buffy had let the plane go without her. After all she had been standing at the departure gate, listening to the staff calling out Marshaa's name, giving her the final call announcement over and over while Marshaa tried to work out if she'd have the bag in blue. Buffy having apologized and spent half an hour running back and forth to the store pleading with Marshaa to hurry up to no avail.

"Oh, well at least you're here now," Sebastian said, understanding everything and smiling to Buffy as he politely gestured his arms towards the two superstars.

"Marshaa dear, of course you remember Mazzi?"

She didn't.

"And this is Adalia Seychan, and this is Rock Mason."

"Oh, hey, yeah," is all she said, not giving a shit and playing with her phone with one hand and holding out her other to shake both of theirs. Then turning back to Sebastian and Patrick, she asked, "Where's Dan?"

"I think you'll find him in his trailer, love. He seems to like it there on his own," answered Sebastian.

Marshaa asked, "Does he know I'm here?"

He did, and seeing her come through the door with the

entourage of people she'd managed to collect since arriving at the airport, he'd disappeared into his own Airstream Classic, which was rapidly starting to smell like his room in his mother's basement. Not that he would have noticed, since he still had his helmet on. Now though, he could see her through his misty helmet standing by the monitors with all these people he'd never seen before waiting in the wings. The supermodel there in amongst them all faffing her long blond hair all about the place and looking beautiful. Adalia standing next to her looking coy, trying desperately not to be out-staged, smiling, then taking a peek at Marshaa's ass as Rock Mason did the same.

Dan's phone beeped and he picked it up and looked at the messages he'd received from her over the last day or so. The first read: 'seems like some peeps think shopping not important!!!!'

The second read: 'here in Vanc….at fucking last!!! Stupid Bitch!!!' And a third that must have just been sent that simply said. 'Where the fuck r u…… 2 many old people.' Seconds later she was at his trailer door.

Adalia Seychan looked on from afar, and if she'd had a bazooka rocket handy she'd have used it on the bitch. *Fuck*, she thought, why had she played it cool with the kid like she had instead of just drawing him dick first to her with sex? The boy should be in her trailer now while they waited for this Swedish guy with the black eyes to finish moving lights around. Then the skinny bitch could have seen Dan, and seen that he was fucking her, and then the illiterate bitch could have gone running back with her stupid bag to 'Chena'.

Then all of a sudden, with her entourage in tow, Marshaa was walking back towards the monitors. Reaching them, Adalia asked with a smile, "Is he not there?"

And Marshaa answered shaking her head completely confused, "No, that's not his trailer, it's a spaceman's."

"Oh okay," Adalia answered. As the words '*dumb bitch*' materialized in her mind, then she heard Rock Mason pipe in as usual, "That's because today we are spacemen baby, even you, you've got off one plane and now you're getting on another, and this one's going to Mars. Before you know it baby, you'll be in one of these crazy suits and space walking with the rest of us."

Marshaa looked around, she couldn't see any space, all she could see was a green screen that was three times the size of the ones she usually had to work her stuff in. She also didn't remember Patrick telling her she had another plane to catch. She said, "So, is Dan not here then?"

And before Rock Mason could spout off any more bullshit, Patrick stepped in, saying, "He's here baby, the king of the world's here. He'll go crazy when he sees you, he's been waiting all day for you to get here, it's all he's been talking about."

How? Adalia thought, *had he been talking 'all day' about the skinny bitch?* All she'd seen of him since he arrived late, as usual, was Dan wearing his suit with his helmet on—and he'd only taken that off to fill his face with food. She said, "Patrick dear, you're too kind, don't lead the girl up the garden path, you know his mind's elsewhere at the moment."

My God, give it up woman and know when you're done, Sebastian thought, as he once again, for what felt like the one hundredth time, wondered what the hell he had gotten himself into. How on earth could she think she could compete against Marshaa for fucksake? At least one thing was certain, the whole circus was taking his mind off of Fluffy—and that was a good thing.

He looked around the place missing his little boy, who'd loved it here—loved running about the place, but not too far. Then out of the blue, Marshaa caught his ear as right on cue to no one in particular, she said out loud, "Hey, where's little Fluffy?"

Sebastian turned around as the words cut through his already broken heart, then smiling and reaching out he took Marshaa by the hands and said sweetly, "The little lad passed on dear; he was such a lovely dog."

As always, Rock Mason piped in his two cents' worth of wisdom, looking around and saying, "You know what I say when I hear a pet dog's died? One less piece of shit to pick up in the park."

Taking a deep breath, Sebastian counted to ten then politely asked, "I take it you're not an animal lover then, Rock?"

"As far as I'm concerned, a pet dog is about one rung down from a model turned actor. You see, what you need to understand is that bringing in dogs or models doesn't make a movie, it's not all about looking good—you need talent."

God the man was irritating and with the upset of losing his dog and an earful of listening to the man's condescending bullshit all day, Sebastian's normally cool demeanor slipped away from him and looking back over he said, "Well from what I've seen so far, from now on you'd be better off playing Goofy at Disneyland as talent's seemingly not on the menu."

Rock Mason sat there in Sebastian's chair as the rest of the group pretended not to have heard and with a smug grin that had a full career spanning some 135 films behind it said, "135 films buddy, come see me when you've got 10% of that."

And as soon as he'd said it, his fate was sealed. Being the man he was, Sebastian had done his homework. And without the slightest hesitation he said, "135 films, of which most where bit parts in B movies until you got a lucky break, since then you've managed one more hit, so it reads to me as 123 shit films, 10 okay-ish ones and 2 which were great and they probably only achieved greatness because you kept your mouth shut, did as you were told, and let someone with talent make you look good."

Rock Mason didn't say anything for a moment and instead just sat there taking it in. Yeah, the guy was right, there'd been a few embarrassments along the way—but hey, that was the price you paid on the way to stardom. Anyway, what did this shithead know about the price of fish? The best he and his shitty little Slave Media company could do with any of the films he'd done good or bad was put a poster together and stick it on a billboard. So, fuck him. He said, "The difference between me and you or any of your people you've bought to this charade is that I have talent and your people pout. I, on the other hand, can be anything that's put in front of me on a well scripted page. You want me to be an astronaut, I'll be it. You want me to be a boxer, I'm there. A paraplegic, I'm there. You dress me up as a turkey and I'll lay a golden egg then knock it out the ballpark. I can sing, I can dance, I can do anything asked of me—except listen to someone pretending to be something they're not. And that someone's you and the crew of pouting kids you're bringing into my world."

"Really, you can dance?" Sebastian replied without the

slightest of upset showing from within.

"Yeah really, you bring that kid out here and let him go one on one with me on the floor and I'll show you. You bring in a dance troupe of nimble fucking sex kittens and I'll hold my own dressed only in my boxers. You know why? Because, I'm trained—trained to perform, not trained to pout. And that's what you've matched me with here on this fucking piece of shit excuse for a production."

Within the hour, Sebastian had shut the production down for the day and had his chain-smoking friend who liked to laugh at Alan's jokes on the lookout for a dance troupe of young nubile girls, and at the same time Clive Sonic's girl on the lookout for an adult size turkey suit along with a golden egg. Yes, he knew fucking with the man and changing things around was going to cost another $200,000 on top of the already spiraling budget, but what did he care? Everyone was being paid and the money was coming straight out of his bank account so he could play with the man for as long as he had him on contract.

****

Mazzi Hegan wondered what the hell was going on. He was there working and completely in charge of the photography of his first feature film and it was going to shit. He'd been lighting it well, he had the crew Roger had brought in for him to do the heavy work, but things were still falling behind and he couldn't seem to summon up the energy to actually care. Now Sebastian had just called all in a fluster and asked for the stage to be lit ready in the morning for a dance scene. A month ago, if he'd heard things were changing at such short notice, he'd have had a hissy fit and all of Vancouver would have heard, but now he just didn't care that much, a bit, but not enough that he'd need to go see his hair stylist to get over it. *Is this it?* he thought, *is this the way straight guys feel when they get fucked about?* He walked over and shared the news with his Gaffer and Key Grip, who would need to arrange the changes, and all they did was roll their eyes a bit and then said, "Sure."

He walked outside and got into his Ferrari and pulled his big boots off so he could hit the pedals properly. The car now had paperwork and litter on the floor. Looking over, he saw Marshaa standing there in amongst her entourage. He put the boots back on and got back out of the car, and said as he reached her, "Hey Marshaa, how you doing, what's up?"

Marshaa stared at him, first wondering who the guy was, then why this slightly effeminate builder who looked familiar was hitting on her. She said, "Hey?"

Mazzi held out his hand and smiled, "It's Mazzi. I shot all your stuff here when we did the Blue Boy campaign."

Then Marshaa got it and recognized him now. She said, "Hey yeah, you're the gay guy?" Mazzi shook himself from side to side slightly, not knowing how to react to that one. The hairs now beginning to grow out on his legs were itching him as he stood there. In his day, he'd have slapped back at her with something like—"Yeah well at least I eat." But now it didn't seem him. So, he just said instead, "Well you know how it is, the more you ham it up and pretend, the more they pay you."

Marshaa stared at him confused, then said with an air of realization that hit like a water balloon, "Oh, so you're not gay. Okay, wow."

Mazzi stood there, moving about in his builder's boots

that he'd never done up. He looked at the girl's legs then took a swift peek at her ass, then her stomach and breasts, her face, her beautiful lips, her hair. *Wow*, he thought, *wow, why had he never seen it before, when all he'd ever seen her for was a skinny dopey bitch?* God he'd like to take her back to his place and spend the afternoon slamming her in his big fuck-you shower with the power heads turned on full.

It was tricky though, this straight world he was getting into now. You couldn't just use 'you wanna come over to my place so I can come in your face' as an invitation as he used to. You needed to be subtle, more discrete. Smiling he said, "Hey, I'm going for dinner soon if you feel hungry."

And Marshaa replied asking, "Have you seen Dan?"

Two minutes later, Marshaa had shaken off this weird guy who looked like a girl but was dressed like a man and had to take his boots off to drive his Ferrari. She made it to Dan's trailer and stood there knocking until the spaceman opened the door. As she stepped inside uninvited and tried to look into Dan's helmet. She said, "Is that you Dan."

Dan nodded and said in a muffled voice she could barely hear, "I can't get my helmet off."

Marshaa looked at the metal clips on the neck area of the space suit and fearing she'd break a nail, pretended to try and unclasp it.

"Why don't you go see someone?" she asked as she tried to look through the misted-up glass to see inside.

As she heard Dan's muffled voice say, "I tried but I can't get down the steps. They say these are real space suits from NASA, but I think they aren't because in those they say you don't sweat."

Marshaa didn't know that line of clothing, but she did

have a jacket that was really good in the cold. She said, "Yeah you need to get them to get you one of those ski jackets, they're really cool."

Dan said, "I thought they'd be back. They came and said something and now it's all quiet."

"Oh," said Marshaa, "you know Seb, he and that old guy had a fight and now we're going dancing tomorrow."

"What?" replied Dan, as he tried again to get the helmet off for real now.

"Seb and the old guy, Rock Mason, they had a fight and now Seb told him he's going to sing for his supper in the morning."

And that is exactly what Sebastian had said as the two grown men parted company, or there about, as Sebastian called out the last word as he reached the door, "Tomorrow we'll see just how talented you really are as you're going to have to sing and dance for your supper and if you don't like it—get the bus home and then go try and sue me for your million-dollar fee."

Dan said, "Oh!" and felt his way to the bed, sat down on it, then laid down on it and looked out at the figure of Marshaa looking like a ghost through the misty visor. He said, "They came to the door and said something, but I wasn't listening, so I said—'sure.'"

Marshaa came over and sat next to him on the bed. She understood exactly what he was talking about. Nodding she said, "I do that too. It makes people go away." Then she said, "You know I've been thinking about you all the time when I was on that stupid wall in Chena and more so on the funny plane on the way back and all I want to do is kiss you."

Wow, Dan thought, as he saw the mist thicken on the

inside of his space helmet. At last things were looking good. Then Marshaa said, "But last time we were together I felt that you thought I was such a slut asking you to come to my room like I did and then I was such a bitch for kicking you out and then you fell in love with that girl and, and, well, maybe it's best, I don't, you know, do anything."

Dan shook his head inside his helmet and reached up and placed his thick padded gloved hand on Marshaa's shoulder. This is all he needed. The most beautiful girl in the world on his bed and she wanted to leave so he'd respect her. He said with his voice echoing around his head in the helmet, "No, it's cool, all's cool. I've been feeling the same way," which, being so pre-occupied with Adalia, was a full-on lie. Carrying on with it he said, "Please stay, I want to kiss you too."

And then Marshaa leaned down and kissed the front of the glass on his helmet, first with a small peck and then again as she felt Dan's gloved hand pull her down upon him and her lips full and moist hit and French kiss the glass.

Dan looked up from inside the helmet as Marshaa's hair fell over the front of the helmet and what looked like a slug tried to break its way in. He could feel the girl now move herself above him, pull herself onto him. Her body on top of his, her hair across the visor, the slug moving around and around in small circles leaving lipstick as it went as he felt the young woman push her crotch into his. Then he saw her fingers cup the side of the visor and hold it as her slug like lips and tongue moved around and around again in circles.

He lifted his hands away from her shoulders and began to try to feel her body but couldn't. Then suddenly Marshaa pulled away from him for a moment and reappeared again kissing the visor first before moving herself up the helmet until her bare breasts lay open and exposed, squashed against the glass, Slowly and surely she began to rub her nipples against the visor as Dan looked up at them squashed against the glass. Around and around they went, as she moved one to the next then squashed them either side blocking out almost all the light. Then as he tried to move his padded hands across her body, he felt the tug at his groin as he felt Marshaa pull at the fly of his space suit, tugging it one way then the next as she pressed her body down on him and her breasts slid about above him on the top of the helmet. Suddenly he felt the zipper go and Marshaa's hand dig into the suit and pull out his already hard cock as her breasts disappeared from vision. Then suddenly Marshaa's face appeared again, looking at him curiously through the front of his visor as she held her hair back with her left hand as she showed him one of the plasters off of his dick.

"It's for the movie," Dan called back through the glass as Marshaa disappeared again and he felt another plaster rip away from his cock. As he called back again, "Aliens get me, and have sex with me, then put them on there." And he saw Marshaa appear again, giggling to herself and giving him the thumbs up as she stuck the first two plasters to the front of his visor. Then he felt a third rip off and saw it join the other two, then a fourth and a fifth and a sixth until they were all gone and he could barely see at all. Then as Marshaa's hand landed on the visor he felt her other surround his cock as she began to wank him, soft at first, then harder as he felt the soreness, from the barely healed sores in his dick left behind by the butter and sugar masturbation mix, begin to return.

Then her hand was gone and he felt her lips around him, soft and tender lips and her tongue that worked its way around the top of his shaft before he felt her push down on him until everything was inside her mouth and throat as her tongue now lapped against his balls. Then suddenly when he felt she must be unable to breath, she pulled off him and lifted her head and smiled down at him from above the space helmet as she let the moist saliva drip from her lips and run down the visor's glass. With a wicked smile Marshaa was gone again disappearing from his limited field of vision. He felt her mouth down on him again until he thought Marshaa's throat would burst or he would also. Then she appeared again, her beautiful face looking down on him with her hair hanging from either side, letting her mouthful of saliva she'd gained from holding his cock in the back of her throat drip from her perfect lips down onto the plasters.

Dan watched as his space suit covered body shuddered and his arms tried to push his gloved hands across her body and breasts as he saw Marshaa disappear from him again for the moment and reappear as he glimpsed her passing naked through an open window left in the visor. Then he felt her climb on him again and saw her hands wipe away the plasters and spit from the front of the glass and her body shift as she stood towering naked above him, her legs tanned and slender, her ass perfect, way above, swaying from side to side as she wiggled. Slowly Marshaa turned and began to lower herself towards Dan's face until her ass, pussy and inner thighs hit the glass all as one at the top of the visor.

Slowly Marshaa slid herself forward, letting her ass and shaved pussy slide across the glass from top to bottom as

Dan's eyes followed, almost as though he was watching a solar eclipse itself. Then as quickly as she was on him, she was off him again, as he watched Marshaa spin around and straddle him, hold his cock with one hand and look at him through the smear stained visor and as her eyes closed, she pushed herself down on him and he felt himself penetrate her.

Holding him there, Marshaa began to lift herself up on him then push herself down as Dan did his best to meet her in his space suit. Leaning forward, Marshaa kissed the helmet again and licked her moistness from where her pussy had just been from its front as she rode and ground down onto his cock. Then, with a little trick she'd learnt from a bushman in Papua New Guinea, she lifted herself up from top to bottom and began to slam herself down on Dan's cock over and over until he could hold it no more and came.

Even though NASA said it was impossible, Dan lay there in his suit covered in sweat with Marshaa spent for the moment laying on top with her right arm across the top of his helmet. *Wow*, he thought, *that was a lot different from the pizza he was expecting when he'd opened the trailer door.* But it wasn't over yet because just as Dan as always had started to think of food, Marshaa was giggling again and lifting her sexy tight body up above him and looking down, positioning herself right above his gaze through the visor she pulled herself apart slowly saying out loud, "Here comes some pussy pie—Buzz Lightyear," as she squeezed out drops of Dan's sperm from the inside of her little slice of heaven and let them fall down onto Dan's visor like a seagull dirtying a windshield on a Sunday afternoon drive.

****

The next morning, for once Dan was not late and in costume early—not because he'd suddenly had a change of heart and decided to get his act together and become professional, but simply because he hadn't left the stage. After a long and patient wait alone in the car park, Belinda had given up waiting and found him in the middle of the night asleep in his trailer, still with his helmet on and his fly open.

Now though it was Chendrill's turn in the morning to get him up after being woken himself by Sebastian who in turn had been woken by Belinda some hours earlier. The decision being made given the hour and the journey time involved to get him home and back again that it would be better to leave him where he was. Now though Chendrill was having to wash his hands after prising the helmet off the kid, who said he was starving.

The stage was set all white now with the green screens gone. A group of Korean girls in track suits kept to themselves as they warmed up at the side of the stage, found at the last minute by Roger and Sebastian and happy that they were being paid enough money to finance their whole trip. The director standing by, looking bemused and wondering why Sebastian had them doing promotional work on the third day of shooting when he knew Adalia Seychan was only available for a limited time.

Rock Mason wandered about looking like Hugh Hefner in a dressing gown frowning as the music started, not saying a word to anyone and ignoring Sebastian completely. The man all pissed off because Adalia had been given the day off, along with that horny little slut, and he had to be here with this idiot kid. This was bullshit, complete fucking bullshit—he was here to make a movie, not a fucking pop video. Fuck he wished he hadn't agreed to be here, taking a film because Adalia's name was attached and signing the contract without his agent. What a fuck up. But then he took a deep breath and thought to himself, *fuck it*, what was he worrying about, he was a pro, they want him to dance, he'll show them how. Then as adrenalin took over as it always did when things got tough, he clapped his hands together and called out, "Okay, let's get this done so we can get back to making a movie."

And with that cue, the four Korean girls took off their track suits, put on their high heels and in their little blue skirts and multi-colored loose tops, they stepped out onto the lit stage area, lined themselves up, waited for the music to start again, and in perfect unison worked their way through a seamless dance routine, full of pouts, hair flips, tiny little bunny hops and wiggly shoulders and asses.

Dan stood watching almost with his mouth open. As did Chendrill, who was doing his best to hide it as Dan's mother was there on her day off after a personal invite from Sebastian. The song finished and as soon as it did the girls stood looking at Rock Mason as if to ask what he wanted them to do next. And as he looked towards the director, he heard Sebastian call out, "That was great girls, lets do it again so Rock and the guys can get more of a feel for it."

Dan didn't need to, in his mind he already had every move down. He looked to Sebastian and said, "No, I got it, can I go in?"

And smiling Sebastian said, "You first and then Rock can follow on after."

With his dick hurting again, Dan walked out in just his

shorts into the lit stage area, lining himself up just in front of the centre of the girls, he stood there, and waited for the music to begin.

Then he heard the 'Beep Beep Beep' of the start of the track and, without looking back to the girls, joined them as their hips moved in three perfect circles and followed it up with a double shoulder shrug and an identical bunny hop first to the right then to the left. Then they all spun in unison, raising their asses in the air for all to see as they moved them around and around in perfect unison. Dan there with them in his element, smiling as he looked back at the crowd watching, playing the fool. Then as the girls spun back with their dark hair flying through the air, Dan was off, moving through them, behind them and back in front in perfect time. Playing with them and the music as he teased them and came in and out of their routine as though it was he himself who had choreographed the whole thing—and then almost as though he had never broken out of the routine, Dan was back where he started front and centre as the song came to and end, but this time with the girls surrounding him hugging him two on each side as he stood there on tip toes with his arms out like Jesus on the cross.

The music stopped and the stage erupted with applause for what was nothing more than a well-organized dance routine with beautifully sweet and innocent Korean girls made better by the playfulness of Dan's dancing.

Looking over to Rock Mason who was only half applauding and was already looking tired of the whole thing, Sebastian said, "Wow, that was fantastic—okay Rock, you're next!"

****

They were still crying with laughter as they sat in the back of Belinda's limo and hit downtown, then as they both settled were quiet for a moment before Chendrill said with a smile, "Sebastian, you surprise me—you can be one hell of a fucker when you want to be."

Sebastian looked at him, still in a serious mood but with tears in his eyes from the laughter, and said back, "Oh, it's not over yet, Chuck. No one calls my friends and I cunts and gets away with it, even if they are the self-proclaimed King of Hollywood."

Chendrill laughed, then smiled again. So far since Patrick had been given the go ahead to make his film, there had been a few egos rubbed in the dirt and the film hadn't even really got going yet. Chendrill felt the part of his arm where Rock Mason had bit him. The Hollywood star getting himself all mad earlier because Dan was everything the superstar had claimed to be. Rock Mason losing his temper straight after being made to stand out there in his shorts with his fat gut hanging out and making excuses as to why he couldn't get his act together—first it was the music and then the Korean girls who he claimed were the problem and couldn't keep time. The guy trying to make light of it as though it was all a big game and he was loving it when the cameras were on him, then once they were off and he was out there again dressed up as a turkey, he'd turned on Sebastian because of his own inability and embarrassment. Calling out in a temper that scared the girls and stopped them dancing, saying how he'd never worked with such amateurs on such a shower of shit show, then losing it all together and attacking Sebastian after he'd called him out for being a fraud.

"Fuck you!" the man had screamed, coming at him with

all his turkey feathers flying and finding Chendrill suddenly there like a wall between them. Then Rock Mason had screamed like a girl as he tried to pass. Chendrill hurting his own ribs again grabbing the man swiftly as the man tried to dodge him, holding him and trying to calm him as the aging, bankrupt superstar tried to kick and scream and wriggle his way free. Eventually sinking his teeth into Chendrill's arm hard enough to get away and ripping off the turkey suit Sebastian had him in and coming back at Chendrill with a performance of half assed Kung Fu manoeuvres he'd learned from doing action movies where they'd have him do the moves in close up and some stunt double do the fight for real. Rock Mason going in hard on Chendrill, trying to be Bruce Lee before getting thumped out cold on the studio floor by Chendrill moments after—because it was a real life fight he was staring in and not a Rock Mason movie.

"What about the fact you are going to have to work with the guy again for the next couple of months and then some?"

"Oh, I'm not bothered, Chuck. I'll let the show play out for a little while longer and let the man run his mouth off a little more while I get things in order, then I'll either keep the thing going or shut the show down. That decision will depend on Patrick—either way Rock Mason will be gone and he can fuck off on the bus back to Hollywood."

Chendrill raised his eyebrows and looked out the window for a moment. Then he said, "If you shut it down, what about Dan?"

Sebastian smiled—it was the first time Chendrill had seen Sebastian truly smile for the last few days. Sebastian said, "Dan will be fine, Chuck. He's an intelligent kid, all he needs to do is grow up and I hope he doesn't do that too soon."

He was right, Chendrill thought. When he was a kid all he wanted to do was get older and be a cop and now all he wanted to do was be a teenager again so as he could start off afresh and get it right the second time around. Sebastian said, "I think it'll be great once Clive Sonic makes mayor and when he does one of the stipulations will be that you get your old job back, on your terms though. I'll make sure that happens."

Chendrill looked to his now close friend and boss in shock. He said, "Well what about you?"

"Oh, Chuck, I'd be no good in the police force, no one would take me serious."

It wasn't what Chendrill was talking about and he knew just that. Then just as Chendrill was about to ask about Mazzi Hegan, Sebastian took him by surprise by saying, "Chuck, can you promise me something?"

Chendrill looked at Sebastian as the man watched the world go by outside the window and then turned to him, "I know you think I'm crazy, but can you promise me Chuck that you'll help my friend Suzy? Even if you don't want to. You know she's really sweet once you get to know her and she's had to put up with so much. She really needs a friend and a helping hand."

Chendrill said back, trying his best to hide the denunciation in his voice, "Do you not feel that the house is enough Sebastian?"

"Oh no Chuck, she's going to leave her husband. I may need to get her an apartment in the meantime if she does."

Chendrill closed his eyes for a moment, then opened them again. *They say a fool and his money are easily parted but Sebastian was no fool,* he thought, *so what was going on?* He said, “I’m sure you’ve thought it through.”

“Oh, I have, Chuck,” Sebastian said back quickly as Belinda took a right onto Pacific and cruised the coast road towards the park. ‘The poor girl’s had it hard and I don’t mean that in a sexy way either. You see she told me her husband’s one of those guys who like to watch his wife with other men. She said it started with one, then two, then you know. She told me she thinks he’s been posting it online.”

Chendrill shrugged and looked out the window to the water with the sun getting lower in the sky. He said, “Yeah it’s what they do these days. It’s pretty weird if you ask me. You shouldn’t get involved; she could always have said no.”

“Oh, I know, but she did Chuck and her husband didn’t listen, he just kept on at her. She said he has a thing for anal sex, Chuck, and I know I’m not one to preach on that subject, but it’s not everyone’s cup of tea. That’s how she’s ended up with the bag.”

Chendrill looked back at Sebastian and he could see the man was serious. He asked, “And she told you all this?”

“Yes Chuck, we talk about everything.”

“What about Fluffy? What did she have to say about the dog?” asked Chendrill, wondering if the woman just sat down with Sebastian and spouted off the way some women can and it was a one-sided conversation the two of them had every time they met.

“She cried Chuck, really cried, she was so sad—we both did.”

Chendrill sat back in his seat and thought about it. The two of them both sitting there on the seawall where they always met, the stripper with her big jugs and the old gay guy both crying their hearts out—her about her ass that had just been damaged internally by her shithead weird husband's friends while he made home movies and Sebastian about his little dog whom her kids had just killed. What a combo. He asked, "You tell her it was her kids who threw little Fluffy in the sea?"

Sebastian took a deep breath and stared out at the bay where Suzy's kids had thrown Fluffy into the surf. The waves now steady and calm. *It was a good question,* he thought, *he hadn't and he knew he should have.* He said, "No Chuck, I was waiting for the right time."

"After you've bought them a condo maybe?"

"Chuck, please, don't get mad at me. I know you think they're a family built out of bad stock, but it's the husband though. I'm telling you, talk to her, meet her, get to know her, you'll see she's a good person deep down. Besides, where else is she to go, Chuck. You want her to go back into sheltered housing with her kids, you want her back wandering around the East Side? You know it's just as dangerous during the day as it is at night. I heard there was a man kicked to death in one of the alleys around there only the other afternoon."

They reached the entrance way to Sebastian's place and Belinda parked outside, leaving the engine running, and sat quietly as Chendrill closed his eyes, thinking again. He had heard about the guy in the alley and he'd been in the area himself not a short time before. In his day, chances were high it would have been him who had been there to investigate—the guy in charge, looking for witnesses and clues until he eventually found the guy wearing the size tens.

"How'd you know about that?" he said.

"It was on the news, Chuck."

"Well promise me you won't be going around there. And promise me you let me know what's going on as soon as you know. Because there's no way I'm having it that a shithead like her old man gets to live in a house you own on his own, watching reruns of his wife getting pounded while you're paying for her to live somewhere else in the meantime. Okay?"

"Yes—you promise me then you'll take care of Suzy, Chuck. She may have been a stripper, but she's still my friend and a human being after all."

****

Chapter Thirteen

Missing the routine of walking his dog first before going upstairs to his penthouse suite, Sebastian went from the front door to his huge white bathroom and ran the bath. It had been a hard week, but now it was almost over. The film had been nothing less than a disaster so far. But he'd had a bit of excitement with it along the way. Now all he needed to do was get everything sorted, see the lawyer he'd found, get all the paperwork done properly, sort himself out personally, then the company, so that in the end if he shut it all down there could be no comeback for anybody—especially Rock Mason, and that would be that. First though he was going to take an Epsom salt bath and lay in it and relax until it got cold. It didn't matter who called or needed him with regard to the film because within a couple of days, it wouldn't really matter anymore.

That evening as he sat out on the balcony with a plate full of white stilton gold he'd been saving along with an open bottle of Screaming Eagle, feeling the breeze in the early evening air as he looked at the view that he knew so well and the water where he'd swam so many times years before with Alan and only once recently with their little dog, which had become their child. The beach there down below, with its slide out in the water and its coast road where aging men cruised on noisy Harleys looking more at themselves than at the road.

With the cheese half gone and the sun almost down, the lawyer had arrived.

The guy full of his own self-importance standing there at the door in his suit and fancy tie with his bald head and beaky nose. The man, Callum Rensberg, telling Sebastian straight off that he did not like dogs, but he was sure Sebastian's would have been an exception. The wine also was okay, as was the cheese, even though both were the most expensive a man could buy. But he wasn't there for comfort or friendship, he was there to do a job, and three hours later with everything witnessed, signed, and double signed again, and with Sebastian feeling as though he could not take another moment in the lawyer's company, the man was gone, along with Rock Mason's career—for now anyway.

Sebastian awoke early. He put on his favourite silk shirt, handmade Italian shoes, and went to watch the sunrise and to hear the birds sing as he took the dawn walk around the seawall. Stopping for blueberry pancakes and cream with an Earl Grey tea at the White Spot on Georgia, served to him by a pretty single mother of two. By 10 a.m. he'd secured a healthy donation to the Vancouver Philharmonic for the services of a pianist and a violinist and by midday he was sitting alone in the pews of St. Paul's on Burrard Street, listening to the melodic tones of Debussy played by musicians at the top of their game dressed in tuxedos. The music filling the air as it echoed around the high walls and the ceiling of the old wood beamed church. Enveloping Sebastian's senses to the brim as wonderful memories rose from deep within, bubbling up, as the soft and honest music played out, drawing goosebumps from his skin, which ran along his arms and legs as the spiritual music passed through him, speaking to his soul.

By three in the afternoon and after finishing a lovely plate of pasta with another glass of fine red wine from his favourite waiter, Sebastian was on his way back towards the park and, making good time and stopping only to help out a family with car trouble, soon he was there, standing high on the centre of the Lionsgate Bridge, taking in the fresh air as he caught the first of the cruise liners passing below as they headed out through the bay towards the inside passage towards Alaska.

And there he stood, as he had with Alan and Fluffy so many years before, looking out from high over the bay towards the mountains across the water and the setting sun. The steady stream of liners passing below with the happy faces of children waving to him, stretching their arms as they reached up to try to touch the returning stretched out hands of the happy joyous man whose life was done and who was about to die.

With his heart pounding and the sun on his face, Sebastian stood and watched the last of the cruise liners pass into the distance, then he climbed the barrier, took the last deep breath of fresh, clean air he would ever take in this world as he felt the wind in his hair, and dropped himself down 200 feet from the bridge's side into the water below.

Chapter Fourteen

Chendrill was the first to hear the news that his good friend had decided to take his own life. An old colleague calling him directly, having pulled Sebastian's wallet and ID from his trouser pocket after hauling his soaked and broken body into a police boat a mile or so into the bay after Sebastian's body had trailed after the cruise liners, carried in the rip from the changing tide. The man who loved boats sitting on the small boat's gunwale surprised to find Chendrill's business card sealed in a small plastic bag inside Sebastian's zipped up pocket—almost as though Sebastian had wanted it to be found.

But what was stranger was the call Chendrill had received half an hour prior to that about his old friend from a lady who sounded old and who'd simply said, "I just spoke with Sebastian and he says to tell you he's fine. He swam out and met Alan and Fluffy on Ambleside beach."

Then as he'd driven back out of town he'd got the call from his old buddy who'd dragged Sebastian's body onto the deck of the police boat. His friend wondering why Chendrill, who was normally so cool, sounded so confused and was asking so many questions, saying things like, "Are you sure it's him?"

He was 100% sure, and had replied, "Pictures don't lie Chuck, I'm sorry."

"When did you find him?"

"Ten minutes ago."

"How did he end up there, was he swimming off of Ambleside Beach?"

"No, he jumped off the Lionsgate bridge, somebody

saw him go over the barrier. They called it in maybe an hour ago. We didn't know who it was until now." Then he paused and Chendrill's old buddy, who patrolled the marine coastline every day of his working life, and who on the weekends sat on his own yacht said, "And Chuck, also, on the back of the card, it says, 'Chuck - Our tears we shed together yesterday were great tears.'"

Fuck me, Chendrill thought as he sat there outside Dan's mother's place at the wheel of the Aston, unaware of any of the journey he'd taken to arrive there. He could not move. There hadn't ever been a time, even with Daltrey, that the shock had hit so hard. The feelings of anger and regret and guilt searing deep wounds as they passed through him. It must have been almost an hour later when Dan's mother came to the window, looked in, opened the door and crouching down said, "Chuck what are you doing sitting out here all alone."

Leaving out the strange call from the lady, Chendrill told her what had happened and took her inside and held her while she cried. Half an hour later, Dan appeared in just his shorts, looking for the bag of Cheesies he'd seen his mother hide a week ago, the kid feeling the silence and looking at his mother's tears, and saying, "Who's dead now?"

And hearing the answer, Dan turned and left his hunt for food to return to his bedroom in the basement, from which, for the longest time, Chendrill heard nothing other than silence.

****

They all met the next morning in the offices of Slave. Samuel Gadot, Sebastian's actual lawyer greeting them individually as they entered. The man who in the autumn of his career now owned the whole top floor of a building next to the Vancouver Supreme Courts, which was home to a company he also owned comprised of some thirty lawyers and articling students—unlike Callum Rensberg, who stood next to him, and who had worked for almost the same amount of years, carried the same law degree, used an office at a friend's firm on the other side of town, and who had spent his entire career chasing ambulances.

It was pretty obvious why two days prior Sebastian had used the man who now stood alongside Samuel Gadot, wearing the same suit and tie he had worn when he'd sat in Sebastian's luxury apartment for an evening and made Sebastian feel dirty in his presence. If he had come to Samuel with the requests for legal documentation of this degree, the alarm bells would have rung and he would have known his regular lawyer, Samuel, would have firstly said 'no' then straight after started asking questions.

But today, what was done was done, and the documentation had been passed over to him and it was now Samuel Gadot's duty as a friend and professional to make sure Sebastian's wishes were honored.

Dan surprisingly sat in black, at the back as he liked to, and stared at the floor as he heard the man who stood there with presence begin to talk.

"No one here can be more upset about the circumstances of us being here today than me. Sebastian and I have been friends for many years. I do though have to speak with you all, as it was one of the man's wishes that everything would be dealt with as fast as possible to alleviate any suffering his departure has or may have caused. Firstly, after reading though the paperwork, I must say Sebastian would like you all to know his passing has no bearing on the incidents or stresses caused in the proceedings that have taken place over the last few days and in fact and truthfully has everything to do with Alan his departed husband who passed on some years back," said Samuel Gadot.

Fuck me. This is going to be a long one, Patrick thought, as he watched the man blabber on and tried to remember if he'd sold the guy a property a few years back. *Maybe*, he thought, *he was the same guy who grabbed that nice place in Point Grey? Yes, he was the guy he'd made it happen for over a weekend.* Patrick looked around the room then back to the high-priced lawyer. *Just get to the bit about the film,* he thought as he wondered about the guy's rate, probably $500 plus an hour, knowing Sebastian, so the way this guy was going on blah-de-fucking-blah-de-dah, he had just made $200 talking about a dog. If the man kept it up much longer, he was going to leave here, grab a taxi to the bridge, tell the driver to drop him off in the middle and do exactly the same as Sebastian had done. Patrick discreetly looked at his watch—he was right, almost half an hour of droning. What was the guy doing, training to be a priest? Yeah, Sebastian was a good guy, but so was Charlie Manson if you caught him on a good day.

Putting on a sad and concerned face, he looked back around the room. There were a lot of red eyes. Chendrill was still looking to the floor, Dan's eyes were closed, maybe asleep, Mazzi Hegan, in his big boots, sitting over at the side, looked fucked up with his hair all messed up as though he'd been pulled in off of a building site. Marshaa was crying and texting at the same time. Dan's mother—crying. Adalia crying also in her big black shades; Rock

Mason—bored. Then he saw Clive Sonic was there also, the guy who was trying to steal his catch phrase and who couldn't count to ten on his fingers—the fucker must have sneaked in late and closed the door with his gimpy hand. He looked back at the two lawyers standing at the head of the table. The expensive one in the Armani suit was now making his conclusions—if he was lucky, he'd get right to what was happening with the film. Then he heard the guy say, "So I'll make this easy, I need to speak with everyone so let's deal with the film you were all doing first."

Great! Fucking Wunderbar, Patrick thought, as he heard the guy carry on, "So, Mr. Patrick De'Sendro. I'm not sure if you remember me but you facilitated a deal on a house for me a couple of years ago. I wish we were meeting under more pleasurable circumstances. But sadly not."

Get to it and stop running down the clock, Patrick thought. Truth was, though, Samuel was there on his own time after having discovered what had gone down with the ambulance chasing son of a bitch after the man called out of courtesy. Patrick was a prick and he'd known that ever since Sebastian had put him on to him and the guy had somehow one weekend talked him into a purchase he didn't want. He carried on looking at a folder he held in his right hand.

"Patrick, it is saying here that you are producing this film Slave is financing, and Sebastian has kindly decided to keep the money flowing for the movie even though he's no longer with us."

Thank fuck for that, Patrick thought, and did his best not to let go of the smile that was behind the facade of sadness. If he was lucky, he could get out of here and go see the latest hooker he'd found who was enjoying riding him.

"However," Samuel carried on, "Sebastian has written a cheque for ten and a half million dollars, made out to the shell company the film has been working under and it's stipulated in Sebastian's will that I'm not able to hand it over unless this morning Mr. De'Sendro can answer correctly without help, a couple of questions. Sebastian states that if you are producing a film these questions should be, as he puts it here, 'No Brainers' and if you can't answer, then you are not deserved of the money. So please, could you tell me—one: what is the name of the scripted lead character in your movie, 'When the Shadows Form'. And two, what happens at the end of the script to this fictional character? Sebastian has stipulated you have 30 seconds to answer."

Patrick sat there for a moment and tried to take in what had just been said. He got it yeah, there was actually little not to get, except the answers correct and if he did not then he could kiss the movie goodbye unless he funded it himself, which was never going to happen—or he could talk someone else into funding it, but how long would that take? The problem was he didn't know what the lead character's name was and since Rock Mason was onboard was he talking about him, or Adalia, or perhaps even Dan? He said, "Well, firstly, I'd like to say everyone has been doing a great job.... Rock.... Adalia, Dan, Marshaa, she's fantastic."

"Please answer the questions," Samuel butted in.

Patrick stood, putting his hands out and looking at everyone in the room, especially Samuel, and said, "Trust Me."

Then carried on with, "If there's one thing I can say…"

To which Samuel Gadot, the veteran of over 5,000 cross examinations in court cases that spanned 3 decades, shut him down with ease, and, cutting in, said, "Thank you." And pulling out the cheque from the folder, he ripped it in four and dropped it into the wastepaper basket next to the desk. Then he carried on with, "Everyone who was contracted on the film, actors, technicians and drivers and all rental facilities will be paid in full, plus a 50% bonus. Except for, I'm sorry to say, Mr. Mason, who will receive zero compensation."

Rock mason sat there and wondered if this was some sort of joke—this prick was playing the clown from the other side of the grave. He looked around the room for some sort of sign that did not look like it was going to come any time soon. He said with his patented smile, "Hey, you have to stop with the funny stuff buddy, this man was our friend, we're hurting here."

But there was no funny stuff and everyone in the room except Rock Mason knew it.

With the skill of a man well versed in public speaking, Samuel moved on quickly and dismissed Rock Mason and Adalia.

Next was Clive Sonic, and he could tell from the way the man had just glanced his way moments before he allowed his silence to let the room know there was to be no more discussion on the subject. Clive was pissed and wished he'd never taken the call from Sebastian now if it was all going to be a waste of time since the fucker knew he was going to throw himself in the drink.

Not only that, from what he could tell he had only been seconds away from passing over the centre of the bridge with his girlfriend when Sebastian had thrown himself off. Had he been moments earlier he'd have seen him and he could have stopped the car and jumped out and grabbed the man as he was about to fall, and if he was lucky he could have allowed Sebastian to pull him over as well, but then maybe he could have gotten a grip on the railing somehow and they could have both been dangling there from the bridge as a crowd gathered and someone could have gotten a video of it all—as they do these days. Clive Sonic, the ex guitar sensation, hanging from the bridge trying to save the life of his friend… But no, Clive's hand, which was damaged in that incident in the Caribbean when he survived being attacked by a stingray, couldn't take the weight of the two men hanging and Clive's grip slowly loosens. Then he could have seen whoever had the best angle on him with the video on their phone and he could have looked into the camera as he tried to hang on, then as others tried to reach his hand he could have let go and fallen down, down, down, still holding onto Sebastian until they both crashed and died as they hit the water below.

It would have been fantastic—he would have been a hero and remembered forever after the clips went viral of him trying to save the life of another and falling to his death were played alongside those with him on stage with his eyes closed banging out 'Boom Boom Love' on his guitar.

Samuel Gadot looked over as Clive had predicted and said, "Mr Sonic, may I call you this as Sebastian has noted that you prefer to go by that name instead of your actual name of Smith?"

Clive nodded, it was fine. As he shook his head slightly looking up, his face conveying the upset he felt inside, he said, “Yes, thank you, Sebastian was good like that, he thought of everything. I’m sorry, I was coming up on the bridge a few second before he jumped and, trust me… I just wish I could have been there.”

Without a word in response, Samuel carried on, “Sebastian, as you know, had a wish for you to become mayor of this city and after his passing he still wishes this to be the case. Basically, it will be yourself or anyone else should you not wish to continue in this venture. If you are, you will be paid $250,000 a year while you are campaigning and while you are mayor. He has also allocated a substantial sum of money for campaign funding for what would be the first, as well as subsequent campaigns, and has already secured the same campaign advisory team as the recently elected U.S. President. So, to me the prospect looks hopeful, you would be, though, legally obliged to ensure certain requirements are met during your administration.”

He turned to Mazzi Hegan, “Mr. Hegan, you retain your shares to the company Slave gifted to you by Sebastian and he hopes you continue to bring your incredible talent to the company and as a gift to you for everything you have done and as an incentive to stay, he has passed on to you his penthouse apartment and also the Ferrari I know you love and has doubled your shares in Slave to 20% of the company. As for the company Slave, Sebastian has asked that Gill Banton be brought in to run the company and I will be negotiating this transition should she be interested. If not, I have other names listed.”

Mazzi Hegan was still not with it. He’d heard the news about Sebastian and gone out on a bender as soon as he’d stopped crying and ended up singing karaoke over in Deep

Cove and woke up that morning with a girl who looked like a guy and liked to swing both ways. Gill Banton though, that fucking bitch coming in with her sexy shoes and ass could be fun. If he didn't like things, he could stage a coup or just sell up and fuck off back to Sweden, after all, he thought, thanks to Sebastian and now owning 20% of a company worth around four hundred million, he was now a rich man.

"Mrs. Tricia Treedle, Sebastian has asked that you be told that he thoroughly enjoyed the pasta meal you made him when you asked him over for a meal recently. He said you have a beautiful home and that, although the house is old, that is what it is—a home. He has, though, expressed a wish for your son Daniel, since he is contracted to Slave, to have a bigger room and since Mr. Hegan now is the owner of Sebastian's penthouse, he has passed on to Dan the apartment in which Mazzi Hegan now resides. He also has given you the option of buying any house you would like to purchase on the lower mainland should you wish to, which he will be paying the property taxes for both residences or any other residence you wish to reside in thereafter.

"Mr. String has also expressed a wish that Daniel is to find his feet in the world and has allocated university funds for this, plus an allowance. He has also released Daniel from his contract from Slave on full pay should he wish. If Daniel should decide to leave Slave, however, then he will no longer have use of the Ferrari."

Fuck me, Dan thought, as he looked at his mother who had started to cry again. This was not good; in fact, it was fucking inconvenient, now he was going to have to clean out his room; and if he was going to be staying at Hegan's place, who was going to keep the fridge stocked up with cheese and shit? It certainly wouldn't be his mum, she'd be getting herself some big fuck-you place over in West Van or somewhere out of the way, and when that happened, how the fuck was he going to get his laundry done, as well as all the other crap? Sebastian should have thought about this shit before he went giving stuff away willy nilly. It was bullshit! Mazzi Hegan's place did have nice showers though, and that big wardrobe which was large enough to rent out to one of those hot refugees he'd seen on TV if he wanted. There was one question though which had been bothering him from the start, and so far it had not been addressed by anyone. He put up his hand

"Yes Daniel?"

"Do I still have the open account with Pizza Hut?"

"Yes Daniel."

"Does this mean I still have to answer to this guy?" asked Dan as he thumbed his left hand in the direction of Chendrill.

"If you stay in your contract with Slave, yes'"

"What if he punches me out again?"

"Then it'll be whoever I allocate."

"You?"

"Maybe me—yes."

And just as Dan was going to ask if this was the case—whether Samuel was going to start hanging around the house and banging his mother—Samuel shut him down, saying, "And lastly this brings me to Charles Chendrill. Charles, Sebastian has left money in trust to cover any expenses arising from everything we have discussed. He has also left you his majority stake in Slave Media and Renfrew Media. He has also asked that all the money from his personal bank account be transferred into yours, which is a sum of just over two hundred and seventy-five million dollars U.S. He has also mentioned that he does not want you or anyone here to be burdened with tax issues arising from his requests and any taxes owed will be coming from the trust account."

And with that Samuel Gadot, the lawyer who as a young boy lived amongst the horrors of Krakow, looked at the piece of shit lawyer who wished he was more and closed the file.

"Thank you," he said in conclusion.

Chendrill sat still for a moment, thinking as he watched the room move and stir, then he put up his hand as Dan had and asked, "One thing Mr. Gadot, I'd like to ask, when were these papers all drawn up and signed?"

And without hesitation. Samuel said, "The evening before yesterday."

It was as Chendrill had thought—Sebastian had left him after coming back from the studio and had this weasel of a lawyer over and drawn up the papers. With the requests Sebastian had been making to Chendrill in the back of Belinda's limo, it all made sense now. Looking to Sebastian's friend and the ambulance chasing lawyer, he said, "So, when Sebastian was drawing up these papers in this manner, did it not occur to you that maybe the man had some sort of intention of hurting himself?"

"Oh," said Samuel, "from looking at the way the papers have been drawn up and the fact that he wanted the show shut down and for Clive's election campaign to start immediately, I would have had no doubts." And before Chendrill could carry on, he said, "But I did not draw up the legal documents—they were drawn up by Mr. Rensberg and delivered to my office yesterday afternoon."

Chendrill stared at the man who knew Sebastian's game plan and decided to not say a word. He said, "You fucking knew, and you did nothing?"

"I was not aware of Mr. String's direct intentions, no."

Chendrill asked, "How much did he pay you?"

And before Callum Rensberg could answer, Samuel answered for him, "I looked into that myself, and it seems Mr. Rensberg was paid a sum of $50,000 for his services. $10,000 up front and the rest to be settled should his client Sebastian meet with an unfortunate accident."

Chendrill stood and felt like throwing his chair at the man standing there with his bald head and fancy tie. He said, "$10,000 for your legal work and another 40 in hush money."

"Well it's not like that, Mr. Chendrill," Callum Rensberg said in a slow voice that whined and grated as he spoke. "We in the legal profession have a responsibility in keeping confidentiality when it comes to our client's personal lives," he said.

"Fuck you and your legal bullshit," said Chendrill, who saw the whole thing as nothing less than assisted suicide. He carried on saying, "You knew exactly what was going down and chose to allow the man to end his life, but I'm fucking telling you now, I will do everything in my power to make you regret for the rest of your life ever deciding that forty fucking grand was worth more to you than my friend."

Then he heard Samuel say, "Mr. Chendrill, don't worry. I have already decided that I will be personally putting the entire efforts of my firm into bringing ethics and perhaps criminal charges against Mr. Rensberg for malpractice and gross neglect."

And from the tone in his voice and knowing the reputations both men had, Mr. Callum Rensberg, the lawyer who'd once had dog shit forced into his mouth by the ex-husband of a client in a divorce case he was handling, left the room.

Chapter Fifteen

Chendrill sat outside in the Aston and stared at the walls of the building he now owned. On the top right-hand corner was the window to Sebastian's office. He was now a rich man, but he would have given it all back for the man to have called him up and asked him up to the office to chat about nothing. In his eyes, the world had just lost something special.

So, it was as simple as this, he thought, when Alan, the love of the Sebastian's life, was on his death bed, Sebastian had asked him if he wanted him to join him the moment their little dog died, and the dying man, being the selfish prick he was, had said yes. And with Sebastian loving the man as he had, and being a man of his word, that was that. Winding down the clock, playing with business and getting more and more wealthy, Sebastian had waited for the dog to die. *Fuck me, what a stupid waste*, he thought as he started the engine and pulled away. He was a rich man, but he didn't feel it. Maybe it just hadn't sunk in yet. Feeling the steering wheel spin though his hands as he turned, he thought back to what Sebastian had said the last time he'd seen him as they had travelled back from the studio. *'Look after Suzy won't you, Chuck, you promise me please?'*

He had promised and he hadn't had his fingers crossed, the way Sebastian should have had as he'd sat crying at the side of his lover's bed and prayed that the monitors would reverse. Or as Chendrill had when he'd been a kid and his mother had made him promise to do his chores or clean his teeth, or to a girl years before when he'd been a player and he'd promised he'd call or not come on her tits.

Sebastian was dead and nothing was going to change this. It was his choice and it was his life, and life went on. Nonetheless it was still bullshit. He turned the car onto Pacific Boulevard and headed past the stadiums towards the East Side. Five minutes later, he pulled up along the road to the home Sebastian had bought for Suzy and her fucked up family to live in. The place was looking good now with its new front bay window and boxes still in the yard. The woman with the colostomy bag and the sob story would be at work now at the school at the end of the road. He put the car into drive and cruised past the house towards the school. As much as he didn't want to bother her, the woman deserved to know her friend had died—if that's what she was.

Pulling into the school car park, he got out and walked into the school's foyer through its double front door, looked at the trophy cabinet that was wanting and stopped at the reception. He smiled at the lady behind the desk who glanced up from her computer and looked as though whatever Chendrill had to say was going to be the biggest inconvenience she'd ever endured. Thinking inside that the woman was a bitch and wondering how many kids over the years had dealt with her and hated her, Chendrill said, "I've a personal message for Suzy Black. If you are able to call her then I'll be grateful."

"She's not here—she's off sick."

"May I ask when she went sick?"

"Who are you?"

"I'm her brother."

"If you were her brother you'd know."

"Not necessarily, when did you last call a family member?"

It was a good point, thought the woman who had a stash of cookies she'd hidden in a box in the bottom drawer of her desk, which was slowly making her ass fat. She hadn't called in a while; in fact, it had been almost three months. She said, "…She called in yesterday morning."

"Are my nephews here?"

"Barely," the woman muttered under her breath, and then not caring, said out loud, "For another couple of years—if they make it."

Chendrill drove back to the house and this time he parked outside. He got out and walked back towards the garden gate. Someone was in—he could hear a shitty Rock Mason action movie playing and could hear the man's voice calling out over machine guns and grenades. It had to be the loser husband who'd taken a short flying lesson a couple of days back. Then the movie went quiet but not off as he saw a shadow at the door and a cab pull around the corner.

Chendrill moved around the corner into the alley at the side and waited as the cab pulled up. The door opened and then closed. Then he heard the clicking of high heels, the cab door opened and closed again, then pulled away with Suzy in the back.

Chendrill walked quickly back to the Aston and caught up with the cab two blocks up, waiting for the chance to pull out onto Hastings and head back into town. He followed it west along Hastings Street, the place changing every block as they came closer to Main Street. Junkies at the side of the road were shouting with their tops off in piss-stained trousers, women with no teeth amongst them all selling their mouths for a score, junk was all around in doorways, shopping trolleys once filled with food now filled with debris pulled from dumpsters and would have been pushed for miles. Dealers on street corners standing there trying to blend in, each with their own patch of ground, selling a ticket out for an hour or sometimes forever.

The cab took a right on Main and stopped outside the strip club.

Here we go, Chendrill thought as he parked up along the road and watched the door. An hour later more people had gone in for the lunchtime show, some had left and headed back down into town on foot or by cab, but none of them had long blonde hair and tight jeans.

He got out, crossed the road and went inside, found a seat in the corner and sat down. He looked at the stage in the centre where he'd found the loan shark and Dan drunk that time before and remembered the kid banging his hand down on the side of the stage.

He ordered a beer from the waitress and watched the girl with the nice legs prance about the stage, slowly taking her clothes off. Then as the daylight came through the front door as it opened and closed again, he saw the Italian come in and take a seat in a booth at the side. Chendrill watched as the man waited for a moment then ordered a beer himself. A minute later Suzy was there dressed like an overaged school girl coming down from up the stairs next to the rear exit. She walked through the bar, sat down next to the loan shark and kissed him on the lips.

They stayed together as the dancer on the stage slowly got naked, twisted and turned until she was down on a silk blanket spread across the stage on her front and back giving slight glimpses of her snatch to men who stared at it as though they had just seen gold.

Another dancer appeared as the music slowed and the DJ revved up the afternoon crowd who were not listening as the girl, still prancing, wrapped herself up in the silk blanket and left the stage. The DJ called out now to 'Give it up ladies and gentlemen for the amazing Lucyyyy!' But there were no ladies or gentlemen there in any sense of the word—in the evenings perhaps, sometimes, ladies on a night out with friends, out for a laugh and something different or the odd couple having fun and looking to get horny so as they can carry it over to the bedroom when they got home. But not that afternoon—just lap dancers and strippers, sad fucks, an Italian loan shark, and Chendrill.

Lucy got up on the stage and wondered why the men were not looking at her as they had the other girl as she spun around the pole in her tight leather skirt that did little to disguise the fact she was bigger than the last girl. The guys surrounding the stage looking up occasionally but mostly they were on their phones. Chendrill looked through her on the stage as the girl danced around as the loan shark and Suzy held hands and talked. Suzy listening intently, nodding as the man spoke. Then with another kiss that was long and full the Italian was up and out, washing the walls with afternoon blue as he left.

Suzy stood, moving along the side of the bar and sat herself down next to a middle-aged man in middle management who'd been staring at her tits ever since she'd come down the stairs. The man unable to resist the pull of her stretched lacy blouse and her purple bra underneath showing through, and the smell of her perfume as she leaned into him and spoke for a while, smiling as she did with her hand halfway up his thigh, telling him this was going to be the last lap dance of her life so she was going to make it good.

Chendrill watched as they both stood and Suzy took the man by the hand and led him to the stairs up to the champagne room. Waiting a minute, he looked around the bar for the next partially dressed lap dancing girl who was about to pass him by and said yes before the girl could even ask.

They walked up the stairs next to each other, the young girl who should have known better in her early twenties. Cocaine can do that though, change a person's perspective and make them hang with the wrong crowd. She said, "It's $40.00 for two songs."

Chendrill saying straight back, "How about we stay in there till I'm ready to go and I'll pay you $500.00?"

The girl stopped midway on the stairs and stood there in her high heels and little knickers and semi top, trying to look sexy at the same time as she said, "It's cash up front. I need it for the guy at the door."

They passed the guy at the top of the stairs whom the girls gave half their money to when they'd fleeced some punter. Chendrill looked at the door which led to the room to where dreams were made. The first song was halfway through and that meant he'd get in for Suzy's second. He said, "Sure."

He paid in cash, five one-hundred dollar bills, of which half went to the house and the other went to the girl's dealer. The bouncer at the door listening to the small earpiece connected to his security radio smiling at Chendrill as he held the young girl by her arm and pulled her to him—the big brute of a man, whispering sweet nothings to a girl he'd never get to sleep with even if he wanted to pay. They went inside. The room was dark; chairs lined the wall along with two speakers, three girls were working there already despite it being midday. Two brunettes, and Suzy with her back to them sitting on her man's lap as they came in. Suzy working her magic, grinding herself down as the man in middle management sat there with hover hands, staring fixated at Sebastian's friend's breasts.

Chendrill nodded to the darkest corner of the room and sat down and pulled the girl down onto him to cover his face. Straddling him, the girl began to grind herself down onto his groin as she leaned forward, letting her hair fall into his face which suited him fine. Suzy there in front of him, now in her panties and bra, pushing down into the man's lap in time to the music as she leaned her head back and stared at the ceiling as she moved. Her bare back showing in the low light of the room.

Chendrill looked at the girl who was on his lap seeing her now properly for the first time, feeling her hands on his shoulders as she moved her groin against his dick. She was quite beautiful with her little six pack and full breasts, her hair long with little earrings that caught the light. One day, he thought, if she ever got her act together some guy was going to be a lucky man and the man would never know about the secret she had. Then he felt her lean in and whisper in his ear, "If you like blondes with big tits you should have waited for that guy to finish."

Then she backed off and pushed hers into Chendrill's face, pulled out both nipples with her right hand and leaned in, lifting herself off his lap, teasing them across his lips, saying, "You like that do you?"

Chendrill did—in fact, he couldn't not. He felt himself getting hard and then harder as the girl dropped herself back onto his lap and grinned at what she found there.

Feeling guilty for the moment for forgetting about Sebastian as the girl looked to his eyes, Chendrill smiled with her as she raised her eyebrows to him. Slowly moving his head to the side, Chendrill looked back to Suzy as she leaned in and spoke to the man she was teasing before her. The man nodded back as Suzy began to take her bra off. Then slowly Chendrill watched as Suzy spun herself around and leaned back on the man as she found his hands and pulled them to her tits.

Chendrill sank back, hiding behind the girl's head. He'd seen her back in the half light and now he could see her stomach as the man in the cheap suit mauled on the breasts of the lady whom Sebastian had bought a home for. Suzy grinding the man's dick with her ass cheeks now as she let him feel her, while she felt nothing and looked at just as much around the room.

As far as Chendrill could see, there were no visible wounds or discreetly positioned plasters covering any form of recently ended surgery large or small. The woman was full of shit and there was no bag attached for it to squeeze into. He heard the girl grinding into him say as she whispered into his ear and pushed her breasts into his now open shirt, "You want to fuck me don't you? You want me to pull it out and slip it into me, don't you?" He did, in fact it would be quite nice, but not here in this shitty room, but back at his place or in a fancy hotel somewhere. Where he could lay her on the bed, pull out his hard cock, and fuck her for the rest of the afternoon.

He answered with a smile, "No."

The girl continued egging him on, still whispering into his ear as she rubbed herself on him, saying back to him, "Slip it in me, get it out and slide it in, I want you to, come on, no one will know, it's dark in here, I love your chest and you're so hard you're making me so excited, my panties are soaked. Come on Mr. PI fuck me, fuck me Mr. PI."

So as not to draw attention to himself, Chendrill gently pushed the girl away from him and looked her in the eyes as she continued to grind herself into him. She smiled. This wasn't the same girl he'd asked a few days back to let him know if the Italian arrived again, in fact she wasn't even there. He whispered into her ear, "How did you know I was a PI?"

And the girl leaning in whispered back, "Because the guy outside here told me you were and said the ones downstairs on the door just said I could keep the other half of the $500 if I could get you to get your dick out and then slap you in the face for doing so."

The cheeky fuckers, Chendrill thought, as he smiled and looked at her and then at the door and then around the room to see if he could spot the hidden camera they must have installed in case some nut job got out of hand. He couldn't see one. *What a strange place to be on the day you discover you've been left a fortune*, he thought, as he looked back to Suzy. The guy she was sitting on having to have just come in his pants as he'd let go of her breasts and was now looking at the floor. Suzy, the lap dance pro, would have known it as soon as he did as well and was now pulling her bra back on and starting to get up. The girl on Chendrill's lap undeterred and still trying to achieve the same and grinding hard with her hands on his shoulders. It wouldn't be much time before Suzy knew there was a PI watching her and Chendrill wondered if his new girl for $500 worth of shitty songs also knew his name.

Chendrill watched as the man got up and, without looking Suzy in the eye, gathered himself together. *It must be a usual sight for her*, Chendrill thought, with her having breasts like that and then letting guys touch them for an extra few dollars. Moments later they were gone and watching the door close, Chendrill leaned in as the girl continued to grind down up on him and said to the girl through her long brunette hair, "Times up."

Suzy had not been there when Chendrill came downstairs and he wondered if she was cleaning herself up after feeling the guy leak. Passing the girl on the stage without looking up, he smiled as he hit the door, and said, "Get your own dicks out," with a grin to the doormen as he walked out into the sunshine.

****

Ditcon was at home and in the middle of a deep, deep sleep and dreaming when he heard his mother calling, "Ralphy, Ralphy, come and have your din dins, Ralphy Ralphy." Slowly he came around as his mother's voice became louder and louder until he eventually woke to see he was in his office with his head on the desk. Stephanie called him again, and said, "You should see this."

He sat up and looked over to the computer Stephanie was using and looked at the screen. It was early morning footage of a guy who was the size of Chendrill limping badly and getting on a bus inside a small terminus. Ditcon asked, "What the fuck is this shit?"

Stephanie replied, smiling at Ditcon as she did, "I think it's Chendrill, it's the Tsawwassen bus depot a few minutes after the stolen US CBP patrol car was taken and crashed at the border and was dumped just up the road from here."

Still half asleep, Ditcon looked closer. In his dream he'd been looking forward to a nice glass of warm milk and a cookie from his mother as he came back to reality. He wondered if he'd had his mouth open while he'd been asleep and said to Stephanie, "Was I out long?"

He had been—and with his mouth open, and he'd been snoring loudly and talking about his mother saying, "Mummy Mummy," in fact it was almost an hour and that's why, out of boredom, Stephanie had started looking at the footage the RCMP had sent about the border breach a few days back.

"No," Stephanie said, lying, and carried it on further, "sorry I didn't even know you were asleep."

Ditcon stood, then sat again. His neck was sore; he rubbed it with his right hand and wondered why it ached like it did. Then he remembered. Maybe he should go clean his teeth he thought, but he'd thrown the old toothbrush he used to keep in the office out some time ago and he kept forgetting to replace it. He said, "you've made my neck ache."

To which Stephanie said straight back, "You've made your own neck ache."

He looked at the screen—she was right, it did look like Chendrill. *How fucking strange is that?* he thought. It must be a coincidence. After all, why would the big cocky fucker be all the way down there at that time of the morning, and, at the same time, be taking the bus? Unless it was him. Looking closer, he said, "I don't think the guy's wearing shoes, he's in his socks." It was a brilliant piece of detective work. Then he asked, "Do you have footage of the bus when it got into Vancouver?"

Stephanie did. In fact, she'd already checked all the

way back to the end of the route the bus had taken and it was where the guy limping in his socks had gotten off. That's where she'd lost him. She clicked the screen a couple more times and there she had him again—the guy who looked like Chendrill in his socks getting out of the bus with his head down. Ditcon stared at the image and made a decision in his mind. *It wasn't him. No way, not a chance.* So, he said, "Yep that's him—I got the fucker, let's bring him in and see what he has to say."

Then Stephanie dropped the bombshell and said, "There's something else I just found out. That guy I told you about yesterday, the one who went off the bridge?"

Ditcon didn't know a thing about it even though he'd been told as he hadn't been listening. Nodding and feeling his neck hurt for real for the first time in a while, he said, "Yep! What about him?"

"Well it was the guy this Charles Chuck Chendrill worked for, the same guy who's been supplying the cars."

Ditcon stared at the girl who had been worried sick about working with the boss, but who now had become his new best friend—kind of. At least until he or she got bored. He smiled. Then he said to her as he leaned back and rubbed his neck, "As I've always said over the years, you need to take coincidences as leads."

And, strangely, as coincidences happened, a few years ago, one wet and windy day, a man's body had been discovered in a garden shed after falling on some garden shears, whilst the man's wife was away in Jamaica. It had been Chendrill who had told him those same words, except Chendrill had said, "There's only one way to look at a coincidence and that's to take it as a bonafide lead."

And as always, Chendrill had been right because, after

all, how often do people pop out to do a bit of gardening on a rainy day? So after looking at the CCTV footage at the airport of the wife leaving and at the family photos on the mantelpiece, it was obvious the two people were very, very similar but it wasn't the wife getting on the plane—the woman had stayed behind and stuck the shears into the man's chest, then taken another plane the same day using the identity of her female lover with her hair dyed.

Ditcon carried on, pleased with himself now, his gut instinct telling him prior that it was Chendrill who'd crossed the border and gotten his neighbours all in a flap. He said, "You see, you've got to follow your hunches, sometimes it's all you have to go on. That's what I did here with this fucking has-been detective."

Stephanie looked at Ralph 'The Thief" Ditcon and stayed quiet. She'd only said they should accuse this big ass Chuck Chendrill as a joke in the first place because she didn't like the fact her boss was being disrespected by the smart ass who drove around in an expensive car.

"Yeah that's why I like being around you. I'm learning so much," she said.

They put out word through the computer system that they needed the location of Basil's car and his whereabouts also. Within half an hour, a few diligent police officers had done just that.

They found Basil in a café just off Howe Street downtown. The border security agent there at a table with Maio and her other friend from Japan. All three of them sitting around a table looking at photos Maio's sister Kaio had sent her of the boyfriend that she'd had when she was in Vancouver. Basil there looking at photos of himself sitting in a bath with all these bubbles and a big Cuban cigar like a poor man's Tony Montana. The friend giggling, like girls do, and saying in Japanese, "He looks like this man's fat brother."

The two police cars sitting outside left as Ditcon's car pulled up and parked illegally outside the café. Ditcon getting straight out, not waiting while his new girl followed behind, saying out loud to her as he opened the door, "Get me something sticky and a double caramel macchiato—and make it marbled."

Without an invite, he sat straight down next to Basil and watched as the two pretty Japanese girls pulled back automatically in their chairs. He said, "I think I've got your man for certain this time, Captain America."

****

Mazzi Hegan still wasn't sure what to do or why as he walked about in Sebastian's penthouse. His life had just turned itself upside down. A few weeks ago, he was happily gay, working as a photographer for Sebastian and worrying about his taxes, and now he was straight and for the moment in charge of the company until this nymphomaniac Gill Banton decided to pull up her wet panties and hop on a plane and get herself up here. On top of it all, he had to decide what items he wanted to keep at the new penthouse apartment Sebastian had just gifted him in his will.

Why the fuck he'd done that to himself, he couldn't understand, making a pact like that with some guy who he'd met at university. *What the fuck?* of all the guys he'd known when he'd liked that sort of thing, not one of them had a dick big enough that it was worth following them to the grave for. But those days were gone, before he'd had a boy's penthouse that had been designed for sex with men. Now he had a man pad with an ocean view that was sophisticated, with Persian rugs and ornaments from around the world that were something beyond trend or style. He'd change it about a bit, get rid of some of the matching plate sets, and women would love it—but the place would still have the air of a single gay man about it, so there was still a chance it would leave them suspicious. He could leave his builder's boots at the door and surprise them when they got inside. That would do the job and erase any doubt. Let them ride the elevator and think they were going to one of the one-bedroom man shacks on the lower levels and end up instead in paradise. Then if he was lucky, he could fuck them on one of the rugs that probably had fleas because of the dog.

But for the moment he just felt like crying as he walked about the place that still smelled of his friend. Sebastian had driven him mad on almost a constant basis but he'd been a good boss. They'd had their spats and tiffs and how many times had Mazzi quit and told the world he wanted to go to Milan, he didn't know—but he could now, he thought, as the idea of selling and leaving crossed his mind again.

Then his phone rang—it was Gill Banton. She said, "Oh Mazzi, I'm so sorry about Sebastian. I've just been talking to Samuel, we're working out a deal. Who's this Chendrill guy who's got all the shares in Slave, the man probably thinks a forty-mil is the size of his dick?"

Wow, thought Mazzi, just like that the woman—like any good agent—was heading in straight for the kill. Knowing only too well that Gill Banton would be in bed with some model as she spoke and something inside Mazzi was wishing it was him.

“What are you doing at the moment, Gill?”

“I’ve been so upset all day, Mazzi, I just had to have a lay-down,” she said.

I bet, Mazzi thought, as he looked out at the view of the bay that Sebastian loved and wondered if he’d ever get Gill Banton up here to his new penthouse so she could see it also while he was fucking her doggy style from behind. He said, “Same Gill, I’m at Sebastian’s place now. He’s given it to me. It’s fantastic, it must be the nicest penthouse in the city,” which it was, “I can’t believe the view.”

"I’d love to see it when I come up, Mazzi,” Gill Banton said, lying—since the man was gay there was no reason to be alone in his new penthouse with him, even if it did have a view. But then she had an idea and said, “Maybe we could have that Dan guy over there with the two of us so as we could discuss his contract?” *If the boy swung both ways it could be an interesting evening*, she thought.

Mazzi sat down on the sofa that was now his and thought about how many times Sebastian would have sat there also, listening to music as he played with his dog. There was no way he was letting Dan near this woman alone—not after the last time. He’d get her up here, thinking Dan was coming, then the guy wouldn’t show and she’d be here on her own. He could get a few glasses of expensive wine in her from Sebastian’s collection and then start flirting. He’d need to do that, play it cool. Not just get his dick out with a chubby on and put it on the table like he had with guys in the past. He had a classy home now and he needed to act that way.

“Yeah sounds like a plan, Gill.”

Then without a word, she was gone. Mazzi stared at the

phone wondering if she was going to call back and after a while realised she wasn't. It was her way. He sat there looking through the window at the view and the seagulls as they passed by, cruising for food. *Gill Banton* he thought, *Gill fucking Banton.* Not long ago, he'd been repulsed by her because she had better hair and nails. Now though all he wanted to do was have his way with her—her and Marshaa of course. He opened his phone and typed in Gill Banton and straight away a bunch of photos came up. One with a hot Peruvian model who looked familiar, then another Dutch guy who she'd just fucked. Then another guy from Barcelona who she definitely hadn't—because Mazzi once upon a time had, and there was no way the guy liked fish.

Then he had the greatest idea. As he had more shares than her, he'd make sure that when she was up, he'd only hire gay guys to model, like Phillipe Tu La Monde so she'd have nowhere else to go but to him. *But no*, he thought, telling himself off, he needed to start growing up if he was going to get somewhere with his life. He needed to be professional. But deep down he knew he was on to something.

****

Chendrill looked at the old lady dressed in black sitting on the chair outside before he entered the doors to the funeral parlor. Standing in the reception for a moment, he looked around at the somber room until the man, who looked as though the years of using formaldehyde had taken its toll, came in from the back.

Sebastian's final journey was about to commence. His now bloated and broken body was wrapped in a shroud at the rear of the facility awaiting cremation. But there was to be no wake or lavish celebration of life, no big bash full of weeping fair-weather friends that one would expect from a man who had spent his life promoting others into the limelight with parties and elaborate openings necessary for the elevation of status from mere mortal to prince or princess.

For all Sebastian had asked for as a final request, which his friend and lawyer Samuel Gadot had read aloud at the reading of the will to anyone who was still listening, were these words which he asked kindly for all who knew him well to abide to.

'I've never liked funerals, ghastly affairs in my eyes, and I'm not going to subject anyone to mine. So, keeping this in mind: please, I ask—no service, no funeral, no ceremony, for me. If you have tears please shed them, yes, and say your goodbyes in a place of your choosing and with those tears wherever you are, know I will be with you. I'm gone and I bid you farewell with these words.' But in those words were a 'get out' clause for Chendrill because although the time and date for Sebastian's quiet lonely cremation was a guarded secret, it was here Chendrill had chosen to say his thanks and his goodbyes to a man who had become a true friend.

The undertaker who dressed in black for a living stepped out from the back and told Chendrill about the backlog he had today in the crematorium because one of the burners was down—when in reality he'd been waiting for the guy who loaded the corpses into it to come back from lunch. It being easier to watch a soap on TV instead of doing his job. The guy in his sixties, wearing one of the two black suits bought for him each year by a wife whom he hated because she was a bitch. The man standing there in the reception with his head down feeling fine inside but looking morose for no other reason other than that's what he did.

Chendrill asked him straight, "What are we waiting for?"

It was a good question. The undertaker looked up at him solemnly, then he turned, walked to, and held open the doors that led out back to the area where people didn't like to go. They reached the ovens, the man asking respectfully for Chendrill to wait—the floor unfinished in the corridor, the place stinking of formaldehyde and the sweet sickly stench that comes from death.

A minute later, the kid who was late back from lunch for no other reason than he was lazy came backwards through a door, pushing a gurney that carried a shrouded corpse. Reaching Chendrill he stopped, looked at him and, pulling out his phone, began texting.

"Is this Mr String?" asked Chendrill.

Looking up at him for a moment then nodding to the label at the foot of the gurney, the kid went straight back to his phone.

Slowly Chendrill looked away from the kid and down at Sebastian's wrapped body.

Not taking his eyes off the screen on his phone, the kid shifted his body weight off the wall and, with one hand, lined up Sebastian's gurney with the crematorium, ready for him to slide inside.

Chendrill looked into the chamber. The burners were ready to ignite but there was ash covering its base mixed with the residue of silicone. Chendrill looked at the kid and said, "Clean this out please before you put my friend in there."

The kid looked at him. "Sorry?"

"You need to clean the incinerator."

The kid rolled his eyes as he finished texting, then putting his phone in the pocket of his black cover jacket he said as he began to carry on, "It's silicone, you can't get it out."

Placing his hand on the gurney, Chendrill stopped the kid in his tracks. The last thing he needed was Sebastian's ashes mixed up with some dead woman's tits. He said, "You need to clean it."

The kid said it again, this time in a tone that had always worked with his mum, "You can't get it out; it's baked in. It's not policy."

Policy? Chendrill thought, *what a load of bullshit.* Chendrill said, "Imagine that it was you going in there because last night you were getting all fucked on E and coke with your friends but instead knocked backed some fentanyl."

"Wouldn't give a shit," the kid said.

Chendrill scoffed, then carried on saying, "Well maybe your mother would care, so, un bake it, turn on the burner, heat it up in there, open the door, and scrape it out."

Reluctantly the kid closed the door, hit the button to ignite the burner and walked away.

Chendrill stood there alone with Sebastian. *When was the last time they had a private moment?* he thought, *it was in the limo*, but Belinda had been there. Nonetheless, it was their time.

"We can't have you mixed up with some chick who was big in the nineties, can we Sebastian?" he said.

He looked over to the door as it opened and the kid

came back down, this time carrying a shovel and a metal bucket stained yellow from cigarette butts. Without a word, he shut off the burner and opened the door, blasting heat and ash out on purpose from the door's vacuum as he did. He waited a second before lifting the shovel and scraping the silicone and ash from the bottom of the incinerator. He looked back up at Chendrill as he dropped the last of the steaming goo into the bottom of the bucket, and said, "Like I said, we're busy."

Chendrill snapped straight back, "Yeah, well you can get busier and go get a broom, be respectful, and clean out the rest of the ash from the poor soul who you put in there last."

"Whatever," said the kid as he walked away, clanking the bucket against the wall as he did for effect. Reaching the door, he called out without looking back, "I'm not the one who turned up here dressed like I'm about to go on holiday."

Cocky fuck, Chendrill thought, as he looked down at his red Hawaiian. The kid had a point. He said straight back, "If you don't like your job, go work at McDonalds."

Without making eye contact, the kid came back to the incinerator and stood next to Sebastian's body lying on the gurney. Reaching in with the broom, he pulled back ash with one slow exaggerated stroke after the other, each time letting some of the remnants of the woman who'd once been so proud of her cleavage fall onto the floor. Eventually when the incinerator was clean, the kid looked up at him. Chendrill smiled and said, "Now how hard was that?"

Without a word, the kid then raised the gurney and slid Sebastian feet first inside and as he was about to shut the door, he heard Chendrill say, "I got this."

The kid looked at him and said, "You ain't allowed, I've got to do it proper."

"Like last time?" Chendrill said as he stood there with his hand on the door waiting for the kid to now leave.

Turning, the kid began to walk away, he reached the door and was almost through when he called out, "Everyone's an expert!"

Chendrill watched the kid disappear and the door close behind him with a slam. He reached in and gently pulled the shroud away from Sebastian's pale and ghostly bloated face. Chendrill looked at him for a moment, Sebastian there with his eyes closed. He kissed his fingers on his right hand and gently touched them to Sebastian's head and after stroked his hair and said, "Thank you, my friend. I will miss you."

Chendrill closed the door tightly, and just as he'd seen the kid do earlier, he reached to the lever on the side, pulled it down, hit the button to ignite the burner, and stood there feeling the heat rise through the burners beyond the metal door and watched through the little observation window as the golden light took over.

A half hour later, he was back outside stepping through the office door with Sebastian's ashes in a box under his arm. The lady in black who was there before was now gone. He walked up some steps and through an ornate memorial garden and headed towards his car. Then he saw her standing there to the side, under a tree, looking to him, as though she had been waiting for Chendrill all along. As he passed, she called out to him, "Sebastian thanks you for looking after him."

Slowing, Chendrill looked over and was about to speak

when he then heard her say, “He is also thanking you for the kiss.”

Chendrill felt the hairs on his neck and arms stand on end as he stopped. He looked over at the woman standing there almost like a ghost herself and remembered Sebastian talking about her from time to time. Not wanting to move closer, he called out as it dawned on him who the woman was, “You’re the one who called—Sebastian’s friend?”

She was Sebastian’s friend indeed, if you can call someone you habitually saw and paid for inane spiritual advice in the form of a palm reading a friend. The woman sitting on a little stool at her makeshift table, outside the shoe shops on Robson Street dressed in her best gypsy clothes and holding Sebastian’s hand. Week after week turned into month after month in which Sebastian had sat and listened as she read his palm, spouting bullshit about Alan being happy and passing on Sebastian’s lover’s kind words. Sebastian, being Sebastian, seeing it all for what it was, but loving it anyway.

Without a yes or a no, the lady simply said, “He’s saying, stay away from Casper Street.”

****

Chendrill pulled out onto the main road holding onto Sebastian’s ashes in the box as he did and thought, *What the fuck was that? Jesus. Fuck. That woman was creepy.* Sebastian had mentioned her once or twice in the brief time they’d known each other, suggesting he should go see her, telling Chendrill how sweet she was and how she knew stuff that she shouldn’t.

But soothsayers weren’t his thing, especially ones that sat on the street with everyone passing by who’d be wondering what the big fellow was missing so much in his life that he felt the need to go sit on a little stool too small for his backside.

It wasn't long after Chendrill headed back into town before he'd gotten two calls. The first from Sebastian's accountant who needed a bank account number to put his money into and then ten minutes later another from the girl on the front desk at Slave who said a lady by the name of Suzy had been in and she'd been crying in the waiting room as she wanted to talk to whoever was in charge. Chendrill said, "Tell her to meet me at the same place she used to meet Sebastian."

Chendrill was back out the door and sitting alone in the park with the sun on his back watching the road and the bench where the unlikely friends had met over the last little while. He wanted to see who was bringing her there—her loser husband or her bigger parasite loser boyfriend, and when she arrived, it was neither. The first he saw of her was her blonde hair waving in the wind as she stepped out of a taxi up at the top of the steps that led down to the park by the water. Suzy coming towards him, looking good in her signature tight blouse and stretch jeans with high heels. Moving down the steps sideways so as not to fall and holding her bag in the crux of her elbow. She moved along past the fountains where children liked to play and hit the seawall—guys discretely looking one way then the next as she passed. Chendrill standing way away, watching everything.

Five minutes later as she sat alone, he was next to her and heard her say as he sat down, "I'm sorry, do you mind. I'm waiting for someone. We always meet here."

And Chendrill said, "I'm sorry to tell you that

someone's not here anymore. He's passed on." Suzy looked to Chendrill as though she had not heard him properly. Then as she realized the guy wo had just sat down in the loud shirt was the person she had asked to meet, she said, "Yes, sorry, I know but it's just hard to accept right now."

Chendrill was too, sorry to have lost a friend, sorry to have had to sit there and not been allowed to thump out the piece of shit lawyer who knew Sebastian was about to end it all and did nothing other than invoice. "Yeah I am too," he said as he took a deep breath.

Suzy looked at him as her eyes began to well up with tears, "So it's true, he's gone?"

"Yep," is all Chendrill said as he looked to nothing out on the water.

"How?"

He told her everything about how promises to Sebastian were sacred and how he'd made one to his boyfriend that they'd meet again, all three of them, once the dog had died. He waited as she shed real tears, gut wrenching tears. Her head in her hands with her hair hanging at the side.

Chendrill waited and watched without offering a hand to console. Then when she was done and Suzy had pulled a small tissue from her bag and wiped her eyes and blew her nose, she surprised him by saying, "Yeah that Alan was always a selfish piece of shit."

****

Dan sat in his room and wondered what it was going to be like having to fend for himself once his mother had stopped crying and called a realtor. Patrick had been all over her about it since it looked like he was going to have to dust off a couple of his favourite patterned cashmere sweaters that had survived the cull. For the moment, she'd said she would wait. But Dan was wondering how long. She hadn't said, 'It's okay Dan if I do move I'll make sure there's a shitty little room in the basement you can live in love.' So, from what he could tell, the computer, TV, sound system and the bench with the red vice that Sebastian had bought were heading downtown to his swanky new pad with its pictures of guys having man-sex on the bedroom ceiling—once that weirdo Mazzi Hegan got the fuck out that is.

What a strange turn of events, he thought, stealing some keys to a penthouse and a Ferrari and ending up owning both, and on top of it all he had Marshaa, voted the most beautiful woman in the world, naked in his basement bedroom sucking his cock.

Pulling his dick from her mouth, 'Marshaa', as she now liked to be called, said, "What's the matter, why can't you come?"

Dan looked down at her as she kneeled at the edge of her bed and noticed she'd put a couple of crusty socks from beneath the bed under her knees. He said, "It's because my mum's upstairs." It wasn't—what would he care, he'd fucked almost everything in the fridge over the years with his mum upstairs, so why should having a supermodel over be any different. After all he was getting evicted soon anyway? But there were two reasons: one, he needed to go to the toilet; and the other was that there was a man looking in the window and he was carrying a hockey stick.

He said, "And there's a guy staring at me through the window."

Marshaa stayed still for the moment and looked up at Dan. She'd seen the curtains were open in the low window but in the heat of the moment she'd forgotten to close them. Now she wondered if it was a Pap who'd followed her there and gotten lucky. She said, “Is he a Pap?”

"No, he drives a cab.”

“Has he got a camera?”

“No, a hockey stick,” Dan answered,

“Oh?” Marshaa replied, as she let go of Dan’s now semi-hard dick altogether and pulled on a t-shirt Dan had not seen for months from under the bed. She turned, looked to the man and called out through the run-down home’s basement window, “You've got the wrong address. We don't take taxis—we have chauffeurs!”

****

It wasn’t long before Ditcon also had Chendrill in his sights after sending out the boys to look for the big guy. When they’d found him, he was talking to some lady with blonde hair over on the seawall in the park at Coal Harbour.

Stephanie pulled the car up and joined Ditcon as he watched Chendrill chatting away with the good-looking blonde. *The dirty bastard, I bet he’s fucking her,* Ditcon thought as he wished he had some binoculars so he could get a better look at the woman. Holding out his hand without looking back, he said, “Binoculars,” and opening the glove box, Stephanie looked inside.

“There aren’t any,” she replied.

And straight away she heard the man tut, then heard him say surprisingly without any hint of frustration or annoyance, “Well, get on the radio and have some binoculars bought to me ASAP.” Picking up her radio, Stephanie called it in and with screaming sirens and flashing lights, the binoculars made their way through red lights and traffic across town. Four minutes and forty-five seconds later, they were with him.

Ditcon took the binoculars from the cop who was good at the wheel without saying thanks, gave the man a talking to for being so fucking noisy, then followed it up with, "Now turn those lights off and get out of here."

Ditcon smiled to Stephanie as they watched the police car pull away. He put the glass to his eyes and focussed in on the happy couple. He was right, the woman had big tits—and long legs, skinny ankles, nice face, big sunglasses on the top of her head. Chendrill was in his usual, standard issue, stupid Hawaiian—the fucking prick. He said to Stephanie, "Can you lip read?"

Stephanie gave it some thought and unless Chendrill was sitting across from her in a bar and mouthing, 'I want to fuck you, right now,' the answer was no. She said, "It's not in my skill set."

Nodding again without looking back and taking his eyes away from the glass, he said, "We need a lip reader." She called it in and ten minutes later they had one.

The lady got out of the police car and still shaking got into the backseat of Ditcon's vehicle and sat next him. Ditcon looked at her—she was older and he didn't like her shoes or her nylon dress. He asked, "You bring your own binoculars?"

She hadn't. This was a pain. He said, "If you're in this line of work, then you need to turn up with the right equipment. You need to keep glasses with you at all times. It's basic police procedure."

The woman looked to her handbag and pulled out her reading glasses. She said, "I'm a school teacher, but my son is deaf. They said it was a national emergency."

Ditcon dropped his binoculars into his lap and looked to the lady who was a school teacher but had a kid who was deaf. *What the fuck?* he thought. What are these pricks doing giving him bargain basement manpower? He handed the binoculars to the lady and said, "If you've got a deaf kid how does he watch TV properly?" It was something he'd always wondered, same for blind kids. Then he said, "Don't worry, there's a guy down there in a Hawaiian. We need to know what he's talking about and the woman with the blonde hair we need to know what she's saying also."

The woman lifted the binoculars to her eyes and as she did she understood what this intense man was referring to when he'd talked about glass. Because of the shirt, she found Chendrill with ease, looked at him and then at Suzy, then to Suzy's breasts. *God, they're big,* she thought—*nice, the lucky girl*, she liked the blouse too, the way the buttons stretched only just keeping them in. She thought about her own and how she'd done the same for her husband when she'd tried to get sexy for him sometimes in the bedroom and how when she'd got him all hot and excited and he'd licked her down there and then made love to her, she had screamed as loud as she wanted without the fear of waking her kid.

Something had been bothering Stephanie, something the woman had said didn't add up. Turning in her driver's seat she asked, "May I ask, if it's your son who's deaf then how come you can lip read also?"

Ditcon said, butting in, "We haven't got time for chit-chat—what are they saying?"

The school teacher, taking her aim up to Suzy's mouth, waited a bit and then said, "They're talking about a house, they're talking about the bay window."

And they were, Chendrill sitting there hearing how sorry Suzy was about the way her husband had thrown Chendrill through the window and was worrying if he was okay.

Chendrill assured her he was fine. He had already gotten it out of her how she knew Alan and had confirmed the fact that the woman had bad taste in men. He'd also found out that the loan shark was an old boyfriend who had a brother who also had a 'friend', and how Suzy knew the brother was gay because he'd not once looked below her chin. She'd said, "They had this thing where they would go to horse races around the province. But I always thought it was an excuse, because from what I could see the horse they had always came last, so why bother unless it was to get away?"

Chendrill asked if she'd ever met Sebastian in the past. She said she had, at parties years before, and he'd been so sweet. Then this year, earlier in the spring, she'd had another row with her husband one afternoon and been walking along the path where they sat right now and she'd heard her name called out and at first she thought it was a man from the bar or some kind of stalker, but then she'd seen the dog and it had all clued in. Not long after that, she'd met the ex-boyfriend again.

So that was the connection, Chendrill had thought as he'd heard the sirens working their way towards the park through the city, then seen the glimpse of light reflecting off the front of the glass flash a couple of times from the side of a car parked on the road up top. With all the commotion, someone up there was watching someone in the park and they weren't being very discreet. The odds were high they were watching him.

Chendrill asked, "What's he do for a living, this ex-boyfriend?"

"Lends money," Suzy answered, without a beat. Then she carried on straight after with, "He's always got cash on him, he's never short."

Then Chendrill asked, "So why had he been hitting up Sebastian for $250,000?"

Suzy stopped talking and looked at Chendrill in surprise. She said, "I'm sorry." But the woman wasn't sorry, not one bit, she was confused. She asked again, but this time in another manner, "He did what?"

Chendrill carried on, the man having enough experience to spot a liar or trickster—there was always body language that showed in their breathing, or a small look to the floor, the rubbing of the neck or the constant touching of their hair and this woman was showing not one sign. She was, from all he was hearing and seeing, just an honest woman and Sebastian hadn't been wrong.

"He was hitting him up for $250,000. He said it was for the horse that died."

Suzy looked away and then back, the woman obviously pissed off, the way they can be when they hear someone they care about has gone behind their back. She said, "I can tell you, the only people who'd have paid top dollar for that nag were the people who made glue. I'll tell you what it was right now—Sebastian went behind his boyfriend's back and offered my Mattia's brother $250,000 for the horse, but what it was really for was for his brother to back off and stay away from the man Sebastian loved. I know these guys were all crazy back then, fucking each other, it's the way they all carried on, even Sebastian, but he saw something more with those two, and it was something he needed to stop. I know he approached Mattia to broker the deal."

Chendrill sat there looking out to sea. *Wow,* he thought. It was the way Sebastian worked—he'd seen it himself—the man threw money at things. It was kind of one of the good and the bad traits he had about himself. He said, "And you hooked up with this Italian again and told him Sebastian was still around and you'd met, and Sebastian was being kind and buying you a house and the next thing the man's going around dragging up the past and wanting his piece of the pie?"

Suzy looked at Chendrill and said, "Yeah, it seems that way, doesn't it? I'm surprised he's still interested in me after he realized what I'd been doing for a living over the last decade or so. But I'm telling you, after I'd told him about the house, I made him swear on my life that he'd leave Sebastian be."

They sat for a moment, both staying quiet as Suzy calmed down and Chendrill took it all in. Then Chendrill said, "Sebastian mentioned to me you had a medical issue he was worried about. How is it?"

Suzy looked to Chendrill and he could tell she was uncomfortable with the question. He said, "Sebastian and I were very close. But not in that way. He was worried about you."

Suzy, took a deep breath and then blushed, then after tussling her hair, said, "Yeah, I've got this bag. I had something happen to me and now I have to wear it for a while, you know, while things heal."

Chendrill nodded, then asked, "So how does having this bag affect you when you're moonlighting at the club?"

Suzy stared at him for a moment, working it all out, putting the pieces to her own puzzle together in her head. She said, "That was you today then? You sent the PI that I heard was there into the club and had me watched, yeah?"

Chendrill nodded, then said, "Kind of."

"Yeah, they said someone had been up in the room.... And now you're wondering how a girl can lap dance when she's got a bag."

Chendrill stayed quiet.

"Well first, we need the money—I know I got this job at the school, but it's wasn't enough and there's not a lot of work at the docks for my husband, you know?"

Chendrill did know. Vancouver docks were busy; there was always work there if you wanted to work hard when you turned up. But if you didn't, the work would go to someone else—unless you were in with the right people. Suzy carried on, "So, I knew there were bills coming up and I didn't want to ask Sebastian as I was so happy he'd found a home for us and I was embarrassed about what happened with my stupid thug of a husband and the window. So I went back for a bit and, well, I took the bag out for a bit and taped the tube to my skin with sticking plaster. You can do that."

"Oh?" Chendrill said, not sounding that convinced. Having seen pretty much all her skin when he'd been in the room a few hours earlier.

"You don't believe me?" Suzy asked. Chendrill stayed quiet. Then with a rush of blood to her head, Suzy reached down to her jeans and, with her long false nails bending as she did, she unbuttoned them, pulled them to the side, and then pushed down the same knickers he'd seen her in earlier to reveal a colostomy bag attached to the bottom of the left-hand side of her stomach. Pulling it up a little she clasped the tube with her long red nails and exposed the sore looking cut in her stomach were the tube entered her bowel.

"See, happy now?" Suzy asked as she pulled up her panties and refastened her jeans.

Chendrill was happy, happy that she hadn't been lying and happy his friend hadn't been proven a fool for his generosity. He said, "Sebastian told me you were leaving your husband. Is this correct?"

Suzy looked at him and for a moment he thought that the lap dancer was about to cry, then nodding she said, "Yeah, I think its best after what he's put me through. You know I should have known it after the first date he took me on and he had us sneak in through the back door of the cinema for free. A week later he had us doing the same in restaurants, although then it was us sneaking out instead of in. I was young then and I took it as fun and exciting. But now I see he was just being cheap, those people working for us, cooking meals and all and all we were doing was stealing."

Chendrill looked away again for the moment and thought about what a slimy fuck the woman's husband was. He'd only been around the couple for a minute amount of time and he could see the way the man leached off of her and used her to get what he needed sexually. He said, "You're very honest."

Suzy looked at him and said, "Yeah well that's me, tell it as it is. If you're with someone who's decent, obviously it's best to keep quiet about some things, but what's the point in holding back if you're asked something and the answer's not going to hurt. That's why I was so open with

Seb."

Chendrill felt the sadness inside her and the sadness inside him, which seemed for the moment to be constant. He thought back to how often Sebastian would have sat here with her and listened to the woman as she let out all her problems. He felt like being honest and telling her that if it were not for her shitty husband and kids, Sebastian would have been around for easily a few more years until the dog died. But what was the point in that? As she'd just said herself, what's the point in being honest about something that was going to hurt?

He sat back and looked at the waters some more, feeling the breeze on his face, then to the mountains on the other side of the inlet with their ski resorts waiting patiently for the first snows to fall. Sebastian had kept his little secret about this promise to Alan quiet, never letting the slightest inkling out of the box. If he had, Chendrill knew he'd have been on it and the man's feelings would not have been taken into consideration. Then he heard Suzy say, "You know, I feel like I have had guys wanting me sexually since I was a teenager and the only one who's ever gone out of his way for me has been a gay guy."

Chendrill looked back to her and waiting as a couple passed before saying, "And on that note, are you going back to your old boyfriend?"

Suzy looked to him as she put a little more together in her head. She said, "You've been having me followed over to Deep Cove have you?"

Chendrill stayed quiet again, and thought so that's where that fuckhead loan shark hangs out when he's not out there selling blocks, sitting out there in amongst the real people who had jobs and pretending to be one of them.

Then he heard Suzy take a deep breath and say, "Well, yeah that's where I go, and if you were wearing a bag for the same reason I am you wouldn't be judging me."

Chendrill looked at her, the woman sitting there with her blonde hair blowing in the breeze. He got it. He'd heard what her husband had said and Sebastian had confirmed it when they'd sat and chatted in the car. Any man who used his wife in such a perverse manner for his own sexual gratification, even without hurting her physically, deserved to see her run to suburbia even if it was into the arms of a shithead like this Mattia the Italian. In Chendrill's eyes, you reaped what you sowed. He said, "Yeah, I get it, don't worry."

Then he saw her turn to him, take a deep breath, and say, "I know what went down with Seb's dog. So, I'm going to tell you something about this other job my husband has that I'll leave with you. Now I know who you are, if you're anything of the man Seb said you are, then I'll know it'll only be a matter of time before my husband gets what he deserves and I can move forward with my life."

****

"What are they talking about?" Ditcon asked again for what seemed to be the hundredth time. The man wondering if he could share the binoculars and have one eye on either side with their heads together the same as he had with his friends when they'd watched people fucking at the point in Stanley Park when they were kids. He asked again, "Anything?"

Staying focused, the school teacher wondered what to invoice these idiots for being dragged out of school under the pretext of a national emergency when all the lady with the lovely tits had been talking about was herself and now her husband's job. Without dropping the binoculars, she said, "They were talking about Deep Cove. Then after they were talking about drug addicts, horses and money, $250,000 to be precise and she's really annoyed about it, and bags they were talking about bags, then the lady showed him her knickers."

Fuck, Ditcon thought. Then said, "The dirty bastard."

"Oh," said the school teacher, who'd just decided on nothing less than $500, then carried on saying, "and she said something about a gay guy. And now they are talking about her husband who she doesn't love anymore because he keeps going down to the United States all the time."

Then it hit Ditcon—it was obvious, the fucker was bringing stuff through the border and using mules to do it. He was getting hot women and guys to do the dirty work and having them stuff drugs in little bags down their pants or wherever. The guy was recruiting drug addicts who could keep themselves together to do the work. And then one had let him down, that's why he jumped the border—he had had no other choice. There was a reason he was driving the fancy car, it was oh so simple once you put it all together. The guy was running drugs. It all made sense now. He said out loud, "Oh my God—how far the mighty fall."

Chapter Sixteen

Rock Mason was pissed, pissed off and pissed drunk and it was no way to be when you had no money and you were sitting in the bar at the Sutton and no one was interested anymore in what you had to say. It wasn't because he'd been telling anyone who would listen about how much of a shitty town this was. Or about how he was better than anyone there or who had ever been there. It was because almost everyone in the bar had seen the video. Be it the guy behind the counter who gave out the drinks, or the other TV celebrities who were staying at the place and wanting to talk about themselves, or the star fuckers who came and went hoping to get laid or to make friends on Facebook.

By now, they'd all seen the video of Rock Mason—the superhero who could do everything, including saving the world—trying to dance alongside the BlueBoy guy. Trying to dance and failing amongst a troupe of beautiful Asian girls, then standing on his own dressed as a turkey, then calling a gentle old man a 'fucking faggot motherfucker' and attacking people while still dressed as a turkey, then ripping the turkey suit off and trying to be Bruce Lee and failing miserably before getting knocked out in one punch by a guy in a Hawaiian shirt. They'd all seen that and other stuff, secretly filmed and released anonymously by a small group of film students recruited and paid handsomely for their troubles by Sebastian.

The man was fucked. Fucked by the video and fucked by the fact that he wasn't getting paid for his pathetic ego-induced performance as an astronaut, and on top of this Sebastian had stipulated that the production was not going to pay the hotel anything over and above the man's accommodation that was to end at midday the next day. And that was why when Rock Mason had stopped spouting off about how he hated Canadians to a bunch of Canadians, he was presented a bill for his overages which included all the meals and drinks he'd been buying for himself and everyone in the bar in an attempt to make himself look cool since he'd arrived with his superstar status generosity that in Rock Mason's mind he didn't ever think he'd have to pay.

But now he did.

The assistant manager handed him the bill with a smile and watched as Rock Mason squinted at the paperwork, which was now almost six pages long. This assistant manager who was about to go home and throw all his old Rock Mason DVD's in the garbage now happily telling him that the amount was $33,434.00 before tax.

Rock Mason stared at the bill that, in his mind, wasn't for him and threw it back at the man then said, "Give it to the guy it belongs to; I couldn't give a fuck."

Then taking back the bill, the assistant manager, who liked to sneak into empty rooms to watch the porn channel, pulled out another letter—this one with a Slave Media logo and 'Attn: Rock Mason' on the cover.

Rock Mason stared at the envelope squinting with blurry eyes, then opened it and said, "Thank fuck for that," as he read the first line at the top of the page which read:

Travel Memo.
Rock Mason - Actor

Then he continued reading:

Greyhound Bus

One-way ticket

5:40am – Departure - Vancouver BC - Bus station

4:05pm – Arrival – Los Angeles CA – Bus Station

Total trip time 34 Hrs 25 Min with one transfer.

****

Chendrill arrived to check on Dan and his mother just before 7 p.m. that evening—not that looking after Dan was his job anymore, but old habits can be hard to change and strangely the place had become very familiar.

He knocked and then opened the door with the key Dan's mother had given him so as he would come see her when she was sleeping. He reached the kitchen and saw a Prada bag hanging from the back of the kitchen table chair. He looked at Dan's mother as she came out of the bathroom in the hall and said, "Is this yours?"

"It's Marsha's, or should I say Marshaa's as she corrected me earlier."

"Oh?"

"She's been down in Dan's room all day with him and she's quite loud."

Chendrill raised his eyebrows. "Yeah that kind of loud, she doesn't seem to care. Thc two have been at it all day. I went down there once when the noise stopped for a bit and Dan told me to fuck off."

"He said those words?"

Dan's mother nodded. She was annoyed and normally the boy would have seen the other side of her temper, but for some reason having a supermodel in the basement seemed to have quelled it.

Then they both heard the door to Dan's room open in the basement and heard Dan's usual pounding footsteps come up them two at a time. He reached the kitchen and without a word he passed them both and opened the fridge. Chendrill said, "I hear you've been telling your mother to fuck off."

Dan answered straight away without looking away from the fridge—the glow from the light inside outlining what was left of the shiner Chendrill had given him when he'd thumped him. He said, "That cabby with the hockey stick's been hanging about here again—go do your job will you?"

"I'm rich now Dan, it looks like you'll need to start fending for yourself, especially if you're telling your mother to go fuck herself."

Dan looked at him, then to his mother, straightened up and stuffed a load of cheese into his mouth. With the words that were barely audible he said, "Oh, well you know how it is, I'm all upset about Sebastian and I needed time alone. Mum just came along at the wrong time."

"What about an apology."

"Looks to me like you're out your jurisdiction now if you're saying you ain't my minder anymore, and since I don't remember you marrying Mum, you can't start asking those questions. So, spare me from listening to your daddy lectures. You know what I'm saying?"

Chendrill wanted to grab the kid who was showing off to the supermodel downstairs and ram his face into the family size coconut yogurt he was about to add to the cheese. Do that, then pour it on his head and send him downstairs to 'Marshaaa' or whatever she'd told Dan's mother she liked to be called.

He moved towards him and Dan's mother caught his arm and said, "Dan if you're big enough to talk to Chuck like that, you're big enough to leave. So, if you don't apologize to me and him then you'll be doing just that and you and your little high-pitched screamer of a girlfriend can go stay at whatever hotel she's booked into."

Dan stood, still licking the lid of the yogurt pot, and he said, "Sure, I will, but you're not being very understanding. You know how I felt about Sebastian. You should have some thought instead of being judgemental. I've never been in this situation before, I'm not old like you two. I'm still fragile and sensitive."

Then, taking them all by surprise, they heard 'Marshaa' who was now standing at the top of the stairs say, "Hey?"

Chendrill turned and looked at the supermodel who liked to scream and didn't look like a supermodel at all, but instead like a normal pretty young woman who'd just spent the afternoon in her boyfriend's room—'Marshaa' standing there in nothing more than the same old sperm stained, creased t-shirt she'd slipped on earlier. Chendrill taking it all in said, "Hi Marshaa, nice to see you."

And Marshaa said as she walked towards him and took his hands in hers, "I'm sorry for your loss. You and Sebastian were such a lovely couple. I know he loved you so much, I could see it in the way he looked at you. I wish there was someone out there who could love me the same way."

And as Chendrill heard those words from a young lady who had his world mixed up, it all made perfect sense—the constant phone calls, the nice wage, the cars, the meals, the walks on the beach, Sebastian calling to have him over all the time, his inability to get fired regardless of losing the Ferraris all the time and thumping out Dan. And as he was about to start to explain to the young lady who, despite her status in this world, at the end of the day was just that, Dan stepped in for him and simply said, "Chuck's not a poof Marshaa, even if he looks like one. He's with Mum. I think you're right though about old Sebastian—I saw it too sometimes."

Marshaa stared at Chendrill, looking at his shirt and then at his dick in his trousers and then to Dan's mother who was almost the same size as her and said, "Ooo!"

****

They laid in bed and listened to Dan and Marshaa fucking in the basement of the house. Dan's mother wondering where her son got the stamina and how at such a young age he had the ability to make love to a woman the way he obviously was to Marshaa—the way she was moaning and groaning for so long. She heard Chendrill say, "We should bang on the floor."

Tricia laughed and felt the embarrassment of how she must have sounded at times when she'd been distracted from her love making by the broom handle Dan used to smash into the ceiling above his bed. She said, "I think it's time for my young boy to leave the nest. I kind of hinted at it to see what he'd do."

Talking into the back of his woman's neck, having just slipped his erection in between the top of her legs, he said, "How did he take it?"

"Well this is all I've heard all day, so it seems as though he agrees." Then she said, "You know, Sebastian's said I can buy any house in town and it's paid for, what do you think will happen with this lawyer who's his friend if I was to buy a really big multimillion dollar house over in West Van, then sell it and buy myself one that I can call home in some nice family area like Deep Cove or on the Sunshine Coast? Do you think he'd mind?"

Chendrill stopped pushing himself against her and thought about it, his girl buying herself a home in a nice family area around Deep Cove, just up the road from that leech of a human loan shark with whom Sebastian's friend Suzy was in love. Maybe they'd all see each other in the park as they took in the view of the water on a sunny day. He said, "I don't think Sebastian's lawyer has a say in it. I'm sure it's exactly what Sebastian wanted, you know the way he thought things through. I'm sure he was giving you that option. I'm sure it's what he wanted you to do, in an around about way, then you'd feel like you've earned it."

She turned to him and kissed him and said, "Maybe I will speak to Patrick after all and have him go look."

****

The next morning, Chendrill called and met Daltrey in a café off Seymour and the first thing he heard her say was, "I heard you're rich?"

Was he? Chendrill thought. Everyone kept saying he was, but, so far, he hadn't seen any changes to his bank accounts.

They spoke for a while about Sebastian as Chendrill looked at Daltrey discretely, checking her burns. They were getting better, a lot less raw than they were and, in parts, he could see new hair growth in places. He asked, "How do you feel?"

Daltrey shrugged, then said, "Okay I guess, better than

when I was on that boat, stealing tuna from the larder, thinking I was going crazy because of that picture of Dan in those ridiculous underpants staring at me. It all seems surreal now."

And it did, almost dreamlike—there once was a time when the woman had been afraid of nothing, but now she was realising she'd bitten off more than she could chew when a real psychopath came into town from overseas. She carried on, "Since you're so rich are you still going to hunt down bad guys?"

It was a question that had been playing on his own mind for the last 24 hours and he had come to the conclusion that it was all he knew—finding bad guys and finding dogs. Shrugging his shoulders, he said at the same time as he wondered how she knew his business, "Don't see why not. Maybe I can work for free now, *pro bono* like Samuel does sometimes. Do the superhero thing and help others who cannot help themselves."

"Yeah, you can wear a cape," said Daltrey as she grinned and imagined Chendrill in a big spandex suit with a Hawaiian shirt styled cape.

Then Chendrill said, "On that subject, I've got Ditcon on my back and I was wondering how you feel about keeping an eye on some shithead loan shark who hides himself away in Deep Cove and his girlfriend who works as a peeler?"

****

Daltrey said yes. How big a shithead this man in Deep Cove was, though, she was yet to find out—as was Chendrill. She needed to start to get her feet back in the water and what Chendrill was asking could be construed as police work since the man, as Chendrill had said, was working outside the law.

She'd been making progress in her own way already, starting off a search for the identity of the young woman who'd saved her life. So far, though, she was drawing a blank with missing persons, and at one point she'd plucked up the courage to step inside the morgue. But that took more courage than she'd thought. With her heart pounding as she'd approached the door, deep in the basement of the hospital on Burrard Street, knowing that the charred body of a young girl who should have been her lay somewhere within, she'd felt herself begin to shake and her breathing become hard. And then after as she'd held a hanky to her nose and stood by the drawer looking down on the corpse that lay there blackened and charred by the fire that the Russian had spat from his hands, she'd cried—cried for the girl who'd worn her name in death and cried for herself for still being alive.

It had not taken long after this for Daltrey to hit the streets with a newfound passion. She'd walked the sadness of Main and Hastings looking for someone she knew was already gone in amongst the heroin and crack laden streets. She'd looked at the young who now looked so old, as the crack or heroin thinned their bodies and souls. Asking questions she knew would not be answered to those who were not listening, through the spaced-out confused cat calls from men and women who had fallen away from a reality they once knew, Daltrey would ask, "I'm looking for a girl who was missing—she was young, younger than me, and strong, a fighter?"

But so many there were, themselves, already missing, missing from families, missing from loved ones and friends who'd grown tired of the evils that came with and from a habit they'd allowed to overtake their lives.

And in amongst these people, Daltrey had roamed, asking, talking, slowly making progress in this world full of filth and sadness until at last she'd found a name from a hooker whose hair and teeth must have once shone.

Bill, Bill from back east, the guy who'd once walked with a girl who was his sister—and now walked alone—as he searched between fixes, wandering, asking after a sister who was missing as he walked the alleys and side roads that surround the centre of Main and Hastings where the fallen now chose to gather and call home.

Daltrey pulled her Audi up outside of her apartment block and looked up at another poster of Dan, wondering how that stinky little fuck had managed to get so high and so far in such a short time when the only place she had gone was down. But that was before and now she was on her way back up again.

She'd sat with Chendrill awhile, spending quality time as he'd waited to get mugged, and it had been nice—her there with him, the pair of them drifting in and out of work with the little bit of idle chit chat. People coming and going, grabbing coffees and stuffing their faces with buns. Chendrill telling her about Dan in his astronaut suit and how he'd told Chendrill the only reason he was keeping his helmet on was so he did not have to listen to Rock Mason's bullshit. Daltrey saying how she thought the man was cool and how much she'd loved the man's films.

What Chendrill wanted, though, would be interesting and for the moment she doubted she'd have the confidence to pull it off—but wandering about in a club for a bit in skimpy clothes could be different. She had the body, but the burn would be an issue. And as for lap dancing, she'd have to see how it went.

She went up to her place and dug out her sexy gear from the bottom of the wardrobe and tried to remember the last time she'd worn it and then for a moment felt sad realizing that she hadn't. Stripping off, she tried it all on.

Daltrey stood there looking at herself in the full frame mirror at the side of the bed and remembered she had actually worn it once before, on the day she'd bought it, and with the excitement of seeing herself done up as she was now, she'd touched herself and watched herself in her bra and panties, stockings and high heels, caressing herself slowly until she'd seen herself come.

But that was then, and she was thinner now—that was for sure, after a week of being holed up eating tuna from a can—but a lot of the girls who worked those places were thin. *Cocaine has that affect*, she thought. She opened the wardrobe fully and found the shoes she'd bought to wear with the outfit and put them on. The black leather heels were loose now on her feet and felt a little more comfortable as she moved freely around her bedroom. She closed the curtains in the room and stared at herself some more in the mirror.

Yeah, she could do it, she thought, suddenly having some admiration for the girls who did it regularly. Spinning around she pointed her ass towards the mirror and looked back at herself. She looked good. She stood up straight and looked at herself over her right shoulder. *Yeah perfect*, she thought. *Wow. You've got what it takes.* Her legs tapering off, covered in tight sheer silk, her soft skin showing at the top of her legs, her laced panties halfway up her delicate bottom. Her curved waist, her spine twisting slightly as she moved her head from side to side for a better view—her beautiful back and her hair that dropped down the small of her back, touching the clip on her bra. She thought of Chendrill and what he'd do if he saw her now, doing a dress rehearsal for what he'd suggested she did after he had told her where the two people he'd asked her to watch hung out.

"Maybe I should just get myself in there into the thick of it and see what comes along?" *Yeah,* she thought. Why wasn't Chendrill right there with her now? Watching as she stood in the darkness. She turned and stood looking at herself front on in the mirror. The light from the window catching her from the side, catching her hair, the muscles on her curved stomach, the tiny bulge from her pubic bone. Closing her eyes, she lifted her right hand and began to touch her breasts, feeling them through the silk of her lacy bra, feeling her nipples, feeling the firmness of her breasts pulled extra tight. She touched the other one and did the same as she opened her eyes. She looked good.

Yeah if Chendrill was here, she'd let him make love to her, she thought. Let him push her up against the mirror as she stood there in her lingerie and heels and she'd let him fuck her against it. She moved forward and still standing laid herself against the glass and took her other hand down below and rubbed herself from outside her panties.

Yeah, she'd let him really give it to her, she thought. She'd surrender herself to him and push herself back to him so as he could hold her, thrust himself into her through his jeans as he touched her. He could hold her, wrap his arms around her waist then feel her breasts, then she'd feel his cock and pull it out and guide it into herself. Daltrey pushed her hand around the side of her panties and felt herself wet beneath. She rubbed the tips of her fingers against her clitoris and heard herself moan as she did.

Yeah that's what she'd do, she thought. She'd let him take her from behind. Let him fuck her really hard and feel his cock push up into her, feel him hold her tight and bite her neck like he used to. She let her other hand drop from her breasts as she pulled it from now inside her bra. She reached down with it and pushing her panties completely to the side, she pushed her fingers deep inside herself as far as her body would let her. Slowly she pulled them out until she could just feel her finger tips there at her opening, then she pushed them back inside against her moistness as her other hand stroked.

Yeah, she'd let him fuck her from behind, she thought as she pushed her fingers inside herself again, over and over until she felt the electricity run through her body making her shudder and gasp out loudly before she moved herself unsteadily to lay down on the bed. She'd wait for a moment until her breathing settled just enough for her to begin to let her fingers touch her body, so as she could do it again. There were no doubts about it, she was beginning to feel better.

****

Chendrill drove the Aston south along Granville and then further south on the highway, which took him straight down towards the border. *If it was him they were watching in the park, then there was a high chance they'd be following him now*, he thought, as he stayed at the speed limit and looked in the mirror. Ditcon was like that—whenever the man got off his ass that is. He'd done well though, he'd give him that. The guy had somehow worked it out that it was him who'd crossed the border. He'd have to prove that though, prove he was there, prove he stole the vehicle. Maybe there could be something in the vehicle that could pin him to the border infraction? But he'd slept with a woman who worked the border on the U.S. side not too long ago, meeting her in a bar in White Rock when he was out with friends and had taken a couple of trips, legally those times, across the border so he could kiss and hold her, and then watch her big tits go around and around in unison as he fucked her on her bed. That would be how his hair, or whatever, may be there, and had gotten into to the vehicle—from him to her, then into the vehicle. It would be a stretch, but he now had the money for the best lawyers who knew just how to stretch things accordingly—it would be all they needed, should it get to that.

But that was a worst-case scenario and it could be something altogether different that Ditcon or maybe that guy with the oily feet had on him—but the latter was no longer a problem.

He reached the border and took a left and traveled along Zero Ave till he hit 272 Street and slowed as he passed the house with its barn set way back from the road. In need of a paint job, blending in and looking the same as all the others.

It was the first time he'd seen it—the place being a guarded secret. The first time he'd heard of the place was when his old friend Rasheed had gotten out of prison and he'd told him he'd 'inherited' it from an uncle. Then months later he'd seen the guy driving around in a new Mercedes. Rasheed was gone now though.

From what Chendrill had heard on the street, a one-way admission ticket to this little haunted house was a cool

$5000 cash, per head, which carried a no return policy. You were picked up downtown in a blacked-out van and you didn't see the light of day again until you got out of another blacked-out van somewhere in Bellingham on the U.S. side of the border.

He carried on past the place and pulled the Aston into a small slip road and got out. He headed north again on foot, then jumped the stream at the side of the road and headed west again through some woodlands. The undergrowth catching his feet as he pushed though the weeds and nettles and fallen branches. Five minutes later, the house and the barn were visible through the trees. Passing the edge of a bog, he kept to the side hidden by the trees and dropped down over a neglected wooden fence and made his way through the back garden and stood against the side wall next to the kitchen's rear door.

He looked at his shoes and wished he'd put his boots on, but it was too late for that. From what he could tell, there was no one around. The rear door was held to the frame with cobwebs. He moved quietly around to the front and looked to the road almost fifteen hundred feet to the south. There were no cars, not on this side of the border or on the U.S. side either. But on the U.S. side they would be there, waiting and watching as they always were.

Chendrill stood silently for a while, then after twenty minutes had passed he moved to the other side of the house and did it again. There was no one there—no rabid dog to warn a sleepy guard or someone coming back from the store.

He walked back to the kitchen door at the rear and pushed the bottom with his foot. It was firm. Then he tried the centre with his shoulder. It was the same. He moved to the windows with air conditioners sticking out the tops of each of them, all of which were cold and dry, and he pushed the frames beneath. There was no give there either, the home was secure, overly secure if that was possible. He was at the right place. He waited some more and thought about how he would do it if it was him. The Americans watched everything along Zero Ave and to come back and forth with a van would only create more scrutiny.

Chendrill moved himself back into the woods and found his way through the bush towards the barn and again stood with his back to it. Chances were high that the place operated after dark when it was running, although it wouldn't surprise him if it ran 24/7. He looked back at the trees and saw a small lane that ran into a gully where it was protected from both sides with a treed canopy above. The width was just the right size for a passenger van or an SUV. He walked to the side where the lane met the barn and studied its cedar shingle side. It all looked the same and weather worn, old dirt splashed up from the heavy rains that came in the winter. There wasn't anywhere to turn or park if you came to the barn from this side. Chendrill walked to the barn's end and began to push his foot into the bottom of the shingles to see if it would give. He moved along towards the centre, pushing hard on each shingle until one eventually gave slightly, as did the next and the next until he reached the other side of what could only be a hidden garage door.

Chendrill stepped back and looked at the frame. He moved in again. Crouching down, he felt along the underside of the bottom line of shingles. In the centre, he found a small piece of wire with a bolt attached. He gave it a pull, snapping it downward, and felt the garage door give at the top and the spring system take over as the shingle wall came out slightly then lifted itself up with ease.

Chendrill pulled the door up another couple of feet and bent his big frame under, stepped inside and closed the large door behind him. The inside of the barn was dark, lit only by a window at the top and whatever light managed to squeeze its way through some joists.

He walked to a door and opened it slowly and saw a steep, thin dark passageway which sloped down, dropping away towards the house. Chendrill looked for a light switch but could not see one. He pulled out a penlight from his pocket and started the walk downwards into the darkness, the small light illuminating only the wall and ceiling that surrounded him and the floor a few feet in front of his feet. He reached a corner where a ladder dropped down from above through a large plastic tube. *With the distance I've travelled, by now I must be under the house*, Chendrill thought as he raised his flashlight and counted the rungs on the ladder as it towered above—twenty-five. He would be roughly 20 feet under now. He looked at the tunnel that was now to his left. The pitch was steeper as it dropped further down under the ground and although the width was the same, the ceiling was lower. The whole tunnel was lined with rotten plywood and strong beams, with a small unlit bulb every 50 feet.

Chendrill headed further into the tunnel, descending lower and lower and feeling the drips of water that had found their way through the cracks as he did. By counting the lamps and judging the degree of the pitch, he worked out he must have been roughly 75 feet deep by the time he reached a line crudely drawn in paint which could only have been the Canadian - U.S. border above. He carried on in the darkness, feeling the air get thinner and colder as the tunnel leveled out and swung to the right and then carried on straight and began to slightly rise again for what he could tell was another 1,500 feet, the small light from his penlight paving the way.

He reached a door, then a staircase, and began to climb up towards what he could see was daylight. At the top was a window high above a heavy metal door with a metal bar along its centre. Chendrill stood at the top and listened, there was no movement on the other side, only silence. Slowly he pushed the metal bar and opened the door.

He walked into another barn not to dissimilar from the one he'd entered the tunnel through on the Canadian side of the border. Except that in this one there was a van with *Washington Farm Produce* written on the side.

Chendrill walked up to the side of it and looked inside. Against the dash were receipts and work gloves and empty blueberry boxes stuffed on the passenger seat and in the center. He tried the driver's door and it opened and reached inside for the receipts and pulled them out. In amongst them was an invoice from the farm with the farm's details written at the bottom in stylish lettering.

Chendrill moved to the barn's side door and opened it slowly and stepped outside. To his left he could see Canada far in the distance to the north and the backs of the camera towers that waited patiently and watched.

You fucking smart asses, Chendrill thought as he looked around the place and wondered who had dug the thing in the first place. Whoever it was had spent time digging deep and going that extra mile with a shovel and making his life easier; only it wasn't a shovel, it was a small diameter tunnel boring machine stolen from a mine up at Williams

Lake, along with a tractor that worked the field right on the border as the mole dug for the three months it had taken to reach the property they'd bought cheap via a numbered company just over half a mile south on the other side.

How many people had been through here? Chendrill wondered. It would be a lot. But knowing Rasheed and his ways, he'd have done it in spurts so as not to allow gossip.

An hour later, Chendrill was back on the other side and sitting in the front seat of the Aston. He put the car into drive and pulled away from the side of the laneway he'd tucked the Aston into. Now he had the means—all he needed was to get this prick of a loan shark down that tunnel and have the border guy wipe some oil off of his toes and meet the guy coming out the other end as agreed and he'll have killed two birds with one stone. But life was never going to be as simple as that for the great Charles Chuck Chendrill, even if he was now a rich man.

Chapter Seventeen

Mazzi Hegan had packed up, cleared out of his old love nest, walked away from his old sword swallowing life and had left it all behind. He was gone and in what seemed the blink of an eye Dan was in, and thanks to Sebastian's generosity in death, he was the proud owner of a gay palace complete with leather sofas, glass coffee tables, power showers, and murals.

Dan hit the button on Mazzi Hegan's music system and listened as The Pet Shop Boys blared out. The silver suit that went with the undies and fitted tight on Mazzi also fit Dan well. He looked at the four Korean dancing troupe girls sitting on Mazzi's leather sofa and smiled. Then he said, "So what do you think of the new pad, you like it?"

They did.

The place had four bedrooms, all *en suite*, which he now owned and hadn't noticed the last time he'd been over and had his nose broken by a man bag. He looked again at the note sitting on the dresser and read it over for the fifth time:

Dan – Keep what you want - Throw the rest to the wolves.

And 'wolves' meant the people in need, Dan supposed. All the clothes, silk suits, as well as the furniture it seemed—and the half-eaten bath loaf. Most of the clothes were super gay though; in fact, all of the clothes Mazzi Hegan had left behind were just that. He could imagine what would happen if he was to drop off a few bags here and there for the guys and girls living on the streets to find.

And the next day, he'd see a bunch of the downtown homeless population wandering about in tight lycra string vests that say 'I Swallow' but what the hell. Clothes were clothes.

Looking to the group of girls sitting there chatting in Korean in the hope that they might put on one of the t-shirts and find some inspiration in the over the top subliminal messaging, he said, "There's clothes as well if you need them."

They didn't—they could see what he was wearing and were cool. The leader, Myuki, said, "Your clothes are too big, not fit."

"These clothes aren't mine, they belong to the guy who lived here before, Mazzi, you met him?" Dan quickly said, putting them straight, and followed up with, "Same with the drawings on the ceiling in the main bedroom."

Then he watched as the girls looked at each other and laughed, and heard Myuki say, "We think that you!"

Dan smiled, he'd given the dance troupe a lightning tour and only opened the door quickly for the girls to see what had once been Mazzi Hegan's bedroom and he hadn't seen anyone glance up to the ceiling to see the drawing, but now by the way they were giggling, they obviously had. He said, "Yeah well, I ain't that hairy."

He'd texted them just after he'd felt 'Marshaa' had outstayed her welcome and in an attempt to get her to leave he'd asked her if she'd help him clean the bathroom and watched her entourage arrive and whisk her off 5 minutes later in a limousine. Not that Dan had actually known where the bleach and rubber gloves were in his mother's home, but it had been a good idea at the time as the supermodel was getting all cuddly and beginning to get on his nerves.

Then not long after, the girls had met him in a pizza joint just off Main Street. Dan there wearing the silver suit he still had on, being stared at with tomato sauce on his chin and the Korean girls all sitting squeezed in together on the opposite side of the table hardly eating. Dan asking as he ate if any of them had family on the other side of the fence and if so what did they watch on TV. The girls not understanding until he'd said DMZ and then they got it. But no, no family over there on the north side. They said as a group, "They not have clothes like you in the north."

Dan doubted they did, but from what he'd seen on the internet, he'd have fit right in on a Friday night in downtown Seoul.

Dan said to the Korean girls as they sat neatly together on the sofa of his new penthouse, "So if you want to move in and stay here you can."

The girls looked at each other, then around the place. Then looking back at each other, they all spoke again together for what seemed like an age as they pulled their long dark hair away from their faces and unconsciously twirled it with their fingers. Then one said, "Can we dance here?"

Dan thought about it for what must have been a second and said, "You worried about the neighbours?"

They were, the place they were staying just on the edge of town had already had enough of the routines they'd been rehearsing over and over at all hours of the day and night. They nodded.

Dan smiled and, looking to the floor beneath his feet, wondered what the people below had heard and gone through on Friday nights since Mazzi Hegan had been living there. Looking up, he said, "I'm sure they've heard worse."

Dan turned back to the music system, and cutting Westend Girls in half, he flipped through some more of Mazzi's collection. Abba, Sister Sledge, Kylie Minogue, Madonna, Diana Ross—*for fucksake*, he thought and wondered if it would ever end.

Then he heard one of the girls call out just as he hit the button for Lady Gaga.

"You have K-Pop?"

Not me, Dan thought but could not be bothered to say 'No K-Pop, no.' He thought back to a video he'd seen on the internet earlier that year when he was watching dance moves and had ended up watching Gangnam style. Then dug deeper. There was a boy band called DNA, there were seven in the band. The lead, he remembered, went by the name of Rap Monster. He flipped through the screen and stopped at Rap, then hit a little folder next to it and the words 'Super Fucking Hot Korean Guys' came up. Dan clicked on it and as soon as he did, the TV clicked on and DNA were on the screen, all looking cool in jeans and baseball caps and from what Dan could tell none of them had yet needed to purchase a razor.

Delighted, the girls got up and moved to the center of the room and seconds later were dancing in exactly the same routine as the boys on the screen. Dan watched the girls as they slowly put their own feminine spin on the routine, Myuki taking the lead and the other girls—Chun Lee, Chun Si and Chun Me—following.

Dan hit another button and another K-Pop song started up which sounded almost exactly the same, but the girls did not miss a beat. Then he hit another, and another as the girls looked to him and smiled. Then he flipped through and hit Frank Sinatra and they stopped.

Myuki looked at him and asked smiling, “You not like K-Pop?”

Truth was, Dan didn’t, but he had a feeling it was going to grow on him.

****

Daltrey took a deep breath and stepped in through the front door of the strip club and smiled at the bouncers as they eyed her up as she passed through. The place was dirty, she thought, as she felt her feet stick slightly to the carpet and the stench of spilled booze hit her nose. Chendrill having arranged it with an Angel he knew for Daltrey to work there no questions asked. The guy owing him a favor from years before when Chendrill had left his name out of a drug deal that had gone south and two Vietnamese had been found, each with a shotgun hole where their stomachs used to be.

The same Angel who now ran the strip club just as surprised as the guys from Ho Chi Minh when the guns appeared, as all he’d been asked to do was unlock a gate.

Within a week, Chendrill knew who had been shot and why and had little sympathy for the two Asians who’d decided to come into his town to spread poison. The Harleys of the two trigger happy bikers put under cover for the next seven years as they did their time in Kent Maximum Security prison. Just as Chendrill had been under cover when the Angel who now had risen in the organization had spilled the beans.

Daltrey found the back room and a locker left empty by a girl who had worked there before and had fallen in love, but would be back soon. The place was clean enough in amongst a sea of depravity and full of chairs and mirrors made dusty with body talc. Then the manager came in wearing a thick gold chain and bracelet, and without as much as a hello said, "You done this before?"

She hadn't, except for a joke, playing stripper and lap dancer, but the person sitting on the chair with the lights off had been a girl who wished she was a boy. She said, "Yeah."

The manager looking her up and down before telling her she gets two songs per lap dance and no more and half of what she brings in goes to him, and no fucking or sucking guys off for extra.

Well you don't have to worry about that, Daltrey thought, as she then heard the guy say without looking back as he was leaving, "Unless it's me—and you don't want to work afternoons on a Monday."

Daltrey watched the man leave then said to herself as she turned back to her locker, "Yeah, I'll get right on that you sweaty fucking asshole."

She looked at herself in the mirror, her long blond wig covering her damaged scalp and makeup hiding the rest. *Fucking Chendrill*, she thought, *what the fuck had he gotten her into?* Get to know Suzy, the other blonde working the room, the same girl with the big breasts she'd seen over in the corner with her hand too far up the inside leg of a business man who should have known better. Get to know her, her and the Italian with the rings who was apparently here all the time, if she could—the guy dating Suzy, or kind of. What was Chendrill looking for? From what Daltrey could tell, he really didn't know yet himself. She did know though that the man now could buy the club outright tomorrow and bring the bulldozer in the same afternoon. But where would the girls with daddy issues and cocaine habits to feed go then, she wondered. After all the devil you know is sometimes better, and how bad could it be?

She stepped outside and looked up the stairs to where she'd be taking Williams that evening, and a stream of his nerdy friends whom Chendrill had lined up for a free evening out on him. Each one armed with a code word that would indicate all was okay and Daltrey could go through the motions of sitting on their dicks—the code being *Hawaiian shirt,* of which she wasn't sure whether it was a joke or whether Charles Chuck Chendrill thought he was being cool.

She stripped off most of her clothes and walked, scantily dressed in lingerie, into the main throng of lights and loose women and sad men, feeling the eyes on her as she went, the girl up on the stage prancing about in her high heels. *Where the fuck was Williams?* she thought as she wandered about smiling like she was loving being there in this stinking shithole in her sexy outfit, some men smiling back, others too drunk to care. The DJ hidden away in a little booth talking bullshit, telling everyone they were lovely people and introducing the next dancer, saying, "Put your hands together ladies and gentlemen for the… Lovely… Asmanda!"

Asmanda? Daltrey thought as she watched the girl climb the steps and step out onto the stage, cross it, then, with a turn and a double back step, come forward again. *Asmanda* wasn't a name. Then she realized she didn't have one for herself, how fucking stupid was she? She was going soft. Soft in the brain, she thought. Yeah, she'd given it a bit of thought and knew she would cross that bridge when she got to it. Chendrill had told her he'd told them her name was Maggie Cross, but she couldn't use that with the sad fuckers in here. *Fuck*. Suddenly Asmanda didn't sound too bad. She looked about, Mell, Shell, Bell… *Belle*, yeah that would do—Belle as in beautiful. Then as if right on cue she heard a guy say to her, "Hey—baby sit down." And turning she saw a fat guy with a bald head and porky fingers sitting there looking up at her. Reaching out he grabbed Daltrey's hand and pulled her down next to him. Then asked, "What's your name?"

"Belle."

The guy smiled, and holding onto his beer at the same time said, "Oh, you're from Quebec?"

She wasn't. Daltrey said, "No, I'm from Victoria."

She looked at the man, seeing him closer in the multicolored light. He had shaved but was obviously having trouble with his razor around the sweaty, fatty flesh under his chin. He said, "I've not been in here before, I like it."

"Good!"

"You're really pretty."

"Thanks."

Daltrey looked away; it had been a while since someone had told her that. Except for Sebastian, and he was probably just saying that to make her feel better. Then she heard him say it again, "I'm not just saying it, you really are."

Daltrey smiled at the man. From what she could tell he must have been in about his mid-forties, but it was hard to tell. He looked lonely. She said, "You're very kind."

"Thanks, you've nice tits."

"So have you," Daltrey snapped back as quick as a

flash. Then followed it up with, "You could work here."

The man looked back at her, not sure what to say or if he had heard her correctly in the noise from the speakers as they blared out a song he could not remember but liked.

"Sorry?"

"You should be."

"No, sorry I didn't hear you properly."

Daltrey leaned in, so he could, then said, "If you started talking to women properly then maybe you wouldn't need to come here to get your dick sucked."

Then she stood and smiled, held out her hand, took his and carried on with, "Baths have taps, give yours a turn."

With that she was off again, moving around the floor, wiggling her little ass as she went, searching for her next victim, looking pretty. She hit the end of the club where the bar was and sat herself down. *Fucking guy*, giving her a compliment like that, *nice tits*, she thought. She looked down at them. Yeah, they were nice, but sometimes she couldn't help herself. Then from behind she heard a male voice say, "Yeah they're nice."

Fuck, here we go again, Daltrey thought as a man in his fifties sat down a little too close next to her. He said, "Yeah they're lovely, I bet they feel great."

Fuck off, Daltrey thought as she looked up and over at the man with the sport coat and shirt and tie. She said, "Go see the guy over there, his are bigger—the two of you will probably get along."

"Oh?" The man said looking surprised at the response from this woman in lingerie when usually they'd have been all over him for a lap dance upstairs. He then said, "You're new?"

Daltrey asked, "Did I ask you to sit here?"

She hadn't.

"No, I was just trying to be sociable."

"Oh, so your tits are lovely, I bet they feel great, is a normal social interaction, is it? Go to the supermarket and say that at the till and see how far you get purchasing your frozen fucking dinner."

Without waiting for an answer Daltrey half stood, shifting her weight to the side quickly, and wacked the man out of the way with her ass. She carried on walking around the club, her nice tits in her lace bra jiggling as she went. *Who's next*? she thought as guys caught her eye. Turning his head as he saw her out of the corner of his eye, a man sitting on G-row along the stage looked away from the girl bending down with her ass out in front of him and said, "Hey?" as Daltrey came along next to him.

"Fuck off."

Then said it again as she heard another guy call out, "Hey Baby," unseen from one of the small booths to the side.

This was becoming fun, Daltrey thought as she carried on, passing the fat guy who'd started the trouble as she did. *Who's next?* she thought as she sat down at a spare seat at the end of the stage as a man with a cowboy hat left for the washroom. Looking up she caught the eye of a passing waitress in a short skirt and asked for a beer.

She looked at the stage, the girl up there smiling at her as she twirled around. The girl had nice legs—and 'tits' for that matter. Her hair cut short in a bob. *How the hell does she get her legs that smooth?* Daltrey thought as she stared up at her and wondered what it would be like to be up there twirling on the stage, spinning around in a pair of tiny knickers that were about to come off. *Fair play to her*, she thought as she smiled back. The girl still smiling as she walked away, ignoring the lewd comments as she moved about the stage, when Daltrey knew herself that if she was up there and someone had said, 'get ya clam out' it would only have ended in a fight.

Daltrey's beer came at the same time as the drunk in a cowboy hat came back to his seat at the end of the stage and, using his silence, asked for it back as he waited.

Go find another horse to ride cowboy, Daltrey thought but instead said, "Oh sorry were you sitting here?"

He smiled, he was.

The guy standing there expecting the girl sitting in his seat in all her glory to show some manners and get up whilst a naked lady watched from above. He heard Daltrey say, "Well, go tell someone who gives a shit."

Daltrey looked back at the stage and then found Suzy who had only just stood and was leading the man she'd been talking to towards the stairs. Daltrey looked back at the Cowboy who she now noticed had a mullet as she heard him say, "Maybe then you would be kind enough to join me, perhaps on one of those chairs they have upstairs instead?"

Daltrey looked away to the girl on the stage, then back to him. This Cowboy standing there smiling, the man had a kind manner, she couldn't deny that, he had asked nicely, he was polite, not sexually predatory in anyway and he was requesting if she would be kind enough to join him, as he'd put it, upstairs, so she could provide the service she was there to do and he was happy to pay her legally to do. So Daltrey said, "It's half price if you go on your own. So why don't you just do that? And when you're done, use the money you saved and go get a proper haircut."

It was going to be a long night.

****

Two hours later, no one dared go near her, not even the doormen, who after the third complaint had come over to ask her to settle down with the attitude. Daltrey sat there at the edge of the bar, still half naked in her high heels and on her fourth beer. The girl with her hair cut in a bob was back up on the stage and they'd been making eye contact again. *She'd give her a lap dance,* she thought as she watched the girl strut about the stage in her white shoes. *Fucking Chendrill, getting her to come here like this.*

She looked around for Suzy. The last time she'd seen her she was popping upstairs to make another $50, but now she was surprisingly back down earlier than she usually was. Then suddenly Suzy turned, caught her eye and held her stare as she crossed the club smiling till she reached Daltrey and sat down next to her in the one place no man would dare to go.

Suzy said, "How about that, two semi-naked women together at a bar and not one gentleman in the vicinity."

Daltrey smiled, the door was open. She said, "Yeah how about that?"

Suzy looked at the barman and asked for an ice water. Then looking at Daltrey asked, "You want another beer?"

"Sure."

"I don't drink, not through choice though, but when I did I kept it to vodka when I was here so these types couldn't smell it on me." Then she held out her hand and said, "Suzy."

Daltrey shook her hand and smiled and said, "Belle."

Keeping a hold of Daltrey's hand, Suzy looked at her

and said, "Belle?"

Apologizing with a smile, Daltrey said, "Maggie."

Suzy let go and took the water and handed Daltrey's beer over to her. She said, "You're creating quite the scene here. You got the manager in a tizz."

"He sent you over to calm me down?"

Suzy laughed and shook her head. Then said, "No—I love it, I couldn't give a shit what he thinks."

Neither could Daltrey. She said, "If he's unhappy and all stressed because of me he can go suck his own dick and take Monday off."

Suzy laughed; she liked this girl with the lovely figure and wig who shouldn't be here. She replied, "He's already been on to you as well has he?"

Daltrey smiled. Then heard Suzy say, "Well for the record, I work Mondays, and if I ever don't, then I can guarantee the only dick I've been sucking is my man's."

Which was who—your loser husband's or your loser boyfriend who lives off drug addicts? Daltrey thought as she looked at the woman's legs, which were longer than hers. Then Suzy said, "As sleazy as the man is, it seems to work for him as there's a few here that just get the primo shifts."

Good for them, Daltrey thought as she looked around wondering which of the girls working the room liked to sleep in after the weekend. She said, "Your guy, he comes here does he?"

"Seems to."

"Lucky you."

Suzy asked, "What about you? I see you like Shannon? She's hypnotic though."

"Oh, yeah well, yes, she has something about her

definitely," said Daltrey, suddenly feeling even more naked and transparent than ever and wondering if the beers were making her that obvious.

Suzy said, "Don't worry, it's normal round here—you can get sick of men. And for your info, I've never seen Shannon work a Monday… Or a Tuesday for that matter. But don't be making assumptions; I think it's because she gets her kid those days, so you know?"

Daltrey wouldn't be making assumptions. In fact, she wouldn't be making anything at the moment, especially a trip back here on Monday morning. Then she heard Suzy say, trying to be kind, "If you're nervous about going upstairs with one of these guys, then you can do one together with me if you want so you can get used to it."

How kind of you. Now put your tits away, she thought but instead said, "Thanks, that's really nice. I'll stay here though. Unless I see someone special—you know."

Then through the crowd she saw Williams coming in the door, all dressed up in a nice white shirt and shoes. Looking at what Daltrey was watching, Suzy spotted him too in the crowd, the lights from the stage making him stand out even more. Suzy said, "Cop."

Daltrey turned to her and smiled, "Really?"

"One hundred percent."

Daltrey looked back to Williams as he wandered around looking through the crowd. She said, "Why do you say that?"

Suzy looked back to her and said, "We never miss them, they're easy to spot."

Well you're sitting next to one, Daltrey thought, as she watched Williams look around some more then spot her sitting there at the bar. Making one more quick tour of the stage he came up the short steps and squeezed his way through a small huddle of people and sat himself down next to Daltrey and ordered a beer.

Looking at him, Daltrey said, "I thought you guys hung out in Starbucks."

Williams turned to her and said, "Sorry?"

Daltrey watched as Williams looked at her, the guy staring her in the eye then eyeing up her stockinged legs and naked stomach as he heard her carry on saying, "What're you ordering, a hot latte?"

Williams looked up. W*hat the fuc*k, he thought, *what was she doing*? He said, 'I'm sorry, I don't understand.'

Daltrey said, "What are you doing in here? You look like a kid, how old are you, 16?"

Williams said, "I'm 24 actually."

"Really, you a cop?"

Williams stared at her, not knowing what to say. Then Suzy leaned over and holding out her hand with a smile, said, "Hi, my name's Lucy. It's ok we like cops too, please excuse my friend."

Daltrey then said, "Would you like a lap dance?"

Williams looked Daltrey in the eye and smiled, this was great, Daltrey playing the part of the hard ass, but why she'd outed him as a cop he didn't know. What he'd do is ask her when he got her upstairs and they were alone, maybe he'd whisper it in her ear while she was riding that nice ass of hers on his dick. *It was going to be a tough one this one,* he thought as he looked at her legs and those lovely breasts she had. He'd need to summon every bit of control he had of his body to not allow the perfectly normal male reaction to occur down in his loins. *Be professional,* he told himself, *go through the motions—pretend you're enjoying it, but no hard on—no hard on.* He said, "I'd love one thank you."

"Great, Lucy can give you one, and watch out because if you blow your load, it's double."

And with that, before Williams could say another word, Suzy was off her stool and clonking in her big high heels as she led him breasts first by the hand towards the stairway to heaven.

Daltrey watched him go and smiled. Yes, she was feeling better and it was great to be a bitch.

****

Charles Chuck Chendrill made it to Dan's mother's home and let himself in. He found Tricia sitting in the kitchen looking at high-end properties for sale on her computer. Standing, she held him and kissed him, rubbed her hands through his hair and said, "I've been looking—these realtors want a fortune if I buy a house then sell it."

Chendrill let his woman go and looked at the old mansion house on the screen. The asking price boldly stating, 'Offers in the range of fifty-five million dollars.'

Chendrill said, "What about Dan—is there room in the basement for him."

Sitting back down again, Tricia said, "Dan's going to live in that penthouse, Chuck. Besides I'm just looking—I can buy this place, but I'd be in debt with the property taxes."

Chendrill leaned in and looked again, the place was nice with a huge stone deck, pool, and a huge garden with steps which went down to the ocean. It was crazy that he could buy it tomorrow and still have millions in the bank. He said, "I think Sebastian said he was picking up the taxes."

Tricia looked at him; she must have missed that bit. Still too upset and in shock to take in what she'd been given even though she'd only met the man a handful of times. She said, "I can't believe this is happening, Chuck."

Neither could Chendrill—the whole thing seeming surreal. As he closed the lid on Tricia's computer, he said, "Truth is, I miss the guy. I genuinely mean that, I can't believe he's gone."

"It was his choice, Chuck."

It was, Chendrill knew that, the man had calculated everything he did all based on how long the dog had left. All for the sake of a promise made to a man who he loved but was probably about to run away with the loan shark's brother until they'd played with the wrong gear stick and crashed the car. *Fucking crazy*, Chendrill thought, then said just that.

"What is Chuck?"

Lying, Chendrill said, "The fact we're both rich."

"You are, I'm not."

"But you will be soon." Then taking himself by surprise he said, "This house, this big old monster home with class, why don't you have Patrick make a lowball offer and see if you get it. Tell them it's cash and it's tomorrow. Tell him he'll have to sell it for free when you do decide to sell and you'll only sell it when he's found a buyer he brings to the table so as there's no one else wanting their usual cut."

Tricia looked at him, then said, "Why would he agree to that? Come on."

"Because he'll still get the fee when you buy it and if he does, tell him I'll fund his movie for him."

Tricia stared at him. "Really?" she said.

Chendrill, shrugged, and said, "Why not? I'll get my money back eventually."

"You hope."

Chendrill shrugged again. *What did it matter*? He thought, the interest on the 100 million would cover it, and it would be a tax write off for Samuel since he was handling all that from now on. There were tax credits as well, Chendrill knowing all about those savings from just hanging around the office and 'not listening' for the last few weeks. *Adalia would be back, but the other idiot could fuck off,* he thought. He said, "Yeah why not, it'll give me something to do instead of looking after Dan. Then maybe we can both live in that big house for a bit and see what happens?"

Tricia sat there for a moment, unsure if she'd heard him properly. *How long had they been together now,* she wondered? She stood again and then walked around the table, put her arms around his neck, and whispered in his ear, "Chuck, did I just hear what I thought I heard?"

Chendrill didn't answer. Instead, he stood and picked her up and took her to the bedroom, then laid her down on the bed. Climbing above her, he leaned down with his arms trapping her on either side of her body. He said, "You don't think I'd let you get away with having the place to yourself, do you? Besides what would you do, that big house might have ghosts."

"It probably has… You never know. It could be fun, we could make love in there and they'd be watching… Have you ever made love to a ghost, Chuck?"

"Yes."

Tricia looked up at him for a moment, then said, "Really, you've made love to a ghost?"

"Yeah."

"Really? You made love to a ghost—how?"

"I'm sorry, no," Chendrill said back, "I thought you said a goat."

****

Daltrey was still sitting at the bar when Williams appeared at the bottom of the stairs looking all sweaty, with his hair ruffled and his shirt hanging out. He looked over to Daltrey who simply turned away. There'd been two other men who'd she'd told to fuck off after they'd come over and tried to sweet talk her during the four to five minutes it had taken Williams to get up the stairs, get ravaged by an older woman, come in his pants, and get back down again.

The girl on the stage was almost done, and for the whole time Daltrey had been sitting there alone, the lady with the silky legs and bob cut had been looking her in the eye. The lady staring as she stripped completely naked and moved seductively across the stage floor until she was on her back with her legs apart giving the front row losers a glimpse of something they'd never get to taste. Then, still looking at Daltrey, she'd gotten dressed. Slowly pulling up her knickers as she bent down, she slipped on a small negligee she'd picked up at Victoria Secret, which hung perfect on her naked breasts and stopped at the top of her slender thighs. Then looking like a goddess, she made her way through the club, passing Williams, no longer interested and on his way out, and over to Daltrey at the bar. Reaching her, she sat down and said, "Did you enjoy the show? The last bit was for you."

They both dressed together in the small shitty changing room where the girls who didn't like Mondays sucked off a sweaty fat fuck and caught a cab back to her place in Yaletown. Shannon sitting quiet as they went, gently touching Daltrey's knee as she looked at her. Her nails natural and perfect. Daltrey smelling the girl's perfume as her heart pounded, getting wetter down below as the cab grew nearer to the Roundhouse Building where the woman had told the cab driver she lived.

They still hadn't spoken when she took her gently by the hand and led her to her room with its trinkets and pillow topped bed. Shannon closed the door and moved closer, taking Daltrey by the neck, gently pulling her towards her. Their lips met softly, for a moment. Daltrey stopped breathing as she tasted the woman's lipstick and felt her tongue enter her own mouth as she closed her eyes.

The woman who'd been sleek and seductive on the stage, moving with elegance and grace as men stared in awe, was kissing her now, feeling her, touching her, undressing her as the woman undressed herself. Then when they were totally naked, still kissing her, the woman took her to her bed and laid her down upon the feather comforter.

Then she kissed her some more as their hands stroked each other's skin, feeling each other's breasts and the softness of their stomachs. The woman reached further down stretching her arm as she did, gasping slightly as she felt Daltrey's wetness. Slowly she moved her fingers up and down as Daltrey let her breath go as she felt the woman's fingers gently stroke her and feel the inside of her pussy.

Shifting her weight, the woman dropped down the bed, softly pulling Daltrey's legs apart as she did. Stroking the tender soft inner skin of her thighs she waited for a moment, savouring what she was about to do, then, with a sly look to Daltrey she smiled and leaned her head down and stroked her tongue up and along Daltrey's warm moistness.

Daltrey lay there feeling the tenderness of her mouth as the woman beneath moved her fingers deeper and deeper inside her, pulling them in and out as she twirled her clitoris gently around and around with her lips and tongue.

Oh my God it was nice, Daltrey thought as she grasped the duvet and felt her insides begin to tighten. This woman, this sexy, sexy woman, caressing her with her softness after she'd gotten herself all horny walking about half naked and being a bitch as men lusted after her. The last woman who'd been doing the same to her, in comparison, had felt like she'd missed lunch and worked as a pipe fitter on an oil rig, which is what she'd have liked to have done for a living if she'd had a dick. But this woman, *wow*, her softness, her beauty, the femininity of her sensual touch.

"Oh my God, oh my God," Daltrey called out as she felt her body suddenly start to go into orgasm. And then it happened, and Daltrey's body began to shudder uncontrollably as she came harder and longer than she ever had with anybody else in her strange and convoluted sexual life.

Shannon sat up on the bed and wiped her mouth with her hand, smiling. Thinking, *wow that was good.* She liked to make beautiful women come, it was her thing. It had been now for some time—ever since she'd discovered she didn't like the white creamy stuff hitting her tits or chin. Beautiful women were it, and if she could find a straight one who was a little bit curious, then all the better. And she did find them everywhere. In hotels or expensive shopping arcades where she'd prowl, eyeing women from afar, then moving in she'd catch their eye and stare deep into them in a way she knew only a woman could understand. Little needed to be said, for words were unnecessary when desire took over. And once she had them in her spell, she would take them back to her place as she had with Daltrey, where she'd undress them, feel them, and eat them until they came. And after she'd scissor them, grinding herself onto them until she'd come herself—as she was about to do with this one who had turned up at the club where she liked to gain easy money to pay the rent. This one who was there unexpectedly—especially sexy not only in her body or bitchy manner, but also because she was a cop.

****

Suzy sat in the corner of the bar and told the loan shark how there'd been cops in and out of the place all day. One of them had been trying to pass herself off as a lap dancer but had turned away almost a grand in money she could have earned from losers like her boyfriend.

This wasn't good, thought Mattia, *what the fuck was it all about?* Yeah, the place was loaded with undesirables such as drug dealers and gangsters and others who delved in certain levels of crime, but he was the only one out of all of them who'd kicked someone to death a block away after coming straight out of the place. He said, "Well it's got fuck all to do with me."

Suzy smiled, that was good to hear. It would be all she needed right now for him to be in trouble somehow and to have to disappear from her life again after all this time. She said, "Yeah, they do that sometimes, you know, come here and check it out, usually after some church going do-gooder has been in and gone home racked with guilt because he's had a decent pair of tits in his face for the first time in his life."

The loan shark, said, "Like yours?"

"Who knows, maybe?" Suzy said as she looked at the stage and wondered if she'd ever be back up there. *Probably not—well not here anyway.* Then she heard her man ask, "So, this chick who was here, hanging about, the cop. What was she asking about?"

Suzy shook her head and looked about the room. Two young guys had just come in and were looking about the place with their mouths open. She'd give them a chance to get drunk and horny looking at the stage and the other girls walking about and then she'd take them both for at least a hundred whether they liked it or not. After all, the excuse 'I've got no cash' carries little weight when there's a cash machine on the wall and your sexual preference and manhood are being questioned. She said, "She didn't ask anything; just told everyone they were losers and to fuck off. Oh, except the guy who runs the place. She said, he asked her to suck his dick."

"Oh," said the Italian, as he looked at the stage as though that was normal. Then he asked, "So where'd she go then, she still here?"

Suzy turned back to her man, whom she'd told Daltrey she liked to suck off, and said, "She left with the headline girl Shannon, she was done for a bit and she took her home with her."

"Really?" said the Italian, looking away from the stage and back at his girl, now intrigued. He carried on saying, "What she took her home to, you know, fuck her?"

Suzy raised her eyebrows as though it was the stupidest

thing she'd ever heard. *What else?* she thought, *she needs help cleaning the bathroom?* But instead, she said, "Yeah she does that."

"Oh?" Then the Italian said, "She ever took you back?"

She hadn't, and hadn't even tried, for as sexy as Suzy was, it was really beautiful sensual women Shannon liked—even ones with an attitude wearing a wig.

Not answering, Suzy let that one hang—knowing guys the way she did and the way they'd get all horny at the thought of her with another girl. Unless it was her husband, of course, who only got turned on watching other guys pound her in the ass, and that wouldn't ever be happening again.

Ten minutes later, the Italian was in an alley across the road waiting for the pair of them to come back. Except when the taxi arrived bringing Shannon back for her finale of the night, Daltrey wasn't with her.

Quickly he crossed the road and stopped Shannon at the rear entrance, grabbing her by surprise and twisting her arm up around her back. He pinned her to the pebble dashed wall and said, "Move or look around and I'll break it. Make a noise, I'll break it. Answer my question and I won't—simple."

Shannon got it, apart from a racing heart at the moment, she was still intact. There was a can of mace in her pocket, but reaching it would mean breaking this guy's rule number one. So, hearing the question was the best option. Trying to sound cool and as though it was normal to be assaulted in the carpark at the rear of a strip club, she said, "Try me, you never know?"

"The cop you just took home and fucked. Where did you drop her off?"

She said, “I didn’t, she went her own way.”

“Who is she, what’s her name?”

“I don’t know, I didn’t ask.”

And she hadn’t asked, but she had checked her purse straight after she’d wiped her mouth and leaned down again, kissing Daltrey’s pubic mound before climbing up and riding her pussy on it for awhile before she’d brought out her little double ended friend and stuffed it slowly into Daltrey’s vagina—then slipped it into herself and played scissors, fucking her hard until they both came.

She said, “She’s hot, she’s small, and she’s wearing a wig because she’s got a burn on her head. Ask around about it. I’m sure your connections go further than beating up women.”

That hurt, the Italian thought. It wasn’t the norm for him to be doing this, but she wasn’t wrong. He said, “So far no one’s been beaten. When is she coming back?”

“She won’t, she knows I know she’s a cop, she caught me checking her out.”

Fuck, the Italian thought. But at least he had something to go on. He twisted the girl with the nice legs who did not like men towards the rear door, keeping her face away from his and said, “Slowly open the door, step inside, and don’t look back.”

Reaching out, Shannon did just that, twisting the door handle gently so she wouldn’t break a nail. She opened it slowly and as she stepped inside, she felt the Italian’s vice-like grip on her wrist give and let go. The door closed behind her and without looking back, she stormed through the crowd and stopped herself right in front of Suzy who was sitting there on a bench by the stage in between the young men who had entered earlier. Looking up at her with her big titties bursting out of her bra, Suzy heard the woman scream, "Your boyfriend's a fucking asshole."

These girls who worked the strip clubs for a living were tough women.

****

Daltrey watched the Italian as he walked back across the carpark and opened the door of his car. *Well, that certainly had been a different way to have found who she was looking for*, she thought. The stripper with the legs having given her one of the best fucks she'd ever had and then the whole magic had been ruined after Daltrey found the woman with her hand in her purse after coming out the bathroom with a jar of leg cream.

And that had been that, relationship over. *But what should she expect, after all, look at where they'd met,* she'd thought as she'd taken a cab back to the club, so she could now wait outside in her Audi.

Fuck that was stupid, she thought again for what must have been the hundredth time. She pulled away and followed the Italian east along Pender Street. *Oh well, it was done—chalk it up as a mistake*, she told herself, trying to shake off her own feeling of stupidity as she carried on, three cars behind. The guy who was having an affair with a stripper with big breasts was moving slowly through the traffic now on Hastings Street, driving a shitty white Civic, cruising it from one end to the other and then back again. Daltrey doing the same, but way back now as she watched. Picking up her phone, she called Chendrill.

He answered and from what she could tell she wasn't the only one who'd been getting laid that evening. She said, "Chuck, I'm following your guy; he's cruising Hastings."

Chendrill saying straight back, "Yeah? He's looking for people, he lends money."

Daltrey watched him as she talked.

Chendrill said, "Did you meet Suzy?"

"Yeah, she's sweet."

"I know."

Then Daltrey said, "You're rich, you should give this shit up."

Chendrill laughed, "I think we both know the answer to that one."

Daltrey smiled. He was right, she did know. "The dealers know him, you can see that. The way they are looking at him after he's driven by."

"If you get the chance, see if he's wearing a new pair of cowboy boots. And if so, can you get me a photo."

It was a strange request.

"Okay?"

Then Chendrill said, "Williams called, he's all upset, said you exposed him as a cop and gave him a knock back on a lap dance."

"Tell him that I knew he had a thing for older women—anyway, I thought Suzy was a better option for him. She could wipe some of that bum fluff off his chops with those big titties." Then she said, "Chuck, I don't think it'll be a good thing if I go back into that place."

The phone went quiet for a moment as Daltrey drove and there were two reasons that she could think of. The first being that Chendrill was feeling guilty for asking her to go in there and abuse herself like that and the second was that he thought she couldn't handle it.

She was right on both counts. But she'd missed a third, and that was that he was still smiling at what Daltrey had just said, about the young police officer who wanted so much to be a man. And also that soon he was going to take her down to LA and have her burns looked at by the best cosmetic surgeon money could buy.

He sat there on the edge of the bed still naked and listened to Tricia in the bathroom sounding like a race horse as she took a pee. Normally it would have been Sebastian who called and disturbed them when they were making love and for a split second when the phone had rung during the throws of passion, he'd forgotten himself and thought it was. But no, it was Daltrey, the young conscientious detective who'd just nearly been killed in the line of duty, and who was now out there working, doing his job for him on the people's coin while he was in bed all evening getting laid. He said, "You do good work, Daltrey."

Daltrey scoffed, *yeah right!* She said, "What do you want me to do?"

"You got his licence plate?" Daltrey stayed quiet, then said, "1 – 0 – 1."

Enough said, Chendrill carried on, "Go home—remember, you don't work for me; you're just doing me a favour."

He heard Daltrey say straight back, "What's the deal with the guy's boots?"

It was a good question and one that needed looking into, even if now he never needed to lift a finger for the rest of his life. He'd heard the guy who'd been kicked to death in an alley was an ex-drug addict. The Italian had been in the vicinity at the same time, Chendrill knew that only too well because he'd stuffed a cheque for $250,000 in the man's mouth a few blocks to the east less than an hour before and if the Italian had been wearing the size tens that delivered the damage, he'd have tossed them the first chance he had and maybe bought a new pair.

Chendrill said, "You know what I'm like."

Daltrey did, and also knew that when he had a feeling then there was a chance he was on to something. He had her following him, but if he felt the man was really dangerous, he'd be doing it himself. So, it was a hunch. Nonetheless, from what she'd seen so far, the guy was a prick and things could get nasty, and they were about to.

****

The Italian carried on along Hastings Street, wading with his eyes through the junkies and dealers, the alcoholics who could not stop, and the poor souls caught in between. There were two things he needed to do now. *One—call the car guy he knew and see how he was doing*, he thought as he cruised around the filth which he, in his own way, helped to keep alive. *And two, find the guy who owed him block payments from last month and had no interest in getting back up to speed with things.*

He hit Main Street for the fourth time and carried along south towards Terminal Avenue, slowing at the SkyTrain station to look at the lost sitting in the doorways and begging for money with their signs at the centre of the road. Then he took a left and another quick sharp one and did the same outside the Central Train Station, where some lucky ones who'd gotten themselves clean would enter and head back east to where they were from to either start afresh or do it all over again.

He wasn't there either, this guy who had once been a good customer but now didn't pay. Then as he headed back towards Hastings Street, he eventually saw him settling into a doorway amongst a few others with nowhere to go. The guy sitting, leaning back now smoking on the street and about to jack up with a hit of heroin he'd just scored not a block from the police station. Sticking the needle he kept just for himself into a vein under his knee, the guy's eyes rolling back into his head as all the troubles in his world melted away and everything became beautiful.

Twenty minutes later, life was shit again.

With one trouser leg still above his knee, he got up and staggered through the streets, bumping into things he had not seen but should have. Crossing roads without a care, arms flailing, shouting at nothing, then he saw him, the Italian, sitting in his car the way he always did—the guy who he owed money to but always gave him more until he could fix things, as he always did.

How long now had it been that he'd gone without paying him what he owed? *A week*? *Yeah it was a week. Fuck he should pay now and get it sorted.*

The Italian sat there in the dark, smiling at him, gesturing for him to come over. He reached the passenger window at the side of the car and held himself up with his dirty hands as he watched the electric window drop, the Italian saying, "Hey buds, what's up?"

The junkie standing there with his hair in his face which was full of scabs.

"Hey!" the Italian getting straight to it saying, "you got my money?"

He did yeah, he had it, had some from his welfare payment and from his sister's he'd been stealing. He reached into his pocket and pulled out nothing. Looking back up at the Italian he said, "Yeah I got it but it's not here. I must have left it back at my place."

His place. A shitty hotel room that cost $400 a month, full of bed bugs and lice. A junkie who left his money at home? It never happened and the Italian knew it, he'd heard it a hundred times, he said, "Get in. I'm going to pick up some cash. You can have some more till you get yourself sorted."

They drove east heading out of the East Side with the windows open because of the smell, the Italian asking, "How old are you now?"

The junkie couldn't recall. He remembered his 26th birthday when his mother and father had come over and were so happy he had a new girlfriend and had straightened himself out after all this time of them worrying about his drug use.

Yeah, he was 27. He said, "Twenty-seven."

But he wasn't, he was thirty-four.

The Italian said, "So, tell me why you have decided not to pay?"

The junkie shifted on the seat as he watched the cars pass by, leaving streaks engraved in his eyes. He said, "I've been looking for my sister and I can't get a job, you know. But I got one lined up, there's this guy I know, real cool guy he's got work for me, then soon as I'm paid, it's yours and we're good."

The Italian saying as he drove and gestured to the parked cars and houses on the streets that ran away north and south from Hastings, "You see them cars? You see them houses? Well they're full of cash and you say you cannot get any for me, but you can get money for that shit you just put into your leg?"

The Junkie looked at the houses—yeah, he would do

that, break into cars, no problem. It wouldn't be the first time. He said, "Sure."

The Italian laughed, then said, "Hey, I'm just joking. What good to me are you if you are in prison?" But this guy was close enough to that as it was and a lost cause.

Then he heard the junkie say, "You seen my sister? I been looking for her; she was here then she was gone."

Not giving a shit, the Italian shook his head as he drove, "Yeah you said." Girls from that area disappeared around there all the time, but not as much as they had a few years back when that Pickton guy had been feeding them to the pigs. He remembered her though, this sister, remembered her looking good for a while as she'd stood there with her brother as they'd both bought blocks. Her in her tight jeans and boots. The pair of them living in the same shithole room at an excuse for a hotel on Hastings. He said, "She working?"

The junkie got it, he understood what the man was saying—'she working?' meant was she selling her ass as they did when they needed a fix.

"No, she didn't do that?"

"You check?"

And sadly, he had, as he'd wandered along the side roads and alleys where the girls hung night and day, rain or shine in short tight dresses and smudged lipstick as they waited for a passing car to stop so as they could do their thing, then go get their next fix.

"Yeah, she's not there, I asked. But she wouldn't either, you know?"

Don't count on it, the Italian thought. How many girls who'd been customers of his had he lost over the years when they'd started using what God had given them to get the cash they needed to buy crack—instead of going through him.

"Have you seen her?" the junkie asked again.

He hadn't, but he didn't bother letting the guy know either way—there was little point.

They reached the bridge and crossed over it heading north, then took a right straight after onto the slipway and headed east into the darkness. Passing through the Indian Reserve where the Italian had never ventured to ply his trade because he knew they'd kill him. Five minutes later he was at his place, parking up in the darkness of his long driveway. He got out and took a deep breath and listened to the night. It was silent. The house on its own next to the huge trees of Cates Park—the inlet to the east at the end of the home's long garden, and only silence as always from the neighbour's house on the other side.

He walked around the car, hearing his feet crunch on the gravel as he did. He opened the door for the junkie and said, "Come on, let's do some shit." Then led him into the garage and stood in the darkness. He asked, "How much you owe me?"

The junkie not knowing what day of the week it was, let alone his balance, he said, "Yeah I got it for you. My sister's cheque will be in Wednesday; you can have that." Then in his best effort not to get his clothes dirty, the Italian grabbed by the throat with both hands the man who thought he was still in his twenties and had been stealing his sister's welfare money and, holding him out at arm's length, held him there until the man went limp.

Slowly he dropped the man down onto a sheet of black plastic he'd laid out across the floor for special occasions. Then standing again, he stood silent, listening to the night.

Five minutes later, he moved again, picking up a bag of quicklime powder and poured it over the body of the man lying there in his shoes with no socks. Grabbing each corner of the plastic sheet, he pulled the string to release the garage door and watched as it swung up above his head, exposing him to the night.

With his left hand, he dragged the man's body out into the driveway and up onto the grass in the back garden. The plastic moving easily now on the grass made damp by the misty night air. He reached the bottom by the trees close to the inlet and stopped. Bending down he found the catch and pulled up the trap door to the pit. Dragging the man's body over, he positioned it at the edge and, letting go of two of the corners, lifted the plastic, dropping the man's body in.

He closed the hatch, locked it, and stood again listening to the silence. There was nothing, except for the movement of the trees, the lapping of the water close by, and the thumping of his heart. *He was getting soft,* he thought as he walked away dragging the now empty plastic behind him. *Letting the kid off like that and not giving him a beating first.* Where were the days when the kid would have been still alive wrapped in that plastic and felt his wrath via a baseball bat or anything else that was blunt so as not to get that AIDS shit flying all around the place. *It was because he was in love now,* he thought. *He'd managed to get back with Suzy, and he was in love. Yeah that was what it was. Suzy was making him weak with her nice ways and her lovely smell.*

He reached the back of the house and opened the top of a steel drum, placed the plastic into it, picked up a can of fuel at the side and lit it, sending a small ball of flame into the night as the plastic quickly burned away.

****

Daltrey's heart pounded as she watched from the edge of the park. She'd climbed through the darkness on the rocks next to the water at the bottom of the garden just in time to see the Italian drop something large into what must be a sceptic tank. She'd passed him on the road as he'd turned without signaling into the driveway of the house. Then turning off her lights, she'd doubled back, entered the park, and in the dim light of the moon found her way through the winding tree-lined lane to the carpark down at the water's edge. The guy was now lighting up a barbecue at the back of the house. The other man who'd come with him would be somewhere around also. But where? If he was, she'd hear them talking. *Maybe he was asleep in the car or he'd gone inside and was sleeping somewhere else?* she thought. Daltrey was right on that one. Except as far as the Italian was concerned, there was to be no wake-up call.

It hadn't been good. Not long back she'd have followed this guy in the darkness without her heart missing a beat—but now, no. She wasn't right and she knew it. The Russian really had fucked her up and even more so now since she'd spent the evening cruising the streets of Main and Hastings Street. The girl who'd given her life for hers only a few weeks back had come from there, had lived there. No doubt on a drug-induced death sentence herself. But the girl had died saving her life and Daltrey still didn't even know her name.

And shame on her for not trying harder, she thought as she stood there watching from the safety of the trees. She'd looked around and asked questions yeah, but in her eyes, she'd done so with her head up her ass. She was only human after all, and not as tough as she or anyone else believed.

Daltrey watched as the man who was in love with a stripper and had lost his edge because of it stood there putting fuel onto a fire, doing his best to keep the flames going. Then, kicking the bottom of the barrel, he sent a shower of sparks high up into the cool night air. With one last check, he walked to his car, got in, and disappeared out the driveway and headed back towards the city.

Yeah go on, get back to the girl of your dreams. Maybe you can lick the dribble left on her from all the guys who she's let feel and lick her tits, Daltrey thought as she moved slowly away from the safety of the trees. She moved through the damp grass, feeling her stockinged feet slide in her boots she'd slipped on as she'd watched the Italian from the safety of her car. They felt good now after an evening of wearing heels. She reached the back of the house and crept around front, then circled the place until she was back where she'd started. No one was there, not a sign, no light. No window opened to let in the night air. She looked at the road and then to her watch; it was past midnight. Fuck she'd been busy—she'd had fun at the club, then had more fun with the girl with the silky legs. Wow, she thought, still feeling it down there. It was a rarity anyone male or female had made her come like that, even if the woman had been a snooping bitch.

She moved around towards the back. Then with the help from the light on her mobile phone, she picked up the track of the man's body from where the Italian loan shark had dragged it through the grass and followed it until it stopped. Daltrey looked towards the trees and then down to her feet. It was pretty much the same area she'd seen the guy dump something into. *Probably a septic tank or a compost pit*, she thought, the guy giving the earth back all the shit he couldn't eat. But with them, mostly, there was a cover of sort and a handle.

She dropped down to her knees and felt the wet grass move quickly through her stockings and moved her fingers through the grass until she found a seam. Slowly she traced it around in a complete square until she felt a latch.

Daltrey moved away, looked back at the house, and then back to the latch. The small semi-circle handle was locked down with a fairly substantial padlock. *Fuck.* A few weeks ago, she'd have been through it with a breeze thanks to the locksmith she'd played to get a set of master keys. She looked back towards the house and the garage built into its side. Then she saw an axe sitting next to the chopping block. *That'll do it.*

Carrying it over, Daltrey stood there in her dress, wet stockings, and boots and took a well-aimed swing hard and fast at the lock, hitting it in exactly the same spot the nice-looking locksmith had told her to, should she ever feel the need to hit one because she didn’t have a key.

Throwing the axe to one side, she bent down again and pulled off the now broken lock and turned the handle 90 degrees and gave the cover a tug.

For a moment, it wouldn't give, the edges so well tapered so as to make a seal. Then, with her legs apart, she gave the handle three almighty tugs and felt the vacuum give as the lid’s seal broke away.

Then the smell of death hit her. The unmistakable, sweet-smelling, sticky stench of rotting human flesh rising up from the depths of a grave. Instantly Daltrey turned her body away, reacting on pure instinct, retching and gagging as the smell lined the inside of her nose and mouth. Covering her nose with the top of her dress, she looked inside the black pit, staring into darkness. Then she leaned down and picked up her phone, which she had placed to one side and turned on its little light, shone it down, and instantly saw the junkie who didn't know his age looking back up at her barely alive, his face white like death itself, his eyes burned red from the quicklime the Italian had covered him with.

For a moment and from the smell, Daltrey thought the man could only be dead. Then she saw his hand move as he reacted to the light. She looked around him, spinning her faint light about as other body parts, along with hands and feet which lined the pit, came into view. Then seeing movement, Daltrey shone the light back onto the man as she saw his hand shift position again. The guy was almost dead, there was no doubt about it. She looked up again and then back at the house, then back down at the pit as she did her best to cover her nose. The pit must have been at least ten feet deep.

Fuck, she thought, what should she do? Call it in and wait, or get the guy out now? No, get him some air to breath, she thought, then call it in.

She stood, walked to the house, looked into the garage and, taking a chance that the guy in the pit was the man in the car, stepped back and kicked the door in.

****

Chendrill sat on the edge of the bed and wondered how he was going to tell Tricia that after they had made love and settled in for the night, he was now going out again. A text had come through from a reliable source that his car was not sitting in the usual pound he'd been stealing it back from, but was now instead sitting safely for the next hour on a back road five blocks down from McGill.

It didn't make sense though, his car was outside. Maybe it was Dan's Ferrari they were referring to, he'd thought, as he sat there in the darkness, having read the text only seconds before. Then he'd stood and walked naked to the window and looked outside to see the Aston was gone.

The fuckers had come and taken it, this time illegally, sneaking it away while he was in the throes of passion—which seemed to be a thing these days. Now though they were keeping it away from the pound so as he wouldn't be able to steal it back. It was a trick, one they often used. When there was a rush of cars badly parked downtown and the pound was too far away for them to pull them all. *So that's what they're up to now*, he thought. *The pricks, taking the feud to another level, using tow truck driver trick 101.* He looked over to see Tricia lying on the bed with one hand propping up her head and before Chendrill could say a word she said, "Pulling the old fuck me and split routine again, are we?"

He was, there was little he could say or do to deny it. He said, "I'll be back in a bit then maybe we can get another one in before my phone goes again."

"You don't need to work, remember."

He didn't and he did, it was a strange dynamic. He said, "Yeah well it's important—I'll be back soon."

Important, like going to get your car so as you can fuck with some shithead's brain important, he thought. His girl wasn't wrong.

He got dressed and within a few minutes, he was sitting with the keys to his Aston in the backseat of a taxi heading towards his car which was apparently hidden five blocks south of McGill.

He reached McGill, asked the driver to turn left, and carried on until he saw the Aston sitting there on a corner amongst old beaters looking out of place. Telling the driver to drop him on the corner, Chendrill got out and watched as the cab disappeared along the road. He reached the car and looked up at the road sign which read Casper Street, then quickly over his shoulder to see the Italian coming out of the darkness as he pulled out his gun and shot him.

****

Jesus Christ answer your fucking phone Chendrill, Daltrey said as she stood with a ladder before dropping it down into the pit.

Giving up on Chendrill, she cradled her nose with one hand and began descending into the darkness of the pit. She reached the bottom and looked at the rotten limbs and skulls scattered around her, then she turned her flashlight to the only other living thing down there. Reaching down, she grabbed the man's arm and tried to get him to stand.

"Don't let me die in here," he managed to whisper.

Daltrey pointed the light from her phone towards his eyes, which looked red and blistered from the lime.

"I can't see properly," he said.

Daltrey lifted the man to his feet and felt her own feet slip on the rotting bodies as she did.

Reaching out with one hand, she put both his hands on either side of the ladder, then said to him, "There's a ladder, start climbing."

The man lifted his foot and began to climb up the ladder away from this netherworld. Daltrey behind him, the two of them climbing slowly, the smell of rotting flesh easing with every step as they grew nearer to the fresh air at the top of the pit's opening.

The man reached the top and rolled himself onto his back and breathed the night air deep into his lungs. Moments later, Daltrey was standing next to him looking down as she wiped the rotting flesh away from her boots onto the grass like dog shit and began to puke again.

Finishing, Daltrey looked away from the pit and took a deep desperate breath of the nighttime air and filled her lungs, blew it out and did it again. Fuck, the smell was still there, stuck somehow to the inside of her nose like some sort of alternative anti-perfume.

She pulled out her phone and tried Chendrill again, nothing. Then she looked up to see the lights of an approaching car through the trees, coming towards the house.

****

The Italian was pissed, *why, oh why can he not get a single thing right at the moment*, he thought. How the fuck could he have lured that big Hawaiian shirt wearing fuckhead to a perfectly quiet area and then forget about the trannies that hung about around there at night? Jesus, he was an idiot, and why the fuck had he not just got on with it and shot the fucking weirdo right there and then, straight after he'd shot Chendrill?

It was Suzy, she was making him like this—it had to be, the loan shark Italian thought, knowing he was completely off his game just because of some random Suzy look-alike woman or whatever she was who'd come around the corner with her short skirt and blonde hair and big come-fuck-me tits. The woman mind fucking him the moment after he'd lined up and put a bullet into Chendrill.

"Fuck!" the loan shark said out loud as he pulled the car back into the drive for the second time that night. "Why the fuck did you not just shoot her as well?" he said to himself as he stopped the car at the bottom of the driveway.

Now Suzy was all angry with him. The woman he'd been in love with his whole life breaking off the relationship and hanging up the phone on him, just because he'd called her on the off chance it was her out there walking the streets late at night and selling her ass.

The woman being at the club just as she'd told him she would be and instead getting all worked up and accusing him of attacking some dyke when all he'd been doing was having a quiet chat.

Fuck, he was an idiot, he thought. But fuck, the business with the dyke stripper was done now, and truth was how many times had he heard Suzy break off their relationship in the past? Many times.

He sat there for a moment trying to think it through as he rubbed the back of his neck and looked at the gun sitting on the passenger seat. Remembering Chendrill lying there on the ground bleeding. He thought, *I've done it now.* Suzy was the least of his problems at the moment. Now he was in real trouble, even if he could pull himself out of the shit with Suzy, he'd shot a guy out in the open and left a witness, and for what? So, he could look like a big shot in front of some shithead guys who ran a tow shop? After all, what had this guy in the stupid shirts done to him? Gotten physical that's what. Then given him a cashier's cheque for $250,000 after, that he couldn't cash at the moment anyway, but would as soon as he hit the Cayman's with

Suzy, but even that was on hold now.

Fuck! Fuck! Fuck! he thought as he tried to calm down and think it through. "Okay, okay," the Italian said as he sat there in the car and looked at himself in the rear-view mirror. "That freak never saw your face." In his mind, he'd done the right thing. Everyone hated that big fuck Chendrill so it could have been anyone waiting in line to shoot the prick. It'll blow over, like it does. Tomorrow he'd go over to the house and tell Suzy she's coming to live here with him, along with the kids. Fuck her weedy idiot loser husband—he could fuck off. She's coming here and from now on there'd be no more bullshit, no more disposing of drug-addicted losers. *He'd fill the pit in with dirt and in the future they could fall on their own swords. Done, that's it. Decision made,* he thought as he took a deep breath and opened the glove box and stashed the gun above it, tucking it in the hole he'd cut in the plastic at the top. Then he got out and looked into the back of the garden and saw in the darkness that the door to the pit was still open.

Jesus Christ! He was such a fucking idiot, he thought. *What the fuck was going on with him today?* He was sure he'd closed it and locked it. Now he'd attracted raccoons again as they were lying next to it in the grass as they liked to do. He walked to the side of the driveway and picked up the long gaffing pole with the spike and hook at the end that he'd found at a flea market and brought home so as he could do target practice on these stinking black eyed fucking overgrown rats that passed through the garden, throwing the pole at them whenever he could—just as he had when he was good at the javelin in the old days back at school.

Taking the pole and balancing it in the palm of his right

hand, he stretched his arm back so the pole's rusting metal hook and spike sat right next to his cheek, twisted his body to the side, took a few quick steps forward, and in one fast, practiced movement he launched the pole through the air in a direct line 200 feet down towards the bottom of the garden and watched it land in the center of the group of raccoon's laying by the pit.

"Yes!" he said out loud, he'd got one for certain. The boy still had it.

Then one of the raccoons stood and dusted itself off. The Italian stared into the darkness as the shape of a small woman in a cocktail dress slowly became apparent. Shit, this wasn't good—*they must be kids*, he thought. Kids out looking for a quiet place to fuck and then they'd come across the open pit in the darkness. Now he'd have to kill them all and throw them down there as well. But what about when they went missing and they brought tracking dogs in as they liked to do? Then he'd be fucked, those fucking mongrels with their big fucking ears and droopy chops would be all over the backyard like flies' round shit. He needed to play it by ear.

He called out, "You need to be careful sneaking about in other people's yards—you could get hurt."

Daltrey had watched as the long spear, suddenly propelled through the air, came towards her and had moved quickly at the last second as it landed, almost sending herself back down the pit. *Fuck*, she was pissed. *The fucker*, she thought, as she looked at the spike sticking in the ground only inches from where she'd been laying. A few weeks ago, she'd run from a madman, but she certainly wasn't going to run now. Not from this fucker. Slowly she stood and for a moment wondered if the Italian had a gun.

Maybe, but if he used it then there'd be neighbors calling the cops and then the RCMP would be here and that's all this prick needed when he'd been fertilizing the lawn with junkies.

Daltrey moved away from the pit; and grabbing the end of the pole, she gave it one hard tug and pulled it from the ground as she called back, "You need to start worrying about who you throw things at," and then stood there waiting for him in the center of the garden.

The Italian slowly walked towards her off of the graveled drive and onto the grass, keeping his eyes fixed on the young woman standing there holding his pole in a party dress and boots. He could see her now in the moonlight—she was a looker. And wearing a dress like that, chances were high it was the same woman who'd been hanging about the club. So, he wasn't losing it, his instincts were dead on and he had been right to almost twist that lesbian's arm out of its socket.

He looked at the man he could now see lying on the ground looking at them both with his face all burnt. Recognizing him as the guy he'd picked up and thought he'd just strangled to death, he took a deep breath. *Jesus Christ! What he needed to do*, he thought, *was get his fucking act together*. He needed to take the pole from this fucking lesbian and knock her the fuck out. Then he'd stick the sharp end of the big toy he liked to throw around the garden into the fucking loser and throw him back down the pit. Then he'd take this bitch into the garage and give his other smaller toy a bit of action. After all, since Suzy had been out of action in that department, it had been a while. He needed to get mean again, just how he'd been in the old days before he'd gotten soft. Back then, he'd have fucked her until he was bored and then before he sent her to join that other loser in the pit, he'd have tortured her until she told him exactly what she and any other fucking cop in this city knew about him.

So, that's what he'd do.

Then surprisingly, Daltrey came at him, lightning fast, bringing the pole up as she did in a posture that could only mean that the direction it would be heading was his head. Quickly the Italian put his arms up to block the stick as Daltrey, at the same time, let go of the pole, and in one swift move while his arms were up, she dove at his legs with her own and scissoring them at his knee, spun her weight around his body and allowing her momentum to bring him off balance, brought the man crashing helplessly to the ground.

The moment he was down and winded, Daltrey was back on him, bringing her right arm quickly around his neck and her legs on top of both of his knees. Then keeping him in the choke hold she'd picked up over a long weekend in Port Alberni, she spun the weight of her body around again, rolling the man onto his back, pinning his legs beneath his ass with hers in between.

And there she held him, feeling the man struggle, unable to move as he fought to breathe. She counted as she felt her forearm jammed deep into his windpipe. One, two, three, four, five, six, seven and at eight he was out cold.

With three jerks of her body she released him from the limpet formation she'd formed around his body and stood. Then wasting no time, she walked over, picked up the long pole the man had nearly speared her with, and with a huge swipe swung it towards the Italian's left leg and stuck the hook right into the man's calf.

Tugging the pole with all her weight, she pulled once, then twice, then on the third felt the man's unconscious bulk begin to give and slide slightly on the grass made wet by the night air. Then just as she saw the man was about to come around, she began to run holding the pole, pulling the man as she did. With all her might she twisted to one side and swung the Italian around through the wet grass in a semi-circle like an Olympic hammer thrower with hairy legs—and let go, allowing the Italian's momentum to take him the last couple of feet, sliding him head first into the death pit of his own creation.

The girl was definitely beginning to feel better.

In a flash, Daltrey was at the edge of the pit, kicking the ladder to the side and slamming the lid down. Reaching down and breathing hard, she twisted the catch and stood on top. Pulling out her phone again, she called Chendrill.

Again, nothing.

It was time to call Ditcon.

****

As late as it was, Ditcon was still in his office, and strangely so was Stephanie, his new driver. Not that they were working. What it was, was this: word had gotten to Ditcon that Chendrill had inherited a fortune. This information had then been 100% confirmed by a lawyer he knew, who'd called another lawyer he knew, who worked for Samuel. And that's when Ditcon had decided to get drunk—not only drunk on alcohol though, but drunk on jealousy also. And in this drunken jealous state in which he'd tried to even the odds in his mind somehow by again trying to seduce a girl half his age with a fetish for domination. A seduction that had only once again failed miserably, but this time ended with his ass sore from being whipped and yet another wet nose and aching tongue after having his ears held crazy tight until he'd hyperventilated and passed out.

Now though he'd settled down and picked up Daltrey's phone call only because he'd just ordered a pizza and thought it had just arrived. As he put the phone to his ear, he said, "If the order's wrong, we're not paying."

We? The tight prick, Stephanie thought as she listened, sitting in Ditcon's favorite chair.

"It's Daltrey."

Ditcon went quiet and listened as the girl who'd just taken down a serial killer breathed hard into the phone. Daltrey carried on, not waiting for the man to speak, she said, "I'm in North Van, next to Cates Park, there's a pit, it's full of bodies."

Fuck, thought Ditcon, as he listened. North Van, Cates Park—he hated driving out there when the doughnut shop wasn't open, and it was RCMP territory, out of his jurisdiction, so he'd probably have to be nice to some spotty faced cop and work this one hard to take the glory. He said, "Cates again hey?"

Being a long way from downtown and set on the inlet next to the mountains, the park had been a favorite dumping ground over the years for people wanting to bury bodies and had seen its fair share of skeletons turn up. He said, "Who's the perpetrator?"

Daltrey took a deep breath and looked to her feet as she heard the Italian stirring below. "Send an ambulance," she said, "there's a guy who's in a bad way." Then she carried on, "the guy who owns the pit is in the pit and I'm standing on the lid."

Ditcon smiled, this was great—no manhunt necessary, he could take the glory, it had been hard work, yeah, but he'd got the guy in the end, he always did.

Then he heard Daltrey say, "Chendrill had me follow him, he's dating an exotic dancer."

Fuck, Ditcon thought, *that fucking prick*, playing detective again while all Ditcon had been doing was trying to fuck him up. And to boot, he was fucking that stripper with the big tits.

Taking a guess, and this time correct—for once in his life—he said, "Yes, we are well aware about Chendrill's relationship with Suzy Diamond." And he was, as after having stared at the woman's breasts for an hour a few days prior, he'd looked her up online and liked what he'd found.

Daltrey said quickly back. "No not Chendrill, the guy in the pit."

This was good, Ditcon thought, *even better*. Now he could bring this Suzy Diamond in and give her a one-on-one in-depth interview about this boyfriend of hers he'd just caught. Maybe he could even console her.

He said, "You next to the park?"

"On the water—to the north."

"Be there in ten minutes."

"Call an ambulance."

"On it!"

But she knew he wasn't, so Daltrey called one herself.

****

They arrived at the same time, Ditcon in a puffed-up state of supreme glory and the first responders from the fire department who went straight to the man on the ground and instantly began to bathe his eyes. Ditcon saying as he looked at them, "What are these guys doing here?"

Daltrey, still standing on top of the lid to the pit, feeling her own skin burning from the quicklime, and feeling the bumping sensation of the Italian who was no doubt at the top of the ladder she'd thrown down there trying to push it open, answered, "You called them, I thought."

Ditcon replied as he looked to his driver, "Where's the killer?"

Daltrey nodded to the grass under her feet and said, "Where he deserves to be."

Ditcon looked to the grass beneath Daltrey's feet and then back up to her. "And there's a pit down there full of bodies along with the guy who put them in there?"

Daltrey nodded. Raising his eyebrows and trying to hide his smile, Ditcon looked to his watch. Then to the sky to the east, the sun was a long way from coming up and that was a shame, as situations like these looked good on camera in the early morning light. He turned back looking to his young driver first, then to Daltrey, and full of pride said, "Well I got the guy in the end!"

Chapter Eighteen

Chendrill woke in the ward of St Paul's hospital and for a moment wondered where the hell he was. Then it all came flooding back—the car, the street sign, Sebastian's message from the afterlife, passed onto him via the strange lady who'd been waiting for him at the undertaker's. A message which he'd taken no heed of until that last moment, when it had suddenly made sense. Putting him on alert. Just enough to see the Italian appearing from the shadows with the gun, giving Chendrill that split second he needed to spin himself away as the Italian raised the gun, taking the shot in the shoulder instead of the heart.

Chendrill had gone down and landed there on the sidewalk looking up, unable to move. The Italian had walked over to him. Then seeing something out of the corner of his eye, he'd moved off quickly into the night at the same moment a woman who looked like Suzy had appeared. The woman with her long blonde hair and big boobs reaching his side and looking down at him as he lay wounded on the sidewalk. Crouching down next to him in her short little skirt, Chendrill had looked at her as the hazy realization hit that it wasn't Suzy. And as she held him and twisted her knees towards his face, the last thing Chendrill had seen before he blacked out was the woman's testicles hanging out of either side of her tight little panties. One thing was for certain, he owed the woman—or whatever she was.

Fuck, he was an idiot, he thought as he felt the wound on his shoulder. Then he heard the doctor coming even before the man, in a hurry, took a peek around the curtain.

"Hey, are you Charles Chuck Chendrill, the guy who found the dog?" asked the doctor.

He was. He asked, "Do you have my phone?"

They did, and the first person he called was Daltrey, who said, "Where the fuck, have you been?"

Chendrill saying straight back, getting it out the way, "Be careful, Suzy's boyfriend just shot me in the shoulder." Then he said, "Maybe it's time to mention this idiot to Ditcon and have him brought in."

Then after a pause, he heard Daltrey say, "You can tell him yourself once he's stopped vomiting."

Chendrill sat there for a moment and listened to movement coming from Daltrey's end. Eventually, she said, "The guy's been throwing junkies in a pit at the bottom of his garden. He thought he was going to put me in it as well—but it went the other way. I trapped the prick in there and shut the lid. I called you, but you'd fucked up, so then I called Ditcon. Problem is that the egotistical idiot took too long to open the pit up and when he eventually did, the fucker was gone."

And that's how it had played out. Daltrey on top, the Italian below crawling around in the mud and slime of rotting limbs and torsos, puking as he found the ladder in the pitch black darkness of his own self-made hell and dragged himself up to stand on his now one decent leg, reaching down to feel the metal spike stuck firmly in the other—the pole now gone, snapped clean at the riveted joint.

Pulling hard, the Italian had screamed as he felt the metal spike come away from the center of his calf muscle. Then still holding it, he reached into his pocket and felt for his phone. It was still there. *Thank god*, he thought as he crossed his chest and kissed his hand straight after as his body unconsciously reverted back to his childhood days when he'd stood happy and smiling as an altar boy and wondered why the Catholic priest was always smiling at him in such a weird way.

He pulled out his phone, turned it on, and looked around as the light from the screen unleashed the horror of what he was smelling and had smelled so bad each time he'd opened the pit to throw in more lime or another poor soul who'd gone too far into the dark side to be able to pay back the money they'd owed.

There was mud and rock shingle all around three sides of the pit, the fourth, though, had a bottom layer of larger rocks that sealed the pit from the outside. Beyond that was a meter round pipe that ran to the rocks at the side of the inlet that he'd laid in for run off—in case, for some strange reason, the trap door closed and he couldn't get out.

Standing on his bad leg, the Italian stuck the metal spike into a small gap in the rocks and started to dig until a minute later they were clear. Then laying down in amongst the filth, he pulled himself into the pipe on his belly and began to crawl through the slime and stench.

Three minutes later, he was batting away from his face the rats that fed on the rot. He pushed away three big rocks that he'd placed on the secluded shoreline himself and pulled himself out completely from his own handmade tomb.

Crouching, he looked at the lights around the place he once called home and then made his way down to the water, stepping in quietly, submerging himself in the dark cold water, and beginning to rub the slime from his body. Then standing again, he looked down at the wound on his leg. It was bad and still bleeding heavily. Kneeling down, he washed the rotting filth still stuck to his hands off in the water then did the same with his leg.

He moved on towards the park, keeping the water just above his wound, hoping the salt would clean it. Then he moved out, wincing with every step as he made his way back inland into the trees until he was alongside the drive. That fucking bitch in the dress was still there standing on the lid to the pit with her arms crossed. Another guy in a suit with a bald head was on the phone standing next to another woman who looked hot.

Fuck he thought, how the hell did he get himself into such a fucking mess?

He looked at the firemen treating the loser heroin addict's eyes and then to their 4 x 4 blocking his vehicle. In the distance, sirens could be heard, more cops and an ambulance no doubt. He moved along to the front of the house and saw Ditcon's car sitting at the curbside. Coming out of the cover of the trees, he reached the driver's side and looked in. The keys were there—perfect. Still dripping wet, he opened the door. He slipped himself inside and sat himself back in the darkness and waited as he listened as the sirens approached. Thirty seconds later, he saw the lights and ten seconds after, the ambulance and police car arrived, deafening the neighborhood as he started Ditcon's car and drove away through the melee.

****

Ditcon was pissed for two reasons. One, because Daltrey was a fucking idiot and should have followed police procedure, used her training and handcuffed the fucking idiot—or better still, shot the fucker. But no, she didn't have her gun or cuffs because she'd been playing undercover slut in the strip bar for that stupid fucking dumb, fucking, fuckhead Chendrill. And two, his car was gone because his dumb-ass driver had left the keys in it. But possibly the most annoying thing about the whole shambolic episode was that his golf clubs were in the back.

"Don't say a word about the car—to anyone. The guy's gone and it's not important how," is all he said to Daltrey and Stephanie as they walked back into the driveway.

Then he said to Daltrey, "Where's yours?"

"In the park. I parked it there so as I could tail him through the trees."

Yeah whatever, Ditcon thought, *big fucking deal, you dumb bitch*. Then he said, "Well the RCMP around here have a lot of explaining to do since they failed to uncover and apprehend another killer we've found living in their jurisdiction. I can't believe they let him escape."

He took a deep breath and shook his head, rubbed his neck, looked at Stephanie, then said to Daltrey, "Go get your car."

****

The first place Daltrey hit after dropping off Ditcon and his driver—who she could tell hated her—was her shower. Then her bath. But the smell was still there. So she showered again and this time scrubbed out the inside of her nose with her fingers.

What was all that about, she thought, this Stephanie woman looking down on her when all she was doing was driving? Let her be the one who outfights a 250-pound monster. The fucking cock-sucking bitch. Fuck her. And she had beat him, this prick who Suzy had a thing for, she thought, as she stared at herself naked in the mirror for not the first time that night. It certainly had been interesting.

She got dressed quickly and forty minutes later, she was standing at the side of Chendrill's hospital bed.

She asked, "Have you told your girl?"

He hadn't. What he had done as he'd woken though was to send a text.

"I told her I'd be late," Chendrill said.

Daltrey said straight back, "She'll be thinking you have another woman."

"Yeah but when she's sees this, she'll know different."

Daltrey stared at the wound in Chendrill's right shoulder. She said, "Maybe she'll think the other woman shot you."

Maybe? Chendrill thought as she heard Daltrey carry on saying, "The fucker nearly got you, hey?"

Chendrill wanted to shrug, but knew he couldn't so he just said, "Still standing."

Daltrey smiled, kind of, but she got the gist. She said, "I thought I had him, but you know—you trap a rat in a drain pipe and if one end's rotten, it's getting out."

Chendrill lay there and thought about the Italian crawling through a pipe, then thought about the fucker shooting him.

Daltrey said, "I saw something tonight I never thought I'd see in my lifetime, Chuck."

Then as the vision of the transvestite kneeling down with her nuts hanging down next to his head as he lay there on the ground flashed through his head, Chendrill said, "Same here."

He owed the transvestite one—that was certain.

Daltrey said, "One thing I will say for Ditcon is, for as much of an idiot as we see him to be, once that trap door was open and it was empty, he was on the phone and had a photo from the club and the lower mainland shut down, and he says it's staying that way."

Chendrill smiled and said sarcastically, "Yeah—good for him for doing his job." Then he took a deep breath that hurt and said, "Well I can tell you there's little point because I'd put Tricia's new house on the line and say the man's still here."

And as always, he was right.

****

In the Italian's eyes, he had done little wrong. Yeah, he'd killed the odd fucker and shot an ex-cop, but the junkies were on their way out anyway and in reality, the State should be thanking him as he was doing society a service. That cop also should have known better than to get physical with a known gangster, *Jesus, fuck me.* And on top of it all, he was in love, and about to, after all these years, get back the girl of his dreams, along with the kids that he knew were both his. All he had to do was lay low for a while until everyone got bored and then wait for his girl to leave her husband, which she was about to do. It had all been perfect until that little slimy gay fuckhead with the poofy little dog had come drifting back in from the past and gone and fucked it all up by buying her and her husband a house.

Now he had another slight setback, as well as a huge hole in his leg.

With his head down, the Italian limped along the street, bought a razor and some scissors from a convenience store and shaved his head in the cracked mirror of the shitty bathroom of a room he found on Hastings Street. The man at the reception window of the cheap hotel only taking cash in advance and never looking up. Then with his new look, he crossed the road and hobbled up three blocks to the charity shop and bought some clothes that someone no longer liked or fit into, stuck an oversize truckers cap on his head, and threw his designer wear that stank of death into a bin. He carried on in great pain back along Hastings Street, limping and beginning to cry out with every step. His body twisting as he moved, he passed an all-night pharmacy which gave a deal on prescription methadone and stepped in, grabbed some iodine, painkillers, and bandages and carried on up the road, passing the shitheads who lived on the street towards the hotel.

He found the entrance to his new home and passed the desk with the manager sitting there in a string vest that he'd ripped at the front from scratching. Struggling with the stairs, he found his room. *The place was a shithole full of shitheads, but a perfect place to lay low*, he thought, as he sat on the bed and pulled the banker's draft from his wallet and looked at it.

He had this $250,000 here and another $650,000 he'd stashed away in the Caymans, and $51,000 in usable money from incorporations he owned here. But he couldn't access that because they may have tallied up his connection and already be watching the system for movement. If he was quick though he could hit the debit machines and pull maybe a grand out on two cards and be gone.

If he was quick.

But they'd know he was still around.

He'd wait, he thought. *He'd wait it out*. Let them think he was long gone and then work a way out of this mess from there.

He looked about the room—the curtains had blood on them, as did the sheet. But the sheet was washed. The walls were shiny yellow from nicotine. He was sure the place stank, but for the moment his nose had stopped working. *Fuck—that fucking bitch*, he thought. *Fucking up his leg*. He pulled down his new trousers and looked at the wound in the cheap fluorescent light. It was bad, but he'd seen worse. Stripping off, he walked to the bathroom and jumped in the shower that was thick with black mold. He turned on the taps and waited for the hot water, which wouldn't come.

"Fuck it," he said out-loud and got in anyway. Then he reached for the soap that wasn't there and then after for a towel that wasn't there either.

Getting out, he limped his way back into the bedroom and dried himself on the bedspread that left him with hair that wasn't his. He sat down on the side of the bed and looked at his leg again. Wincing at the pain, he pulled the wound apart and then screamed out loud as he poured a splash of iodine straight in. Falling back, he lay down and looked at the ceiling, wondering if someone would care enough about his screams to check.

He waited, listening for doors to open, footsteps along the old wooden floorboards of the corridor that would stop outside his door to see if he was okay. Nothing. He spun around and looked out the window through the shitty net. People outside were sitting in doorways, some high on crack, some selling second-hand junk they said was theirs. Some doing both. That guy that kid saved, Clive Sonic, there in the distance, lit up on a billboard in the night sky. The man with the smile, looking cool, Saying, 'Trust Me' to anyone who cared to look.

Fuck off! the Italian thought as he laid back down and stared at the fluorescent light with its burned out ends and dead flies stuck to its grease and wondered about Suzy. How was he going to explain this one to her? He should call. Twisting the dyke's arm was fixable; having a pit with the odd dead loser in the garden where she'd sat with him and had barbecues, that was going to be a tough sell—it was work though, so maybe she'd get that? Maybe, but sometimes women could get funny about the strangest things.

****

The light was just coming up on a new morning when Chendrill pulled himself out of the bed and walked to the window. Somewhere out there was a group of men who had conspired in various ways to close his curtain. It was a strange feeling. One that sat there in his stomach and gave a real-time wake-up call. Twice now in the last month someone had tried to remove him from society. *Maybe it was time to grow up*, Chendrill thought. He could settle down with his new girl and ride it out for the next 50 years—if he was lucky enough to get that far and become a cool guy in his nineties. It would be hard though to do that, sit back and know there were people out there wandering around who'd had a part in orchestrating his downfall.

The Italian was at the top of the tree, but who were the others and how much did they actually know? He'd find out soon enough, he knew that. Someone sent the text about where the car was sitting hidden to his guy in the know. He called him up. The phone went for the longest time before the man answered and said, "You get it?"

"Oh, I got it alright," answered Chendrill, "right in the

shoulder, from some Italian."

His man, who Chendrill now paid but hadn't before when the man had owed Chendrill for getting him a suspended sentence instead of spending two years in a holiday camp, was now silent for a moment. Then, confused, he said, "What?"

Chendrill hated saying it, but he said it again, "The car was there, but there was this Italian loan shark with it, and he had other ideas."

"This is the guy they're looking for?"

The guy was on the ball.

"Yeah, but not because of me. It turned out he was starting his own cemetery in his yard. Where'd the info that sent me there originate?"

"A text. I'll send it to you."

It came up and Chendrill read it.

The Aston's at Raymur and Casper for 2 hours.

Fuck, there it was again, Casper, why had he not listened to that woman who was trying to warn him, why hadn't he just looked where the street was, just for curiosity even? he thought. Then he carried on talking to himself in his mind as he stared at the name on the phone. Hocus pocus, that's why. That's what you get for being small minded. You, big dumb fuck.

Putting his phone away, he said, "Well they weren't lying."

The Italian wasn't following the car and hoping to see Chendrill arrive though, he knew that. The thing was planned. After all, the guy had been busy driving around Hastings looking for a certain person to feed the lawn with.

The fucker would surface soon, they always did, Chendrill thought as he watched the clouds begin to pick up the low sun. And when he did, he'd make sure he spilled the beans.

There was a slight knock at the door and without waiting, it opened. It was Dan's mother and seeing her man standing there in his hospital gown she came straight over. She said, in a manner that only someone who had spent their working life in patient care could, "You'd be better if you didn't walk about."

Chendrill turned and smiled. It was good to see her and as soon as he did, he felt an overwhelming sense of guilt.

Tricia walked over and held him, and in her embrace, he could feel his woman's anxiety. She said softly, "Chuck, I think it's time to stop this." She looked at his legs—still bruised and scabbed from before. Then she said, "Last time it was your legs, this time your shoulder, where do you think the next injury's hitting Chuck?"

Time to stop?—she wasn't wrong, Chendrill thought. How long had he been fucking with these guys at the tow shop even though he knew they were all connected? Even if that wasn't the actual reason the Italian had decided to set him up—after all, he hadn't been particularly nice about handing over Sebastian's money—*but fuck him*, Chendrill thought as he held his girl without speaking and felt the blood rush from his stomach. *Fuck him. He had tried and failed, and if you're going to do something, you do just that—if not, watch out.* He'd been there in the hospital long enough. It was time to go, so he said to his girl as she held him and worried about him, "You didn't bring me a new shirt by chance, did you? The one I had on has a hole."

****

Carl the big fucker of a tow truck driver who could use

his neck as a pillow was shitting himself. Yeah, he had an old Buick Sabre with a veteran plate and a disabled sticker attached to the back of his rig which normally would have made him smile. But today, more so than any other day in his life, he was terrified.

Everything he had worked for, which amounted to a job at the tow company and a shitty rental home in Surrey, was now in jeopardy just because he'd let his ego get the better of him. The guy had met the Italian by chance at the football, knowing him from old when he'd done repo for one of the man's friends. Big Carl the tow truck driver, standing there with a beer in one hand and a hot dog in the other, trying to be cool and asking him stupidly, "What's it gonna cost to whack the big fuck who wears the loud shirts."

The tow truck driver who didn't need a support cushion on a plane all pissed off, having had enough of this Hawaiian shirt wearing motherfucker making a mockery off him within the tow trucking industry. The tow truck driver in bed at night so pissed off now that he couldn't even have a wank. Lying there whilst his wife snored and farted in her sleep. The guy dreaming and fantasizing about killing Chendrill himself or paying a hit man to do it so as he could feel like the gangster boss he didn't have the chops to be.

He could do it, yeah course he fucking could, he'd lay there thinking. In his eyes, no one needed to know he'd paid the guy or was involved in any way, but if the man was to suddenly disappear then anyone working at the depot who'd been smirking at him, or leaving toy Ferraris in the lot like they had, would all think *hey, the big guy Carl, watch out for him—don't fuck with that guy Carl.*

But just as he was expecting the Italian with the rings to smile and deny that killing people was what he did or used to do, the man had said, “Tow his ride and leave it where I say and let’s see what happens.”

Now the man had gotten what he wanted and wished he hadn’t. *Fuck, fuck, fuck,* he thought as he sat at the lights next to the charity shop on Hastings and felt the big diesel engine of his rig chug away.

He’d gone in to pull the Aston the previous night. Big Carl getting the call from the Italian just as he was about to go home late after ruining people’s evenings. Big Carl the tow truck driver going in stealth-like, getting up some speed at the top of Dan’s mother’s road and turning his tow truck’s engine off so he could coast in towards the Aston. The guy stopping, cutting in at an angle in front of Chendrill’s car, and in one practiced move he had the luxury car on the back of his rig and then dropped it off again in that quiet area where the trannies liked to hang out.

Sixty minutes later, he was home feeling like a king and coming on his wife’s face as she liked him too do. Then off to bed feeling smug. Now though, in the cold light of day, not even twelve hours later, the whole of Canada was looking for the Italian prick—wherever the fuck he’d gone. How long was it going to be before they caught on to the fact that it was him who dropped the car off right next to where the idiot had to have shot him?

He’d had enough calls to tell him the guy who’d been fucking with him was in the hospital with a gunshot wound. So how long would it take for the detectives, whose job it was to put people away, to find out and put two and two together and come back with him?

“Fuck!—Fuck!—double fucking fuck!” Carl called out

as the lights changed and he pulled away and passed the shitty hotel where his partner in crime was hiding with a festering leg.

He reached the yard on McGill and felt the eyes on him as he pulled in—thinking he would look big, but now feeling as distressed as the veteran whose car he'd just towed. He dropped the car and threw the keys on the counter just as he always did and walked inside to the rest area at the back to grab a coffee to calm his nerves. Passing the open computer, he looked at the screen—someone had been searching. The top of the search screen read:

Accessory to attempted murder prison sentences

He stopped and read in amongst it all one line that sent a shiver through his body and caused his stomach to hit his mouth. It read:

25 years to life.

He carried on into the back room and thought for a moment that he was going to vomit. As the words, *Oh God—oh God, please no, please no*, flowed through his mind.

He opened his phone and typed in the same search. Seconds later it was all there for him to see. Half sentences—full sentences—joint principal—conspiracy—life imprisonment—words in Latin, others he didn't understand. One thing he did understand though was that there were no doubts about it—at the end of the day if he did not get out of town, he was going away for a very long time and where they would send him he couldn't bring his tow truck.

****

The first thing Chendrill did after he picked up his car was to go back to his apartment to charge his phone, and the next thing he did was call the tow truck office on McGill Street.

He said, "Please could you make an announcement to all your drivers that a Chuck Chendrill's on the line and wants to talk to one of them."

But there was little point in Chendrill waiting for someone to come to the phone because moments after the dispatcher had happily said exactly that over the tannoy for all to hear and gossip about after, Big Carl was out the door with his fat neck bouncing up under his chin, heading for home.

He was about halfway there when the realization set in. *How can I go home?* Carl thought, as he sat there covered in sweat with his heart pounding, gunning the tow truck with the rattling chains back towards Surrey. He couldn't run—look at the Italian they were looking for him all over. If he kept heading east, he'd be picked up. He could hide but where and who with? He could take the missus, but she liked her TV and why would he? She hated him anyway.

He pulled off the highway and sat for a moment as if he was working, considering his options. Go west, hang out on the Island? No good—they'd be onto him. Same for the North and East. South... it was an option. He could hit the border now and go through and disappear. But they could have a picture of him there if Chendrill was already on to him. It was a possibility. And if not and he got through, they'd still be looking for him because eventually they'd know he was there. *Fuck*, he was an idiot, a fucking idiot.

He should have just punched the guy in the face like he used to at school—given him a slap and been done. But no, he wanted to be one of the big boys, wanted to be a gangster, and right now it was painfully obvious he didn't have the guts. An Angel? Not a chance. How the fuck did those guys operate and not seem to give a shit?—the way they walked about like they owned the place and could care less.

Because they were in and he wasn't—that was the difference. And to be in you needed to be strong and he was almost crying and all he'd done was tow a car and send a text to a killer.

Yeah, that's all he'd done, he thought, as he sat there trying to stay calm and watched as the traffic filed past. Yeah, but if he thought like that, pretty soon he'd be thinking that in court when the judge put the hammer down on the best years of his life—and then someone else would be coming in his wife's face, in the same way she liked him to.

Fuck, he told himself, act now, do something now and get ahead of the game—sneak out, get to the States, do it so no one knows you're there, change your name. He could go to LA or New York and tow real cars for a living. Big celebs' cars, then just send back a postcard of Dustin Hoffman's Rolls on the back of his rig and let them work it out up there in the coffee room on McGill who'd sent it.

He pulled out his phone—he knew someone he'd met a few years ago when they'd chatted in a bar and both got drunk together. The guy knew someone who had a tunnel and it was operated by associates; it took you under the border. No questions asked, with a one-way one charge. All he needed to do was call. Chances were if he did, he wouldn't need to pay as the guy had said he could slip him through for free because he was a good guy and was connected. He remembered the man, sitting there with a double Jack and Coke and saying, "Anytime—anytime, call me and you're through."

Flipping through the contacts, he found what he was looking for—it said 'Tunnel guy,' no name.

He dialed and seconds later it answered. The voice on the end sounded the same as the man he'd spoken to years earlier, even if he was eating. Carl said, "Hey, it's Carl, we met in Lefty's a couple of years ago. How you doing?"

No Answer. Carl carried on, he said, "We had a competition, we were seeing if we could drink a beer whilst we had a full one balancing on top of our heads."

Then the guy said, "You the guy with the neck?"

Unconsciously, Carl felt his neck and rubbed his forefinger through the fold, pulling out a lump of wet dead skin on the end of his nail as he did.

"Yeah, that's me."

Then the guy said, "What do you want?"

Carl got straight to it. He said, "Your travel business, I was wondering if I could call in the favor and grab a ticket?"

The man on the end of the phone saying straight back, "Yeah sure—five grand cash—one way—there's a bus going tonight—have the money in an hour and once it's picked up, I'll call you with where we meet half an hour before it leaves."

Fuck! Carl thought, *five grand was a lot*. And if he paid it that would leave him half the savings he had in his bank. Taking a chance, he said, "When we spoke, you said it was free because the top of my head was flat."

Carl listened as he heard the guy on the end of the phone laugh, then heard him say, "Yeah you're right. I did. I remember. It's $5000—if it's too steep, grab your passport and you can cross for free at Peace Arch. Call back in thirty minutes if you've got the money, if you haven't don't."

And with that the phone went dead.

Carl sat there and looked back out towards the traffic again. Five grand, but there was light at the end of the tunnel—quite literally. It was a move and it was a slick one. Fuck you *Charles Chuck Chendrill and your big fucking car and shirt.* He thought, *fuck you.* Big Carl was back and he had a plan.

****

Dan sat on his new leather sofa and ignored another text from 'Marshaa'; then straight after, a long, long one that had taken almost two hours to write, which came all the way from a mansion in Beverly Hills where Adalia had been sitting by her pool.

He said to the girls, who were all in a line standing at the other side of the room, "Try it again and this time instead of doing the little hop all together one way, try to do two to the left and then the other two of you go to the right."

They looked at him—he was great at choreography, but the English was getting in the way.

Myuki said, "You show!"

Dan got up, still holding the button to the remote control for the music. Lining up, he hit the button, did the move, skipped to the left, paused the remote, rewound it a bit, and did it again on the other side. They all watched, then got it.

He sat back down and hit the button again, watching as they all did their little bit and moved perfectly. It was great, and fuck these girls were so sexy. He said, “Want me to order in another pizza?”

The girls looked around and smiled. They’d seen him get through five already and it wasn’t even four in the afternoon. But what the hell? Then he said instead, “Or should we go out?”

Ten minutes later, they were all squashed into the Ferrari and heading towards Micky D’s. Dan looking at the new ‘Trust Me’ posters all over town depicting Clive Sonic as the man to have as mayor—glad to see the back of his own campaign. The girls loving the attention as they played the music on the stereo as loud as it could be. The Ferrari cruising along through traffic with Dan smug at the wheel and not giving a shit about the noise.

He pulled off the road and dipped the car under the Golden Arches and parked up diagonally outside the window as he liked to do. There was a chance that Melissa was working; and if she was, Dan was hoping to drag her back and get her dancing with the girls—then, if he was lucky, into his room for some fun, along with the rest of them, if they were willing. So far, though, they hadn’t given any sign that they were interested in anything other than dance routines. But how long would that last? They were young though. And being young himself, there was every chance it could all come together for him if he waited. Long gone were the days of shoving his dick in a girl’s face as he had with Daltrey and the blind chick with the dog which bit him.

Adalia Seychan had taught him that, and taught him

well.

They all sat down at the table, Dan sending Myuki up to put the order in with a stack of bills he did not count. The girl coming back with a tray full of food and the change.

He asked, "You happy?"

They all nodded, how could they not be? They had free accommodation in a penthouse where they could dance 24/7 if they wished—not only this, but their landlord was a superstar who paid for all the food, even if it was junk food at the moment.

"Maybe we should get some to go as well, for later?" suggested Dan.

The girls looked at each other, then at the car, then at the fat guy at the counter with a pillow for a neck and big gold rings on his fingers.

Big Carl the tow truck driver picked his order off the counter and walked towards a table with his tray as he watched the girls and the punk kid who couldn't park his Ferrari properly and wondered if it was the same one he'd been towing and where he'd gone wrong in his life. How the hell could this dozy looking fuck have four chicks and a Ferrari and he had a fat assed wife? But that didn't matter right now in the scheme of things, as he needed to get out of town. He'd been to the bank and pulled all his savings. The guy who he knew once and had gotten drunk with years back had told him to be near the window that looked out onto Main Street. He looked out the window, past the Ferrari, and saw the guy sitting there on the corner on his Harley, waiting.

Fuck that was quick, he thought, the man on the phone telling him that when he saw the guy pull up, he had one minute or he would be off. *Fuck,* he thought, *how long had he been there while he'd been sitting there staring at this loser and his skinny Asian girlfriends*? Standing, Carl quickly took off towards the door, his fat legs rubbing against each other and his ass showing as he did.

He hit the double door with the palm of his right hand and ran out into the carpark with his neck wobbling and his open jean jacket blowing in the wind. He reached the Harley. The guy in the small skullcap helmet sitting there looking at him as he came. Reaching him, Carl panted out of breath. Digging into his pocket he pulled out the envelope that read five on the front, handed it over and without a word the biker was off, thundering away at full throttle with his big cowboy boots positioned high on the foot pegs of his Harley, carrying what equated to almost one hundred tows from the downtown area.

He walked back under the arches and entered the door and looked at Dan who was staring at him as he did. Unable to keep his mouth shut, Carl said to him as he passed, "You're lucky I'm on my day off, parking like that."

Dan wondering why the fat fuck couldn't mind his own business said straight back, "At least I can fit in it."

Big Carl, the tow truck driver who thought he was tough, was angry enough now to get into it with anyone, even this skinny big-mouthed idiot. But the kid was lucky he was on the run from the law—wanted for attempted murder. Maybe he should just go over there and tell the prick just that, then deck the fucker. What difference would it make? He could be out of there in a heartbeat before the cops came along and tried to revive him. Yeah, he'd do it—fuck it. He'd knock the cunt out, show him who's boss in front of his girlfriends in their little shorts that didn't fit, who were now taking turns to eat fries out of the idiot's mouth.

He stood, took a deep breath and began to walk over when he saw Charles Chuck Chendrill pull into the carpark in his Aston.

Chendrill got out of the Aston and, with the briefest of glances at the tow truck, stepped inside. He looked at what Dan was doing and then to the girls and, feeling the pain in his shoulder, went and sat down at their table.

"How you gonna find this cabby with the turban who's stalking me if you keep getting yourself shot?" Dan said.

"Maybe it's a good thing this guy's still chasing you and you'll think about it next time you decide to do a runner on a cab?" Chendrill said back.

"Maybe you'll do a runner next time someone pulls out a gun?" It was a good point.

Chendrill said, "Sometimes electricians get a zap, you know what I mean? Comes with the territory."

And in a way, it did, and Chendrill knew that. When he signed up, they'd been upfront and said the job can be dangerous but that they did try to train you and prepare you for an unfortunate situation or incident. Which was more than they did if you took a job working the night shift in a convenience store—not that he ever would have.

Nonetheless, a gunshot wound was disturbing, especially for Dan, who surprisingly was getting used to having the big fucker around.

Chendrill carried on saying, "Besides the guy missed. Just grazed me." Which was an extension of the truth and they both knew it—Chendrill because it hurt badly still. And Dan because his mother had told him.

"Who did it?" Dan said.

Chendrill got straight to it, "Some Italian guy and a fat fuck who drives a tow truck."

Dan looked at the table where the guy he'd just been lippy to had sat and saw he was no longer there. He looked out into the carpark at the tow truck which wasn't moving. Dan said, "Like that one?"

And Chendrill answered straight back as he looked to the truck parked up by the road more closely. "No, not like that one—that one," he said.

Dan smiled. This guy, who he'd become friends with and who, according to his mum, he had nearly lost the night before, playing it cool. He said, "Really?"

Chendrill looked back and nodded. Then said, "100%"

"The same guy?"

Chendrill shrugged. Then said, "Where was he sitting?"

Dan showed him and said, "Right there."

Chendrill stood and looked at the table and the mountain of food the man had just ordered sitting there completely untouched. He walked over and looked at it. Picked up the tray and bought it over to Dan and the Korean girls' table.

"What if he comes back?" Dan said.

"Oh, there's no chance he's coming back. Not while I'm sitting here at least."

Dan stared at the back of the tow truck, the vehicle looked dirty and menacing with all its chains and hooks hanging free. Turning back to the table, he looked at the girls who had no idea what they were talking about and said to Chendrill, "What are you going to do, stake it out and wait for him to come back?"

Chendrill smiled, it was the logical thing to do. But where was the fun in that? He said, "No, why would I want to do that to the man when I can sit here and let him watch me eat his food?"

****

Carl stood behind a bus shelter on the other side of the road and peeked through at Chendrill, Dan, and the girls in their tight shorts who he'd love to fuck. All of them smiling and joking as Chendrill ate the tow truck driver's meal. He thought back to when he'd last eaten. It was first thing this morning, long before reality had set in that he was now an accessory to attempted murder—back then when he still had some sort of semblance of a life.

Then he saw it coming along the road, the big commercial wrecker tow truck he used to drive and cause havoc with whenever he had the opportunity to switch lanes for no reason. The big beast in all its grandeur cruising along Main Street with some schmuck he hated from the depot at the wheel. Long gone were the days of such glory when there was nothing he could not tow. Then it slowed, took a noisy right with its engine blasting smoke up and out of the dual stacks on either side of the cab. The tow truck crossed the road, stopping traffic as it did and pulled up into the Micky D's carpark at exactly the same time as the police car he had yet to see arrived.

In one practiced move, the tow truck was in front of Carl's truck and the driver was dropping down to the ground from the cab. Walking over, he talked to the cop in the car and then walked back over to the cab of Carl's tow truck. Pulling out a slim jim, he quickly opened the driver's door. Seconds later he was inside, then at the back of his own truck, noisily dropping the crane. The driver then hooked onto the front of the tow truck and hit a lever, pulling its front tires off the ground. With one more trip inside the cab of Carl's truck, the guy released the hand brake and was back in his own vehicle, revving the fuck out of its huge Detroit Diesel engine and dragging Big Carl's pride and joy out onto Main Street straight past where Carl was hiding behind the bus stop and off to the police compound followed by one of Williams' friend's in his patrol car.

****

The Italian didn't know what time of night it was later that evening when he was woken by the sirens blasting outside his window. His head ached and he was sweating badly. He sat up and looked at his leg, which was swelling and still hurt. Then he looked at the bed and to the bed bugs crawling on the sheets and across his stomach.

Quickly he batted them off and stood on his good leg and stared at the triangular shaped bite formations on the fleshy part of his gut.

*Fuck me, that's disgusting, h*e thought as he swiped the remaining bugs off the sheet and onto the linoleum floor and smashed them to death with his shoe.

Fucking things. Checking himself in the mirror for more, he put on his trousers and hopped himself barefoot and shirtless downstairs to the reception. Calling out to the guy on the reception as soon as he hit the last step, he said, "Hey, fuck me, the room's full of bed bugs!"

The receptionist, who never looked up, did just that and said nothing. Before the Italian could say another word, he pulled out a can of bug spray and put it on the counter in front of him.

The Italian picked it up. Standing there with his top off,

he looked at it and said, “This is for roaches, not bed bugs.”

Without looking up, the receptionist brought out another can, a different color from the first. The Italian took it and kept the other and called out as he walked away, “You need to find me another room.”

He reached his room again, hobbling all the way, lifted the sheets, and sprayed both cans onto the mattress until both were empty. Then with the smell and taste of the insecticide in his mouth and lungs, he opened the window. The night air came in through the bloodstained curtain. He looked out and felt the cool air on his face and forehead. He was still hot, too hot. He went to the bathroom and put his head under the tap for a moment—the cold water helping, but not for long. It was time for a shower again, he thought, as he turned on the taps, hoping the hot water would be there this time. Giving up again, he got back in and felt the cold water like ice on his boiling body, then getting out, he reached for the towel that didn’t exist.

Fuck he should have got one when he was down there, and some soap, he thought as he hobbled now angry and naked to the door. Opening it he screamed out down the corridor towards the stairs, “Towels—get some fucking towels and soap up here.”

He closed the door and felt his head spin as he did and with just the one leg working properly he wondered if he’d be able to stay up. He held onto the door, then the wall, then the bed, and lay down again and with his head spinning, passed out.

****

It was almost midnight when the power bar on Carl’s phone went red. It had been ringing with calls from his wife and guys from the towing depot all evening, but none from the guy who could drink a pint of beer with another balancing on the top of his head.

He was cold and wished he had the dirty fluorescent jacket he kept behind the driver's seat of his tow truck—that, and his charger.

They could trace his phone, he knew that, but they hadn't. They had his rig, but that was that fuckhead who was supposed to be dead. But he wasn't, he was alive and well and had been sitting in McDonald's with some homo and four chicks eating his food. *Fuck, he was hungry.*

He looked along the road on Robson Street, which was now blocked for pedestrian use and remembered towing a vehicle that had stopped for a moment right next to the Art Gallery. The guy had chased him all the way to Georgia Street on foot and he'd lost him at the lights and left him in a cloud of diesel fumes after he'd heard the guy screaming.

How long had it been now? he thought. All day, all night it seemed, and all he'd had was a Subway sandwich. Then just as the last bars of power began to disappear, his phone went and a voice simply said, "Go stand on the corner of Burrard and Robson," and hung up.

That was two blocks to the west. He knew the area well because it was full of cars every afternoon after three when the parking law changed. He moved off, waddling his ass as he did and hit the corner just as a farm vehicle with blacked out windows in the rear pulled up on the other side of the road.

He crossed over, and as he reached the passenger side, the door opened and Suzy's husband let him in.

They pulled away, with no one speaking. Carl recognizing the guy at the wheel and wanting to chat. The husband saying nothing, except, "Go sit in the back," as he handed him a hood.

Big Carl, the tow truck driver who wanted to be a gangster, moved through to the back, squeezing his fat gut between the seats, and saw six other hooded people sitting on the floor—two of whom had to be children. He sat down. Then from the front of the van he heard Suzy's husband call out to him again for him to hood up or get out.

He travelled south straight down Burrard with the hood on his head, feeling every bump on his ass through the hard metal floor. Then from what he could judge, they took a left and a right and found Granville then they stayed on it heading south again until he could hear through the open window planes coming in to land at the airport. From there, they hit the highway and carried on further south for twenty minutes or so, then he felt the vehicle slow and take a turn, then a sharp right and then left and carry on, stopping every thirty seconds or so. *They had to be on Zero Ave or close,* he thought, as he felt the vehicle pull away and then slow and start up again, over and over.

Another thirty minutes passed. Then he felt them turn, hit gravel for ten seconds and come to an idle as the driver got out and got back in again and drove them inside some kind of building.

Moments later, he heard the back open and the man who's face he couldn't place say, "Keep the hoods on and get out."

Looking at the ground, the tow truck driver shuffled his way along the metal flooring of the van and wondered if all this nonsense was worth it. He heard one of the kids begin to cry and then the mother scold him to silence in a language he could not place. Then he got out and stood looking down at his big greasy work boots with their steel toecaps.

A hand grabbed his and placed it onto what must have been someone else's shoulder and then he felt someone touch his and hold on. They started moving like cattle down a slope as the air became stale. Fans started and as they kept walking downwards the air became cold. There was water on the compacted gravel floor. They reached the bottom and he felt the downward slope change and begin to rise. Slowly they carried on in a line—the kids sniveling, foreign words coming from in front and behind. They reached the top as the temperature changed again and the dampness left the air. Then there were some steps—they climbed them, passed through another doorway and entered into another big building with dust on the floor.

He heard the back of a van open up, as the door clonked, and drew a breath of relief as he saw the bumper and U.S., Washington State license plate briefly as he climbed into the back. He settled down as the doors closed and he heard other larger one's open. Then the new vehicle started and pulled away, stopped, then started again as the wheels crushed the gravel beneath them as they carried on along a track.

Then the vehicle came to a sharp stop in the gravel and there was noise. Gunfire, men screaming, women and children screaming also. He heard the driver's voice shouting, "No! No! No!"

Dogs began barking and in a matter of seconds, the rear door was open again and someone had hold of his boots and he was being dragged out feet first onto a dirt track where he landed face first in the dirt.

****

Basil stood and felt the oil between his toes as he wiggled them in his shoes in the darkness. What an operation it had all become—him up there in Vancouver working tirelessly digging deep to find the guy who'd stolen their border vehicle and headed north bouncing across the border in it. Basil out there, working alone undercover in a foreign country, hunting day and night, putting in huge overtime until he unearthed the secret that now culminated in busting up a massive border breach and the uncovering of a highly sophisticated tunnel system.

At least that's what he'd be telling them and what his time sheets reflected.

But what the hell, no one could take away from him what he'd achieved even if all he'd done was take a call from Chendrill that same evening and been told to get his ass down to Zero Ave and to watch two particular addresses for activity—one being on the Canadian side and the other on the U.S. side. It was simple, if you see a farm vehicle hit the one on the Canadian side, then get ready on the other because like rabbits they'll be coming out the hole on the other side—and they'll be moving fast.

And that's what he'd done so far that evening—that, and get his feet rubbed by Maio. His new girl there earlier with her little bottle of massage oil with its squirty top and her little stick, Basil with his eyes closed and a smile. Then he'd gotten the call from Chendrill; and with no time to slide his socks on, he was out the door.

He'd passed Suzy's husband driving the farm vehicle—with half a dozen illegal immigrants and one tow truck driver in the back and Williams on its tail. Basil driving so fast on the highway as he headed south that he hadn't noticed either. Then he'd tucked himself away on Zero Ave, sitting there with his hands on the steering wheel in his car, nervously wiggling his oily toes and feeling his heart pump in his chest. Unconsciously sinking his head down into his shoulders like a turtle as he waited until the van eventually came and disappeared though a side lane into the correct barn—just as Chendrill had told him it would.

Then a minute later, with his oily feet slipping in his sockless shoes he'd rushed out the car and jumped the border himself and alerted his colleagues at the border security services as they arrived all pumped up with their guns out to arrest him. Basil waving his ID, pointing, and shouting as he battled to keep his shoes on his feet.

"I'm an intelligence officer—U.S. Customs and Border Protection—get the fuck out of my way! There's a breach! They're going through a tunnel—call me a SWAT team and take me to that farm, right the fuck now!"

For Basil, who so far had done pretty much nothing exciting in his life, it didn't get much better than that.

Chapter Nineteen

Charles Chuck Chendrill put down the phone after calling Basil and sat on the sofa at Dan's new place, which used to be Mazzi Hegan's and stared at the Korean girls' asses as they revolved slowly around and around to the music. Dan mesmerized, sitting there with him, both with their hands on their knees as if it was a Sunday morning at the launderette.

"I don't think they are ever going to stop," Dan said.

Chendrill hoped they wouldn't. He said, "Are they always like this?" They were, dance practice went on at all hours, and in between they ate and took turns flirting with Dan. But now there was another man in the house, and he was older and sexy.

So, it was time to tease and the girls were having fun with it.

Chendrill asked, "Do they each have their own room?"

Dan smiled and said, "Yeah kind of, but so far they've been all sleeping with me in mine."

Chendrill broke away from the girls' hypnotic revolutions. "Really?" he asked.

Dan smiled and said straight back, "Yeah I think they like looking at Mazzi's erotic art on the ceiling."

"Oh?" said Chendrill and wondered what the art was and why he'd never in his life been as lucky.

Then Dan said, "But they won't let me fuck them. They just cuddle and then sleep. And when they do, they snore—especially Myuki."

"Oh?" said Chendrill as he got it. He said, "So, that's nice they've friend zoned you then—in a big way?"

Dan smiled, he hadn't really given it much thought—as he was having so much fun. But as always, the big guy wasn't wrong. "Not for long, I hope. You see, Myuki keeps looking at me, I got the feeling," he said.

He's got the feeling, Chendrill thought. The guy who only a little over a month ago was knocking one out into his mother's socks now had a feeling and was sleeping in a boudoir designed by a gay man with a troupe of Korean dancers Sebastian had somehow found just so he could shame Rock Mason.

Fuck, he wished he was Dan's age again, and said, "I'd better go."

Dan said, "Yeah you'd better before Mum comes around and you get shot again."

Oh yeah, that, Chendrill thought, as he felt the sting in his shoulder and remembered the Italian pulling the gun on him.

He said, "Yeah and I doubt she'd fuck it up either."

Still making light of the incident when deep down he knew he'd been lucky twice now, Chendrill stretched and stood, felt the pain in his shoulder worsen, and wondered if the wound was bleeding under the bandage.

Seeing movement behind them from the reflection in the windows as the girls looked out at the view from the penthouse, the girls stopped their dance rehearsal and came over to Chendrill as he made for the door and smelled their sweetness and looked at their painted toenails as each one waited in line to kiss his cheek.

Yeah, he wished he was Dan's age again.

****

Chendrill drove back towards Dan's mother's home and

wondered how things would have panned out had the Italian not got his aim wrong or if he'd been a real pro and shot the woman with the stretched panties who somehow scared him off. They'd be another meeting at Slave no doubt, but he had no will so what would have happened with all his new money that he had yet to see?

He hit 12th Street, headed east, and called Williams with his right hand as he sat at a red. Williams sitting there happy and excited as he answered and the first thing he said was, "God, I wish I could have crossed the border and been there when the shit hit the fan. How the fuck did you know?"

It hadn't been hard; in fact, truth was it really couldn't have been easier, and the suspicion had been there for Chendrill for a while now—ever since Suzy's husband had blurted out that he'd left the door open on Zero Ave. Then after when Suzy had said he had a job going down to the States. In the end, though, the woman had gifted the little fucker of a husband's illegal activity to Chendrill anyway as they'd sat on the bench by the water. After all, in Suzy's eyes, it was what the man deserved after getting his kicks out of watching strangers rape her ass.

He said to Williams, "You just have to listen."

Williams out there working for free all day on his day off and loving every minute of it as he'd cruised about in his own vehicle and on his own time, picking the tow truck driver up in his sights as he'd left the yard on McGill and headed towards the highway. The young cop who wanted to be legendary like Chendrill letting his idol know that the guy was about to make his neck bigger as he'd settled down in Micky D's for some lunch. Then, on Chendrill's instructions, Williams had arranged a tow.

Following the guy after, Williams had called Chendrill again with updates as the man wandered around the city like a lost puppy and eventually sat in Robson Square before getting in a farm produce van and headed south.

That's when he'd made the call and sent Basil with his feet covered in oil flying out of his favorite foot massage chair.

Chendrill hit the road that he'd used so many times when he'd been to see Dennis. *What he would do*, Chendrill thought, as he headed east in the darkness and looked at the road, was contact Dennis again, see how his wife was and see whether she'd skipped town. He knew the woman would—*but would she if Dennis was now a partner in a huge dentistry*? Chendrill doubted it. *But he'd do that,* he thought as he drove. He'd call Dennis in the morning and offer him just that and then he'd have a word with Samuel about the man's license and see how the people who took it away from him could handle a law firm with seemingly unlimited funds.

He made it back and let himself into Dan's mother's place and was met in the corridor with a hug and another kiss on the cheek. Tricia said, "I thought you would never come home."

It was a good point. He said, "I was with Dan."

Tricia said back, "I know, sometimes I wonder what the two of you have in common."

It was around 8 a.m. when Chendrill woke to find Dan's mother messing with his dressing.

She said, "I'm sorry, but it's bleeding." It was and quite badly. She carried on saying, "You should have stayed in hospital instead of stealing food and looking at chick's asses."

Fucking Dan, Chendrill thought, as he sat up and looked at the sheets that would need to be thrown out unless the washing detergent could live up to its promise.

"Really?" he said.

"Like I said yesterday, you need to grow up, Chuck."

He did. He said, "Then I'd be boring."

And Trish said straight back, "You've got a fortune in the bank to keep you from being that. Make sure you're here to enjoy it instead of pretending to live some weird superhero life."

Chendrill thought about that one. He'd been called a few things in his day but a superhero… he wasn't that. He said, "Okay, you win, I'm staying put and house hunting with you until I'm better."

But almost as soon as the words had left his mouth, his phone rang and it was Basil from the CBP telling him he had a couple of other interesting people in the van along with the husband and this guy with the fat neck. And then moments after he'd put down the phone, Suzy called.

Chendrill pulled the Aston up outside the house that Sebastian had bought for his old friend whom he used to like to chat with at parties.

They sat at a table next to the new bay window—the framework looking better now since it had been fixed up. Suzy sitting there all emotional in her loose top feeling guilty, crying tears of frustration more than of upset for her husband, who she'd just discovered was sitting behind bars in a U.S. Federal remand center.

"The guy rarely worked, you know, but when he did, he'd say it was tunnel work, but I didn't know he was doing this. I took it for granted it was at the docks just as it has always been," she said.

Chendrill stayed quiet. Given that the woman had been the one to give her husband's nighttime activities up to him only the last time they had met, it was an odd thing to say, but women could be like that. Especially if their kids were in ear shot. Say one thing one minute, completely deny it the next. He'd seen it years before whilst dealing with domestic abuse, when often the women had called because her husband was beating the shit out of her and then denied he'd done just that when the police arrived and the kids were there. It was shitty, but it was life and he understood. Chendrill said, "He knew what he was doing, and besides I have to tell you, I was involved in instigating this investigation into the tunnel they were using."

Suzy looked to him for a moment, taking in what the man in the loud shirt was telling her. Then she said, "I knew you'd look into him after what he'd had the kids do to Sebastian."

Chendrill took a deep breath. He said, "He told you, did he?"

"No, my youngest did. It's disgusting. The sick asshole, he didn't have the guts to go speak to Sebastian himself, so he sent the kids instead."

It was then that Chendrill got it and it was an angle he had not yet considered. At the end of the day, it was easier on the kids for the woman's husband to fall on his own sword. The woman playing him to help give the man the little push he needed. After all, had Chendrill started to dig deeper about her husband initiating the assault on Mazzi Hegan and then after for having her kids attack Sebastian and kill his dog as per their father's instructions, then the boys would be in trouble with the law themselves and could have easily been sentenced for assault as juvenile offenders—or at least have been pulled into court and coerced into testifying against their father. In Chendrill's eyes, she'd played a good move as even if it had just come down to a day trip to the supreme court for her boys, unless the father was a pedophile or was constantly beating them and their mother, then no child should be put through testifying against their father and have to live with it forever after.

Chendrill said, "It turns out that in the bus he was driving there were two known terrorists. So, maybe the person who tipped off the authorities did the world a favor."

In genuine shock, Suzy put her hand to her mouth. *How could it get any worse*? she thought and asked, "He was driving terrorists?"

Chendrill said, "It's yet to be proven. You know what these people are like. They like to make things bigger than they are."

Then Suzy took Chendrill by surprise and said, "Well let's hope it is true and then we can take some of these monsters off the street and at the same time I can get on with my life."

"Oh?" said Chendrill, as he wondered if she'd also heard about the other love of her life.

Then before he could say another word, Suzy asked, "Have you seen the news?" Without waiting for an answer, Suzy carried on, "My mother always said I had bad taste in men—it looks like I get a clean start though. It's a good thing, I think."

Chendrill stayed quiet for the moment. Then Suzy said, "You know he's still here in town?"

Chendrill nodded, he suspected as much—the man was

injured, after all.

Wondering if the guy was in the basement, he asked, "The Italian? How do you know? Has he called?"

Suzy nodded, then said, "You know he's not a real Italian. He looks it and pretends to be, but he's not, he just liked the persona I think, liked people to think he was part of the Mafia—you know, I don't even think he's ever been to Italy."

Chendrill smiled and felt the heat of embarrassment drift though him. It was funny and kind of humiliating at the same time, getting hit by such a loser it seemed—even if he had been burying junkies in the lawn. He stayed quiet and watched as Suzy sat there looking at the floor. Moments later, she said, "He has SIM cards that he throws away. I know it's him because he always sends a text with random numbers just before he calls for real. He's been doing that, except now he's skipping the numbers and just getting straight to it."

"Saying what?"

"I don't answer, it's just random messages, so I've not paid too much attention, but the ones I have heard he's begging one second and saying let's meet the next. You know, stuff like that and drivel, sounds like he's in pain. As I said, I don't answer now."

Chendrill nodded and, unconsciously rubbing his wound, said, "Did he say where?"

"If he does, I'll tell you. But I know he's downtown somewhere. I'll forward them to you. I want that idiot out of my life as much as I want to divorce the other one, which now it seems will be pretty easy. All I want in my life now is to be here with my kids in this home that Sebastian bought for me, that's all I want."

Then she said, "I know you hold all the aces now Chuck and I know if it wasn't for my husband and kids, Sebastian would still be here. But please don't take my house away. I've been honest and this is the first real home I've ever had."

Chendrill smiled., He'd made a promise to Sebastian to look after the woman and her kids and it was the last thing on his mind, but obviously the first on Suzy's, though the woman had dealt with all the other issues first before she'd gotten to her own. He said, "You ever thought of a career in dentistry?"

****

Chendrill got back into his car and headed back downtown. He hit its core and, seeing a rack of women's flip flops by the doorway of a 7-Eleven, he stopped. The sliding door opened so fast with a *swoosh* that it made Chendrill wonder if Captain Kirk would appear. He looked at the rack, the flip flops all there in different colors some with flowers, some without. Trish liked them; it was what she wore around the house and what Dan would wear also when he couldn't find his shoes. He spun the rack and looked further, what he needed was a pair any man would be too ashamed to wear unless they hung with Mazzi in his old days on a 'girls' night out.

Buying them, Chendrill then headed south again towards the private hospital where a surgeon had worked miracles on the love of Dennis the dentist's life. He parked up outside and walked into the fancy reception and asked to be shown Alla's room.

He knocked on the door and, as soon as he entered, he wished he'd brought flowers.

Dennis was there, as was Alla. But they weren't talking. Dennis said, "Hey?"

Dennis stood and took Chendrill's hand. "What happened to your shoulder?" he said.

Chendrill smiled, he looked over to Alla, "Hi Alla."

The woman wasn't answering. Dennis got to it. He said, "Alla's had both her operations. The doctor said she should be up and walking soon. There's money left over from the operation and they are recommending we stay and go through physio so as Alla can start walking again. I say yes, but Alla, bless her heart, is saying she can do that on her own and we can save the money."

Chendrill looked at the Russian woman with the beautiful face. She was a tough bitch, there was no doubting that. He said, "What are we talking about money wise?"

"$50,0000," said Dennis.

Chendrill understood, it was a lot of money. He also understood the fact that Dennis wasn't worried about the money but rather about the fact his wife was likely going to head south with the $50,000 as soon as she had taught herself to walk again.

He said, "I'll pick up the physio, Alla. You keep what's left for a rainy day." Then he said to Dennis, "When you've time could you please do me a favor and visit a car dealer and pick out something fancy then go find yourself a big apartment downtown that you'd like the pair of you to live in. Then once you've settled in, I'd like to talk to you about opening a business with me."

Dennis stared at Chendrill, not taking it in at all. He said, "What are you talking about?"

Chendrill told him again, this time filling in the minor

detail about the amount of money he now apparently had and watched as Dennis had sat head in hands in silence as Chendrill's plan for a huge surgery downtown that he'd love Dennis to front once the lawyers had secured his license unfolded.

It was good being Sebastian.

Chendrill left the hospital and headed back over the bridge downtown. He'd played the messages the Italian had sent his girl over and over and backwards. The man was in a bad way, there was no doubt about it. The way he breathed, the way he lost concentration, and the way his temper would burst when he was pleading. But in the background, there was always a lot of other things going on, ambulances and cops flying by, buses passing powered by electrical cables that sparked, people calling out drunken or drugged out nonsense, cars and trucks sitting or honking at lights.

Suzy was right, the man was downtown. But it wasn't in the core where people shopped and partied and ate expensive meals in franchise restaurants where pretty waitresses with cleavage all asked, "So how's your night going?" for better tips as they'd been trained to do. The Italian was in the East Side, in a place where no one gave a shit and the man was familiar with, a place where he knew he could hide in plain sight and be close to his women. He was in an area populated with pimps, drug addicts, and prostitutes, along with the insane and the frightened who should never have been offered outside care away from the hospital. He was in a place where no one looked and society tried to sweep under the carpet.

Chendrill drove the Aston and cruised Hastings Street with all the windows open, once and then twice, and then a third time even slower. He stopped at each light and parked, taking in the sounds and ignoring the drug addicts that came over to lean on the car.

From what he could tell, the Italian was on this road and not on any of the others which ran parallel. For the others were one way and from the messages, the traffic flowed both directions. Also, there were constant occurrences of street people fighting or screaming or just plain talking.

But there were a lot of cheap hotels with rooms that covered a section of Hastings Street which ran for at least eight blocks.

He carried on driving, looking at each of the hotels, counting off each one as he did and an hour later, he had it down to just three.

The first was a bigger establishment which looked good if you were booking up via the internet, but most people who did were gone the next day. The next was above an old church and housed the homeless on a monthly basis and the third was along from the charity shop which did the same but was running a 'no vacancy' sign and had been for months.

Chendrill parked up and walked up the street, the people leaving him be as he did. He looked at the big poster of Clive Sonic and smiled as he remembered the first night he'd met the man at Sebastian's. Then he stopped on the opposite side of the road and leaned against the inside of a doorway which smelled of piss. Seconds later, he was out again and that's when he heard Daltrey's voice say, "Yeah I did that as well."

Chendrill turned and smiled, his old friend standing there at the side of a bus shelter staring right at him. How the hell had he not seen her. She said, “You took your time—I was wondering when you would figure it out.”

And how had she? Chendrill thought. What process of elimination had she followed to come to the same place?

He said, “I take it he’s over there then?”

He was. The Italian was up there on the second floor, waiting it out for the police to get bored.

Daltrey said, “Yeah, you see that window on the second floor with the light on, he’s in there.”

Chendrill asked, “How do you know?”

“Because the lady in the pharmacy told me there was this guy with a bad limp who keeps buying painkillers and iodine. And if I had a bad leg and I was hiding, I’d pick a place next to the pharmacy that took cash.”

“That easy?”

Daltrey shrugged. But the truth was it hadn’t been ‘that easy’. She hadn’t slept. After finding Ditcon’s car via CCTV camera recordings as it headed back downtown, she’d lost it in a multi-parking facility opposite the SeaBus terminal along with the guy who everyone thought was Italian except Suzy. She’d then checked all the hospitals and clinics for leg wounds and then every all-night pharmacy in the vicinity until she eventually found one which had sold medication to an Italian-looking middle-aged guy with a limp. That information coming to her quicker than she’d thought it would as soon as she’d started threatening to have methadone licenses pulled for any of the pharmacies she questioned if it turned out they’d neglected to mention a mass murderer had been in their shop. After that, it was a basic similar Q&A on every sleazy no questions asked hotel in the area until eventually she’d made eye contact with a guy who refused to look up.

She looked back to the entranceway of the hotel that didn't even have a name and said, "That and the friendly guy on the desk over there told me." Then she asked Chendrill, "How did you work it out?"

To which he replied with a smile, "It was easy, I saw you."

Daltrey said, "He's in a lot of pain. When the traffic goes quiet for a bit you can hear him calling out."

Then she said, "I'm waiting to see if his girl turns up. I want to see if Suzy's as innocent as she seems."

Chendrill said, "She's not going to, don't worry. I spoke with her and I can tell you this relationship has run its course."

Daltrey looked at him.

"You did, did she know he's here?"

Chendrill nodded then looking up to the window said, "Not exactly, but he'd been calling her and leaving messages. She turned them over, that's how I found you." Then he asked Daltrey. "Any news on the guy you saved, how is he doing?"

It was a good question and one that Daltrey was still trying to get her head around. The guy was fine, if you call being strung out on methadone and quicklime burns after being strangled fine. But he was alive. One thing was troubling her though was that she'd heard the man tell the paramedics his name was Bill. She said to Chendrill, "You know that saying, what goes around comes around?"

Chendrill waited for Daltrey to answer her own question and when she didn't, he got it. He knew that Daltrey had been looking for a guy whose sister was missing and maybe last night she'd found him. Daltrey although cool on the outside was obviously still hurting bad, but at the same time trying to tough it out rather than take it easy in the way she should have been. He said, "I'm sorry I asked you to get involved. I'll look into who this guy is, don't worry."

Deep down Daltrey was glad Chendrill had gotten her involved but stayed quiet—deep down, she knew meeting the man she'd saved and sitting down with him was on the agenda once she'd dealt with the guy who'd tried to spear her and leave her down his pit. So instead she just looked to the window of the room where the Italian was hiding. Chendrill joined her watching the curtains in the room move in the breeze, then said, "What do you want to do?"

And all Daltrey had to say was, "Let that fucking monster suffer."

Chendrill looked at her; for someone as tough as Daltrey was, the comment was out of character, he said, "You know it wasn't him up there who burnt that girl to death."

And without taking her gaze away from the window, Daltrey replied, "Yeah, I know, but you weren't in that pit."

****

Mattia the Italian loan shark woke again and this time he wasn't sure why he had. He was hot though. The window was open and there was a strong breeze coming in, but he was still really hot—fever hot and his body hurt and his head was aching like a motherfucker. *Jesus Christ*, he thought. He looked at his phone, but the battery was dead. Then he looked at his stomach to see the bites that were there had gotten worse and turned into what looked like a rash that covered his whole abdomen. Then he saw his crudely bandaged covered in purple from the iodine he'd been pouring onto it. Lines of black were visible, rising below and above the point of impact where Daltrey had swung the spike into it.

Standing, he held onto the wall and hopped towards the bathroom and pulled out another four painkillers from the jar and, taking water straight from the tap, he knocked them back.

That'll do it, he thought. What he'd have to do was head to the train station and jump on the next train out of town and hit the hospital where his friend from school worked. He'd been here now for at least five days. No one had been around and he had had that call from his brother and his uncle who used to take him fishing. His mother had also called to see if he was okay. It had been good to hear from her. And Suzy, she was coming over soon.

He hobbled back to the window and looked out and then down. The group of guys were there, looking up at him as they always did. He called down to them, "Hey, I know you, you owe me for a fucking block!"

But that's not what he said—for the man's words were gibberish and only coherent to himself. The conversations with his family and old friends were just dreams and nightmares from the past and the feeling that Suzy was coming over in her high heels was nothing more than wishful thinking—for the man was dying. His veins slowly filling his body with poison as the infection in his leg boiled his insides away and the septicemia sent bacteria and blood clots into his vital organs as he tried to walk in a daze up and down in his room and out on the street below, dragging his leg as he did. Calling out and blending in with the people who lived on the street, who had seen and heard it all before.

He began to cough, slowly at first and then hard, as he lay back on the bed as many others had in that same room shortly before they had died—some owing him money. Long and harsh rasping coughs that were soon forgotten as the heroin or crack poisoned his predecessors' veins very much in the same way the poison was now filling his. The guy on the desk below hearing and seeing it all before and making a killing, literally, from one month in advance of rentals handed over by unwitting short-term guests who lived and died amongst the horror that was the downtown East Side.

Still staring at the window Daltrey took a deep breath, then she turned to Chendrill and said, "It's best we go get him and have the hospital clean the man up so we can ask him who the other poor souls I was treading on in that pit were."

Then as they were about to cross the road and head up into the seedy hotel where the owner hoped his patrons would die at the start of the month so as he could re-rent the room, the Italian came out into the street. The man shirtless and limping badly, dressed only in his trousers and shoes with no socks. His head shaved, his body and face sweaty, his torso covered in bite marks from the bed bugs which fed off him while he slept.

Chendrill said, "Oh my God."

Looking back to him, Daltrey said, "Yeah, like I said, he's been in and out all day. He gets to the end of the block and can't get any further because of the pain. Then I think he forgets why he's left the room because he gets confused and starts shouting at people."

Crossing the road, Chendrill and Daltrey followed. Chendrill in his Hawaiian, Daltrey in her big boots and jeans. Both of them standing out more like cops than ever in this world, where the sick and the helpless lived and read the streets better than they ever could. The Italian reached the end of the block and stood there with his hands against the wall and his head down, breathing hard as the sweat ran into his eyes.

He called out, "Okay, Suzy—let's go."

But Suzy wasn't listening. He tried again—this time calling to a woman standing next to him with her boyfriend in the bright Hawaiian shirt who wasn't listening either. Sinking down, he dropped to the ground as the pain in his leg overtook his stability and he sat for a moment, then he dropped further and laid down with his back on the sidewalk. His head resting on the ground in amongst the needles, dried puke, and piss. His eyes looking up and seeing nothing—only shapes and streaks of light as his head spun from the poison that flowed through his veins.

****

It was around the same time that Big Carl the tow truck driver felt the poison run through his veins also. Except his poison was not actual or physical—this was the poison of pure fear, that toxic combination of cortisol and adrenaline constricting blood flow and stopping his breath. The source of his fear were the others who shared the tight space within the remand center he could now call home—for a while at least. These men who were far more vile and nastier than him. Men large and small, who'd spent so much of their lives so far in one cage or another that their tough look wasn't a look at all, it was just what they were and needed to be to survive in their world. These were institutionalized men, who had grown up in a system they no longcr feared because most had long ago accepted it as part of who they were—they were it and it was them.

Not like the wannabe gangster who sat with them now, out of his comfort zone and on the verge of tears, a man who'd spent his life driving a tow rig pretending to be the same.

It was just after eight the following morning when Suzy's husband opened his eyes as he waited in his cell for a lawyer that he hoped his wife would spring for. The cell now suddenly full of men who wanted to know why he was there and wearing women's flip flops. The leader of the group, being the biggest native Indian Suzy's husband had ever seen, was the one with the questions.

First, he asked if he was comfortable, then as Suzy's husband nodded back, he said, "Good, that's important, you see we like our new friends here to be comfortable."

The husband who liked to watch his wife get fucked in the ass sitting there still nodding and looking at the man's size and looking at the pink plastic flip flops on his feet. The big guy watching as he did and asking why he was there.

Suzy's husband telling him, "I crossed the border."

"Oh, wow you're that guy? Great, you're the guy who's been bringing terrorists into our country?"

The husband took a deep breath. They weren't wrong but he didn't know who was in the van. He was just the guy behind the wheel. They needed to know that. He said, "Yeah, I understand you think that, but I was just the guy who drives—you know, not the guy who arranges it all."

Then the big guy said, "You eating the food here, though aren't you? You know, you're here and you're a Canuck and that's cool, but you're still eating American food?"

Oh, so that's what it was Suzy's husband thought, they wanted a tax, they wanted his food for the short time he was going to be there on remand, before his wife or the guy who owned the tunnel sent a lawyer over and fixed it. He said, "I've no need for that, there's water. You take my food or some, you know, I'm cool."

The big Indian who ran the place then said, "What is it you're offering? All or some I'm confused."

"I mean take it all, you can have it all."

"Cool," the Indian said with a smile. But it wasn't over, not by a long shot. He said, "What you got for my friends then?"

That was it, Suzy's husband thought, he didn't have anything else to trade. He said, "I can ask the wife to bring some smokes if you want."

"Sure, that's great."

Then the big Indian asked, "You like dogs?"

It was a loaded question and one even the husband's small brain, which was running at full alert, could pick up on. "Yeah, I like dogs." Suzy's husband nodded as he replied, then said it again, "Yeah I like dogs."

"Big dogs, you like big dogs?"

"Yeah I like big dogs sure."

"You like little dogs?"

"Yeah I like little dogs."

"Why did you have the little dog killed then?"

Fuck me, this wasn't good. How the fuck could this big fucker have heard about this? Suzy's husband thought. Feeling his stomach rise up into his chest, he said, "You referring to the dog that the guy who was fucking my wife had?"

The big Indian smiled, then said, “Yeah.”

“That wasn’t me,” Suzy’s husband replied as he looked around the cramped cell for a safe passage that was never going to appear. He said, “That was not me, it was my boys. They got carried away that’s all.”

“That’s all?” asked the big Indian.

“Yeah, you know, kids are like that.”

“Yeah,” said the big Indian who’d known Chendrill from when he was a kid and lived on the reserve in Canada and went to the same school. He said, “Sounds like bad parenting.”

Suzy’s husband jumped on this one, throwing his wife under the bus straight away, saying, “Yeah, their mother, she’s been a bad woman you know. Out all the time, at the club while I worked—you know.”

“Worked doing what—bringing terrorists into our country?”

“No, at the docks.”

“Oh,” then the big Native Indian said, “You like gay people?”

He did, yeah—he was liberal, he had gay friends, one had just bought him a house to live in, explained the stripper’s husband as he nodded. Then he heard the big Native Indian standing there with all his friends say, “My friend Bash here, he’s gay you see, and I heard you beat one up, hit him in the head with a baseball bat and fucked him all up?”

Suzy’s husband took another big breath and swallowed. How the fuck did these guys dressed in orange overalls know what had been going down up in Vancouver? He said, “That wasn’t me, no.”

"Your kids?”

"Maybe?"

"Your wife again?"

"Yeah."

"Bitch, eh?"

"Yeah."

Then the big Native Indian said, "You like that Clive Sonic guy?"

Suzy's husband didn't like him no, in fact he hated the guy, hated his song Bam Bam Love or whatever the hell it was called and he hated seeing pictures of the guy all over town telling him he was going to make changes for good and other stupid shit. He said, "Yeah I like him; he's good."

The big Native Indian saying, "What's that saying he's got—that slogan?"

"Trust Me."

"Yeah that's it—you trust me, do you?"

"Yeah."

"You trust him, this politician singer guy Clive Sonic as well?"

Suzy's husband nodded.

Then the big man asked, "You trust him enough to let him fuck your wife in the ass?"

Suzy's husband stared at the big man with his mouth open—which was now bone dry. He asked, "Why would you say that?"

"Because, I heard through the grapevine you like anal sex."

Suzy's husband stayed quiet, he looked at the group and then to the door. Then back to the big Indian with the questions. Then heard the guy say, "You've got little feet, I like your shoes."

Suzy's husband stared at his feet in the flip flops with

the little flowers on the straps and saw that his toenails needed cutting.

"Thanks, it's all the warden here said they had, so I got lumbered."

"No, I heard they were a gift from some guy who wears those fancy shirts and drove the truck for that guy whose dog you killed. They say the guy had a courier company deliver them special, just for you."

Suzy's husband felt his stomach turn as he looked to the flip flops and put two and two together and came up with Chendrill. The big fucker who'd thrown him through the window for no reason—now the guy was setting him up with an even bigger fucker. Then he heard the big Native Indian say, "My friends like guys with little feet, you know what they say about guys with little feet?"

He did, he'd heard the same joke all his life ever since he'd reached adulthood and his hadn't grown as they should have. He said, "No."

"Oh," said the big Native Indian, then carried on with, "they say guys with little feet like anal sex."

Suzy's husband smiled, that was one he hadn't heard before. He shook his head and said as he tried to make it a joke, "Yeah giving it is good—you know, to girls."

"To your wife?"

Suzy's husband smiled and nodded then said, "Yeah, she likes it."

"Oh? I heard you like it too?"

"Yeah, I like it too—you know, giving it."

"How about watching, you like that too do you, you get turned on watching a group of guys ploughing down your lady's alley?"

Suzy's husband stayed quiet—there seemed nowhere he

could go and nothing he could say to change the subject. Then he heard the big Native Indian say, "Well you know, funny thing is, you and I got a lot in common, because I like to watch too. But in this world, there's one thing I know and it's that you can't have everything you want. You can't be one sided on these things in here, not if we're all going to be friends."

Then with a smile that lit up the room, the big Native Indian said, "Especially with you wearing them sexy shoes like you are, I think we're all going to get to know each other real well—Trust Me."

The End

With many thanks to Justin Gouin.

Paul Slatter grew up in London, England and now lives in both Canada and Thailand.
He is married and has four children.

Printed in Great Britain
by Amazon